Memoirs from DEATH ROW

RAYMOND ANDREW CLARK

MEMOIRS FROM DEATH ROW

About *Memoirs From Death Row*

Memoirs From Death Row is a collection of fictional stories written by Virgil Shelton, a fictional character, housed at the Tennessee Department of Correction's Death Row.

These are his completed short stories, along with the circumstances involving his acts leading to his death sentence. *Memoirs From Death Row* is the flagship of these different stories each with its own brand of suspense and unexpected conclusion.

Print ISBN: 979-8-35094-323-8
eBook ISBN: 979-8-35094-324-5

Special Note from the Author:

Drugs, alcohol and smoking are dangerous to your health. These are fictional characters and the contents about their behavior, language, lifestyles, locations, dialogues, are purely for entertainment and literary purposes.

Dedicated to

my loving mother,

Lennie S. Clark

"The greatest storyteller I have ever known"

and

The Clark Family Legacy

CONTENTS

1. Memoirs from Death Row 1

2. Where Angels Lay 41

3. Momma Brown's Crack House 67

4. The Recorder 101

5. Unwell Letters 151

6. The Spirit of the San Xavier del Bac 187

7. Courage Under Fire *(New York City—Terrorism)* 205

8. Pimpin Ain't Easy 241

CHAPTER ONE

MEMOIRS FROM DEATH ROW

THE WEATHER FORECASTED LIGHT SHOWERS WITH A PERIOD OF occasional heavy rains. I was relieved by the meteorology report. A soothing rain would prevent any nocturnal disturbance to me. It was a perfect combination between solitude and rain. They both worked in rich harmony for me. I enjoyed the soft rhythmic tapping of the rain drops pounding against the window, while I intensely studied in the quietness, reflecting on my measured reality that time was compressing my existence. I really needed to enjoy this moment; disillusionment would come within 13 hours. I wouldn't be destined anymore to enjoy days like this—I mean days that I had long dreamed about as a boy, growing up in Madera, California.

I held my head back, touching the cold, unassuming cement slab that anchored four corners of my Lilliputian cell. After 16 years on Death Row, this final depository was cold, placid, uncomplimentary harsh, but brilliantly conceived as a threshold staging area for a person's eventual transformation of life to take place. The room offered no benevolence—nothing that provided any impression of hospitality just before.... before you really think about your misgivings, the unfulfilled what ifs, and if only I had listened to my mother, uncle, brother, someone—anyone.

I lit up a roll-up, an unfiltered cigarette. The brief illumination caught my attention to a barely readable scribbling on the wall across from me. "Buck was here." I bristled, "Well fuck you, Buck, you ignorant bastard. You should have at least written out your full name." I thought, "Besides, who does he think would give a horse's ass if they knew he was here, the dumb son-of-a-bitch". The moment grabbed me. I quickly waved off this unwarranted slur.

This was part of my problem—being a preposterous jerk, always critical of someone else, but not quickly rationalizing my own behavior. I have done so much time across the states, looking at assholes like me in every prison. I can even calculate how many cubic feet of cement I have paced back and forth on, until now. This is the last of them… where all pathetic jerks come, I reasoned. This becomes our final pacing ground.

I soon realized that my mind was rambling now. This wasn't good for me. There was an unsettling problem I had to sort out to hopefully arrive at a harmonious solution inside me. Recently, before they moved me in here, I had been thinking good thoughts—wondering how Paul felt sitting inside that cold, Roman prison and whether God could touch me the way (not the exact way he touched Paul) but a certain way that I would know, without a doubt, that it was the Lord. But in the tight deliberation of my thoughts, something conjured up this notion that maybe I had to revisit that moment; consequences resulting in this death sentence—a denunciation of my acts. Maybe this was going to be my road toward Damascus. I had been working on my Christian image for years—squeezing the Bible; selecting the right scriptures from Psalms and Proverbs, the precise verses that marveled those wide-eyed, death sentence opponents who immediately claimed victory about a changed man and fueling the political crusade against death sentence advocates about eliminating capital punishment. I paralleled this course of action with my state paid lawyers who kept me alive, not because they really believed I was innocent but because the system paid them exceedingly well to keep me alive only to finally lose at the bitter end. "I'm innocent," I have proclaimed all these years. "I was set up by my fuckin' charge partner," I cried.

"Are you alright?" a voice quickly severed my thoughts. I cleared my throat pontifically, "Why certainly. I was just evaluating all the possible scenarios that could occur, delaying this inevitable possibility rather indefinitely, thereby dismissing the hopes and aspirations of those death sentences advocates, bracing themselves for a celebration in honor of my death."

"Hot digady," Stoney said with a gleeful laugh. "You sho' got a gifted gab." It was old Stoney Fox, the correctional officer that worked this last area. He was a special person. Not anybody in their right mind would want to work here. He was profoundly religious and saw the good in everyone before they went on. He worked two Death Row walks for over 35 years, seen 41 executions, and could recount in graphic detail each and every one of them.

Stoney possessed the most visional image of how Heaven looked and how the angels would be waiting for you. Unlike the Chaplain, we all believed that old, black prison guard had spoken directly to God, Allah, Christ, Mohammed, Buddha and even the Virgin Mary. And if you were an atheist, Stoney even had an audience with Satan and knew exactly how the demons would greet you in Hell. They say he was the last person a condemned man wanted to see since he employed a clever method for getting everyone under self-control, particularly those who were terrified of death, especially the ones like me.

"I'm hanging in there, Stoney."

"That's right, young fella, hang in there, and kee-pa prayin' to the good Lord. You don't know how this will end up."

"I'm doing that."

"Good. A young fella like you deserves a chance, especially when he knows the good book like you do."

"You reckon?"

"Why sho."

"I hope so."

"Just kee-pa listenin' to that phone to ring. Saved a plenty of folks. Some never came back."

"Really?"

"Really," he paused with a wide grin, "T'ank them folks gonna stop killin' one day. Killin' ya'll ain't never bought nobody back. No sir, that's for sho. So just kee-pa hangin' in there, son."

"Thanks Stoney."

"Well, I'll be movin on. Be hollerin, at ya in a bit, alright?"

"Alright, Stoney."

A heavy sigh moved over me as I watched the old colored guard walk slowly away. After a moment, I cut a malignant glare deep inside the wall again, but this time my contentious mood swung away from the expletive graffiti on it. I began thinking about the Apostle Paul and his past reputation for persecuting Christians. I then shifted with an uneasiness. This wasn't quite right. My motive was crystal clear, with some specious excuse to the Lord, I moved to a more suitable course. It wasn't that I had all the time in the world.

Time was a premium for me, and any irrelevant pathogens had to be dismissed in my mind. This wasn't about Paul. I was a murderer without cause, without compunction, without mercy, without provocation and religion had nothing to do with my despicable endeavors.

Soon, my original thoughts reappeared about something I personally considered to do after I was baptized seven years ago. The baptism was nothing but another ploy for the Christian support groups. I deduced my plan simply to buy more time from Tennessee's Lethal Injection. It was a dead cinch, 'can't miss' proposition that any homicide investigator would undertake by grabbing a scoundrel like me to clear up another unsolved murder. This would provide my lawyers with the best legitimate excuse for an indefinite stay.

By now I realized, without my help, the cops would never solve these murders. The modus operandi was inconsistent with the way I operated. I still remember the unpleasant circumstances of how, regretfully, our paths took which ultimately caused their deaths.

It all began when I was nearly freaked-out on bourbon and acid in a local hillbilly joint just outside Des Moines, Iowa. It was filled with shit-kicking music and red-neck colloquialism. My partner in crime thought I was in Tucson, ready to run some coke out of Hermosillo, Mexico, with some gringos I did time within the Arizona State Correctional System. I initially had that intuitive feeling not to trust these wackos, but my take was a cool ten grand for just providing a three-day shuttle service. I figured it had to be a monstrous load of coke, maybe 100 kilos at least.

The delivery was to some Italian dude pimping the shit out of the Orlando area, mainly to tourists looking for some fast action after their Disneyworld adventure. They said he felt safe coping south of border, especially where he had worked with the Mexican Cartel so well.

At any rate, it was a deal too good to be true. Undoubtedly, I was dead right! I previously forgotten that I told Emilio de la Fuentes that I had $1,500 to buy some coke and the conversation led to this job. The motherfuckers got me high and stole my dough, leaving me high and dry in some piss ass motel room outside of Tucson.... so much for the Hermosillo job.

I then hitchhiked my way up north to Des Moines with a country music lovin' truck driver. I was too embarrassed to let my partner know I had been laid and played. Naturally before departing and thanking him for his generosity, I had stolen his 357 Magnum that was hidden underneath his seat. With the ten bucks he gave me, I headed straight to a roadside stump called Gussies.

It took less than three hours to get completely shitfaced while bullshitting with the local yokels. I was now anxious to be on my way, so I nudged the gun closer inside my waistband and headed out determined to get my dough back.

Before I could frame my next thought, about a quarter mile from Gussies, I slowly staggered down a lone dirt road, stopping abruptly in my drunken stupor at a candy red Chevy and two people standing by it. My cheekbones flushed with a maniacal glee. The poor bastard was struggling with a lug wrench, trying to twist off a stubborn lug nut. As I stumbled toward them, the young blonde woman gave me a suspicious gaze.

I looked briefly around. The area was utterly silent, the road was isolated, and I had suddenly found my dough. "Let me help you," I mumbled semi-incoherently.

The woman hesitated a brief moment, but the young, crew cut guy didn't. "Sure, sure! I am catchin' the dickens trying to get these two lugs nuts off."

"No problem. Mechanic work is second nature to me." I remembered stooping down, staring at the fresh spare tire. I was home free I reasoned. Within a minute or two, all the lug nuts were off.

"Thank you, sir. I guess we can manage now," the young woman said weakly. I exchanged glances with her. I shuddered momentarily, trying to mask my nefarious intentions.

"Aim to finish what I started, ma'am. You'll be on your way shortly."

"B-but," she protested.

"Hold your tongue, honey. Let this nice man finish and we'll be on our way," the young man interjected.

Smiling to myself, I tightened the spare and jacked the Chevy to the ground.

"Will five bucks be okay?" the young man asked. "It ain't much, but it's best we can do."

"Nah, nah," I said. With a quick glance around the terrain, the utter stillness of the night continued to be my best accomplice.

Now this was the part that still remains a mystery to me. Previously, I had been a journeyman thief, but I severely underestimated my apprehension for violence. In an instant, I removed the 357 Magnum from my waistband pointing it directly at the guy's head. They made it so damn easy, standing there motionless like store mannequins, staring expressionless through a spiral vacuum far away in some unknown abyss.

Two shots suddenly barked out quickly recoiling my hand backwards, as my eyes blinked from the swift moving bullets that each slammed hard inside their skulls. Their bodies simultaneously fell to the ground like cotton ragdolls. I remembered the woman's neck twisting again from the third shot, bringing her eyes finally shut. It was an unmistakable gory scene and the stench of the gun powder smoke circled the air with an evil silhouette that seemed to be prancing up and down over their featureless bodies from the sudden cool breeze. The apocalyptic violence caused me to vomit. Bending over, my gut seemed to be racing up my windpipe. I coughed, wheezed, gagged, and wheezed again. Staggering against the car, I momentarily steadied myself, wiping away the thick drool from my mouth with the back of my hand. My body suddenly grew limp. I was quite distinctively numbed from the shooting. I suspected the speed and ferocity of the act, coupled my alcoholic and drug-induced minded, perhaps made them seem non-human to me at the time.

"Motherfucker," I quickly moaned to myself. This was now becoming a real psychedelic trip. I could feel the rush surging inside my body. An unexpected, bizarre sensation engulfed me with a twisted combination of anxiety and fright. I started gasping uncontrollably as I nervously raced through his wallet. "Holy shit," I thought. "I killed these poor sons-of-bitches," I groaned, suddenly wiping a mountain of wild sweat from my forehead.

I remember dragging their cold bodies deep into the woods and tossing them down into a shallow ravine. Returning to the scene, a truck suddenly came roaring down the road. I fell back against the car hood, lowering my head, trying to conceal my face and portentous behavior. My eardrums vibrated from my heart pounding so hard against my chest. It was then I realized, in my malicious exhilaration, my underwear was sagging and soaked with smelly crap. I stood holding my breath until the truck raced by me without the slightest awareness of my dark frame and unspeakable dark deed.

Moments later, I gave that old Chevy the ride of its life. I secured a measly twenty-seven bucks for my unorthodox behavior. I liked that term "unorthodox behavior" because I could mentally digest that notion better than thinking I had just committed a cold-blooded double murder.

After a few hours of driving southwest, I was feeling distastefully icky from the crap inside my underwear. My high was nearly evaporated when I pulled up by a small farmhouse just off Highway 25 near Kent, Iowa. I really didn't want to think about this one very much, except she was a little, old colored woman. I suppose I could have just let her remain tied up after I bathed, but I didn't. I wanted to resurrect that thrill again to satisfy my exuberance for malice afterthought that appeared to be thoroughly saturated inside my head. I remembered closing my eyes on this shooting, unsympathetic about her plea of not finishing her Bible study in the book of Isaiah. She continued to moan before a lone shot silenced her petition.

"Ouch," I snapped, quickly tossing the roll-up to the floor. The cigarette burned my fingers, unplugging my concentration from the cement wall. I sighed momentarily, lighting another roll-up, recalling how I could have traversed my steps back there again blindfolded. To be honest, I was beginning to regret killing those three people, especially the two women. This was going to be bad luck. I was excessively superstitious. I had scolded myself for not simply robbing them and stealing that fancy Chevy. It would have been rather easy to clean up and change clothes. When I aimed that gun at her, I remembered how she gave me a look of blistering disgust, thoroughly upset that I interrupted her Bible study. For a long time, I had been curious about the book of Isaiah. I guess I read all sixty-six chapters a hundred times or more, memorizing each chapter and verse, wondering if this was the scripture she was deliberating on that evening. The Bible fell harmlessly to the floor when her head rocketed backwards from the impact before I could determine where she had stopped.

I took a long drag off my roll-up, fish puckering five, neatly blown smoke circles from inside my mouth, watching them disappear as they cascaded up against the wall. By now, the raindrops were pelting hard against the window but, before I could gain a measure of increased comfort, I realized another hour had vanished. Reaching over, I grabbed my Bible squeezing it. I decided to say a short prayer, but at this point, I couldn't concentrate—my lawyers would be here soon. The prolonged waiting was beginning to make my skin crawl.

This was the closest I've ever been—deposited in the last cell, the dead man's closet, only a few steps from the execution room.

"You alright, lad?' Stoney asked, circling around the narrow corridor.

"Just a little chill," I replied.

He shook his head sympathetically, almost as though he perfectly understood my reaction.

"You gombee alright, son. When most of them get this far, they get a bit edgy, even the ones that cuss and fuss. Everybody dies differently, especially when they were using 'ole smokey', the electric chair. Good Lord, I'm glad them folks over there made things little easier. Ya know, this doesn't make a mess out of things. Them ole undertaker fellas didn't like to pick up some of those real bad ones."

"Can we change the subject?" I said sharply.

"Why sho. Didn't mean no harm. No sir, ole Stoney gombee prayin' that you'll be alright. Them lawyers can really work a miracle. They say you got some goodin".

"I hope so. I am sorry I shouted at you."

"That's okay. But I came back to find out what you wanted for dinner".

"My last supper?" I sighed.

"Well," he took a long pause, "just a special dinner. You can have anything you like. We can even get you a beer but we really don't tell the public about that—them Christian folks and politicians, and victims' families would really raise cane about that."

Moments later, after giving him a list of things I wanted to eat, I watched the old guard shuffle slowly down the corridor. I cannot fully express in adequate words how the terror flowed throughout my veins when Stoney mentioned that dinner. I was really fucked up even discussing the subject with him.

Before long, my thoughts rotated back to the old woman's farmhouse. I still remembered, just as plain as day, wiping the Chevy spotless of any fingerprints and thoroughly doing the same in the old woman's farmhouse. Hell, I knew how the crime scene, forensic technicians worked. I changed vehicles and drove her 1978 Ford pickup all the way out of Iowa, heading for my rendezvous point with my partner in crime, Cherokee Ace. As I drove toward Tennessee, my spirits rose, not as one would believe, leaving Iowa; but my sensitivities about the killings wasn't quite apparent at this point; and, meeting a real criminal specimen now occupied my thoughts.

Unlike most of the cons I was acquainted with, Ace was diabolically ingenious—a clean shaven dude, half German Irish and Navajo. I guess my attraction to him was because he always remained a sanctimonious white-collar crook with a penchant for violence. I knew some of those killings he bragged about were no German fairytale. I believed, for instance, the crimes I did in Iowa were Boy Scout material to him. He would have really left that small area in utter pandemonium.

In the past, I always regarded doing time by flying under the legal radar scope. I took the position that rapes and murders, that real sick shit, wasn't going to be my trademark; therefore, my aberration in Iowa would never be discussed with him or anyone else for that matter. Previously, I made it perfectly clear to him never to contemplate any reprehensible action with me. He knew I always maintained a close but unobtrusive watch over him when we did a job. I simply gave him my professional experience and every single aspect of what's necessary to do a commercial burglary and we made good money from it. After that, we split up and rendezvous at some later date and different location. This time it was in Tennessee.

I remembered dropping off the old pick-up somewhere in Missouri. I then started hitchhiking to a small town called Dyersburg, Tennessee, about an hour or so north of Memphis. Hell, I was up for this number. I've never been to Memphis before and thought I would drift on down there after the heist and see Graceland, eat some real barbeque, and wander down on Beale Street. I really love the blues and planned to stop by BB King's joint. My highlight would be Graceland and visiting Elvis' mansion. There was nobody like Elvis, he was the real king of Rock n' Roll.

I was fully preoccupied about Graceland the afternoon arriving at Dyersburg; when, at the motel, a strange monotonous tune, 'Hit the Road Jack', was repeatedly swirling around inside my head. I was listening to that song and my intentions were to take my remaining nine bucks and get the hell out of Tennessee. Unfortunately, Ace knocked at my motel door and the rest was pretty much a sad affair.

It was small jewelry store that had plenty of cash according to Ace. He cased it out for several days. During the day of the job while fumbling for a match inside Ace's room, I stumbled across a nickel-plated 38 revolver hidden well inside a towel in the nightstand. I shifted uneasily, relieved I had thrown that 357 Magnum away in a small lake near the Missouri border.

When Ace returned to the room, I wasn't feeling that irresponsible sense of immunity this time. For some reason, the concealed revolver was disturbing to me. I still remember our terse exchange.

"What's up with the gun?"

"What do you mean?"

"You know what I mean."

"Do I? So, I guess I'm fucking clairvoyant now."

"I should hope not but the gun… inside the drawer… hidden between them towels?"

"Take it easy. I bought it from some guy in a poker game in Buffalo."

"You know how I feel about that. If the cops catch us with a gun, it's going to be a problem for us. We're ex-cons."

"Not for me, it ain't."

"Dammit," I thought to myself. Here goes the fuckin' song again, 'Hit the Road Jack', ringing like a damn alarm clock inside my head. I eventually went along grudgingly knowing that staying in Dyersburg was my worst mistake. It was supposed to be a burglary but, when we arrived at the jewelry store, it was open.... the owners were very much inside the premises.

"What's going on?" I asked.

"Some fuckin mix-up. They were supposed to be gone."

"Well, it's off man," I sighed.

"The hell it is," Ace snapped.

"You piece of shit," I moaned to myself.

After a short debate. I insisted that my role would be limited by simply remaining inside the car. I still remember that cold, frigid stare and squinch look around his eyes as he glared at me. I wasn't willing to engage in no armed robbery and remained steadfast about that point.

He sat there, in a long moment of silence, staring at the jewelry store. Perhaps twice or maybe a third time, an urge rushed up inside me to leave him there, right there inside his car and hustle quickly away from Dyersburg. However, my lousy greed would overwhelm that unwell premonition since the purpose of my rendezvous with Ace was for money. Besides, I was broke. So, like a damn fool, I nestled deep into the driver's seat watching him casually stroll toward the jewelry store.

Somehow, I was beginning to get that nervous tension when he entered the store. I had a lukewarm feeling that this caper was really going to be fucked up. Call it what you want but every criminal has a sixth sense when things are about to go wrong. And, before my mind could work through the progression of my negative thoughts, I heard four or five gunshots.

"Ace.... you... low... life... son-of-a-bitch," I screamed.

In an instance, without trying to determine what occurred inside the jewelry store, I started the car and was off searching for the fastest exit away from Dyersburg and the fuck away from Ace.

As I drove down the street, I began thinking about what my mother would often say, "God moves in mysterious ways." I just left Iowa committing three senseless murders, coming to Dyersburg to do a simple burglary; and ran into this insane bullshit with a maniac who just committed a murder in broad daylight.

My eyes slowly opened at that point. It was the rain—the rain was now dancing lightly against the narrow, thick window. The sound was only a whimper. I was now lying back on my bunk—not awake, not really asleep, but somewhere in between. That period in Dyersburg was worse than a nightmare. I managed to escape initially by heading north on Highway 51. I thought maybe I had escaped being just a few miles from the Kentucky border. The plan was to wipe his car clean of fingerprints and hitchhike to the West Coast.

But a flicker of my inclination for avoiding capture was suddenly dashed. I should have guessed as much—an omen, a real bad omen—crept up inside me when I saw a sign that read NORTHWEST CORRECTIONAL CENTER on Highway 78. I remembered then why I always hated being in small towns. They were perfect places to build prisons. They build them out in the middle of nowhere—where there was endless terrain.... treacherous footing.... acres of open farmland—all prerequisites to provide ample opportunity for a wayward escapee to be struck in the back of the head by a lone bullet from a skilled prison marksman or his ass torn to shreds by angry blood hounds.

It was there in a small town called Tiptonville where my flight was officially doomed by a group of state troopers' roadblock. A couple of days later in the Dyer County Jail is when I fully realized the gravity of my situation. I was initially relieved that my conscience hadn't been sagged low enough for me to confess those Iowa murders to Ace. He had nothing on me and I intended to cooperate fully with the police but it wasn't like that at all.... nothing remotely the way I figured it would be. To my utter astonishment, I was being charged with three counts of first-degree murder. Ace had executed the jewelry owner, his wife and their seven-year-old granddaughter.

I sighed, trembling in the dark silence of my thoughts. It was far too late to feel distressed about things. But, somehow, your mind nevertheless drifts away.... thinking about ideals of starting fresh, shaking off the filth, alcohol, drugs, and torrid periods of a lascivious lifestyle.

It's crazy to have dreams like this—but it's all a dream. On Death Row, the reality of your predicament emerges through your dreams and the darkness reminds you of your solitude—not the improbable state of living but the probable stretch toward dying.

I still have images of the judge's granite face and cold eyes as they fell upon me, almost revengeful while detailing in a rather peculiar, but elegant manner, my lengthy criminal history, which distanced me farther away from my credibility in the eyesight of the jury.

Ace was particularly clever in repaying me for leaving him. In a well-developed, uncompassionate tone, he told them about my plans to burglarize the jewelry store, panicking and leaving him behind after he shot each victim. My fingerprints were discovered inside the store, on the side of the countertop, but they had been there the day earlier as Ace insisted I go inside with him. It never occurred to me to wipe the side of the countertop after I looked at a dazzling 16-carat diamond ring. Like my mother often said, "God moves in mysterious ways."

It was an oppressive day for me, and the jury eventually found no mitigation. Despite my testimony, they were satisfied arriving at their conclusion. I remembered shaking my head in a dubious manner when the verdict was read by the judge. Death by lethal injection is what he said. It was as though I was hearing something inaudible and inconceivable from a long way off. I was now condemned to death—dying for something I didn't do.

"Here's your supper, son," Old Stoney's voice returned me to my reality. The rain had finally stopped, only my solitude remained.

"What time is it?" I asked.

"About 6:37 p.m."

"Damn," I thought. Five hours have passed by. "Heard anything from the lawyers?"

"Not yet but I know they're working hard. They'll be here shortly. Ya know how those courts are. Just kee-pa prayin. Gotta good meal for ya. Five crispy fried pork chops, a platter of French fries, avocado salad, four dinner rolls, a peach pie, ketchup, Louisiana hot sauce, and one Bud Lite beer—everything that you requested," he grinned.

A moment of profound silence followed between us. I then sighed, a latent of uneasiness fell across my face. I was hungry but had no appetite. The nervousness and dread produced a cold shiver throughout my body. "God knows," I thought, "this is a helluva time to die."

"You alright, son?"

"I-I don't really know."

"It's okay.... whatcha feeling is alright."

"It is?"

"Why sho."

"You think......?"

"I know whatcha you're thinkin," he interjected. "Sometimes a man thinks he's finally ready. He then gets that funny feeling that he ain't, so he must try to get that understanding about dying. Nothin' you doin' is different from the rest of us—we all gonna die one day, exceptin' you know when your time is a comin'. So, it ain't nothin to be scared about, just go on if that what it is. They go real fast.... like taking a sleepin' pill. I'll be there if you like—like all the rest of 'em".

"You will?"

"Sho I will. Just tell the warden you want old Stoney there. He'll understand."

Undeniably, there immediately seemed to be a strong murmur of confidence returning to me. In fact, I had become suddenly hungry. A temporary suspended interest about dying left, as I slowly ate my dinner. Again, my mind wondered about my inevitable predicament.

I recalled about ten years earlier, while my mind was in a combined state of phlegmatic and unmindfulness, did I receive some information about an organ donor program. For a moment, the concept seemed highly offensive to me; however, I realized it was my selfish part, the unenlightened, uniformed, unforgiving, and uncaring division of my soul. Inasmuch as I often struggled to substitute the perplexity of my greed and selfishness, I was never, even as a small child, able to elevate my thoughts toward giving anyone a modest token of appreciation without something in return.

Perhaps much of my final decision came from Connie Dawson, a cold-hearted, demented sociopath, child rapist and murderer, whose crime was so ghastly that prison guards ferociously taunted him, creating moments of illusionary freedom for him, and hoping with uncanny impatience that he would take the bait; thereby, properly allowing them to slaughter him in a like manner to a degree much further beyond the suffering he created for his little victim and her family.

Dawson was executed precisely five months after Cherokee Ace eight years ago. Despite Cherokee's unnerving disposition, he was a pure misfit at doing time and Death Row had all but unglued his fragile state of mind. He suffered from an acute level of claustrophobia, which perhaps expedited his frequent quarrels with his attorneys, reassuring them of his competency and to dissolve anymore lingering appeals. I still remembered that fuckin' exalting look of superiority on his face when we caught a momentary glance at each other. He cocked his head in smugness, confident that I would be joining him soon.

But, like the prison officials, I also despised Dawson who reminded me of a diminutive, horn-rimmed glasses wearing weasel that was inexplicably nervous toward any authority. Although Dawson was void of any human empathy, somehow, he managed to temper my feelings since he cradled me with an endless source of reading material.

It was through this relationship with him that I decided to inquire about being an organ donor for the Mayo Clinic.

Dawson privately confided to me that he agreed to donate his entire body to the University of Tennessee's Forensic Research Department in Knoxville. Considering what he had done, the entire criminal justice process along with society had flamed a trail of unmitigated hatred toward him. Ironically, after his execution, the university declined to accept his pathetic remains.

At any rate, this was nothing but a half-baked scheme of mind, something to provide another measure of irrefutable proof to my Christian supporters that I had changed.

After completing a mammoth-sized medical questionnaire, I became a designated donor for my heart, kidneys and liver. Basically, this was now going to be a simple piece of strategy. My Christian support across the region was growing stronger. My next step would be to expose the three murders in Iowa, if or when my appeals had been exhausted, and if the Governor denied my clemency. How easy the whole matter seemed to me until I was abruptly asked by the prison officials if I would be willing to donate one of my kidneys. Perhaps this amazing development would become the most astonishing thing that ever occurred to me.

Immediately, this request complicated matters for me. It was my concealed reluctance that haunted my guilt and despair and my initial decision to admit the inescapable fact that this was never my real intention.

However, without ever mentioning it, I suspect my thoughts waved through the division of my soul—the good spirit versus the bad spirit. My decision was finally made again with another ulterior motive, while avoiding to place more stock in the prison officials' perception about me being engulfed with cynicism, selfishness, and self-indulgence, I agreed to the initial medical evaluation to determine my suitability for the transplant.

"Mr. Shelton," a voice echoed inside my eardrum, promptly breaking me away from my thoughts. It was old Stoney along with two officers standing at my cell door. I quickly snapped awake, shaking my head to orient myself. "Your lawyers are here. I come to escort you to the interview room with them," Stoney said.

But in the comparative quietness, a dull expression seemed to be working over the two officers' faces. I hesitated a moment, immediately sensing some unwell vibrations that caused me to think irrationally that they were perhaps staring at a corpse. My mind was suddenly jolted by every nuance of my imaginative thoughts about them.

"Is everything alright?" I asked, shifting my eyes evenly at Stoney. I had never seen these two officers on Death Row before—never! This was the moment that shocked my senses, inducing my phobia about dying or being executed in a sterile, white room, while spectators eagerly gazed at me wondering how I would react to these precious moments of my advancing mortality.

Now in an agitated state, before Stoney could respond to my question, I repeated, "Is everything alright?"

"Why sho. Whenever the warden believes we're getting close, these officers kinda take over, maybe two or more, if necessary."

"Getting close..."

I said, "What do you mean?"

Smiling and nodding, Stoney said, "Now take it easy, son. It's just a prison procedure—anything under three hours without notice, we're required to begin our preparation, but that doesn't mean.... "

"....Mean I am gonna be executed?" I interrupted with a quick ululation.

"No, it's not."

Stoney's reply should have calmed my nerves; however, I had suddenly become so frightened of the officers' presence.

"Now, now....," Stoney said, obviously sensing my certain uncontrollable fear. He then stepped closer toward my cell door quickly letting go a dry smile. "Remember my sayin' earlier, son? That's why ole Stoney comes here with these nice fellas, we understand.... understanding is the best thing in the world. Everybody gotta job to do, and you gombee just fine."

At the moment, I felt somewhat better, but not fine. How in the hell could I be fine—like feeling good, relieved, or satisfied? I might be executed within three hours and there wasn't a fuckin' thing fine about this. The whole process was unmercifully screwing with my head.

Three minutes later with my hands cuffed and feet shackled, I penguin bounced, two-stepped inside a small room that had an unusual smell of heavy bleach with a strong disinfectant agent. Instinctively, I sensed it was all part of the equation—a hospital scent, somewhere sick people might be (even a critical care unit) or maybe even close to the area where the execution would occur. My nostrils suddenly flared as I drew a deep questioning breath but before my thoughts would zoom out of proportion, I quickly shook my head suppressing this unsettling feeling. My eyes then settled down, catching the composition of my two attorneys' Lincolnesque faces.

"Terry couldn't make it," Warren said.

"I don't give a rat's ass about Terry not being here," I emptied out a quick tirade. "Why have you guys waited so long to talk with me? I'm going fucking nuts."

Ignoring my agitated state of mind, Warren Eppington, my lead counsel, continued. "Terry is waiting on another Motion for a Stay from the Sixth Circuit."

I then lowered my head, flushed scarlet with embarrassment, now too ashamed to make eye contact with them. "I'm sorry," I whispered.

"That's okay."

"And the Governor?" I asked wearily.

He then gave a heavy, deep sigh. "The parole board is very conservative about these crimes. They declined our clemency petition. The Governor's Council is meeting with him. We really don't know; the warden is standing by. The Governor's Office will probably wait until a decision is reached by the Sixth Circuit on our stay request. If that's denied, he'll act—and it will be anybody's guess what he will do. There is strong opposition against us, but we do have our support."

Meanwhile, after a few minutes conversing with Warren, Don Proctor, his law partner, sat quiet and composed. From time to time, our eyes would meet almost transferring subliminal messages. It was something he wanted to say, and it was something I wanted to hear. Throughout what followed, Warren shaped the last remaining time of what Terry's legal strategies would be, but I was beginning to have no illusion about this effort. Maybe the quiet demeanor of Proctor was unknowingly diminishing my hope.

Eventually, turning, I single-mindedly decided that I couldn't leave without the benefit of Proctor's appraisal about my dwindling options.

"So, what are you thinking?" I asked.

"I'm thinking maybe...."

"Maybe, it doesn't look good?"

"Hope."

"Hope," I exclaimed.

"That's right, hope."

"My mom has hope."

"Hope can sustain you."

"Like Paul."

"Who?"

"The Apostle Paul—Paul had much hope and faith. He was in prison still writing the epistles. He wrote First and Second Timothy while in a Roman prison."

"That's good. Speaking of writing, how's your short stories coming along?"

"I call them my Memoirs.... Memoirs From Death Row. I also keep a journal about everything. You'd be surprised what's in it. I want you to send it to my mom. She'll know what to do with it, if...."

"If what?" Warren asked.

"If I'm not here tomorrow," I sighed.

A few minutes later, in my mind, the room gradually become a labyrinth in several ways, confounding my ability to communicate and listen effectively. Quickly, Warren noticed the subtle change in my behavior.

"You alright, Mr. Shelton?"

"I need to get out of here." Turning, I looked around, grimacing from a sudden wave of acid that had surged up from my stomach. I swallowed dryly, motioning to Stoney to enter the room.

"Get me out of here," I cried.

I swiftly realized what was occurring to me. It was a time compression matter that I was battling inside me. My memoirs had to be completed, thoroughly saturated with an indisputable profundity of a cleansing of my mind, while leaving the Iowa matter for someone else to discover rather than my open confession. There remained only a faint notice of optimism, but an ever-growing feeling of ominousness perhaps making me believe I had to accomplish everything within three hours.

"We'll take you back, son," Stoney spoke in a voice slightly above a whisper.

Warren nodded in agreement. It was now only a waiting process.

Returning to my cell, I had become sufficiently paranoid. The rain had completely stopped, making the rich harmony of its sound absent from my thoughts. Somehow, meeting with my attorneys was a predictable outcome. After 16 years, my perception maybe was solidified when I caught Warren's rigid features in my peripheral vision. It was really him that had given up hope. The plethora of legal challenges was monumental. He had done something most lawyers avoid doing with their clients on Death Row—he hadn't become too personally involved in my case, but rather in my life and, with the exception of Iowa, I shared everything with him.

Lighting up another roll up, I was now trying to properly manage my thanatophobia, a term a prison clinical psychologist described to me several years ago. It's an acute fear of dying. Although I received nightly medication to control my anxiety, the thought of death was always accessible in my subconscious mind.

My diagnosis wasn't dissimilar to others who felt the same way on Death Row. The prison officials were used to that reaction. Even if a person was diagnosed with manic depressive psychosis, passive-aggressive personality, panic-disorder, obsessive compulsive disorder, and even martyrdom, the United States Supreme Court had settled many legal arguments about these psychological and psychiatric disorders by detailing that many of us will have mental issues and stress, even acute stress, for that matter. Stress was an acceptable behavioral characteristic in the evolutionary process of an execution.

The court understood Death Row inmates' apprehension about dying, coupled with the lengthy appeals through the state and federal court systems, the endless constitutional issues, collateral attacks on procedural matters and countless legal arguments. This was an exhausting psychological process that could create these symptoms after years on Death Row. And yet, for these prolix legal challenges if, at the end, an individual is evaluated as being competent despite a disorder, it is the only criteria that matters in allowing the will of the people to be accomplished.

As for me, the hour of my marathon reality has nearly arrived and society's craving for justice will be satisfied despite my acute stress.

A few minutes later, I took my last drag off the roll up and tossed it into the toilet. The impact slightly rippled the water. My eyes froze, staring semi-catatonically at the cigarette butt floating around the water. Soon, before I realized it, I was composed and ready to write again. My thoughts now returned to the transplant surgery.

After months of preliminary tests at Vanderbilt University, it was apparent that I was a perfect match to an ailing man living in Baltimore,

Maryland. Although I was terrified about donating my kidney, somehow, I managed to muster enough courage to undergo this procedure. Besides, how else could I increase my Christian support base unless I agreed to this sacrifice?

Eventually one day I was transported to Vanderbilt, not for a scheduled test, but a meeting. Filled with a strange mix of emotions, this unusual summons had caused my paranoia to nearly leap out of bounds. I was perplexed and wondering if after all these tests, I proved be an unsuitable donor. It was at this point I believed a mental transformation occurred inside me. Somehow, I could feel the prospect of utter disappointment if the surgeons changed their minds.

I remembered finally arriving and being placed inside a small holding area. As I sat in the quietness and before I could manifest any more negative thoughts, the room's door suddenly opened. My head turned slowly toward it. My hands began to tremble almost nonstop while both fear and uncertainty stuck me simultaneously.

"Mr. Shelton—Virgil Shelton?" the man asked in a reserved tone.

"Yeah, that's me," I answered.

"Nice to meet you sir."

I hesitated a few moments, while my eyes rotated over the faces of six individuals standing in the doorway. Intuitively, without being told, I quietly realized why I had been taken to the hospital. It was my meeting with the potential kidney recipient.

Standing between my physician and three officers was a feeble-looking colored man, hunched slightly forward, with salt and pepper strands and a receding hair line. His dark eyes were set deep inside his head. He wore a jacquard sweater that seemed to drape over the edges of his drawn shoulders with a deer painted on the front and tan slacks. He looked both exhausted and enthusiastic at the same moment. Staring intently at me, the man's lips slowly split open into a soft smile as he spoke first.

"This here," motioning next to my door, ".... is my wife, Helda. Next to her is our oldest daughter, Kimberly. My name is Paine—John Paine."

"Ma-am," I nodded to each one.

"They were against it at first but I told them I wanted to see you and thank you firsthand. I know the good Lord is really gonna bless you. We're some prayin' folks. My whole church is gonna be prayin' for ya."

I was, in fact, nearly overcome by this unimaginable moment. Indeed, I must admit I was really stunned.

"Are you alright with this?" Doctor Peterson asked me.

"Yeah....yeah....it's no problem."

"Good. If everything goes well, the operation hopefully will certainly give Mr. Paine some longevity. Your genetic make-up is extraordinary. A real medical phenomenon has occurred in this process."

That day was the beginning of establishing my broad Christian support base. After the transplant, I did find an enormous amount of self-pleasure in seeing me accomplishing something positive, without any second-guessing my motive, and resisting those undesirable, racial traits concerning any prejudice toward saving a colored person's life. Somehow, I was feeling that some good qualities about me had been exposed. This feeling of elation would continue especially when I realized that Mr. Paine's church, a membership of nearly two thousand, was undertaking an incredible campaign for a new trial for me. Inexplicably, this operation had become my gold mine—I had struck a rich vein of human compassion by saving a man's life who was their beloved elder deacon. Mr. Paine also retired from the Baltimore City School system as the maintenance superintendent which paralleled other support from many teachers and school administrators.

As the months continued, I was somewhat vitalized by the galvanizing efforts of Helda Paine. I became invigorated by dozens of weekly letters and money for a legal defense fund.

What was happening slowly began to energize me through a gut instinct that these colored folks could eventually raise enough political upheaval that possibly could influence the court to grant me another trial. I even had bizarre visions of Reverend Jesse Jackson meeting with me, so thoroughly satisfied of my innocence that he would contact all those colored preachers and politicians he knew across the country about my case. But after eighteen months, my impish, irrational euphoria and delusions of grandeur had come to an unthinkable end.

Perhaps the second most amazing coincidence occurred to me on a Friday afternoon. I'm still confounded just thinking about the infinitesimal odds of something like this ever happening to anyone. It was a letter from Jennifer Pryor, who was a choir member at Mr. Paine's church, that unveiled this supernatural moment for me. I still remembered my eyes blinking with incredulity and my blood felt like it was draining from my face. My mind was locked frozen staring at two unbelievable sentences in her letter, which read:

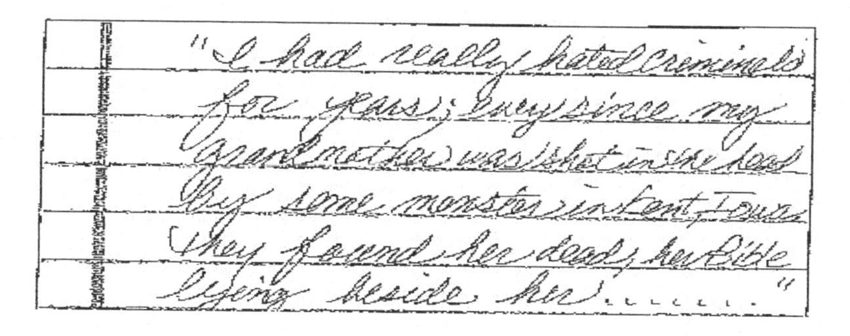

"I had really hated Criminals for years; Every since my grandmother was shot in the head by some monster in Kent, Iowa. they found her dead; her Bible lying beside her......."

Almost without thinking, I dropped the letter and flopped a belly slam on my bunk. My mind reeled in astonishment as I was feeling strangely disembodied, contemplating those indelible, haunting memories about her—impressions that perhaps were neither, but premonitions—periodical admonitions about events in my life I wanted to purge. Somehow, as incredible as it sounds, this letter was my warrant giving me notice that justice was overdue, and the Iowa murders finally placed themselves deep inside my battered subconscious. Her words only confirmed that the Kent slayings could never be mollified in my mind.

In reality, these two sentences just stolen the very plan I encumbered for years to extend my life on Death Row. I stirred on my bunk nearly paralyzed in utter disbelief. "How could.... I-I-I mean... how was anything like this possible?" I asked myself. "How?"

This was Pryor's third letter to me. The first two were brief, too brief as an afterthought. Although she participated in donating money to my legal defense fund, I sensed some unusual cautiousness in the tone of her letters. For some reason, something that was never apparent to me, I wrote her back without noting my typical proclivity but with an unbridled tolerance expecting that an artful person would encourage her to write again. Perhaps her occupation as a computer science teacher stimulated my interest.

Startled by these two sentences, I quickly realized there was a disquieting terror that suddenly engulfed me. This was recompense from God, not an indication of an obscure coincidence. Her grandmother had reached me from her grave, a stunning closure to the thing that was so frighteningly familiar to me about why I had studied the Book of Isaiah so much. I was being confronted with something extraordinary, perhaps even supernatural, beyond anyone's comprehension. I felt exactly like that wayward coyote who killed a bear cub years ago only to finally be cornered by the spirit of its mother bear—like a haunting illusion that had become real, very real.

This was her personal retribution, maybe for all three of them, without an arrest, prosecution or even a sentence. She didn't require the meticulous work of a zealous police detective or the much-celebrated assistance from America's Most Wanted. This was the power of the Almighty coming to convict my soul. I was finally captured!

I never encountered anything quite like this. Undoubtedly, I realized my fate was doomed. Nothing could ever convince me to incriminate myself about these murders and destroy the stalwart reputation I cultivated with Mr. Paine's church. I wasn't thinking any such thing—it was still that Christian image I had to uphold. If necessary, die secretly while seeking forgiveness but outwardly portraying a victimized composite of a man denied his fair market of justice. Foolishly, I really believed I could reconcile everything with God.

I expelled a long, deep breath. "I'm be damn," I sighed. I returned the letter inside the envelope and placed it inside my Bible at the beginning of Isaiah. I remembered for a few seconds and a strange feeling moved over me about that old woman's eyes, her face and just where she stopped in Isaiah. Naturally, that day has haunted me ever since. I became psychologically deranged from it, trying to determine what passage she was studying. Insightfully, I recognized in some weird form, this verse was relevant to me. From that day on, I never looked at Ms. Pryor's letter again nor did I send her a reply.

"Mr. Shelton.... Mr. Shelton...." It was old Stoney's voice, crackling with a tone of lamentation. I quickly disengaged my thoughts, lifting up my head searching for his eyes.

"Your lawyers want to see ya, son. The warden also told the chaplain to come over. He is on his way."

"No!" I said sharply. "Tell the chaplain that's okay. Thank him for everything."

Stoney's eyes narrowed. He shook his head as he quickly reported my request over his walkie-talkie.

By now, I knew there wasn't much time left. I was more perceptive about my condition. Even though my heart was beginning to pound inside my chest, I knew there wasn't anything else I could do.

Four minutes later, I was returned to the sterile interview room but only Mr. Proctor remained. Warren was visibly absent from the scene.

Mr. Proctor stirred in his seat; his head shook imperceptibly. I then experienced a sudden horrible moment of new, raw panic.

"Warren told me to express his regrets. He couldn't stay, he has an important case tomorrow, a lengthy deposition he had to study," he sighed, with a look of mute appeal on his face.

"They turned our Motion for a Stay down?" I asked wearily. He shrugged his shoulders, "I'm afraid so."

"What about..."

"The Supreme Court?" he interjected. "The high court won't intervene. Chief Justice Rehnquist's court has been tough on these death penalty cases that request a stay. The Sixth Circuit wasn't persuaded by our argument and denied us relief. They considered it to be a rather thin constitutional issue." He studied himself before speaking again. "God knows we tried, Virgil," he said with a deep sigh.

"And the Governor? What about him?"

"That's why I called for you. About ten minutes ago, the Governor denied our clemency petition. Warren tried to speak with the Governor directly, but his attorney told him that his decision was final." He shook his head, "I'm sorry....so sorry, Virgil."

I then swallowed nervously wondering if there was anything else that could be done. Proctor looked at me questioningly, "We've done everything—I mean we didn't leave any stone unturned. It's been a long arduous, legal battle. We really tried everything."

"So that's it?"

"I guess so," he groaned. "I'm so upset about this. I don't know what else we could have done." He sighed staring at me for a long moment and then said, "Do you have all your affairs in order?"

"Yeah."

"What about your memoirs?"

"The prison will mail them. Stoney will see to that," I replied, turning to him (Stoney).

He nodded. "Don't mean to rush ya'll, but we've gotta go now." I then felt a strange chill as I heard his words.

"Me too," Proctor said. He reached out to shake my hand, "God bless you Virgil." "I hope so," I replied weakly. Proctor's eyes suddenly darkened. There was a lost expression on his face.

"Tell Warren and the other staff members, I appreciate everything they done for me," I said.

Proctor's jaw tightened as he extended out his hand. "You'll be just fine. I'll be out there giving you strength."

"Thanks," I shrugged.

We shook hands and embraced for the last time. Moments later, as I walked down the narrow, gray corridor, my mind re-worked every inch of the surrounding. It was important to me because this was the last time I would see this bland environment.

My mind then kaleidoscopically shifted to my mother, uncle and brother's faces all merging together speaking in unison from a sense of desperation. I should have listened more, understanding the nature of their dark, eerie warnings that someday— surely a day like this would come soon, even sooner than I would imagine—if I continued on my insidious path. My mind ached for another chance, maybe another life, maybe anything except what was about to happen. "I'm going to be executed tonight," my voice moaned inwardly giving the distressing news to the rest of my body. Funny, your thoughts all seemed to be one gigantic collage when you realize death is inevitable.

A minute later, when I returned to my cell, my personal belongings were packed in one single bag. My Last Will and Testament had been prepared two years ago and sealed inside a plain, white envelope. Looking around the room, I had nothing but a few commissary items and my memoirs. Perhaps my mother would have them published one day. I never really gave her much—mostly a heartache. I spared everyone the burial expenses as the state would cremate my remains and send her the ashes if she wanted them. I had later changed my mind about donating any more organs. My objective to Mr. Paine had been achieve.

"We're ready, son," Stoney said wearily.

"My memoirs?"

"I'll pack 'em," Stoney replied. "Would you like me to finish them?"

I cocked my head slightly, surprised by his unusual question. "How could he finish my stories?" I wondered.

"Huh?" I winced.

At that moment, the warden appeared with four officers, all walking with a quick military gait toward me. Without realizing it, my knees buckled. I suddenly felt a cold fist closing over my heart. The moment was like bad news striking hammer blows all over my body. My stomach contracted in a tight ball.

"But Warden….," I cried out. And before I could utter another word, he spoke. "Virgil Shelton, this is going to go alright. Trust me on this. But before we proceed to the execution chamber, I have a statement to read."

It had only taken a minute or so for him to read my death warrant. Tonight, the People of the State of Tennessee will have their reconciliation. This ominous moment had finally arrived. God knows my legs felt like lead.

"We're here to help you, Virgil. It's time to go," the warden announced.

There was no reaction from Stoney, not even a flicker of a movement from him. In fact, everyone, all four correctional officers, stood semi-frozen staring at my every movement. Unmistakably, I realized the execution was now set. Very soon I would be deceased. Within seconds, someone whipped a chain around my waist. Soon, my ankles were also tightly secured.

"Are you sure about the Chaplain? He's standing by, Virgil," the Warden asked. I shook my head. "Nope. Just have him call my mom as soon as it's finished. She's probably sewing—it helps her nerves, but she'll want to know real quick. I think she'll call her pastor. After he speaks to her, she'll want to tell the others."

"No problem."

"And tell Chaplain Burgermesiter, I thank him for everything he's done for me."

"Sure. I'll be glad to," the warden answered.

I then turned and looked at Stoney. "Will you walk next to me, please?" I asked breathing hard.

Grabbing my right arm, the diminutive officer smiled as he waved the other officers away. "He gombee alright," he nodded to them. "Ole Stoney by his side now. We can walk alone. There ain't nothin' about this matter Mr. Shelton can't handle. The Lord gonna get him right." He then gave me a gentle tug. "Let's go, son. I'll finish your memoirs."

Wordlessly, I stared at him confused about his statement but too alarmed to explore its implication. Numbly, I lumbered down the short corridor with him. It was as though my mind went through a pitch-black void trying to suppress the fear I was straining to compress inside me and, before I realized it, I was being lifted onto a cold, rigid gurney.

I cleared my throat nervously as I felt my legs tickle from the cold leather straps laced tightly across my wrists and ankles. "Oh Jesus," I said to myself. "This is it."

I suddenly felt an unsuspected urge to crap and vomit all at once but something told me to resist these urges—hold it.... hold it.... hold it—a voice rotated back and forth inside my mind. I shook my head, waving off this feeling. It really shouldn't matter how my body would initially react to death. In either case, who would really care if a hefty deposit of crap was discovered inside my underwear.

I blinked my eyes trying to adjust from the bright, phosphorescent ceiling lights and, suddenly, a faceless feature of a strange man looked squarely into my eyes.

"This will only take a few minutes. I am going to place an IV in your vein. A fast-acting barbiturate will be first injected inside you to make you sleep. You won't feel a thing. The other drugs will stop your breathing and heartbeat."

I made no response, unclear whether his statement was necessary or maybe he was trying to make me feel calm.

I then turned. The warden had a pensive expression on his face while on the telephone. He was speaking with the Governor, I surmised; however, before I could ponder about a miraculous stay, he had slowly placed the receiver down on the hook.

"Nothing has changed," he sighed.

Motioning to Stoney, who was now standing by a thick curtain, instinctively I knew what he was doing. It was going to be his forty-seventh execution. He was preparing for witnesses to see it.

The worst thing for the victims is their impatience with this long, legal process. Critics often say the process creates cruel and unusual punishment on both sides. Somehow, in the overall scheme of things, we manage to tolerate it.

Sixteen years ago, I still remembered the Wilkerson's family members' faces in Dyersburg. Ace had severed a part of their lives and included me in this nightmare. My execution was the final chapter in their lives, finally releasing them from the perpetual tension about my quest to escape this manner of justice.

A bead of saliva glistened across the corner of my mouth. My eyes watched the curtain while I languorously tried to lick the drool away.

Now something incredible occurred. There were several other individuals besides the Wilkerson family and Proctor.

As I turned, looking for someone to explain who they were, Stoney walked over to me.

"They're here," he said. "Waiting for you to speak to them." Suddenly, there was a sharp gasp from a black woman who stood up.

"Stoney," I pleaded. "What's going on? Who are these other people?" I asked. He then edged closer to me cocking his head suspiciously.

"Ya know who they are."

"I-I-I don't understand you."

"I told them to come. It was me that got them here."

"What do you mean?" I asked intently.

"It was your thoughts. I hear your thoughts—all of 'em. Been hearing condemned men's thoughts for thirty-five years. That's why I came here with you, ya know, to get things real right for you, son."

"But.... I-I-I- still don't understand," I moaned softly.

"Don't ya—?"

"No!"

"We don't have much time left. I told them about Kent, Iowa."

"I.O.W.A.", my eyes flew wide. "What about Iowa?"

"About how you murdered Ms. Jennifer's grandmother. Told the Davidson and Corey folks about you changing that flat tire and wanting money and such. You remember now? That Red Chevy you stole after killing that boy and girl? You know. Ya remember, don't ya? These are their parents."

"Oh Gawd," I screamed.

"That's why I'm gonna finish your memoirs, son, ya know, to make everything right. Now tell these nice folks that you're sorry. Ask them to forgive you son, please!"

"Yesss," I yelled out, incapable of repressing a flood to both guilt and tears. "Yesss," I screamed. "I'm so sorry for what I did," I sobbed. "I'm sorry," I wheezed and coughed, over and over again.

Stoney then leaned over, even closer to me. So close, I could smell the blandness of his breath. I tried to search for an explanation in his cold eyes—searching for an explanation is one thing and trying to get ready to die is another. I simply conceded the point.

"Now repent son. Repent to the Lord," he whispered softly in my ear.

"I'm getting sleepy, Stoney.... I'm getting soooo sleepy. I'm scared, Stoney, real scared." I could feel the barbiturate working swiftly inside me.

"I know, son, but you gotta repent before you go to sleep," Stoney replied.

"I-I repent.... Stoney. God, pleaseeee.... forgive me," I moaned.

"That's good, son," Stoney said while patting my chest gently.

"Stoney!"

"I know son, she told me what that scripture was—it's Isaiah 54:17."

"No weapon that is formed against thee shall prosper; and everyone that shall rise against thee in judgement thou shall condemn. This is the heritage of the servants of the Lord, and their righteousness is of me, saith the Lord."

"But just before you shot her, she mumbled this last verse:

"Therefore, will I number you to the sword, and ye shall all bow down to the slaughter: because when I called, ye did not answer; when I spake, ye did not hear; but did evil before mine eyes, and did choose what wherein I delighted not."

"Isaiah 65:12."

"That's right son—Isaiah 65:12."

"Ooooooo Gawd, I did do evil in God's eyes. Yes I did," I sobbed heavily. "Please tell them I am really sorry, Stoney.... pleaseee. I was gonna confess it because I was only trying to stay alive. But I-I-I really couldn't do it when I got Ms. Pryor's letter. I know killing those people in Iowa was so bad," I cried, nearly choking on a thick layer of saliva that had formed inside my mouth. "Stoney, will God ever forgive me for what I did there?"

He then shook his head, making a sidelong glance at the witnesses. "We gonna pray that HE does, Mr. Shelton. Surely, we gonna pray—all of us is gonna pray for ya, son".

"Finish my stories, STONEY.... F.i.n.i.s.h.... my.... Stor.... Orrrrr.... reeeeeee.... eeeeee.... eeeeeeeeeeee," Shelton said as his voice faded away with a prolonged slur.

His eyes slowly closed, leaving only a deep hollow groan—a death grumble in his throat punctuated with several short and successive grunts. A few moments later, his chest gave one mountainous heave releasing his final breath. Less than three minutes later, the heartrate monitor echoed a loud, eerie alarm with a single line stretched across its screen.

And soon the attending physician confirmed what everyone realized—that he was dead.

The viewing room had been gripped tight like a vice, almost hypnotic while the spectators watched with near intrigue-like necrophilia as the unprocessed cycle of death slowly integrated itself toward the process of its completion. The cold eyes of the witnesses blinked excessively, perhaps none of them actually knew how they would feel watching him die but, in the abstract, the bittersweet revenge that had massaged their hate for 16 years failed to give them the expectant gratification of justice.

Jennifer Pryor's previously scorching look had now given way to a stricken expression of horror. She, too, like the others, were utterly astonished by what just transpired between the old guard and Virgil Shelton. Speechless everyone now recognized why they came and the significant connection with each other and, no one was feeling a viable consumption of regal satisfaction as they all gave Stoney one final, long appraisal stare.

The old guard stared evenly and soberly at each of their faces. He seen these faces before—it was like all the other times that he nurtured their internal grievances while giving them that final opportunity to hear those secrets—repressed deeds well hidden inside the cranial chambers of a killer's mind.

Stoney then slowly turned staring down at Shelton's lifeless remains. The old prison guard shook his head slowly. It was his calling that he perfectly understood would continue on Death Row—a conduit who remained a willing servant to some unexplainable power that allowed him to consume the thoughts of condemned men's secrets while knowing, in every instance, that it was he that would finish their memoirs.

Leaning over, his face etched with an incurable sadness, he strained to withhold a tear as he uttered his final remark, "I will, son.... I will."

MEMOIRS FROM DEATH ROW

THE FINISHED STORIES OF VIRGIL SHELTON

ALOON
BARBE
Emma's House
WOMEN
STABLE
WHERE ANGELS LAY
by : Raymond Andrew Clark
Short Fiction Story
Approximately 8,500 words

CHAPTER TWO

WHERE ANGELS LAY

HANK JACOBS WATCHED THE BARN BOY STRIP OFF THE SADDLE and bridle from his chestnut Colt. Without a word, he tossed two silver dollars at his feet. He looked at Hank, a painful gaze. Hank's face was drawn, thin, and his eyes burned from days of heavy trail dust. They set deep inside his head—cold, killer, black eyes. For several moments, his body stiffened, and he said nothing, absolutely nothing as he studied the little Mexican stable hand. He coughed slightly. His throat was still raw from the hot, Texas sun near the Mexican border, and he was annoyed that he rode into El Paso so late. He planned to be there earlier, a day earlier, to kill a man.

He sighed, turning around to glare at the full moon. It was almost ten o' clock. Anxious cowhands rode past him galloping towards the Santa Rita Saloon and Emma's whorehouse. Somehow, he could feel the nervous boy staring at him. He enjoyed turning his back on people; his instincts could sense their every move… heartbeat… tenseness… conviction… eyes… Turning he could see the light close. He was always ready to kill them before they change into the darkness. It was unending moments of the darkness when they each decided to kill but, he was always faster. The lack of hesitation gave him the edge.

"Bed him down good, boy. Aim to leave before noon tomorrow."

"Si, senor."

"Brush him first. He likes a good rub before his sweet oats."

"Si, senor."

His eye swung down to his boots. He patted them twice, kicking the last bit of trail dust from them. Glancing back, he saw the little boy walk slowly toward the last stall. He then paced slowly toward the Santa Rita Saloon. Snapping his Lancaster 4-barrel shotgun open, he tossed four shells inside it. A scatter gun would empty out a crowded bar, he thought.

The stale sweat had sufficiently dried on his face. His stride quickened as he considered how many times he would shoot this murderer and cattle thief. It needed to be quick. Slow agonizing deaths unsettle him, not his conscience, but his poor aim. He enjoyed killing outlaws, fugitives, society's scoundrels for a living. Hank was now the most feared bounty hunter the west had ever known.

For a moment, there was a slight flicker in his eyes. He stopped in his tracks. "Jason Clayton's horse," he moaned. He instantly recognized his horse. He grinned, a subtle grin. "Gonna kill him, too," he muttered. His face changed rapidly as Hank thought for a moment. His muscles relaxed as he worked the tension from his body. Last time he made a miscalculation about Clayton. Just a hairbreadth twitch of a movement altered his shot. It felt awfully good when he squeezed the trigger. Awfully good. "Dammit," he said as the bullet whistled out the barrel. "I`ll be," he flinched. The bullet scraped across Clayton's scalp as he ducked and coiled, racing for cover.

There was a long pause as Clayton's wild eyes searched the thick terrain for his assailant. Hank remained quiet. Already in his mind, he had undoubtedly missed his chance. Clayton was too fast for an even-up showdown. In fact, he was lightning fast—the only man he knew that was faster than himself. Ol' Clayton cussed at him releasing a hail of bullets that ricocheted off every rock and tree near him. The rocks shattered and bark splintered as debris flew in every direction at once.

He kept yelling and screaming but Hank maintained his composure. Clayton was trying to rattle him with the barrage. "Reckon you had me," he yelled. "I'll find ya." Clayton chuckled ignorantly.

Hank remained silent. He knew the silence was killing this bank robber and horse thief. That reward of $500.00 was always disturbing him. Somehow, Clayton believed the price should have been more—a thousand more—likely ending with a wire tag looped around his big toe.

Hank would wait nonchalantly, hiding safely out of Clayton's range and sight. He knew time was on his side. He was patient—killing always required a strange level of twisted tolerance. That was the difference—patience.

Clayton laughed. "C'mon." His six-shooter barked again… and again… and again… snapping a volley of shots that rained everywhere. Clayton's horse snorted, momentarily spooked by his uncontrolled craziness. His leathery face contorted as the last shot fell harmlessly in the dust but, Clayton was no fool. He had plenty of ammunition left. He now was dug in waiting five minutes… fifteen minutes… and finally a full hour. Soon, his thin layer of patience had significantly worn.

The nervous Clayton rushed out from the brush, leaping up on his horse and quickly rode away. That was thirteen months ago near Tombstone. This was tonight near the Mexican border—a different town and different time. This time he did not intend to twitch.

This journey had ended in El Paso, Texas, a place where Horace Grimms was also hiding. He followed the rumors, whorehouses and Grimms' whiskey trail to the border. Grimms was a gun-for-hire, but mostly a pathetic killer, indiscriminately killing without cause, without compunction. Time after time like replaying it over in his mind, Hank analyzed how Grimms' eyes would be set the moment he fired the first round inside his thick gut—a bullet that would combine both the end of Grimms' life and his nightmarish pursuit of him.

He was wasting no time; already his finger rubbed across his blue steel, six shot Colt 44. Hank cocked his head looking intensely. He then bristled from a sudden warm breeze. Rubbing his fingers together, he raised an eyebrow that caught a movement near Clayton's horse. His head spun in both directions, searching for an ambush. He gazed down the long street, once... twice... a third, and finally a fourth time. His eyes caught glimpses of every single movement. Turning for a half a minute, he stared again at Clayton's horse. And then—there it was! He saw it now, a drunken cowhand staggering to his feet from behind the water trough. His dogmatic vigilance and unflappable concentration was perhaps unusually guarded.

Hank warily watched the drunken cowpoke as he nestled down in a chair outside the saloon. His back then pressed against a dark wall, concealing his dark frame and his even darker thoughts. A smug grin worked across his face as his tongue rotated the black tobacco around inside his mouth. A quiet spit leapt from his mouth and fell quietly on the dusty boardwalk. He was feeling a surge of both adrenaline and ecstasy. He braced himself for this long-awaited event. "I'll be damn," he thought, "I'll kill both of 'em tonight." He grinned.

He stood still, never a movement, never a sound, just staring at the people going in and out of the saloon. About an hour had passed when he finally moved away from the wall. His eyes narrowed. He glanced briefly, right and left, as he strolled nimbly quick across the street. He gazed down at the drunken cowhand. He had now lifted his groggy head staring into Hank's coal-black eyes. He squinted his eyes as Hank lowered his wide black hat shielding his cold face. Suddenly, an unwell premonition moved inside the cowhand.

Intuitively, he seemed to understand why Hank was there. Relieved, his shoulders collapsed. He sighed a breath of comfort.

"I ain't lookin' for you." Hank said to the cowhand.

Drawing a long breath, another, and quickly another one, the cowhand said, "I reckon not."

"That horse (pointing at Clayton's horse), you know where that man is?"

"Uh huh!"

Hank smiled. This was going to be easier than he thought. "Where?"

"Whiskey," he grinned. "A pint of rot, cost you four pesos, but can you spare two bucks? Ya' know, a few numbers on the Roulette," he giggled.

"Sure." Hank reached inside his breast pocket and tossed a ten-dollar bill on his lap. "Keep it! There's a second piece to it, another name, there's two of 'em."

The cowhand looked at Hank for a moment. He wasn't fooled. The nature of his subtle inquiries was keenly understood by him. Tucking the ten-dollar bill inside his shirt pocket, he soberly gestured down the street. "Down there," he pointed, "Ol' Emma's whorehouse, that's where he went to. Took old Grace Early with 'em. She's a whore," he snickered weakly.

"The other man. They call him Horace. Horace Grimms. A big fella, maybe wearing a big brown hat, brown and gray snakeskin boots, with two pearl handle Colts. He rides a big black colt, with tan patches on its right behind and a fancy calico spread on his saddle."

"Huntin' him too?" his grubby face asked nervously. He said, "Whiskey, I guess I'll get that drink now," he mumbled. He stared straight ahead not wanting to meet the tall man's gaze.

After a few moments, Hank moved closer to him ignoring the hysterical laughter and carnival sounds inside the saloon. He made a weird, unfriendly, raspy half-chuckle as he spoke, "I'll kill ya. Kill ya worse than dead." All doubts leaped from the cowhand's mind. He knew with certainty that Hank meant every word.

"I ain't sayin nothin. Just a drank. Ol' Charlie Moore won't be no problem. No sir," looking up at him, his face etched with desperation. "Hey Gringo, I don't want no trouble… ridin' out south in the mornin', a little place called El Porvenir—that where I'm from, just south of Juarez. Goin' to a juba t'morrow. I'm one of the dancers, ya know. I ain't gonna say nothin—not a word, I swear on my mammy's grave, no sir, notta word." He then slowly edged himself up, slightly bent over and unsteady on his feet. Then balancing himself, he asked, "Hey mister! Reckon if Ol' Charlie can go now?"

"Go on, ol' fella," Hank whispered. "Go on and remember my sayin."

"Yes, sir." At that moment, the old colored cowhand moved slowly between the swinging saloon doors, disappearing into a haze of smoke and noise.

Hank stared at the cowhand; his lips pressed tightly together. He was obviously annoyed at the unexpected question. Registering a look of mild disgust, his gradual body language made the cowhand suddenly uncomfortable about his statement. The ol' cowhand suddenly turned near the entrance of the saloon doors. "I'm just gonna get me another whiskey now," returning again to the entrance of the saloon door.

Suddenly, his eyes took on a near trance-like expression as he stared blankly ahead. He then raised his right hand feebly, quite possibly trembling as well. Pointing he then said, "He's down there, too, both of 'em—down at Ol' Emma's whorehouse."

Hank worked a feigned expression on his face. It was his death mask. Turning his head, one last discharge of tobacco rushed from his mouth clearing it completely. There was a sudden icy chill that raced through the cowhand's body. An eerie feeling of coldness was squeezing the alcohol from his pores. He shuddered and shook from the strange sensation. This was getting too damn dangerous, he believed. Hank's eyes weren't the eyes he wanted to see anymore.

The nail-biting silence gripped the frightened cowhand as he watched Hank's hand grip the shotgun barrel tighter. His chest heaved up and down, beads of wild sweat formed on his forehead. He understood the only thing that stood between him and those two men was his mouth. If he knew that, so did the stranger in front of him. Rubbing his haggard beard, the cowhand walked back inside the saloon.

Her eyes were closed but she wasn't asleep. A long blonde strand hung down her forehead. It draped over her nose and curled underneath her lips. She shook her head, grimacing at the smell of his foul whiskey breath. She smelled a stinking odor that reeked the room with rotten sour that oozed from inside his mouth. A big man, with a rough coarse beard, salt and pepper hair cords sealed with a thick, waxy pomade that semi-covered a large bald spot on his head. His pot belly, hairy chest heaved up and down while his snoring sprayed tiny mists of Tequila Whiskey scent from his nostrils.

She felt used, abused and saturated by his body filth. He had deep scars across his chest. Long scars that ridged a horrifying puffiness on his body. She remembered him bragging that he had killed 47 Indians, mostly mountain Apache, a few Sioux and the rest, he wasn't certain about. The boasting also included women and children. He was an ex-lawman, and now an ex-bounty hunter on the run. A $5,000 price tag loomed over his head.

He also told her that a small Apache war party ambushed him two years ago near Copper Creek early one morning. It was six young braves that tracked him for miles. They buried their sharp buffalo knives deep inside his chest, rotating a trail across it. He screamed, gasping as the blood raced over his chest rushing down both sides in dozen directions. Closing his eyes, he knew this was only the beginning of his terror. However, almost miraculously, his wraithlike wails met the anxious ears of a small Calvary detail tracking the wayward braves from Fort Bliss; their eventual rescue saved his miserable life.

She shook her head slowly from side to side. She tried to resist crying but small tears moved slowly and then faster down her smooth cheekbones. She sniffled and sniffed quietly again, concerned that he might wake up and pound lecherously inside her youthful body again. She froze and her mind raced away from the whorehouse back to Philadelphia where she was born. Her life was better, much better than this.

She still remembered the excitement on her mother's face when her father told her they were moving to Arizona. Her father was a dentist with a bright future in dentistry. They left for Tucson five years ago, the four of them, including her younger sister. It was a risky proposition by the town to help finance a large dental program in the southwest. At first, things were going well, better than anyone had expected but tragedy wasn't far behind them. Her mother and sister suffered from a serious bout of tuberculosis and died months later. She, too, suffered as well but miraculously survived.

It seemed so incredible, but their deaths melted her father's dreams. Soon, he became an alcoholic. His dentistry skills eluded him as patients began complaining and, later, they simply stopped coming. The town finally sealed his fate by terminating their agreement and closing down his dental office. After much debate, her father couldn't obtain enough town support to carry on. This was 1873 and Arizona was a long way from joining the union and, thus, no appeal was available for him.

Three years later, the insidious tragedies were continuing to repeat in her life. It was one lone evening and she would never forget the cold, hard, wet driving rain. She had an eerie feeling when she heard a lone rider stop in front of the cabin.

The knock unsettled her. It was the town marshal. Her eyelids now fluttered as she remembered his painful expression. "I'm sorry," he said. "Your pop was shot point blank in the chest. He died inside Clancy's place. A bar girl shot him. Argument over some money but don't know for sure." She sank to her knees sobbing as the tall man patted her softly on her shoulder. "Got a place to stay?" he asked.

Suddenly, a movement caught her attention disconnecting her thoughts. Her body grew tense. She strained to listen for another sound. Again, another movement and this time she felt a presence move by her bed.

Gradually opening her eyes, the room was pitch-dark. It had been her ideal, the darkness. She didn't want him staring at her while she undressed. She lifted up her upper body, supporting it by her elbows. She was silent for a moment. This was insane, but somehow, she believed something was inside the room. Turning, she stared at the large man. He was still asleep.

"Something is wrong," she said quietly. Slowly, with a near perfect cautiousness, she moved easily from the bed. Her thoughts were all connected to the sound. It was indescribable and inexplicable, but it was audible—she was certain of it.

She kneeled, slipping on her bra and panties. Next, she picked up and wrapped herself inside her gown. Quickly, she gingerly tiptoed over to the dresser. She stared around the room, perplexed and disoriented. As she pondered her next move, the pearl handle Colt pistols' glitter caught her eye through the intense darkness. He strapped them across the bedpost close to him. The perspiration was beginning to form on her temple. Her heartbeat increased, pounding inside her chest so hard that her eardrums vibrated. Something was about to happen inside this bedroom. She just knew it.

Now terrified, her puny left hand moved ceaselessly across the top of the dresser's surface. Now almost frantically but quietly, roaming until her hand stopped—it gripped her small, red Bible. She picked it up, clutching it to her body, while praying. It was the only thing meaningful left in her seventeen-year-old life—her mother's red Bible. Her body was now chilled by a combination of fright and uncontrolled speculation.

She had been mysteriously awakened by something, something that was still inside the bedroom with her and this drunken cowboy.

She blinked, hearing another movement near the door. She shook, now nearly hysterical, as mop-sweat dripped from her hands. She abruptly felt a deep pain inside her stomach. She wanted to scream but something sealed her mouth.

"On the floor... the floor... the floor... get down quickly," a voice drilled alarmingly inside her head. Her eyes ping-ponged as she looked at the door, now the sleeping cowboy, and now the floor. Quickly and quietly, she fell on the floor curling up in a fetal position still praying... praying very hard.

BAMMMM!!

The sound raced through the room as though a locomotive had roared by it. The loud, ear-splitting reverberations came with inglorious rage as the wooden door shattered in half by the incredible force of Hank's shotgun. Her body now safely concealed on the floor as shots thundered from a competent aim.

BAMMMM... BAMMMM... BAMMMM!! Three separate, distinct rounds charged angrily at Grimms' body without bothering to comprehend if the bed occupied anyone else. Her stomach knotted. Grimms screamed one loud, incapacitating yip-yowl as the blasts tore pieces of his flesh throughout the room. Nothing on the bed was spared from the flesh-seeking pellets that suddenly turned the bed into a bloody, ghastly human collage of separated pieces of Grimms' torn flesh.

"Oh, God," she said shaking. "Oh, Jesus," she sobbed.

It was over within ten seconds but perhaps more like ten minutes... ten hours... ten years or maybe ten lifetimes in her mind. Her eyes were still sealed shut and the red Bible is now almost welded to her chest.

She could now hear the neurotic screams of panic-stricken women running throughout the house. Death was also very prominent somewhere else inside the large, two-story adobe frame, square-shaped villa. Emma Smith, the owner, rushed from door to door screaming with uncalculated fear and disbelief. Drunken, half-naked cowboys, staggering, twisting, and spinning as they struggled to dress while both fright and agitation rocked their dull senses. Shock and surprise gripped Emma as she cringed from the unthinkable scene—a nightmarish sight of double human carnage semi-annihilated by an unimpassioned fiend. She thought only raw hate spun by a pernicious evil could kill like this. The scene was uncontrolled chaos as the uninhibited squeals evoked a general alarm, even past the deafening noise inside the Santa Rita. Anxious cowhands raced toward the whorehouse with crazed speculation and trepidation about what could have caused such a scene at Emma's.

"Somebody go get the Marshal," Emma pleaded. "My God," she gasped. "He's still here. Right here! He's down by the front door," she screamed.

Meanwhile, still partially dazed, the young woman struggled to her feet. During the rabid commotion, she had seemingly been forgotten. She had been dumped in El Paso days earlier by a young cowboy who crossed the border. Stranded, broke and exhausted, her eventual refuge came under the safe haven of Emma's place; a spot that somehow, unexplainably, was a magnet that drew other young women under similar circumstances to Emma's whorehouse.

Still clutching her small red Bible, she stumbled through the web of confusion inside the hallway. The hammering screams became a mild whimper as the women began running down the stairs to safety.

It took her a few minutes to fully comprehend what had just occurred before the shootings. As she moved down to the first floor, a young black-haired, Spanish-looking woman called out to her.

"Sara," she paused, "Sara Palmer, are you okay?" she asked, with an accent.

She frowned. "I'm all right." Not stopping, Sara continued past the large sitting area, continuing on through the bar, and still on to a small room near the kitchen and four adjacent rooms.

Sara clamped her eyes shut. She was trying to contemplate the aura of suspense that pulled at her subconscious mind. This was certainly no illusion to her. Sara's pale face strained to revisit that sound somewhere in that room. She tossed her head backwards, brushing back her strawberry blonde hair. It fell midway to her back; an even edge just recently trimmed by Emma. It was her customary practice to personally groom and pamper the women she referred to as her "Angels."

In the distance, she could hear Emma complaining to the Marshal about the damage to her two bedrooms and lost revenue. It was Friday night—the whorehouse's best night. Her twenty-three women would entertain both cowboys and gauchos north and south of the border.

In the midst of her complaint, Emma seemed to ignore the tragic nature of the two men's deaths. Both Jason Clayton and Horace Grimms' bodies had been perfectly destroyed by a lethal killing machine. As her sarcastic complaints continued, it was obvious that the Marshal failed to provide her with a solution. It was only when Hank gave her a $100 bill, with the promise of another $200 upon receiving his reward money, did the matter end.

Sara's thoughts then slipped back into the bedroom. She laboriously fought to understand what had occurred to her and why. There was something standing over her. It had made the Tequila whiskey in her system ineffectual as its presence moved past. In some convoluted way, it was speaking to her—guiding her from the bed, nudging her over to the dresser as she grabbed her Bible and prayed. It was all so well-orchestrated to move her away from a certain death.

It was now nearly 3:00 a.m. The whorehouse was silent again. Sara had curled up in a chair asleep still clutching her red Bible. Gradually, very gradually, her eyes opened to a faint sound. She studied it for a moment not sure what it was. Unfolding her long, slender legs, she quietly touched them to the floor. Still listening intensely, she now recognized the room where the sound was coming. Someone was playing a piano in the last room. She hesitated for a moment and then moved with deliberate and well-precise steps closer to the lightly touched sounds of the piano keys. As she inched closer to the room, she began to believe, utterly without deduction, that perhaps this wasn't real—like the supernatural experience in the bedroom.

She stopped outside the door. Her heart momentarily fluttered as she grabbed her breath. Closing her eyes, she took a long breath, relaxed and tried to remain calm. With one hand, she turned the door knob pushing the door open ever so slightly a few inches. Again, she paused holding her breath.

She shivered. Obviously, the person had noticed the door opening because the music stopped, she believed. She hesitated in her spot waiting to hear a word or sound. It didn't happen. She now could feel someone on the other side of the door. For a brief moment, an impulse jolted inside her body with a wild notion to run—run like hell, she thought. "No"! Something in her head told her, "No, don't go!" "Oh Jesus, help me," she muttered to herself. "What's happening to me?" she asked barely audible.

She quickly drew her shoulders up as she sensed pressure on this opposite doorknob. Someone was holding it. She suddenly began to imagine several hair-brained thoughts. It was finally luring her to this isolated room to destroy her with hellish pleasure. Sara's mouth was dry; her knees buckled as the door stretched her small arm. The door now moved sufficiently open as she continued to squeeze the knob, now drenched with crazed sweat. She braced herself, ready to be killed at any moment. Suddenly, a round head quickly darted from behind the door post frame. She gasped! Leaping back quickly, the movement produced uncharted fear inside her body.

"Yes, ma'am. You alright?"

Their eyes met each other's gaze. It was a young Negro boy, dressed in a black suit, white shirt and black bow tie. He flashed a wide grin at her. It was an energetic smile that exposed his unsoiled, white teeth. A small gap wedged his bottom front teeth slightly apart. His full face encircled two large, almond-shaped brown eyes. He was frail, perhaps 13 years old or so. His hair was oil black, combed back with tiny waves in neat rows. He was brown-skinned, almost mulatto looking, but not quite.

Sara looked at him speculatively. He then stepped backward without uttering another word but, somehow, she believed he was inviting her inside the room. She paused, rubbing her temple slightly, perhaps attempting to insure she wasn't sleepwalking.

"Never seen you before," she said. Smiling, she walked slowly inside the room. "I'm all right." Her muscles relaxed in her neck as she answered his question.

"You must be Helen's boy. She so sweet. This place couldn't run without all the cooking and cleaning she does around here." The boy smiled and said nothing.

"You play so well."

"Yes, ma'am."

"Been playing long?"

"'Bout six years, ever since I was seven."

"Who taught you?"

He grinned. "Taught myself. Asked the Lord to teach me."

"Huh," she giggled. "I'm sorry, did you say the Lord?"

"Yes, ma'am. Always praying to God so one day I just asked HIM to teach me," he smiled.

"Well, I'll be. What can you play?"

"Anything I hear and like. I make up my own music."

That's amazing. Really amazing—I'll be," Sara said, now relaxed as she sat beside him on the piano seat.

"You know what else?" he said with an unusual glee in his face.

Sara shrugged her shoulders. "What else?"

"I know secrets. The Lord tells me things."

"What?" she snapped. Chuckling innocently, she then said, "What does the Lord tell you?"

"I knew that man was coming here last night. He was gonna kill those two men. I saw him coming to your room."

"My room?" Both surprise and alarm fell across Sara's face from his bizarre statement. "Are you sure?" she asked with much doubt in her voice.

"Yes, ma'am."

The room was silent for a moment. Stunned, Sara then asked, "How did you know that?"

"The Lord, I told ya." He casted a strange stare at her. She bristled sharply from the expression. Still perplexed, there was an odd feeling moving inside her—the same feeling she had just before the shooting occurred upstairs. She was beginning to recognize his voice. It was maybe the same voice she heard inside her head uttering the admonitions to fall to the floor.

She looked quizzical at him, confused. This wasn't possible for a little negro boy to possess such an incredible gift, she thought. He heard all the commotion, perhaps even overheard a conversation about her from one of the women, she believed. He was just being coy, making a mockery of her, she thought—or was he, she reconsidered. She sighed.

"My momma always read the Bible to us. She really loved the Lord. I do, too," she said with a faint smile.

"I know."

"You know?"

"Uh huh."

Her hands curled the Bible tighter as if she was contemplating her next question or even trying to assess the strange character of this mysterious colored boy.

"Why me? I ain't been so grand. I'm in a terrible place like this. When my Poppa was killed, I didn't have any place to go. Didn't know my aunt's address in Philadelphia. I was taken in by Mrs. Daisy. They owned a ranch nearby us. I was fifteen years old." She stopped momentarily, shaking her head.

"Her old dirty husband started doing nasty things to me." She paused. "After so long, I finally told her. She didn't believe me and threw me out. Been drifting around ever since. But, I always been carrying my red Bible and praying to God every single day; praying he would send me back to Philadelphia to my kin folks. A cowpoke told me he was gonna take me but he came here instead and left me to do some cattle rustling across the border. So, I guess that's that, reckon," she sighed.

"I reckon," the boy repeated. His small fingers struck a light note on the piano. He then turned and grinned at her.

"You want to go to Philadelphia today? The stage leaves this morning at 7:00 a.m. It will take you to St. Louis. The train will then take you all the way to Philadelphia from there."

"Hardly. That takes money for a ticket. I can go eventually, but I've got to do some back work, ya' know, to earn some money and my keep."

"No, you don't?"

"Whatcha mean?"

"Ticket."

"A ticket."

"Look inside your dresser. It's there—right there!"

Sara hesitated before replying. She pulled herself erect. Her body froze while her mind raced to absorb the shock of his statement. Far back in her mind, she remembered her mother reading about spirits, angels and miracles in the Bible. She was aware that sometimes spirits worked through people and even animals. She sighed. Her body had become flushed with jubilation.

"Are you...?" She abruptly stopped before completing her sentence.

"Uh, uh," he remarked.

She winced. "Did you know what I was about to say?"

"Yes, ma'am, but I ain't no angel. No, ma'am."

She laughed. "I guess that was a silly thought." She shrugged. "Is this some joke?"

"No, ma'am. Just look inside your drawer. The top one." He then turned staring at the piano. "I've got to see Helen in a few minutes. You take care, Miss Sara."

"My name!" She snapped. "How did you know my name?"

He shrugged. "I heard someone calling you."

"Hmmmmm." She winced. "Well, nice meeting you and what's your name?"

"Paul, Paul Tracker."

"Good." Sara stood up and walked over to the door. She then turned and stared at the strange boy. "So, Paul," she smiled placing her right hand on her hip, "if my ticket isn't there, that's okay. Can we be friends? I really need a pal."

"Oh, yes, ma'am. Friends forever and ever." He giggled softly. They both laughed. "Well, I'll see ya' later."

The boy then slowly turned facing the piano. He looked rigid and formal looking. His mind seemed now to be somewhere else.

"When you find your ticket, top drawer, don't say nothin' to nobody. Ol' Miss Emma will make you stay and force you to pay wages for your keep for a long time. You just quietly go and sit peacefully inside the stage office. She won't know. Catch the stage and thank the Lord, all right?"

Sara nodded. "I will."

Closing the door, Sara waved good-bye, believing their paths would cross several more times. She relaxed with her mind settled from the mystifying conversation with the remarkable Negro boy. It was too premature for her to jump to any conclusions, but she intended to check the dresser drawer.

As she moved toward the kitchen, another sound grabbed her attention. She instantly recognized that it was coming out of Helen's room. Apprehensive, Sara was closed-mouth as she inched closer to the door. Now listening through the door, she could hear the soft moans of Helen. She was weeping.

'Miss Helen?" she whispered pressing the side of her face closer to the door. "You all right, ma'am?"

Moments later, a small seam in the door streaked vertically. It opened up to a brown-skinned, heavy-faced woman. "I'm okay, sugar." She wiped her tear-soaked face. "You go on. Just some sad news from the telegraph office yesterday. Gone on baby, Miss Helen will be all right."

"All right."

Sara moved slowly away, her mind was now running about the strange boy and the dresser drawer. She hustled quickly upstairs. Arriving inside her bedroom, she bristled rethinking whether she should even enter it. Sara's eyes were set. She would suppress the ungodly sight of the bloody scene from her mind. She commiserated for a long time.

There was that strange feeling again, without pin-pointing its connection, but somehow, she felt it was related to the room and the boy. Her mind locked, sealing the grisly scene somewhere else in her head. Sara pushed the door open racing to the dresser. She pulled open the top drawer. At first, she didn't see it. Her face become swollen and scarlet. She stepped back as the disappointment was beginning to stir inside her. A final and complete tug of the drawer exposed a white envelope lodged, almost concealed in the corner of it. In an instance, she grabbed it shaking her head. Her hands trembled as she flipped it open and removed a ticket. A ticket... ticket... ticket..., the word rattled and tattooed inside her head. "Jesus," she said, shaking in disbelief. She was absolutely thunderstruck!

For a few seconds, her thoughts were composed of the smiling, mellow features of the boy. It was his gift—a mysterious and unfathomable connection with God—that rocked her conscience. She wept for a brief moment. This had become a mental cliff-hanger for her, pushing her own sanity between the vortex of humans and spirits. Somewhere in the scheme of it all, she realized, with unequivocal and irrefutable evidence that he, without question, was her guardian angel.

Hearing Emma's voice, the reality of her next move was now apparent. Grabbing one of her two outfits, she quickly raced to the bathroom. A fast bath and a swift change of clothing had now prepared her to leave. This was now going to be a delicate matter. Emma maintained strict control over the women. Her iron clad grip was reinforced by a four-man security squad.

Sara returned to her room. Dawn had now arrived very quickly. It was almost 6:00 a.m. and most of the women were still asleep. She moved quietly downstairs, still wondering what she might tell the lone guard posted at the front door. She smiled as the lanky man stared at her.

"Are you comin' for these?" he asked, holding a pair of pearl-handled Colts. The Marshal forgot 'em. Miss Emma said one of ya'll would take 'em to the office." She nodded. Taking the gun belt and two pistols, she casually strolled by him.

After dropping the gun belt off, she hurriedly walked another quarter of a mile to the stagecoach office.

It seemed like forever but the stagecoach finally arrived. The stop was brief as it just obtained a fresh team of trail horses. Trembling, she was hoping someone wouldn't contact Emma. Moments later, the driver barked out a loud command to his anxious horses who responded by snorting and grunting as they galloped in unison down the long dusty street.

That was nearly twenty-five years ago as Sara Lee Harris, now an evangelist, yawned and stretched her long legs upon hearing the train conductor yelling, "El Paso... El Paso, Texas." She was traveling with her husband and two teenage boys. This was the last stop on a fifty-nine-day revival across the southwest area. She and her husband were preaching and teaching the New Testament and Gospel.

It was now 1903. Both the United States and Mexican railroad had reached El Paso helping to create a land and population bonanza. As for Sara, she was both nervous and tense. Her mind still contained all the images of drunks, fights, vulgarities and lawlessness in the town twenty-five years ago—and Emma's whorehouse. She also remembered that horrible Friday night, the insane killings, and the little negro boy who saved her life. A life that eventually was pre-destined for her to spread the ministry and her personal testimony for eleven years from coast to coast about her stage encounter. She had often wondered about Helen's son, a boy that she never had an opportunity to formally thank or even say farewell to before her departure. It seemed utterly impossible to believe but it was true—every single detail was still fresh in her mind.

She insisted that they go directly to see if the whorehouse was still there. Despite her family's supportiveness, Sara seemed apart from them. There was something that she needed to resolve in her mind.

Within a half-hour, they arrived at the villa. It was slightly worn but well preserved. She then turned to her husband and said, "Will you wait here? I need to do this alone." He nodded, motioning to the boys to remain inside the carriage with him.

From the inside, someone followed the tall, long-legged blonde down the long walkway.

Soon, Sara was ringing the doorbell. A smallish, rotund, white woman with silver hair answered the door.

"May I help you?"

"Yes ma'am?"

"Is Emma here?"

She smiled. "Oh, Lordy. Do come in." She waved at Sara's family while closing the door. Turning, she looked delighted to see her.

"Is that your family?"

"Yes, it is."

"Handsome fellas. Any girls?" She laughed. "We're partial to them."

"No, maybe later."

"That's nice." She paused. "Did you know Emma Smith?"

"Yes, ma'am."

She smiled. "Emma was sweet in her own way. Never agreed with her business—the girls, the men, the drinking and such." She frowned. "She's been dead almost fifteen years now. Left this place to her daughter. She lived somewhere in Illinois. Came down to the funeral, stayed three days and sold the place. Left like a whirlwind. Ain't seen or heard from her since."

"I'll be."

"It's a home for young women now. We got different angels," she said with a snicker.

"Thank the Lord." Sara mumbled. "Is Miss Helen still here? And her son?"

"Heavens yes! Lordy, lordy... couldn't run this place without Helen. She's the girls' nanny. Everybody love her to death. Don't remember anything about a son. Didn't know she was ever married, let long having any children but I've only been here ten years. Miss Helen is out back. We got lots a girls come by. I know she'll be glad to see 'ya."

Sara smiled as she walked away. Now moving through the house, she could still hear the irrepressible voices, laughter and the drunken smell and scent of horny cowhands.

She was cautious approaching Helen's room. Just before knocking, her door suddenly opened. Helen's face lit up.

"Can I help you?" She smiled. It was obvious she didn't remember her.

"Yes, ma'am."

"C'mon in, honey." She stared at two young girls washing dishes. "Ya'll gone finish them chores." They both nodded and giggled as they stared at Sara.

Helen's room was hardly what she had expected. It was much larger, even longer, with a big spacious window. Their eyes met evenly. For some reason, Sara seemed fidgety.

"I'm sorry. Maybe you don't remember me. I worked her a long time ago. It was for only three days."

Helen nodded.

"Do you remember the night those two men were so horribly killed here?"

"Good God. I'll never forget that night."

"I was inside one of those rooms. I left the next day."

A flicker of surprise radiated across Helen's face. She shook her head as the memory surfaced in her mind.

"Child. Me and Miss Emma always wondered what happen to you." A wide smile worked across her face. "Well, I'll be. Don't you look so beautiful."

"Thank you."

Immediately, something caught Sara's eyes. It was sitting on Helen's nightstand. It was a small photograph. There was a short period of silence then Sara walked over and stared at it.

"He was wearing these exact same clothes that morning."

"Who?"

"Your son. I spoke with him. He was in the other room playing the piano. He warned me that night—made me get up, dress and take my mother's Bible. If I hadn't got out of that bed, I would have been killed. Christ, he saved my life. He said God told him things—secrets he called it." She then walked over and picked up the picture. "He even told me where my ticket was, that's how I left. I heard you crying that morning. I hoped he comforted you." She smiled. "Is he all right?"

Helen shrugged. She then slumped in a wide chair. Her mouth dropped open like a large sea bass. Her expression reflected unrestrained dumbfoundment. She rocked—first back and forth, then side to side—moving and now reeling as she seemed taken back by Sara's statements.

Sara realized something dreadful had occurred, perhaps the gruesome reflection of that grisly night had evoked some weird effect on her. Helen continued to shake and shudder.

"Are you alright?" Sara asked. A growing worriment settled over her face. "Excuse me, please. Miss Helen, did I say something wrong?"

"My father—that's my father in that picture. He was 13 years old then. It's the only picture I have of him. Left us when I was a little girl to join the Union army. He fought in the Civil War. He was wounded in his back. The bullet paralyzed him from his neck down. He was up in Ohio in a government hospital. The government took care of him. We moved to Texas after the war. I met Miss Emma in Dallas. That's how I came here to work for her."

"Oh, no, that can't be. I spoke to him. It was a boy, this same boy that's in this picture. I'm sure of it."

"But, it's true. My father died the same day those two men were killed. I got a telegram from the telegraph office earlier that day. I was crying all day. He always told me that his spirit would somehow find me. I could feel his presence somewhere that night."

"Your father??? This... is... your... father...?" Sara said slowly as she gulped spastically.

"You don't believe me?", Helen moaned. Small tears rolled down her face as she stared at the picture. "My daddy played the piano. He just taught himself. My momma always told me that God talked to him. She told us his mind could go places that he had never seen. The Lord took him there he always said to us. My daddy was always talkin' to the Lord. Just sayin', "No, sir; Yes, sir" and carrying on just like he was really talkin' to one of us."

She slowly rose, walking over and picking up a small box. Opening it, she pulled out and old faded telegram. It was a meager looking note. "Kept it all these years. Here read it:

"Helen Tracker.
Sorry to tell you that your father, Paul Tracker,
passed today, peacefully, Friday at 2:35 pm.
Please contact the hospital for arrangements
of his remains and personal items"
Chaplain R. E. Edwards
Colonel—Union Army

Helen then took the picture from Sara's trembling hand. She was meticulous as she gently removed the picture from the frame. Turning it over, there was a handwritten notation which read:

"To Lennie,
Love,
Paul Tracker—1854".

"Lennie was my mother's first name. Gave it to her the same year they were married. I was three years old at the time."

Sara was in complete awe. She stood frozen staring at Helen. This had become an unexplained phenomenon, detached from any rational or scientific description known to mankind which had occurred in her life. Without question, Paul Tracker's spirit had arrived that evening changing the course in her life.

Today that night had finally climaxed for both women. Without knowing why, a spiritual pendulum changed the course of their lives as it swung Sara's certain death to a life of full, unrestricted ministry. A ministry that included a mysterious baptism of a tall, feeble looking, barely mobile man one evening in Wichita, Kansas. The man heard her sterling testimony, a story that slammed his conscience with those horrible images that Friday night in a whorehouse, in El Paso, Texas. He understood the terror and near hysteria that was recorded in her memory. Bristling at the account, he was old—his arms and legs hurt crippled by years of arthritis and rheumatism pain.

Her testimony was one which he created that warm night. Unknowingly to her, Sara baptized Hank Jacobs, nineteen days earlier. A lonely man, broke and haunted by a sickening evil, deep inside a killer's mind. Sara would never forget the pained expression on his face as she smiled at him.

"God bless you sir", she said.

He nodded. "Done killed... killed a lot... killed real bad, more than I can remember," he replied. He then shook his head, "Reckon the good Lord will forgive that?" His anxious faced looked agitated and exhausted.

"God is merciful, even toward a cold-blooded killer," she answered.

"That I be—ma-am. That I be. Sorry for that evening, Miss," he said, while his lips trembled and hand shook. "Sorry! Sorry for a lotta bad things." He was then helped by two men to his seat.

Sara would miss the connection as she continued on with the baptism service.

Her moment had come full circle as both women sobbed moving towards each other, hugging and weeping in the center of the room. Helen father's spirit had come keeping his promise to her, while saving Sara's life and perhaps the destiny of other young women—'Angels' as Miss Emma liked to call them—forever.

Momma Brown's Crack House

Raymond A Clark

CHAPTER THREE

MOMMA BROWN'S CRACK HOUSE

THE STEAMY AUGUST HEAT WAVE HAD THE CITY ON THE BLUFF singing the blues. The lyrics of the stifling humidity angrily descended upon Memphis working its way throughout the city's steaming barbecue restaurants, while mopping southern sweat, sauteed the brows of foot-stomping, head-twisting blue singers that fascinated wide-eyed tourists who hustled up and down Beale Street with their all-night itineraries.

Across town, air-conditioners and ceiling fans roared in the Orange Mound neighborhood. The community was sagging, not solely from the ridiculously hot temperatures, but an unrelenting crime wave that worked in harmony with the oppressive heat. It was suffocating the residents nearly paralyzing them into submission.

Strangely enough, the menacing heat failed to intimidate the anxiety level of two local teenage thugs. Parked under a large maple tree in a rusty and wrecked 2000 black Infiniti I30, their truculent intentions separated them from the heat. They were too preoccupied by a single-minded agenda of robbing a crack house. Two cold Colt 45 double malts rested tightly in their sweaty hands. Their heads were bumping in cadence to several of their favorite gangstas rap songs.

They grinned at each other in silence, relieved after two days their determination wasn't squandered.

Looking through the rear-view mirror, a further confirmation of their plan now was emerging. The driver smiled, shaking his head with regal satisfaction. "Dee-Low, looka' here man, there's that fat-ass Sandy—the bitch comin' down the street."

Grim-faced, Dee-Low raised his red ball cap slightly above his bloodshot eyes. He shook his head wearily, "That's the third time in the last half hour."

"Yeah, just like yesterday," Trimmers said with an ignorant giggle.

"Huh-uh."

"Should I holler at her, ya know, see if she can cop an eight ball for us?" Trimmers asked.

"Hell nawwww, you dumb-ass. Then the bitch gonna t'ank somethin' up. Just be cool cuz."

Dee-Low squeezed his square chin pondering about how many rocks Sandra Parker was buying.

Delois Ivan Mitchell, aka 'Dee-Low', tilted his head back, his eyes staring toward the roof of the car. He took a long inhale wiping the heavy sweat away from his bumpy forehead. He was slightly nauseated. A bewilderment cloud loomed over his head about his rapidly approaching predicament, the climax of his freedom if he flunked summer school—passing grades were a stipulation on this third probation.

Dee-Low took another deep inhale. Nothing was right in his short life. He was nearly eighteen but he was beginning to feel old and the anxiety of being successful had absolutely nothing to do with an education but everything to do with him getting paid. Perhaps the latest verbal tirade with his English teacher, Mr. Armstrong, confirmed what he wanted to be, a gangbanger, hard core rapper with pimping whores and slamming Cadillac doors.

He lowered his head, sniffing haughtily at his last exchange with Mr. Armstrong. The heated argument occurred when Mr. Armstrong looked at him with a mixture of disgust and revulsion.

After failing to complete his fifth homework assignment, Mr. Armstrong frowned at him and while peering down his nose at him contemptuously, he said caustically, "If you ever want to hide something from a niggar, put it in a book." Mr. Armstrong turned away and repeated the statement again with a look of delight in his face. He then turned back facing the classroom with a momentary flicker of an annoyance glance snapped toward Dee-Low. He said pointing directly at Dee-Low, "You—you're a living product of that racist and degrading statement!" and shrugged slowly walking down a narrow classroom aisle. He sighed deeply, "I'm sorry if the statement offended anyone, it wasn't intended to be offensive, but a profound reminder that illiteracy is a serious problem among black teenagers, especially those who simply fail to comprehend our written language." He paused for a moment, his faced etched with sorrow.

Dee-Low felt a sudden urge to punch him squarely between his pouchy chipmunk cheeks. Twice he shook his head, stress lines raced across his forehead. His face was tight, pinched from the increasing notion that this snobbish, fleshly wattled bastard just disrespected him in front of his friends.

It took him a few minutes to figure out what to say, he closed his eyes and open them again. A chilly silence suddenly gripped the room. The moment made Mr. Armstrong feel uneasy. He could sense Dee-Low's irritation growing.

Dee-Low then shrugged angrily and said, "I ain't no stupid-ass niggar!" He frowned, suddenly slamming his English book to the floor. "Fuck this book and fuck you, too." He then stood up; his eyes looked venomously around the room searching for someone who disagreed with his assertion. "Anybody t'aink I'm stupid?" A predatory expression worked across his face. The classroom was quiet. No one opened their mouths for a reply.

Dee-Low's face gradually softened, and then slowly worked into a broad smile. He knew why they didn't respond. It wasn't that he personally intimidated them, even though they were afraid of him—his violent moods, treacherous demeanor, abrasive behavior—but none of these characteristics were as dominant as his influence was over Trimmers who was real homicidal. He was a real gun freak, especially for the exotic, automatic assault weapons that could extinguish multiple lives in a matter of seconds. He was a psychotic, weasel-like teenager who suffered from an acute schizoid personality which produced periods of extreme shyness and aloofness.

Oddly, these psychological conditions weren't present when he possessed guns which created a new and frightening personality within him—a dangerous and deadly psychiatric problem of an extreme homicidal nature and compulsion to kill people and other living things.

Trimmers would take his arsenal of weapons deep into the northern Mississippi woods and literally shoot every animal that moved. His juvenile rap sheet contained three shootings, four assaults, one attempted murder, and several brandishing incidents—all with guns. He had been to reform school twice and juvenile detention countless times. After his last reformatory sentence, he dropped out of school and was on state probation.

Dee-Low learned to cultivate a peculiar friendship with Trimmers, aka Edward Davidson Jr., by establishing a near like primordial allegiance that he selfishly created when they were incarcerated together in reform school. Regardless of what anyone thought about their relationship, a bizarre intimacy was formed. Trimmers gained a measure of self-importance around Dee-Low. He accepted being his 'main-niggar' a responsibility he took seriously. In fact, so serious that he was willing to do anything to demonstrate his loyalty to him, including murder.

Before long, all the students in the Shelby County High School system knew about their unsavory reputation and the grapevine stories permeated throughout the hood about two niggars acting like John Dillinger and

Machine Gun Kelly, bumping in that old black, Infiniti I30, and wearing matching 'wife beater' tank tops. The word on the street was simply that these two gangstas were dangerous—real fucking dangerous.

The remarkable silence had caught Mr. Armstrong by surprise. He no longer stood perfectly erect. The student's apprehension was now obvious and, at this point, he understood that perhaps he gone too far or maybe even screwed up. Although he wasn't aware of Dee-Low's relationship with Trimmers, he was familiar with signs of unhealthy body language. By now, Dee-Low's monstrous glare and veins throbbing in his temple was a sufficient notification for him to immediately soothe this amount of unimaginable tension downward.

Mr. Armstrong cleared the lump in his throat, "I'm sorry if I offended you, young man, really I am," he sighed.

Dee-Low refused to speak. His eyes chased Mr. Armstrong's features, running up and down the middle-aged man's pudgy frame. For a brief moment, Mr. Armstrong's heart fluttered inside his chest. He struggled to compose himself and to resist the urge, a fast-approaching sensation in his mind that Dee-Low was about to harm him, to blaze a trail to safety as his best option. But he pushed this impulse away. He would never regain the respect of his students if he bolted away leaving them in an uncertain situation.

Mr. Armstrong shrugged, "Again, I was way out of line. I'm sorry," he repeated. "Real sorry."

Dee-Low flashed a superior grin. Looking around the classroom, his eyes shined with pleasure. At the same moment, Mr. Armstrong knew he had cop-deuces. The students all shook their heads greenly. This was the moment that required him to salvage his authority in the classroom.

After a long moment or so, the look of uneasy puzzlement gave way to the surging adrenaline that raced throughout his arteries. He then moved slowly in the middle of the classroom but never taking his eyes off Dee-Low.

He winced, looking now at Dee-Low's smoldering gaze. "I think you need to go to the principal's office. I'll meet you there. You can't be in this class any longer."

"Fuck the Principal's office and fuck you," Dee-Low barked out.

"I think you…."

"I'm goin'," Dee-Low interrupted. "Not cause you say leave, I'm tired of this bullshit," Dee-Low bitterly replied. "You don't have to suspend me. Fuck it—I'm outta here!"

The classroom erupted with a combined reaction of elation and defiance. Mr. Armstrong's face was flushed with indignation as he watched Dee-Low swagger out the classroom, with his fist pumping like a piston. "Y'all be cool," he said with a tee-hee-hee chuckle.

"Here she come again," Trimmers' voice suddenly dribbled passed Dee-Low's thoughts, rebounding his mind back to the moment. He raised his head, studying acutely the casual strides of Sandy who was walking along in an unassuming manner of satisfaction.

Suddenly something caught her attention. She abruptly stopped on the opposite side of the street. She hesitated a brief moment glaring directly at the black Infiniti. Her eyes narrowed with suspicion. She was rethinking in her mind whether the Infiniti had been there earlier.

"I believe the bitch spotted us." Trimmers grumbled.

"Just be cool…. be cool, cuz," Dee-Low muttered.

There was an incriminating look on her face. She turned slowly twisting around her bovine figure. For the next few seconds, she had to make a quick decision. There wasn't much time—she could either return from where she just come from or ignore the occupants inside the Infiniti and continue on to her destination. She frowned, paranoid about the rocks hidden inside her panties. A prickling sensation moved up her spine. Closing her eyes she winced inwardly, wondering if the Memphis Vice Control Cops were secretly staking out the area.

"Fuck," she moaned to herself. She was already out on bond for a dope charge. Another arrest would really compound her already fucked up life. She was a rat-tat-tat—Mississippi junkie, part-time prostitute, occupational thief, and a full-time crack head who migrated to Memphis allegedly for a new start, but eventually settling in for the same old script. This was all she needed, someone or something fucking up her already fucked up life and latest hustle.

During these short moments, a set of ivory mini blinds surreptitiously rotated open slightly allowing a pair of raven eyes to descend tightly on the black Infiniti. They were also watching Sandy's frequent trips to and from a small, one story, red brick bungalow a few houses away.

Meanwhile, Sandy licked her puffy lips. Her mind raced back to her dilemma. She shrugged shaking the cobwebs inside her head about the Infiniti. It was clear now in her mind—she realized who owned it.

An edge of tension raced over her. She swallowed dryly as her right hand moved slowly up to her bra. With a quick pat, her hand felt the switch blade knife that she had deposited snugly between her breasts. "Em black bastards," she fumed to herself. "They been watchin' me. I betcha watchin' me every time I cope some dope… they been sittin' there watchin' me like some ole thievin' ass cockroaches."

Sandy shook her head. For some reason, her anxiety level evaporated like the confusion that swirled inside her head. She lowered her sunglasses to the bridge of her nose and, with a part wiggle, she shimmied and swayed her mountainous buttocks across the street.

Dee-Low pushed the electric button on the door panel. The window moved down sluggishly… then slower… and then it stopped midway. He frowned, then gently placed his hands on the window, easing the window low enough to allow his head to duck out a few inches. Looking at her, he unbuckled a big alligator smile flashing his three initials on his upper front gold teeth—D L O.

Sandy rolled her molasses eyes, feeling somewhat defensive approaching the Infiniti. "What's up, baby boy?"

A loud hyena cackle flew out of Dee-Low's mouth, "Uuuuuuuuu, what's up big Momma?"

She smiled wryly, stepping closer toward the Infiniti. Bending over cautiously, her gaze weaved passed Dee-Low, settling gradually on Trimmers' face.

"Hmmmm, thought so," she huffed. "Whatcha killers doin around here? Lookin' to kill somebody?" Her humor fell dead, like a stone being dropped in a sandpit. There was no movement in their dry faces.

"Why?" Trimmers said with a crazed look on his face. "You gotta contract for us or did you smoke up the down payment?"

Sandy bristled at the remark, "Uh huh, I smoked it, 'bout the same way your mammy..."

"You fat bitch," Trimmers bellowed reaching under the car seat, interrupting her before she completed her sentence. There was no illusion in his mind she was making reference to his mother.

"Oh sheeit," Dee-Low gasped, quickly lunging over toward Trimmers, his face stricken, while he struggled to grab his right arm. His face edged with tension as he knew his maniacal road dog was trying to get his gun. He had stolen a custom-made, long barrel, .38 caliber revolver with a silencer in a car burglary a day earlier.

Screaming in exasperation, Dee-Low yelled, "Be cool, cuz!" He huffed straining to hold

Trimmers' right arm tighter. Sighing, "Just... be... cool...," he grinded the words out between clenched teeth.

Trimmers' eyes blinked excessively. He really wanted to shoot Sandy, not once, but several times—shooting the living daylights out of her fat-ass, he thought.

"Sho' you okay?" Dee-Low's voice softened, his breathing was hard and heavy. For a long moment, both men's bodies were frozen. Dee-low still felt slightly uneasy loosening his grip on Trimmers' arm.

"I was just kidding. Didn't mean no harm... I-I-I."

Dee-Low's head swung quickly around; his eyes brimming with anger. He was pissed.

Sandy knew just how crazy and temperamental Trimmers could be. Playing the dirty dozen to a niggar like Trimmers quite possibly could be playing her way into a casket.

"What's wrong with your silly ass?" he hissed at Sandy. Sandy shrugged. Her face drawn and the small hairs on the back of her nappy neck stirred. Certainly, she was fortunate this time, better yet, maybe blessed that her guardian angel (not Dee-Low) had created this intervention.

In the edge of calming the situation down, Dee-Low saw an elderly woman standing on the porch of a red bungalow. He wasn't certain she overheard the commotion between Trimmers and Sandy.

Sandy sensed Dee-Low's attention drifted away from her. She turned and quickly acknowledged the old woman.

She smiled broadly, "Heyyyy... everything is all right."

The woman's response wasn't immediately forthcoming. She hesitated as if she knew or wasn't quite certain whether Sandy's response was conveying the truth.

"Who's that?" Dee-Low asked.

"Momma Brown—she's been livin' over here for years."

"Oh yeah," Dee-Low remarked, with a long, searching look on his face.

Sandy began swiveling her head; a dubious expression worked across her face. There was something disturbing, perhaps even alarming, about their presence on this quiet street. She knew these wild, uncontrollable street pirates were ready and willing to practically do anything to get some money.

"You been goin' to her house?" Dee-Low asked.

Sandy eyed him skeptically. She was nearly thirty-two and much wiser… far wiser and more streetwise… compared with these undisciplined thugs.

"Whatcha' call yourself doin'?"

"Nothin."

"Nothin!" Sandy repeated.

Dee-Low snickered, "We just tryin' to cope some dope, ya know."

Sandy hesitated a moment. This was some fuckin bullshit, she thought. She shook her head, smiling and now realizing why they were parked on the street.

"What ya'll niggars doin'… watchin' me or somethin'?"

Dee-Low's face hardened. "Hell naw. We ain't been watchin your fat ass. We just been kickin the bo bo."

"The bo bo," she huffed. "Bo bo, my wide ass. Y'all niggars tryin to do something," she sighed, placing her hands on her hips. "Y'all ain't thinkin about nothin' around here?"

"Whatcha mean?" Trimmers snapped.

She shrugged, poised, waiting for Dee-Low to engage himself in the conversation.

Dee-Low grinned benevolently. His eye and thoughts were focused on Momma Brown, who remained standing on the porch. Soon, a large German Shepherd pushed himself out the front door nudging up beside her. She began shuffling around the small area with a walking cane.

"What's up with her?" Dee-Low asked.

"That's her dog, Biscuit. She nearly blind."

"Oh yeah," Trimmers remarked.

"Yeah, she's been in the neighborhood for a long time—a really long time."

"Looka here, "Dee-Low said. "I need an eight ball, and if you cop it, I'll buy ya a twenty-dollar rock."

Sandy's apprehension was quickly erased. She would expose herself and confirm their suspicion that Momma Brown was running a crack house.

"I-I-I can turn it."

"How much?"

" 'bout one hundred fifty," she quipped, her eye dancing with joy. "But I can get it for less than that, maybe a hundred."

"Cool."

He paused, turning his attention to Trimmers. "Yo, you cool with it?"

"Yeah," Trimmers said, with a tight smile. He realized Dee-Low was playing this greedy, crackhead heifer. Her cautious regard for the personal safety of the hood was gone. She was hustling real tough—a walking mule connected in with Momma Brown, running crack errands day and night.

A twenty-dollar rock was enough to detour her apprehension in another direction. Dee-Low exerted much enthusiasm for the deal, quickly ruffling through his pockets. He removed two tangled up bills. Folding and creasing them out, it was a hundred and a fifty dollar bill.

Sandy's face was giddy with joy. Her lips were moist. The twenty-dollar rock sealed her careless behavior with a strong exclamation mark concerning the activity in Momma Brown's bungalow.

"That's hundred and fifty."

"Uh-huh."

"Get it for a bill, and bring me back thirty," Dee-Low said testily. "Don't fuck with mah bread, you understand. Get the twenty-dollar rock from the fifty."

"Okay, okay!" Sandy nodded excitedly. "I'll be back in a few minutes, but y'all drive down the corner, away from the house… away from this area, cause somebody might be watchin' us." She paused, looking around like a schizoid dope fiend. "I don't want anybody to know my business. I'm comin' right back."

"You better," Trimmers snarled.

Sandy's refrigerator frame shook with a mocking laugh as she bent down and made a helpless gesture. "I ain't running away with this monopoly money. No sir, not to worry 'bout this little bit," she giggled.

Before Trimmers could react to her remark, Dee-Low said in a raspy chuckle, "Y'all chill this bullshit. Gone on, get my dope."

Both men's eyes followed Sandy's beefy frame across the street. After walking a few steps, she hesitated a brief moment obviously irritated about them still parked under the maple tree. It was apparent that her nervousness was generated by their immaturity or perhaps it was cause of them being too bold and nonchalant about the transaction.

A cloud of suspicion loomed up inside her, despite her desire to smoke that rock. Even in her most desperate moods, she wasn't ready to compromise Momma Brown.

Down at the bungalow, Momma Brown and Biscuit were no longer on the front porch; however, the entire exchange from the beginning to end among the trio was no mystery to her.

Over the last several months, she developed a fondness toward Sandy, but her display of goodwill was always predicated on the type of consumer that invested in her business. She enjoyed masquerading as a shy, somewhat feeble-minded woman, rather unsteady in her balance, partially blind, and, at times, exceedingly generous. This was her clever profile that made what she was doing so appealing. In spite of the growing crime rate in Orange Mound, her business was always under the radar. Her mind was analytical, much like the stock market. She knew beforehand how much dope she would sell and when to stop.

Meanwhile, feeling nearly distraught, Sandy made an angry dismissive gesture, motioning several times for them to leave. There was a shine of displeasure across her face. She was unwilling to advance one single step closer toward Momma Brown's house.

Dee-Low shook his head. His gaze retreated from Sandy's face. Besides, everything they needed to know about Momma Brown was established. This was going to be easy, except for the German Shepherd, who Trimmers would most likely shoot. There wasn't much to it.

Dee-Low finally waved back at Sandy, and the black Infiniti pulled away slowly.

Gradually, Sandy's face relaxed. When the car moved along side of her, she resumed her pace and, without breaking stride or turning her head, she said, "Y'all meet me at the Burger King on the corner in about ten minutes."

Both men nodded. Dee-Low made a soft rap of his knuckles against the door panel. In the same instant, Trimmers turned up the radio volume. The music blared out of both sides of the windows. Laughing, he floored the accelerator with a feeling of being airborne. He watched with a menacing glee through the rear-view mirror, the polluted smoke exhaust gushing out from the black Infiniti dual tail pipes. The copious outflow dampened the street with a dark film of black ashes and silt. The black Infiniti roared down the narrow street with a trail of fumes chasing it.

"I sho wanna serve that fat, stinky-ass junkie," Trimmers shouted over the ear-splitting music. "Hope her funky ass is at the house when we come in cause I'm gonna waste that bitch."

Dee-Low laughed, "Man, fuck that hoe! We gonna rob that ole woman, and hope like hell, she gonna be cool when it go down. She ain't gonna tell the police—'somebody took mah money and crack.' She just gotta go to some senior citizen joint."

Several hours later, the creepy shadows of a full moon cascaded over the black Infiniti.

A succession of rapid coughs suddenly broke away the unwell silence that occupied the black Infiniti during the early morning hours. It was nearly two o'clock in the morning. Dee-Low shook his head in irritation from the coughing and wheezing Trimmers was making when he tried to swig lustily on his last quart of beer.

He frowned. His head felt like a bag of cow shit. The crack, alcohol and weed were beginning to ping-pong inside his head. Looking at Trimmers, he grimaced at the stale taste inside his mouth. It felt like the varsity track team rushed through it—with sweat socks on.

By now, Trimmers seemed to settle down from his tumultuous coughing. He studied him for a moment, sighing moderately at the sight of him polishing his revolver. He then snapped the cylinder opened once… twice… a third time.

"What's up with you?" Dee-Low inquired obviously annoyed with his road dog.

Trimmers' response wasn't immediately forthcoming. His usually expressionless features were caught by the moonlight's beam across his smooth, caramel face. There was a freakish smile that spread wide, arching his cheekbones high on each side of his face.

Deep-Low repeated his inquiry, "What's up with you?" but this time rather sourly. "We gombee kinda cool with that heat. Ya know, she's just an ole lady."

Trimmers smiled nastily, "She gotta dawg—I'm scare of big dawgs, especially them police lookin' dawgs. And if somebody else is in there, I'm just gonna shoot them." Trimmers faded Dee-Low's idea. He had now come to a point of no return. No matter how it worked out, there really wasn't many options for him. He knew his words would be drifting into nothingness trying to persuade his psychotic friend to avoid any violence.

Looking ahead of what was about to occur, he recognized that Trimmers was steadfast on shooting or maybe even killing someone in Momma Brown's house. The dilemma of his fate was cast when he embraced Trimmers as 'His brother's keeper.' He was undeniably sealing his friendship with a would-be lunatic waiting for the moment to saturate his abnormal craving to watch a person die.

This was the disquieting bond that he sought. Maybe its appropriateness could be rationalized in some of Memphis' gang-infected schools but he was no longer in school and their private initiation could eventually lead them to death row.

"Come on man, let's go," Trimmers spoke returning Dee-Low to the moment at hand.

Dee-Low sighed wearily. "Yeah... drive over on the other side of the street, we'll walk over from there."

Dee-Low didn't really have a plan, just a funny intuition that this jack move wasn't quite right. He stared mindlessly while Trimmers drove to a street adjacent to Momma Brown's residence. The black Infiniti pulled up behind a blue Ford SUV, concealing its dark frame and the darker thoughts of its two occupants.

Dee-Low's mind was spinning. It was too late. Trimmers wouldn't accept it—the very thought of backing out of this deal and fucking off half of his hundred and fifty dollars wasn't worth mentioning it to him. Even though they smoked an eight ball, Trimmers wasn't interested in crack. He was a killer and killers simply needed to kill.

Dee-Low slowly lifted his gaze over the dashboard. Removing his red ball cap, he covered his head with a black and white polka-dot bandanna. He then stared at a large rubber *Freddy Krueger* mask, but unlike the demonic creature in Midnight on Elm Street, this was no dream. He shrugged, thinking how useless the mask would be—there would be no witnesses left. Momma Brown and her dog were going to die this morning. A towering feeling of emptiness loomed inside his head. Bitterness and anger converged over him both at once. No one was missing either one of them—missing like a parental concern significant enough to call the police and express their understandable anxiety about their teenage sons weren't home... safe... sound... and fast asleep.

Their incorrigible behavior finally led them to this unholy juncture. In the aftermath, surely the forensic evidence would reflect the brutality of their deeds, the senseless and unnecessary crime that would never erase society's reprehensible perception toward them. They would become Memphis' newest murderers—repugnant black, teenage castaways that deserved whatever was befitting them, not only an expeditious trial and a first-class execution, but a Friday noon, well publicized and nationally televised lynching on the town square.

About an hour later, both young men shuffled quietly over to the next street. Their figures moved quickly, darting in and out between cars. With eyes hawkishly keen, they listened quietly, ears tensed, straining to hear one sound—any movement that caught their attention; and, there was.... nothing.

The air was perfectly still. The night closed its eyes to their nimble footsteps. Clutching their rubber masks, they moved in a circuitous route, almost with an extraordinary manner of calmness, edging closer toward Momma Brown's red bungalow.

Within a few moments, they were crouched outside of her back gate. Slowly, with painstaking caution, they removed the rubber masks from their waistbands. Dee-Low took one last questionable stare at Trimmers as if he wanted to say, "You're sure you wanna do this?" but there wasn't a mitigating return gaze. He quickly tossed away this thread of compassion that abruptly ran through him.

Quickly placing the masks over their bandannas, the transition was smooth. They did it before, many times, but this was different. They raised the ante from aggravated burglary and assault to home invasion and, quite possibly, first-degree murder.

Dee-Low took his last reflective sigh about the matter. He understood that Trimmers' self-effacing behavior would cause everyone to believe he wasn't the leader in this crime. The thought gave him a momentary absence of life's feel, the kind of feeling were many black teenage males experience living in the hood without fathers and no viable black, male role models. Sometimes life for them was short circuited. The current of hope and aspiration had been extinguished in their lives making the proposition of dying more palatable. They often made no distinction between the two—life or death.

Trimmers moved closer toward the back gate, arching his head slowly over it. He temporarily adjusted his mask. Hs head turned sideways surveying every inch of the small back yard. Stooping down, he muttered, "It's clear—nobody's back here." Dee-Low nodded. He looked up, his eyes briefly scanning for a heat sensory light that might abruptly expose them. His eyes shifted downward. There were no early warning devices ahead of them.

Trimmers then moved to the gate post. Within a few seconds, he worked free a loosely wrapped rope that secured the gate to its post. The gate swung slowly opened with a mouse squeak. Trimmers quickly caught its cry before another sound escaped from it. Holding the gate firmly, he looked sharply at Dee-Low as both men's shoulders softened. Noise and light were never kind to burglars.

After catching the gate just in time, Dee-Low eased by him settling on the cold cement steps of the back door. Trimmers inched the gate back ever so slowly trying to avoid another squeak. Securing the gate to the post, he wrapped the rope to it returning the gate to its original position.

They looked briefly at each other, recognizing the only thing that separated them from the money and rocks was a wooden door.

"She ain't got no security door, not even no iron bars on the back windows, damn. Man, Momma Brown's ass is wide open in the cut," Trimmers whispered.

"Yeah, this is kinda crazy," Dee-Low replied.

For a few minutes they both remained motionless waiting for a possible response from Biscuit. By now, Trimmers was anxious to get started. It was going to be a thrill shooting that big ass German Shepherd. The very thought sent a chill racing up his spine. Removing the revolver from his right pocket, his mouth spread into a tight grin. It was the silencer—it was perfect for this job, he thought.

"I can shoot the door lock. Maybe once, or twice and then we just kick that bitch open," Trimmers said in a low, raspy chuckle.

Dee-Low paused. "Whata about the dawg?"

"Fuck the dawg, he's gone—just like that, gone."

Dee-Low stiffened perceptibly. "Okay, okay… I'm cool, Fuck it, let's go."

Trimmers was now holding the .38 caliber about ten inches from the door lock. Both men covered their eyes attempting to avoid any ricocheting metal fragments striking their faces.

And then suddenly, "Peck, peck, peck." Three rapid sounds of compressed noise tore open the round, silver plated lock on the back door. At first, a bright yellow flash leaped from the silencer's nozzle, followed by a small swirl of smoke that twisted up from its tip.

"Come on," Trimmers whispered excitedly. "Come on."

Dee-Low paused, sweat was streaming down both his armpits. Turning his head, he looked at the adjacent house and then made an about face to the house facing the backyard. He winced confounded by the complete darkness, something he didn't anticipate, or at least how the noise seemed to be swallowed up by it.

Perplexed, he swung his attention back to Trimmers, who was still holding the pistol firmly in his right hand. Without saying a word, Dee-Low suddenly grabbed Trimmers' left arm, "Go ahead, you got the gun."

Trimmers moved belatedly, still surprised that the German Shepard wasn't there challenging them at the back door with his ears pinned back, snarling and barking ready to die for Momma Brown. But that fact never materialized. An eerie calmness of uncertainty came over both teenagers.

"Man, this is some bullshit," Trimmers whispered. "Not a fuckin' thing happened," he moaned.

Pushing the door slowly open, Dee-Low hesitated slightly, still waiting for the dog to come charging at them. He bristled, the nicotine smell from Trimmers' tobacco breath crossed his neck and circled around to his nose, giving him chill bumps. Stopping, he half-turned, mildly annoyed by Trimmers' halitosis. "Damn cuz," he winced.

Trimmers shrugged meekly, stepping back a few inches. Dee-Low then turned around his eyes trying to adjust to the small kitchen.

"Okay, we're in," he whispered. "Come on, you go first in case that fuckin' dawg comes out of nowhere."

Both teenagers were now listening intently, slipping on a pair of rubber gloves as they tiptoed further inside the small house. The gloves were another brainy idea from Dee-Low, a precaution to avoid leaving their fingerprints, something useful he learned from watching CSI, especially the Miami series.

As they crept passed the narrow kitchen, their eyes blinked with incredulity. They stood directly in front of the living room, and with the exception of a single white chair sitting in front of a window, the room was completely empty.

Impulsively, Trimmers moved passed Dee-Low, with his arm extended outward. He pointed the gun down the narrow hallway. "Damn, the ole lady and the dawg must be gone, or something," Dee-Low mumbled to himself.

Moving behind Trimmers, he was beginning to feel impatient, maybe even paranoid.

"Man, let's hurry up," he said icily. "I don't like this shit."

"Uh huh," Trimmers replied.

Within a few seconds, they both reached the first bedroom door. Their exercise of restraint disappeared. Trimmers didn't hesitate, using his left hand, he turned the doorknob and pushed the door opened wide. Waving the pistol frantically, they both rushed inside the bedroom. Shocked, their jaws dropped. Like the living room, the bedroom was completely empty. They looked at each other in stunned silence.

It only took them a fragment of time to realize something was terribly wrong inside the house. Without a flicker of caution, the two wayward teenagers stormed wildly throughout the small bungalow. Their frantic search concluded in a rear bedroom that contained a small fold down bed and seven white wicker chairs.

A few seconds swept by. They both slowly returned to the living room. They seem uncharacteristically uncommunicative. The condition of the bungalow surprised them and surprised the heightened expectations they marveled about for two days watching Sandy's relationship with Momma Brown. Everything seemed so well planned out, even with the rubber masks and gloves. Now, it appears, they were deceived, played like little toddlers.

Yanking off his rubber mask, Dee-Low's face was drenched with sweat. He tried to restrain himself from the growing frenzy that was boiling up inside him. Walking toward the back door, he pursed his lips, shaking his head. He spoke hotly, "I believe that fat-ass bitch was playing around with us, ya know, maybe told granny to take a hike, or something."

"But don't she live here?" Trimmers asked quizzically. Dee-Low shrugged. "I t'aink so."

"That's where Sandy was goin those two days."

"I know. I know!" Dee-low angrily responded. "We gonna check thangs out in the mornin, cuz."

Trimmers shook his head, a pained expression formed over his face. For the last two days checking out Sandy and Momma Brown's bungalow, all his eggs were in this basket. Repeatedly in his mind, he spent his share of the money several different ways—a new car stereo and speakers, rims, clothes, and another gun, a pearl handle, blue steel, .25 automatic from Dunton's Pawn and Loan Shop. He sighed, "I sho like to shoot that fat hoe."

Dee-Low frowned. "Just be cool, let's check it out." In a relatively quiet moment between the two, Dee-Low was back tracking about the unexpected dilemma. It was becoming clear to him from the condition of the house, Momma Brown didn't live there. She was using it as a front. But the house was too clean for it to be used by junkies smoking, snorting, or shooting up dope inside it.

"But it looked so real—like it's her house," Dee-Low said, rather dejectedly.

"That ole lady fooled the hell out of us," Trimmers quipped.

Still frowning, "Yeah, but we comin back, cuz—we comin back," Dee-Low repeated.

"We gonna find out t'morrow whata fuck is goin on. She don't get away."

Trimmers eyes glinted with pleasure, "That's what I'm talkin about," he said, turning a cold eye. "Y'all t'aink she gonna call the police?"

"Naw, and report what? Ain't a fuckin thang here but we know she gombee back. The place don't even smell, she comin back," he smiled wickedly.

"Let's grab a hat, cuz, before somebody sees us."

It was nearly ten o'clock in the morning, the heat rays from the sun danced across Dee-Low's haggard face. The morning came too suddenly as it wouldn't permit these two rag-tag bandits enough time to properly digest ten of Krystal's thin cheeseburgers, four large fries, two cherry pies and two strawberry milkshakes. Dee-Low was crammed up in the back seat. His stomach growled, a biological notice that a bowel movement was forthcoming.

Meanwhile, Trimmers was snoring and farting in the front seat, his mouth gaped wide open, his breath was still reeking.

For a moment, Dee-Low was almost resolute about wanting to call his mother, maybe she was concerned that he hadn't come home but why would she be? He remembered what she told him during their last argument, "You just like your no good ass daddy! You ain't no good ridin or walkin. You need to get your trifling ass outta my house!"

"It's hot in this motherfucker," Trimmers groaned, with a thick yawn, breaking Dee-Low's isolated thoughts about his mother. "Roll the back window down some moe."

Dee-Low's head jerked up; he pushed the electric window button. Glaring outside the tinted windows lowered, he surveyed Krystal's parking lot. It was Friday morning; another scorcher was on the way. People were already sweating as they zig-zagged from the heat to Krystal's ice cold, air-conditioning fast-food joint.

"Looka here, I'm gonna take me a healthy shit—then we need to hustle back over to Orange Mound to see what's up with granny. If we see Sandy still coping from her, we just gonna park at the Burger King. Then we gonna walk down the street, and if she's home, bum rush her old ass, kill and rob whatever mother fuckers whose up inside that joint. Nobody gonna hear shit with that silencer you got on that bitch."

Trimmers chuckled loudly, "Man goin take that shit! Take a big one for me, cause you gonna see my shit later on cuz—some real freaky deeky shit when I dust a mother-fucker's asshole, running up inside that joint."

Two hours later, the noon sun stood over Memphis, throwing a blanket of smothering humidity that covered the entire city, punishing indiscriminately its residents with summer-like Sahara Desert temperatures.

Unexpectedly, before going to the Burger King parking lot, Dee-Low decided to return home for a brief period. Strangely, while home he momentarily regretted his bizarre statement to Trimmers suggesting they kill everyone inside Momma Brown's home. He shook his head; it was a terrible mistake. This was an unsettling moment, since he set the stage for a brutal murder. Trembling on the edge of his error, he squandered a misplaced opportunity for him to rework the robbery and insist no one, except the dog, be harmed. By now, the anatomy of this crime was etched too deep inside Trimmers' demented mind.

At the same time, entering his mother's cramped, tiny apartment, he was still looking for a way out. Maybe his mother would insist he stay home, piss him off about something (perhaps school), anything that would divert his attention to the up-coming crime. However, that period passed by quickly. She wasn't home and Trimmers was becoming impatient.

And now, here they were parked under a shaded area at the Burger King parking lot. They were flat broke, probation violators, high school dropouts with juvenile records, petty crooks on the verge of committing a major crime and possibly murder.

"Come on, let's go," Trimmers barked, stuffing the revolver tightly beneath his red wife beater tank top. His face was beaming. He checked it for the umpteenth time. He then reached underneath the front car seat pulling out a medium size box filled with ammunition for the revolver. His eyes sparkled when he grabbed a large handful of bullets, wedging them down in each pocket. He cast a thin sinister stare at Dee-Low. "Just in case," he smiled. "Don't wanna run out. Ya never know what's up inside granny's crib," he snickered.

By this time, Dee-Low's moment of reluctance was gone. He refocused his thoughts on the home invasion. A few minutes later, they shuffled over to the corner of the street where Momma Brown's house was in viewing distance. Nestling under a tall pine tree, they each lit a cigarette and could visually outline all the activities on the street. They were both poised, concentrating intently about how they were going to handle the situation.

For a nearly an hour, they watched Momma Brown's bungalow and soon two men emerged from it. Moment later, two vehicles pulled up in front of the bungalow, a sleek black, Cadillac Escalade with custom rims, followed by a stylish BMW X5, both parked with their engine running. Undoubtedly, they were dope boys, because the Escalade displayed two televisions in the back of each rear seat head rest. Each vehicle had heavy, designer tinted windows, characteristics of players and dope boys.

"Man, look at em' rides," Trimmers moaned. "They goin to Momma Brown's crib. She servin these folks today," he spoke with a heightened pitch in his voice.

With their curiosity elevated high, the teenagers cautiously moved closer down the street, while searching for a better location in case they recognized one of the two occupants. Slowly, very slowly, they edged ever closer, stopping abruptly for another smoke. They were both amused by the prospect of how much money and cocaine was inside Momma Brown's bungalow and so self-assured that Dee-Low's only weapon was a medium size hunting knife.

Suddenly, their mouths flew wide open with surprise when Sandy's dumpling body backed out of the BMW. She paused a brief moment and looked both ways but apparently was too preoccupied to notice the two wayward teenagers spying on the vehicles a short distance away.

In an eerie way, their presence wasn't entirely unnoticed on this quiet, narrow street. There was someone watching them… tracking their lurking steps… their surreptitious behavior. It was the same pair of eyes that understood their ignorant and naïve intentions a day earlier. These eyes recognized that they were severely outclassed with their hoodlum ambition.

Yesterday, their eyes wanted desperately to speak with them, issue a judicial warning, but what the notice say, and in what manner could these eyes warn hunters engaged in stalking its prey for two days.

After watching the teenagers a few more minutes, the eyes closed, the mini blinds were slowly pulled together in alignment, sealing the eyes far away from hunters about to be hunted.

Meanwhile, the teenagers stood frozen, mentally exercising a full composite of everything and everyone associated with the bungalow. At the moment, Trimmers was struggling to contain his excitement. Several times, he cleared his throat excessively. His eyes stared in fascinated bliss. His mind was pushing the envelope, wanting to crash the premise with blazing bullets, killing and slaughtering everyone in sight. His mouth, lathered with a thin layer of frothy sweat, revealed the diabolic intensity of his thoughts.

A combined total of eleven cigarettes later, the two teenagers watched a small group, looking half-smashed with demure giggling, lumber out of the bungalow. Sandy was conspicuously anchoring up the rear.

"Man, em' mother fuckers really got down," Trimmers said with a silly chuckle.

"Uh huh," Dee-Low's whispered replied.

"We need to go in there as soon as they leave," Trimmers announced.

"Don't worry. We will," Dee-Low answered.

Moments later, the teenagers watched the Escalade and BMW pull slowly away down the street with music blaring loudly from both vehicles.

They stood silent for a several minutes. The afternoon heat soared to its murderous temperatures of 107 degrees, untangling the teenager's stalking instincts. Their flimsy wife beaters tank tops were drenched in mop sweat. Even under some partial shade, the ugly summer flies caught scent of their sweaty odor buzzing and biting them with zeal and determination.

"Ouch," Trimmers cried. "Man fuck these niggas—ass flies," he groaned. "We need to get this shit over with, man." He spoke with disgust.

Dee-Low allowed his mouth to spread open to a soft grin. He was trusting his instincts now, feeling that Momma Brown sold those dope boys plenty of crack.

The equation was simple—if she sold a lot of dope, it stood to reason she was holding plenty of cash, dope and Sandy was her main mule.

The moment arrived for both of them. Their reprehensible nature seemed to gallop along, pointing toward the climax of an unthinkable crime. They strolled across the street, moving closer toward the red bungalow. Their malignant thoughts flushed with excitement when they contemplated the potential booty waiting for them. They were intending to find that trap room this time in her house—they wouldn't leave without the money and crack this next go around.

For Dee-Low, it was the image that he craved—a fancy ride, his pockets lined with Benjamins, an endless line of shake joints and whores dangling on each arm. On the other hand, Trimmers wasn't motivated by the material glitter. He would be immensely satisfied in quenching his obsession by replaying back and forth inside his mind the unimaginable moments in Momma Brown's face when she received the first bullet from him. He was merely saturated in pleasure when thinking about enhancing both his demented image and reputation as a stone-cold killer.

They were almost at the red bungalow when a movement grabbed their attention. They abruptly stopped in their stride. Their eyes settled on an elderly, black woman who walked out the front door of the bungalow. She was busy chattering to himself, completely unaware of their presence and upcoming coyote assault.

"Hmmmm. Momma Brown got some moe company, another lady in there with her," Trimmers whispered.

"We ain't gonna leave no witnesses," Dee-Low said sourly.

Trimmers shook his head, "Ya damn right, cuz."

Shortly, another elderly, black woman with salt and pepper hair, wearing a light blue cotton dress, with large flowers neatly designed on it emerged from the front door of the red bungalow. The women seem self-absorbed while talking and laughing with each other.

"Must be three of 'em," Trimmer said.

"Yeah, but that ain't no problem," Dee-Low replied.

Before long, the two women returned inside the bungalow. During that period, neither teenager took a moment to realize when the women failed to regard their presence with suspicion. With combined minds in monolithic thought, they distanced themselves from considering the strange calmness surrounding the bungalow. Even their morning burglary of the premise never punctuated a clue in their delinquent minds that something was wrong… very wrong.

Without hesitating any longer, Dee-Low's dark eyes swept up and down the narrow street. Only a small, gray and white cat brazen the heat scampering across the street, stopping underneath an old brown truck for some momentary shade. There was no other movement that caught his eyes.

Seconds later, the two teenagers were moving along the side of the bungalow—the same route they used earlier that morning. They crouched down, creeping toward the back gate. Dee-Low stared into Trimmers' cold eyes. He was now certain what he saw in them—Death! With a heavy sigh, he whispered to him, "All set, cuz?"

Trimmers merely nodded his head. Gradually, his muscles tighten. Reaching inside his waistband, removing the revolver, "Come on, let's roll", Trimmers muttered. Quickly, Trimmers unwrapped the rope that secured the back gate, the same procedure that he used earlier, even catching the gate before it let go another mouse squeak. Within seconds, they were in the back yard.

Their eyelids were stiff, wide with tension. Creeping up the cement steps to the back door, Dee-low immediately noticed the bullets hole were still there in the lock and door. Turning around, he gave a quizzical stare at Trimmers. "They ain't fixed and changed the door lock. The bullet holes are still inside the door."

Trimmers listened and nodded, slowly moving up the steps beside and now past Dee-Low. Grabbing the doorknob, he gradually but delicately turned it slow… stopping… and then slowly, like a safe cracker listening intensely to every sound a dial on a safe would make from its turning rotation. With one final turn, the doorknob abruptly stopped. Trimmers squeezed the doorknob tightly. He then tilted his head wedging it flush against the door. His face strained, while he listened intently for a sound inside the kitchen. His body heaved up and down but no noises came from inside the kitchen.

With a quick flick of his wrist, he checked the revolver in his right hand for the last time. Trimmers' face shine with ecstasy. Dee-Low sighed tensely, with a quick shake of his head, he nodded. "Okay," he mumbled.

Trimmers gave him a wink, studied himself, and with lightning swiftness, he pushed the door opened, charging insanely into the kitchen. Dee-Low stormed behind him, waving the hunting knife.

Surprisingly, the kitchen was empty, the noise of their entry didn't immediately produce any response from the old women. But within a fleeting second or two, Trimmers rushed toward the living room entry with frantic energy.

And suddenly, "IIIIIIIIIIIIIIIIIHHHHHHHHHHHHHRRRRRR-EEE", scream.

Something extraordinary happened. From out of nowhere, a white, heated liquid flew out from around the corner directly into Trimmers' face. He let go a horrific cry, dropping immediately to his knees, both hands spread wide open. The pistol simultaneously fell to the floor.

"IIIIIIIIIIIEEEEEEEE! IIIIIIIIIIIIEEEEEEE! IIIIIIIIIIIIIEEEEEE!"

The gut-wrenching scarlet screams surged out of him in octaves of maddening waves. He then fell forward with both hands covering his smoldering face, kicking and screaming hysterically, while patches of his sandy skin sagged onto his hands.

"I can't seeeeeeeeeeee," he screamed unmercifully. "I'm blind… I'm blind… I'm blind… I'm blind!" he bellowed while kicking and screaming.

Before Dee-Low could react, his eyes became saucers. He gulped spastically, staring at Trimmers' violent contortions and rapidly disfigured facial features. Panic-stricken from Trimmers' repulsive sight, he quickly turned around in full alarm, realizing the only way to avoid what was happening to his friend was to run—run like hell, run like his life depended on it.

Dee-Low could feel the blood pounding inside his eardrum. His heart was performing paroxysms inside his chest. Turning, his legs sprinted toward the back door, but something excruciating hot, like hot lava from a volcano, touched the back of his head. He howled and hissed as the skin from the back of head literally felt like it was peeling away.

Both teenagers were now screaming and recoiling in horror and suddenly, Trimmers let out a strangled cry followed by three loud thumps—thump… thump… thump. Trimmers' exploding cries abruptly stopped with a sharp jolting period.

Meanwhile, Dee-Low's mind studied him for a quick moment and instinctively knew something awful occurred to Trimmers. He immediately sensed someone was standing over them. His face was saturated with raw sweat and tears.

"Don't kill us," he wheezed. "We didn't mean nothin—just foolin around. We lookin' for somebody else," he moaned. "Y'all, please let me go. We gotta get to a hospital. Whatcha done to us?" he asked, his mouth filled with a thick spew.

"I guess we fucked up your self-made cataclysm for Momma Brown, didn't we?" An eerie question with an icy voice broke passed his moaning.

Dee-Low, still grimacing, slowly turned over on his right side, his eyes brimming with tears. He sniffed, coughed and coughed again, trying to clear the blur in his eyes. He began blinking excessively, There were three shadowy figures standing over him.

"Momma Brown," he moaned.

"Right here—right here, sugar," a voice replied.

Dee-Low flinched. The voice wasn't from an old woman or the voice he thought he heard came from a deep and heavy tone, and it sounded like, almost like...

"Here I am sugar," the deep voice repeated. "Y'all come here lookin for me? Momma Brown and her ole lady friends, didn't ya?"

Shaking his head in disbelief, Dee-low's eyebrows shot up in surprise. He winced, quite stunned by what his eyes had given focus on. There standing over him, it was all a charade, with their fake breasts, make-up, reading glasses, padded buttocks and wigs.

Dee-Low's eyes took on a wounded look grimacing. He asked meekly and rather innocently, "Where's Momma Brown?"

"Right here—I'm the one in the middle, sugar."

Dee-Low slowly examined the broad shoulder black man, puzzled, but then he realized they had been wearing disguises all along. It was a clever deception, masquerading as old women to conceal their identity, while maintaining a low profile, led by the quiet and unassuming Momma Brown.

"We been watchin ya'll the last few days parked in that black Infiniti." Before Dee-Low could compose his simple-minded thoughts, his eyes drifted to Trimmers' motionless body on the floor. He winced as his eyes caught sight of a large wound in the back of his head. A thick flow of dark red blood oozed out from his scalp down the side of his face and dripped into a small puddle of blood by his neck. His eyes were frozen, covered by a thin layer of gloss. Dee-Low sniffed and more tears filled his already soaked face. He knew, without asking the question, Trimmers was dead.

"Pleaseeeeeeee man.....Pleaseeeeeee man," Dee-Low wheezed, a thick flow of nasal mucus hung from his nose. "I ain't gonna say nothin about this," he sobbed hysterically. "Pleaseeeeeee, don't kill me."

The three large frame men's faces were waxed with indifference. The man in the center, the affectionate, sweet, old Momma Brown actor, stepped a few paces toward Dee-Low. He was unmoved by his pleas. Bending over him, he spoke pointily, "Ya the nappy head leader of his bullshit plan, ain't ya?"

"Nah sir.....Nah sirrrrrr," Dee-Low voice slurred, wiping the drool above his mouth. "Nah sir."

"Stupid... y'all little niggars just fuckin stupid! Ya'll ain't gonna fuck up our operation—we had it too long for that to happen. Besides, didn't ya come for Momma Brown? Did you come to kill us? You come in here with a gun and a knife—busting down the door like some fuckin bad ass outlaws." He then stood up, turning and looking at the other two men. "Well, ya found me, sugar... You found Momma Brown and her friends."

The early sunrise rose ending the last day of August. A new month was beginning and the first day of September's morning light came with a mild northern breeze from Canada that chased away most of the humidity across the Mississippi River. It also meant the start of college football. The locals were optimistic about the University of Memphis Tiger Football team's upcoming season. Still others were anxiously waiting for the fall program of the University of Tennessee Vols football season who were selected number eight in the coaches poll of America.

The new dawn lifted away the dark clouds that hung over the city. The early light gave way to a crowded Burger King parking lot. Police, crime scene technicians and reporters from both the television news outlets and the Commercial Appeal were combing the area for witnesses and other possible information in the parking lot.

Meanwhile, on a couple of streets over from the Burger King parking lot, Sandy was up early, a normal junkie habit, knocking at the front door of Momma Brown's bungalow.

The curtain pulled back slowly, and then the door opened a few moments later, "Hi sugar," Momma Brown said with a wide grin.

"Heeeeey, Momma Brown, you got anything this mornin?"

"Yeah, whatcha need, sugar?"

"Gimme five for fifty. I gotta deal for you later—somebody comin from St. Louis with plenty of cheese. He wanna bird. I'll come alone to cop it."

"Sho sugar—now you come right on in and have a cup of coffee with me," Momma Brown said with a broad smile, stepping back to let Sandy inside. "A little cool, glad we gonna to get some cooler weather," as Sandy walked by her. "Yes ma-am, yes ma-am," She replied, glancing down the street at the police cars. "I heard they found two black dudes inside a black Infiniti. Someone said they had acid poured over them and they were beaten to death."

"Sho nuff! Did ya know 'em?" Momma Brown asked.

"No ma-am, I really didn't know 'em. Seen them around a time or two," Sandy said. "Just some dudes I guess trying to get over and got caught up," Sandy quipped.

"That's too bad. I'm really sorry to hear that, sugar," she replied with a look of indifference.

The Recorder

by: Raymond A Clark
short story fiction
Approximately words

2004

CHAPTER FOUR

THE RECORDER

MUTTERING PEEVISHLY UNDER HIS BREATH, SERGEANT FRANK Rosenburg's mouth tightened into a stubborn line. His eyes raked slowly over a crime report of a missing fourteen-year-old girl. A spasm of irritation moved over his liver-spotted face—something was wrong with the initial report. It was like studying a jig-saw puzzle. His eyes blazing for that one single piece of information to make the picture whole inside his mind.

He hesitated a moment as his eyes intensely analyzed the kidnapper's circuitous travel route. This was going to be a difficult investigation, maybe impossible, but anything was possible if he could flush out one solidary clue hidden deep inside Lester Phelps' head.

He had worked these cases before and the day after always seemed to be the worst. That's when the sensation of panic becomes utterly contagious, his arms blossoming with goosebumps as the early pressure mounted on the unit to find the missing child. The parent's trembling voices grew wild with endless scenarios of what might be happening, especially if a demented, sociopathic rapist was involved, then anything and, most likely everything, was possible. And, of course, he realized the media would examine every statement, action and procedure he undertook in the opening salutation of the case.

Although his boss told him to ignore the pressure, especially any media pressure, he almost anticipated himself never-the-less sauteing his sweet ass inside a human pressure cooker of ridicule and cynicism every day that the child was missing. Every second… minute… hour was an eternity of sweat he ingested inside his stomach.

Rosenburg expelled a long breath and faced his partner. "You think I oughta again? We don't need to pamper this creep."

"Well, it's been a couple of hours maybe? What do you think?"

"Carney, are you shittin' me? That's why I asked you for your opinion," Rosenburg winced.

Carney shrugged, shaking his head. "Guess so, he hasn't asked for a lawyer. I know the bastard has killed her… I just know it."

"Hey, take a breather on that," Rosenburg snapped. "Let's not speculate on that point until we know for certain. She's alive as far as we're concerned. We really got to play it that way."

"But…"

"No damn buts."

"Alright," Carney sighed.

"The son-of-a-bitch is coy… real coy and fickle at the moment. We gotta do that good cop/bad cop routine with him. Change our procedure a little bit," Rosenburg said.

Meanwhile, in the adjacent room next to the two detectives, separated by a two-way mirror, sat Lester Phelps. He tilted back in the chair with his wrists handcuffed behind him. His face twisted in pain, oblivious of the tight handcuffs turning his knuckles white, but from those irrepressible images of Chelsea Marie St. John. The veins on his face were standing out in livid ridges along his temple and forehead.

Phelps was mumbling, barely audible, too low for the intercom to pick up his voice. He was breathing hard now. His mind already re-working back to the day of the kidnapping. He had deliberated for days stalking Bonnie Chesterfield, a pint-size, fleecy brunette with braids and autumn leaf eyes.

Her café au lait complexion sufficiently aroused him especially when he discovered her parents were an interracial couple. There was some unmistakable quality about her that was stimulating him in an unusual manner which stroked his schizophrenic condition into an insatiable urge to act irrationally. He been suffering for months with a post-traumatic stress disorder that was successfully being repressed by him for years. Living in Boise, away from the megalopolis areas of Los Angeles, was a perfect antidote for him. It had been easy assimilating with his psychological condition in southern California. He stalked so many young women for years in his mind.

The temptation was so irresistible. On many occasions he almost surged at the urge to cradle an adolescent girl and secretly deposit her for his personal, sexual consumption but he seemed to resist these burning temptations carefully. He was familiar with the stories about how pedophiles were treated in prison.

His employment with the Los Angeles City School System didn't make things easier for him. Perhaps it was those young, black and Latino girls he fantasized about who he perceived were sexually taunting and teasing him that eventually exhausted both his restraint and will power. After eleven years, it was time for him to consider relocating. He felt relieved his decision to move to Boise with his cousin Alfred was a positive step.

Leaving the school district was a strange departure for him. He was an introvert without many friends or relatives. However, he considered Charlene Harris, a busty, thirteen-year-old black girl, with large biscuit eyes and Aphrodite face who always cast a wide smile at him, a secret admirer. She was also someone he believed he could trust. He told her privately he was leaving. They were alone, alone with his fantasy, alone by the boy's gymnasium's restroom—a perfect location—a perfect moment in time to touch her hand first. But the notion of touching him, even his hand, made her laugh, because it wasn't at all what he imagined as she quickly scampered away.

In the interrogation room, both detectives continued to work the case. Rosenburg's tongue raced between his lips as his mind visually retracing over Phelps' getaway route. Unlikc Carney, he wasn't satisfied with these facts; something was missing. A slight shudder ran through him. He then slowly stood up walking over to a large pin map on the wall.

He looked suspiciously at the map. With his eyes wide, unblinking, he began to gaze at the map of Boise, moving down to Route 84 south, passing through Mountain Home, and ending on Route 26 East between Gooding and Shoshone. It was between this location were the Gooding Police Department arrested Phelps who was driving a 1996 brown Toyota Four Runner.

Until now, everything seemed to point directly at Phelps. Even the eyewitness account detailing the precise physical description of him. Looking back, he also remembered Ms. Morton's eerie description of how Phelps drove slowly besides Bonnie Chesterfield, abruptly stopping, opening the passenger side door, suddenly grabbing the unsuspected teenager, her face chalk-white with terror as she briefly tried to struggle with him. Within a few moments, Ms. Morton said it was over. The vehicle door slammed with a loud punctuation roaring down the street leaving behind Chesterfield's velvet backpack.

Ms. Morton recalled gritting her teeth, shaking her head as she raced nervously toward the center of the street. She anxiously struggled with her eyeglasses, trying to adjust them as she strained looking to obtain the license plate number on the sports utility vehicle moving swiftly away eastbound, but there was no rear license plate.

For a moment, she thought she was going to collapse but the dizzy spell passed.

"Oh, my gawd," she cried, screaming for help.

Ms. Morton's eyewitness account was certainly irrefutable, despite the fact he was wearing a green baseball cap and thick sunglasses. She was familiar with Phelps who was employed at Cedars Glass Factory, less than two miles from the middle school. She recently has been receiving Workers

Compensation from an on-the-job injury at Cedars and, Morton admitted, she was secretly an admirer of Phelps. She was not a docile person. She initially tried to ingratiate herself to him.

She was impressed by his reserve, quiet and unassuming behavior. Her life was in much turmoil—men, the wrong men, the wrong decisions about men—created much consternation inside her mind. But despite her lousy judgment, there was always that possibility, especially if the right man had come along, her attitude might change.

She believed he was different as he wasn't from Boise. She was frustrated with dating cowboys and hillbillies. Perhaps his southern California values provided him with some class, a real gentleman, something that seemed extinct in her life. She always vowed to never date a married man, nor a co-worker, but she was having a ridiculous fantasy toward him to the degree she would make this an exception.

After a few weeks of early pleasantries, she became aggressive believing she perfectly assessed his body language properly. She remembered how surprised he was when she gave him a sudden embrace one day and pressed her sinewy body close to him, pushing her right thigh keep between his groin, hoping to arouse him.

He responded frighteningly spontaneous—quickly shoving her away with unbridled force, fanning the air with his hands in a show of incommodious disgust. She still remembered him glaring demonstratively at her; his body stiffening in apprehension.

"I-I'm sorry," Morton said. "I shouldn't been so forward. Forgive me, please accept my apology," she whispered.

Phelps shivered, looking at her scornfully. "He snapped the question at her, "What the hell is wrong with you?"

"It was just an innocent hug," she replied. "Damn!"

"Don't touch me," he cried. "Don't ever touch me again."

"Okay… gee whiz! I'm real sorry, Mister Phelps. You won't have to worry about that ever happening again."

However, Morton wasn't familiar with the 1966 Toyota Four Runner. There were other reasons why she was thoroughly convinced that it was Phelps inside the vehicle.

Morton had previously been surprised by his unexpected behavior toward her. Although she never considered herself to be a striking woman, but her make-up, perfectly coiffed red hair, buxom breasts, rock-hard legs, and toned features have always been manipulative assets for her with men.

Now, she tried to ignore Phelps' over-reaction toward her. Besides, it was his prerogative. Maybe she misjudged his kindness and respect toward her. In reaction to his behavior, she was first startled and initially believed her conduct was too premature. Nevertheless, she remained curious about this self-effacing man from southern California.

Without discussing the incident anymore with him, she wanted to avoid another unpleasant encounter and prevent a tendency for her to be unusually self-centered about herself. But there continued to be an unexplainable fascination with his pattern of withdrawal from other women in the factory that she concluded he was either a wimp, homosexual, or maybe somewhere in between. After six weeks, she merely dismissed her unfounded infatuation toward him.

And then one Wednesday afternoon, Phelps had been granted a half-day personal leave. Oddly, it was also her first day on workers' compensation leave. She remembered leaving the Human Resources department and politely offering him a ride as he waited at the bus stop. He seemed so agitated by the gesture that he shook his head in blatant disgust, quickly shuffling down the sidewalk.

She quickly realized that it was his behavior that was ridiculous and not her own unfitting advances. Rather than accepting his continued rejections, Morton seemed to be quietly developing an annoyance toward him that was slowly creating an ungovernable obsession inside her head.

Her unmistakable disappointment about a relationship that never occurred propelled an unusual impulse to know more about him. Daily, she drove near the factory with a peculiar sensation to observe precisely what he was doing after work. With growing intrigue, she watched him initially wait at the bus stop and leave when he was certain everyone had left the factory.

At first, her suspicion hadn't been apparent about his usual routine—going to Chippy's Diner ordering a grilled cheeseburger with tomatoes, fries, and a strawberry milkshake. He then would quietly stroll three blocks to a nearby park, sitting on a park bench while watching the activities of an evening girls' softball practice.

On the fourth day, his pattern continued and instinctively she knew something wasn't quite right. With an eagle-eyed intensity, staring at his every movement on that park bench, she finally shook her head in bitter insolence. "For God sakes,", she mumbled. "He's fondling himself. The poor bastard is stalking those little girls. The creepy fuck is a child molester."

"This is crazy," she thought. "There is a piece of ass all over the factory and he is doing this shit." Now absorbed with self-satisfaction, she had exonerated herself. It was never her. She been guilt-ridden, initially believing she offended him so deeply that he wanted nothing to do with her or any women in the factory, but now it all made sense, perfect sense, about his capricious behavior toward her.

Morton's accounts had become a substantial element of proof. Rosenburg was assiduous, quickly developing an entire composite of Phelps' profile and possible motive. Normally, this would be an open and shut case. Notwithstanding the missing girl, there remained several loose ends to satisfy his analytical method in his follow-up investigation. For one thing, Phelps didn't own a 1996 brown Toyota Four Runner and, strangely, the department hadn't received a stolen report about one since the time of the kidnapping around 4:47 p.m.

About a half-hour later, Rosenburg and Detective Carney arrived at Phelps' residence, a dingy duplex he rented next to Alfred Singleton, his cousin. Neither man was home. The neighbors hadn't seen them, and suggested the police officers try Alfred's automotive repair shop a few blocks away. Quickly moving to the automotive repair shop with two patrol units, the shop was closed. Again, a check of the immediate area produced the same results.

Rosenburg was now becoming hasty and anxious, knowing every second the girl was missing were liability moments against them. In the flurry of events, he hadn't taken a moment to examine the teletype printout on Phelps. He'd been given a National Criminal Investigation Check (NCIC) printout on him. Surprisingly, Phelps had no criminal history—no arrests, traffic violations, civil suits, liens, nothing—absolutely nothing was recorded in the NCIC printout except his registered fingerprints as a school employee for the Los Angeles City School District.

Now, increasing the pace of the investigation, Rosenburg was a perfectionist or at least he wanted to be extremely thorough in his mind. He was a compulsively detailed investigator, driving his co-workers crazy with endless questions about police reports, why wasn't this or that done, etcetera, etcetera. Everything had to thoroughly satisfy his exigent, inquisitive nature to a degree that almost alienated them. In fact, most cops hated working with him, but Carney was different. He was like the incomparable Edward (Ed) Norton, the screwball sewage worker on the long running and immensely popular Honeymooners series starring Jackie Gleason.

Rosenburg's criticism merely rolled off his back and yet, Rosenburg wasn't a Jackie Gleason; far from it—there was no comedy in his behavior. He was a modern-day Sergeant Joe Friday of Dragnet with an uncompromising disposition regarding only the facts.

Rosenburg received permission to examine Phelps' personal data record. Although he directed the unit secretary to contact Phelps' last employer in Los Angeles searching for any minute details about his character from his last supervisor, he was also paralleling this action concerning what he could learn at Cedars. He was skillful in persuading the plant manager to extract Phelps' personal data record from his personnel file thereby eliminating a potential prosecutorial problem with the confidential nature of his personnel record, without his consent, or a search warrant.

While studying his personal data sheet, his body suddenly stiffened and his eyes looked straight ahead. His concentration was severed by what smelled like a loud, cheap perfume. The aroma was directly behind him. Someone was staring at his back.

"Can I help you?" he asked without turning around.

"Maybe… I'm not sure if I should say this."

"Fine. Off the record, then."

Turning, his eyes quickly settled on a stout white woman, maybe in her early fifties with a leathery complexion, perhaps from either excessive tanning or years of sun exposure. She was short, not much over five feet, which explained why her head arched backwards staring up at his six-foot, four-inch frame, and soup-strainer mustache.

She seemed nervous, pulling back her maple sugar hair and snapping it secure in a ponytail with a rubber band.

"What exactly do you want to tell me?"

"I don't want no trouble."

"Well, I won't cause you any."

"That guy… the one you're looking for."

"Phelps, Lester Phelps."

"Yeah. I think he doesn't like women."

"You don't say."

"I'm sure of it. But the plant manager really likes him. They think they're too many women working around here anyway. He works good. I mean he does his job but he's so weird."

"Weird?"

"Yeah, weird. I see a lot of those weirdos when I was visiting L. A., the place is full of 'em, just like him."

"What else can you tell me about him."

"I think he keeps a diary."

"A diary?"

"That's right. I've seen it."

"You have?"

"Don't get me wrong. I'm not nosey or nothin', but I've seen him writing in it all the time. It's a small black notebook he keeps in his back pocket. If you didn't know it, you wouldn't pay much attention to it. Ya know what I mean?"

"Yeah. I got it. Anything else?"

"Nope. Not offhand but remember I know he don't like women, at least not grown ones," she said with a half snicker.

"Anything else?"

"That's it. You ain't carrying one of those small tape recorders on you? Don't want my name mentioned in any of this mess."

"It won't be." Rosenburg smiled. "You have my word on that."

"Good."

"But, just for my off the record notes, can you tell me your name, in case I need to holler at you again? Off the record, of course."

"Why sure. It's Hazel, Hazel Murphy. Mssss. Murphy, but all my friends call me Hazy," she said with a flirtatious smirk. "Wouldn't mind if you called me Hazy."

"Well, here's my card, Ms. Murphy," Rosenburg replied, shaking off her unsolicited invitation. "My home and cell phone numbers are on the back. Call me anytime, okay."

"Okay! Even if you're at home?" she grinned.

"Sure! My wife won't mind."

She considered his statement for a brief moment. Her shoulders collapsed slightly as if his reply disappointed her. "Okay," she said. "My break is almost over. I've gotta go."

Less than a half-hour later, the two detectives were sitting in the Chesterfield's living room. At this point, Rosenburg would now choose his words carefully. He had to be both positive and philosophical with them.

Positive about the level of police resources committed to this undertaking, along with how the 'Amber Alert' operation worked, and a list of search volunteers, flyers, posters, and the widening media support that had been all galvanized in these initial phases of the kidnapping.

Philosophical about the combination of psychological problems they were experiencing at the moment—a restless anxiety, panic, fear, frustration and hate all emerging together with a twisted impulsiveness absorbed by a feeling of guilt. Added to this was a nagging doubt that despite this colossal effort, there may be still not enough done to save their daughter.

Sitting across from them, the room had become unusually quiet after their arrival. Everyone seemed to be hesitant—just a hair breath instance—unsure where to begin but Rosenburg recognized that and understood they were waiting for their guidance.

He then nodded to Mrs. Chesterfield. With white hair, semi-styled flip without the long bangs, her face was sweetly expressive, almost girlish but not quite. Certainly, she was much older that her appearance and, despite her obvious stress, she looked fit.

"We're working as fast as we can. We have a possible suspect and the information about him is very reliable," Rosenburg said delicately. "My department is doing everything we can do to solve this matter quickly—I mean everything—including the amber alert, media, posters, volunteers, the works."

"Who is he?" Mrs. Chesterfield asked, moving beyond the police logistical information.

"We believe he works at Cedars Glass Factory. He has been identified by a co-worker. She saw the kidnapping. His name is Lester Phelps. Do you know him by any chance?"

"Hell no!" Mr. Chesterfield bellowed.

The room suddenly grew silent as the stocky black man stood up; his eyes filled with dark portent. "Hell no," he repeated. "We don't know the bastard and we certainly don't know anybody who would do this to us."

"I'm sorry," Rosenburg's voice lowered an octave. "We just need to cover the bases."

"Well, I understand Mr. Rosenburg, I really do. My husband is really tired. To be perfectly honest, he hasn't slept a wink since all this happened and neither have I much."

"I can just imagine," Rosenburg replied. "We hate things like this."

"Thank you," she sighed.

"We're trying to get a photograph of him. I should be getting one any moment from the Los Angeles County Sheriff's Department where his fingerprints are on file. I'd like you to see it. Maybe you might recognize him—someone that you have seen around the school or somewhere, anywhere."

"Good enough. Anything we can do to help—anything," she said, her voice gradually cracking. Her head casually twisted backwards and, without warning, she suddenly wailed out, "Dear God...." She had broken down, no longer capable of holding back her emotions. Her face was now flooded with a stream of tears rushing down her cheekbones, circling underneath her chin, and intermittently dropping onto her green blouse. "Please help up, we don't know what to do. Don't let anything happen to our baby," she sobbed, dissolving into tears. "Please don't..." as she continued shaking her head.

Rosenburg understood immediately the difficulty he was faced with. A missing child's bereaved mother is nothing a cop ever wanted to encounter, especially if he knew the child was murdered.

There was an uncomfortable moment of silence among the four people as Mrs. Chesterfield continued to weep. Both detectives felt a stifling coolness as Mr. Chesterfield remained silent. His blood appeared to be drained from his face and only a cold penetrating chill remained. His dark eyes set fixed staring at them.

Seizing the moment, Carney slowly cleared his throat. "I think we oughta go now. We're going to keep you folks posted on our efforts. You can believe this, and I speak for Sergeant Rosenburg as well, we gonna turn this city upside down searching for your daughter, the entire state, if necessary."

Mrs. Chesterfield nodded. "Thanks," she said breathing hard and shallow.

"The school gave the officers a photograph of Bonnie, but we appreciate it if you have any more, the more the merrier, especially a recent snapshot. We like to spread it everywhere, the patrol units, search teams, internet posters, media," Carney said.

"Sure, sure! I just happened to have a recent one I took three months ago. It's a very good close up of her," Mrs. Chesterfield replied.

Five minutes later, both detectives left the Chesterfield townhouse. As he walked toward their sedan, Rosenburg glanced at his wristwatch grimacing. He shook his head; it was eight thirty. Bonnie Chesterfield was now missing nearly four hours since the reported incident by Ms. Morton, he thought to himself.

Staring up at a quarter moon, Rosenburg frowned taking his last sip of black coffee. It was that 9:55 p.m. brew. He made a mistake. Five minutes later he would have missed the second shift restaurant workers' coffee. They couldn't make a good brew even if their lives depended on it. His mouth was caffeine soured, feeling that he had a cup of diesel fuel. He then leaned back onto the car hood, stretching his angular frame against their unmarked police sedan. Carney, on the opposite side, belched. His upper lip sneering from the acid bubbling up inside his stomach struggling to digest a greasy, double cheeseburger and two root beers. Both men were exhausted, but their fatigue wasn't a sign of them being ineffectual. This was only a momentary respite.

Sitting the empty cup on the car hood, Rosenburg's mind was continuing to work this case nonstop. Something was wrong. He just had and old-fashioned hunch. Since Phelps didn't own a vehicle, where did this 1996 brown Toyota Four Runner emerge from, especially since the department had continued to be silenced by the lack of not receiving a vehicle theft report? His curious lament about the sports utility vehicle was quickly interrupted by a radio call from a patrol unit. The broadcast reported that Alfred Singleton was detained about a block from his automotive repair shop.

Less than five minutes later, the detectives drove up to an unmarked special patrol unit still with it small rear amber light flashing. Pulling up on the passenger side of the vehicle, Singleton had already been deposited in the back seat.

Rushing out of the unmarked sedan, Rosenburg, without a moment of hesitation, lumbered over to the vehicle. As he moved closer toward it, Singleton suddenly screamed in exasperation, "Can somebody tell me whatafuck is going on? Why have these assholes got me handcuffed in front of my place?" he shouted with brutal contempt. "This is my fuckin place of business! I'm a taxpayer! I pay your fuckin salaries!" he hissed and fumed.

"Take it easy, Mr. Singleton. I'll take them off," Rosenburg replied, exchanging questioning glances at him.

Within a few moments, the beefy mechanic was nudged out from the police sedan and the

Wrist-biting handcuffs were removed. Frowning, flushed scarlet with anger over his face, Singleton bellowed, "Gonna call my lawyer about this," wincing as he massaged the tiny steel teeth mark impressions around his wrist.

"Sorry about the handcuffs. Sometimes they put them on too tight."

"What's this all about?" Singleton bellowed.

"We're looking for your cousin, Lester Phelps."

"For what?"

"We're working on an investigation. A young girl was kidnapped earlier today."

"Kidnapped! And you think…."

"We have an eyewitness."

"About Lester?"

"That's right."

"Hmmmm."

"Do you know where he is?"

"Sure, I know where he is."

"Where?"

"He works for me part time. I told him to go up outside of Gooding and drop off some parts for me."

"Is he driving?"

"How else is he going to get there?" Singleton snapped.

"Hey smartass! I need some information about the vehicle. You can give it to me here or downtown. It's late… I'm not going to fuck around with you about this," Rosenburg responded.

Singleton sniffed haughtily, "You guys don't think…?"

"The last time—the vehicle. I need the information about the vehicle," Rosenburg huffed.

"Okay, Okay," Singleton's eyes widening with innocence. "It's a 1996 brown Toyota Four Runner. It belongs to a customer of mine. I had him test drive the Toyota. I put a new transmission in it."

After providing Rosenburg with the license plate number and registered owner information, he placed an immediate "ALL POINTS BULLETIN" out for Phelps and the sports utility vehicle, along with the description of Bonnie Chesterfield, to the state police.

It was now eleven thirty that evening. Rosenburg's eyes were blood shot. His head was drowsy from a lack of sleep. They had now been working since seven o'clock in the morning. Somehow neither man wanted to leave their smoke-filled office. Gradually, Carney had fallen asleep. He was a diabetic. The double cheeseburger and root beers were in contrary with his physician's advice. He had raised his sugar level again.

By now, Rosenburg had become anxious. He placed both hands to his head and began rubbing his alabaster hair, while staring at his notes. Next to them was Lester Phelps' photograph. Somehow, he was certain they had their suspect and, if he was still in Idaho, it was only a matter of time. His mind then swung to the young girl. He felt a numbness seeping inside his chest. The premonition about her still being alive wasn't forthcoming to him that clearly. It was a moment that was utterly unsettling to him. He initially thought about revisiting the Chesterfields with Phelps' photograph but remembered they were exhausted. Tomorrow would be a better time, he reasoned. Besides, Carney had some serious health problems and the short rest was beneficial.

It was now 12 a.m. Rosenburg's eyes were half-closed, his head slightly lowered, but he wasn't asleep—black coffee and insomnia would keep him awake.

Suddenly, the sound of a telephone ring raced through his head like a loud locomotive whistle. Both men sat quickly erect. Rosenburg took a deep breath. It was from the communication center. He had told them to contact him immediately if anything developed in the case. Connie Stapleton was working and understood the sensitivity of the investigation. She knew they were exhausted and would only call if there was something urgent at this hour.

"Missing Persons, Sergeant Rosenburg."

"Hey Sarg."

"Connie."

"This is she."

"What's up?"

"Well, I got some good news and some bad news."

For a terrible moment, Rosenburg was slightly annoyed at her statement. She ought to have known better and focused her inhibitions about the pressure on them. He sighed moderately. "Connie," he groaned.

"I wasn't thinking. I'm sorry, Sarg," she sighed.

"What do you have?" Rosenburg asked.

"They got him. They just arrested Lester Phelps," she said with an exhilarated glee in her voice. "He was asleep inside that brown Toyota in a rest area. They found several open containers on the front seat, mostly Budweiser beer. The girl wasn't there. They checked the surrounding area, but a witness told them he drove up in the rest area alone."

Although she was wrapped inside a heavy camping blanket, her small body still shivered despite the rotating sound from a space heater operated by a portable kerosene generator running only a few feet from her. After a few moments of being acclimated to this strange environment, she slowly twisted her neck, squinting her forehead up and down, trying desperately to move the black bandana over her eyes a fraction of an inch upward so she could obtain a glimpse of her surroundings. Both her wrists and ankles were tightly bound. In the process, her forehead ached from the violent encounter with the steering wheel when her abductor forced her inside the vehicle. She tried hard to fight him but he was strong as an ox, so crudely powerful that his grip on the back of her neck soon rendered her unconscious.

Without much success, she then shifted her hips grimacing momentarily from the number of bruises throbbing all over her legs. Her lower back and knee joints were burning with an excruciating pain like she had been a contortionist folded up and stuffed inside a small trunk for several days.

After a few minutes lying motionless, her mind began to search for clues about this mysterious location.

Suddenly, she abruptly paused for a split moment, relaxing her entire body, concentrating, suppressing everything else inside her mind. She was now listening intensely, her heart pounding against her chest, for any aggravation to her stomach and immediately between her thighs. The questions now rattled out: Was she sore? Was there any excessive moistness? Was there any secretions? Was there any vaginal bleeding? Was she ....?

She then gradually relaxed, relieved—rotating and eliminating these horrific thoughts one by one—almost certain now that she hadn't been raped but she still felt violated. And now, her mind quickly resumed to where she had been swiftly deposited. Instinctively, she felt isolated at the moment but strangely not alone.

She sniffed slightly, wondering from the smell of the moist dirt, airy subtle breeze, and thin cold air that she had recognized these peculiarities before. There was a hollow sensation in her mind, something distinctively vast, even the twisting wind currents coming from multiple directions all at once, took her only a few more minutes of stern contemplation that she might be inside a cave chamber. It was the limestone smell of petrified, rock-ribbed walls and the faint sound of flowing water. She intuitively believed there might be a small lake, river or even a waterfall nearby.

Ironically, she was a biology student who was fascinated with the strange underground landscape of caves filled with speleothems, beautiful shaped mineral deposits. Her mind could also visualize the Gypsum Powers, delicate spiral crystals that sprouted from porous rock. She concentrated further, sensing the Helicities, strangely twisting cylinders that grew from the walls, ceiling and floor of caves, believing they were also present, which solidified her conclusion that this ominous location was perhaps a cave.

A small tear trickled down from her right eye stopping half-way on her cheekbone. At fourteen years old, she was so profoundly unprepared for this nightmare.

Immediately, she thought about her parents. By now, her father would be giving the police his lethal-looking stares, a barrage of endless questions about their investigation procedures and driving like a maniac all over Boise. Her mother's sharp tongue would keep a balance of things, but she might be a basket case. She sensed they were both saturated with grief and would do anything to find her. She was certain of it.

Her mother's face then came into her mind. It was a sight of desolation and despair. She bristled momentarily from a subconscious thought, "I know she thinks I'm dead now," a strange voice whispered softly inside her ear.

She took a deep breath trying to shake away this unwell feeling. Expelling it, she began coughing and wheezing from the cold, damp dirt rubbing up against the side of her moist face. Somehow, the moment gave her a strong inclination to survive. She felt amazingly determined to be free. Straining to untie herself, she twisted her wrist back and forth, back and forth, against the tightly wrapped duct tape. Beads of perspiration formed on her forehead. Sweat trickled down from her armpits as she pulled and coiled her nibble body.

Then for a while, her triumphal resolve seemed to be slowly disappearing. Her withered elbow ached from the intense strain placed on them. She tried desperately to free herself, but her body gradually grew loose and limped. She was now inexplicably exhausted, feeling utterly helpless and vulnerable with absolutely no other thoughts about escape. With her thoughts now spinning, she shuddered slightly hoping the blindfold, with its unnerving darkness, wouldn't make her go crazy. Almost certainly, she had to remain calm, in self-control, waiting until she could figure out her next move before her abductor returned.

Bonnie continued to lie still on the ground for several more minutes, silent, unmoving, until her ears suddenly caught sound of something moving. Her facial muscles twitched nervously. A fast-moving chill quickly rushed up her spine. She swallowed dryly finding it almost impossible to scream, almost impossible to speak, almost impossible to think rational, except he might return soon and kill her.

Nevertheless, she continued to remain frozen, intently listening to the bizarre movement circling around her. Although she knew that many cave-dwellers lived inside caves, this was no rat, raccoon, or even a salamander. She was positive about this. By now, her heart was hammering inside her small chest. She wanted to let go a maniacal scream, but her hysteria continued to be silenced by the subtle movements. Despite her youthfulness, she was demonstrating a remarkable level of courage. For several more agonizing moments, she continued suffering from this paralyzing fright, this monstrous nightmare her abductor was psychologically placing her under; so intense that her mind wanted to cry out in a voice of raw with terror.

And then, seemingly out of nowhere both shock and surprise fell upon her from a soft voice which suddenly dissipated this sickening wave of horror welling up inside her body.

"Are you alright?" an engaging voice asked.

"Yes," she replied hoarsely.

Shimmering and full of suspicion, Bonnie paused for a moment. She was undeniably too frighten to compromise herself, not knowing if this was some cruel hoax.

"I'll help you… help you get out of here.".

"Pleaseeee," Bonnie wheezed, abandoning all thoughts of reservation. "Help me get out of here," she cried.

Meanwhile, it was now three thirty in the morning. Rosenburg contacted Connie Stapleton notifying the dispatcher that they had finally arrived at the Gooding Police Department. The brown Toyota had been towed, deposited inside the police garage, waiting to be dusted for fingerprints and other evidence by the crime scene technicians from Boise.

Stepping outside of their sedan, Rosenburg looked up toward the dark sky. He bristled momentarily. The night was bitterly cold; the wind was blustery. Pulling his up his collar around his neck, he had an unsettling feeling about Bonnie Chesterfield, wondering if Phelps left her shielded from the early morning brazen elements or maybe sprawled underneath a light layer of foliage, raped and strangled to death. He suddenly caught himself, disregarding his worst premonition about the young girl. Hopefully, it was the former, maybe she was safe… maybe he hadn't enough time to do anything harmful to her… maybe he had another motive… maybe there were too many possibilities, too nefarious for him to consider.

As they walked inside the small police building, Rosenburg stared at Carney. His partner was weary. They had now been working non-stop for almost twenty-four hours.

It was a stroke of good fortune that Phelps was arrested in Gooding. Carney worked there for three years before joining the force in Boise, that was nearly eighteen years ago. He always maintained contact with the guys which naturally alleviated any jurisdictional squabbles and bureaucratic red tape.

Rosenburg and Carney waited about fifteen minutes while Phelps was being fingerprinted and processed. Things continued to be tense. Both men privately were feeling the same trepidations.

Rosenburg then looked at Carney and said, "Hope I hadn't screwed up."

"What?" Carney was clueless about the remark.

"I told Connie, I would call Captain Riggs."

"What's wrong with that?"

"I didn't call him."

"Are you fuckin nuts?"

"I didn't call the media either."

"Now, I know you're fuckin nuts."

"The guys here believe it's just a stolen auto."

"This is no good Rosey, no fuckin good."

"Maybe," he sighed. "Maybe… but we need to talk with him first. Remember that hunch I have?"

Looking both amazed and angry, Carney said, "I can't believe this shit! How could you not let the Captain know?" he sighed. "Does your hunch cover my ass and retirement?"

"The girl is missing, don't know this guy's mental state, we need to check him out before the media bombards this place. Just thinking about her. I need you to work with me on this, at least for our first interview. I'll take the heat on this, okay?"

"My Irish ass."

"I will," Rosenburg insisted.

"Heat spreads both ways," Carney groaned.

For a long time, both men stood silent. Rosenburg knew his partner of seven years was digesting what he had told him and the implication about violating departmental rules and regulations. But Carney's silence wasn't necessary his rejection. Carney trusted him. They had been through a lot together. Rosenburg stood by him during a painful divorce, co-signed for a personal loan to consolidate his debts, and even saved his life by shooting a wayward drunk about to stab him in the back during a bar room fight. Although he believed in the police Code of Ethics, law enforcement was everything to him. But somehow, in spite of this factor, his relationship with Rosenburg would make rules and regulations subordinate to his feelings toward Rosenburg.

Shaking his head, "You know, I suppose I'll follow you anywhere, cover your ass, even if we were in Beirut. I mean, I ain't got no blind loyalty. You also covered my ass before, plenty of times," he paused. "You know what I am saying?"

"Sure. I know what you're saying! This is strictly my call. Your reservations are duly noted."

Carney sighed heavily. "Well, in that case, deal me in. Besides Captain Riggs is just bucking for a chief's job somewhere. This media crap is right up his alley," he said with a low cynical laugh.

"Maybe. But we need to level our best shot at this creep before anybody interferes with us."

Ten minutes later, Phelps' booking process had been completed. Before interrogating him, the detectives stopped by the property room to inventory his personal property. While the clerk was giving Carney the sign out property tag, Rosenburg was contemplating. His memory was immensely broad, long as an elephant's trunk.

It was Phelps' diary—that little black notebook—the one Ms. Murphy referred to with all those frequent notations recorded inside it. The prospect of the police finding it and placing it with his personal property could make him terribly vulnerable and could be some powerful evidence against him, especially if he recorded the events regarding the kidnapping and Chesterfield's whereabouts.

Over the years, Rosenburg had investigated another man like Phelps, a possessed soul who unleashed a bizarre number of recordings in a small notebook. He suffered with the Oedipus Complex, a sexual attraction of a boy to his mother with accompanying feelings of hostility toward his father. He still remembered reading the hundred and thirty-seven pages of scribblings, squiggles, lurid sexual fantasies, irrational excitement, misanthropy, hostility and, finally, the deliberation of a murder. The last six pages outlined how he cogently planned to kill his father, cutting him up in pieces, and disposing the carcass in the hog's pen, but he didn't have enough nerve to do that. Instead, he buried the remains in a remote location on the family farm. They found his father's severed skeletal remains precisely where he noted it in his diary.

As he walked up to the property window, he bristled a moment subdued by a surge of superstitious dread. He then shook his head in commiseration, trying to resist feeling the same malignant thoughts when he read John Henderson's diary that ultimately Phelps' conclusion wouldn't be the same.

Frowning, Rosenburg looked every bit surprised as he watched Carney inventory Phelps' personal property but the small black notebook wasn't among the inventoried items. He shook his head as Carney read off Phelps' personal property items:

- ✓ $27.65 in currency
- ✓ One Ironman wristwatch
- ✓ Idaho Driver's License
- ✓ Social Security Card
- ✓ A fingernail file
- ✓ One black comb
- ✓ One black lizard-skin billfold, containing several miscellaneous business cards from merchants in Los Angeles and Spokane, Washington.
- ✓ One clothing receipt for a pair of house shoes
- ✓ One fast food receipt from Chippy's Diner
- ✓ One pair of Niki sunglasses

Reconciling that last item with the property list, Carney turned looking directly at Rosenburg with a sigh of resignation on his face.

"It's not inside the Toyota. Everything is accounted for. He gave them his consent to search the trunk, even though he isn't the owner. Nothing was seized. Everything inside it belonged to the registered owner. Maybe, our folks will find something inside it, if she was there. I know we'll find something, a hair, fiber, anything to place her inside that Toyota, confirming what Ms. Morton saw, but no one has seen a black notebook."

Rosenburg felt sick. He was almost certain they would find it in Phelps' possession. But for now, he wasn't going to make this investigation complicated. It was time for them to speak to Phelps.

"Are you ready?" he asked Carney.

"Ah, are you kidding me. I've been ready the moment we walked in here."

About forty-five minutes later, both detectives were sitting directly across from Phelps.

Rosenburg glared directly at the fifty-two-year-old white man who was slightly built with an egg-shaped head, gunmetal eyes, slack jawed, with a dry line mouth, coal black hair, clean shaven, except for a moustache and a chiseled nose. He wore a short khaki windbreaker, green shirt, denim jeans, jackboots, and a green ballcap. He didn't appear to be particularly strong. In fact, he seemed rather puny at first glance.

For some reason, there was a peculiar intensity among the three men, almost electric, as the detectives used the moment to get organized. They sensed their initial questions would define their relationship with him. It was important to cultivate a sympathetic posture, psychologically attempting to gain his trust but mindful that there was a missing girl and his cooperation would be beneficial to everyone.

Rosenburg then shook his head adamantly nodding at Carney to turn on the tape recorder. He then let go his usual sanctimonious, bullshitting ass smile before he spoke.

"We're from the Boise Police Department. My partner and I work out of the Missing Persons Unit—here's our business cards. My name is Sergeant Rosenburg and my partner is Detective Carney."

"Missing Persons," Phelps remarked, as he examined the business cards.

"That's right," Rosenburg replied.

"Is that why I'm here? Is somebody missing?" Phelps asked.

"I'm afraid so," Carney answered.

"Who?"

Rosenburg sighed, "Bonnie Chesterfield. Somebody kidnapped her yesterday in Boise."

Phelps eyes suddenly widened innocently like the proverbial cat that ate the canary. "Kidnapped!" he exclaimed.

At this point, Rosenburg regarded him with suspicion and said, "I need to admonish you, ya know, for the record and your rights." Rosenburg didn't need to use a printed card. He had read the Miranda Warnings a thousand times.

> *"Before we ask you any questions, you must understand your rights. You have the right to remain silent. Anything you say can be used against you in court. You have the right to talk to a lawyer for advice before we ask you any questions and to have him with you during questioning. If you cannot afford a lawyer, one will be appointed for you before questioning if you wish. If you decide to answer questions now without a lawyer present, you will still have the right to stop questioning at any time until you talk to a lawyer. Do you understand what I have just read to you?"*

Phelps was silent.

Rosenburg then repeated the question, "Do you understand..."

"... sure," Phelps interrupted him. "I understand," as he winced.

"Having these rights in mind, do you want to talk with us?"

Phelps shrugged. "I guess so. It's about... uh..."

"Bonnie Chesterfield."

"Okay, what do you want to know?"

Before Rosenburg could respond to the question, the door, previously closed, suddenly flew open with the crime scene technician waving at them.

Rosenburg nodded, motioning for Carney to turn off the recorder.

"Excuse us for a second," he said to Phelps.

Quickly closing the door behind them, it was Nora Anderson, the crime laboratory shift supervisor. When she wasn't studying crossword puzzles, working on her Mary Kay business, or weary from a hung-over, she was the department's best crime scene technician, maybe the best in the entire state.

"Have you guys started?"

"Not really," Carney answered.

"Good."

"You got something for us?" Rosenburg asked.

"Plenty."

"Great!"

"We found several fingerprints on the dashboard."

"Good."

"But that isn't all. We got what appeared to be a small, dry blood spot, fibers, maybe hair, and possibly a tiny fragment of skin tissue off the steering wheel. We found other fibers and definitely hair strands in the back fold-down seats. There was also some duct tape, a flashlight, three cans of chili and five separate pieces of heavy cord rope, long enough to tie up a small person. We took photographs, made a diagram, and we're taking specimens we collected for forensic examination back to the laboratory to analyze it.

We've got the girl's DNA. I'm also having the truck towed to Boise so we can give it a thorough going over."

Rosenburg and Carney knew they had to work fast. Nora wouldn't tolerate any consideration of insubordination or departmental rule infractions. Although she wasn't their supervisor, she had plenty of clout with the upper brass in the department because she had solved so many cases and became an outspoken advocate in cases like this. Her credibility allowed her to be direct and forthright in her decision regardless of who was investigating a case. Rosenburg was no exception. The Toyota was a crime scene that was bound to hit the media soon.

Returning to the interview room, Phelps looked obviously agitated. He then cast stare at them in mock defiance. Carney scowled back at him.

"Are you alright?" Rosenburg asked.

"Hell no!"

"Neither are we."

"What's next?" Phelps asked.

"Where we left off. Turn on the tape Carney."

Phelps shook his head.

"Are you going to answer my questions?"

Phelps' eyes were unreadable from a wordless stare.

"We know Bonnie Chesterfield was in the Toyota. We got an eyewitness that saw you, can place you there, right there with the Chesterfield girl. If she's alive, maybe we can work something out, mitigate this matter with the District Attorney," Rosenburg said.

Phelps continued to shake his head.

"Dammit Phelps, the child's parents are going crazy! Trust me. I can work out a deal, but we need to find her. This will help all of us."

Phelps' face suddenly grew haggard with worry. He clamped and unclamped his teeth, stress lines formed on his brow.

"Listen," Phelps said helplessly. "I need some help. I know you believe I kidnapped her, but it was only in my mind. I fantasized about them all the time, especially her."

"Bonnie Chesterfield!" Carney snapped.

"Yeah. I know it ain't right," he moaned. "But I-I-I kept watching her wondering what it would be like…"

"… having her for yourself," Carney interrupted, but Rosenburg shot a prohibited gaze at him. It was no time to ask leading questions. Carney stirred and breathed hard; his mouth crimped in annoyance.

"I didn't kidnap her. I might have thought about it… maybe even dreamed about it… I have dreams about things like that."

"You ever acted upon your dreams?" Rosenburg asked.

Phelps glared at him.

"Maybe acting out of fantasy, but later changing your mind. Perhaps what you thought would stimulate you, didn't occur?" Rosenburg said.

"I never would! I swear, I didn't kidnap her."

"Did you drive directly to Gooding?"

"Yeah. I did exactly what Alfred told me to do. He was running late, that's why I got sleepy coming back. Maybe it was the beers, so that's why I pulled over at the rest stop."

Rosenburg looked at Carney. "What about the rope, and duct tape in the back seat?"

Phelps bristled. "I feel sick and my head hurts. I guess I had too much to drink. Can I get some coffee and a smoke? I'm a little nervous, so I need a break before I say anything else."

"Did you buy the rope and duct tape?" Rosenburg asked, ignoring Phelps' request.

"Yeah, but it was just a game. I-I mean it was part of my fantasy."

And suddenly—"Cut the fucking crap, you sick son-of-a-bitch, where's the girl? Did you fuck her, and kill her… you piece of living shit?" Carney yelled.

"Cool it… just calm down Carney," he sighed, looking bewildered and perplexed. "We're gonna take him to Boise. Maybe we'll need a break, okay?" Rosenburg said, as he looked at his exhausted partner.

Carney hunched forward. "I'm sorry," he moaned. "I guess I do need a break," lowering his head, obviously embarrassed by his outburst. "I apologize to you, Mr. Phelps. I am really sorry for the comments I made toward you."

Phelps shrugged. "I understand. I know I come across like a real creep."

Trembling, by now her heart was pounding hard inside her chest, her face became a mask of terror as she quietly followed the mysterious girl who moved swiftly, waving only a small flashlight. Meanwhile, Bonnie's head swiveled from side to side, still frightened her abductor might return. Her eyes darted manically picking up objects out of the gloom. She swallowed dryly, profoundly relieved that she had been rescued. Thinking back, her mind sought for a rational explanation, something that made sense about what she had seen. She was encircled by a small campsite. Her pulse quickened at the bizarre scene—a large box containing an assortment of canned goods close by her, next to it was a police scanner, three ten-gallon cans of Kerosene, blankets, a case of bottled water, a box with soap, towels and face clothes, toilet paper, dry cereal, a first aid kit, more duct tape and rope.

She shivered. A strange electric cackle of dread moved throughout her body knowing that someone had planned to have her there for a considerable period. Somehow, she just knew it.

Meanwhile, three hours later in Boise, Phelps was sitting inside the interrogation room; his hands cuffed behind his back. He had only offered a token response to Rosenburg's questions. The interrogation stopped momentarily. He was tired and his brain, numbed from a lack of sleep, undeniable affected his ability to remain abreast with Rosenburg's quick pace, verbal assault upon him. But Carney was scrutinizing Phelps' features for clues, unconvinced by his unresponsive behavior, and by now he was thoroughly convinced that Bonnie Chesterfield had been slain. Finally, out of sheer frustration, Rosenburg agreed to stop the questioning. Besides Phelps hadn't requested an attorney to represent him. No matter what the circumstance, Rosenburg was adamant about resuming their interrogation as quickly as possible.

After inquiring with Carney whether or not he should resume questioning Phelps a third time, a telephone call interrupted his momentum. It was from Hazel Murphy, the Cedar Glass Factory employee.

"Missing Persons, Sergeant Rosenburg."

"Sergeant Rosenburg, this Hazzy. You remember me, don't you?"

"And how could I ever forget?"

"I was just wondering."

"What can I do for you?"

"Well, it might not be nothing."

"You might be surprised how we can make nothing into something. To me, everything is important, even the most trivial matter. Sometimes it can be exactly what's needed to break open a case."

"And, like I asked you before, keep my name out of it... except I heard about the $25,000 dollar reward offered today about the missing girl."

"Well now, I wasn't aware of this," Rosenburg responded.

"Yeah. It was on both the television and radio this morning from some anonymous source. Isn't that wonderful? I could really use it."

"I bet you could."

"But don't get me wrong, I would have called anyway."

"Oh, I believe that," he said with a wheezy chuckle.

"I'm serious."

"I'm serious, too. And if this turns out to be something, especially if it ultimately leads to Bonnie Chesterfield's whereabouts, you deserve the reward, especially if it's strictly about information where she is being held."

"Well, I don't know about that."

"What do you have?"

"Like I said, it might not be anything, but the other day, the same morning before the girl was kidnapped, our section was on our morning coffee break. I could have sworn I saw Clara Morton reading Phelps' little black notebook or a book just like it."

"What?" Rosenburg snapped.

"My eyes popped wide open, because I was certain it was Phelps' diary."

"Are you sure?"

"Of course, I'm sure. Listen, we've worked together at Cedars for ten years. Clara doesn't read anything—books, newspapers, tabloids, or even gossip columns—nothing. When she saw me staring at her, she seemed startled and slipped it inside her handbag. Hell, it might not be anything, but I thought I should tell ya about it."

"Did you say anything to her?"

"Not a fucking word, excuse my French. I pretended that I didn't see a thing, spoke to her and went to the vending machine. She looked kinda twitchy, like maybe something was wrong, or angry at herself. I'm really not sure, but that little book she was holding was bothering me... that's why I called you right away, because I might forget."

"Is that it?"

"Yeah, except..."

"I know—you don't want your name mentioned."

"Exactly!"

"Thanks, Hazzy. I'll get back with you."

"Well, it's nice hearing your voice again, Sergeant Rosenburg," she said, changing her voice in an adorning tone.

"You betcha," he sighed. "Really appreciate this information. You take care of yourself." Rosenburg ended the conversation, hanging up before she could respond.

Baffled, Rosenburg took a deep breath. He looked across the table at Carney for an uneasy moment. His suspicion swung away from Phelps. Something was wrong—extremely wrong.

Morton was his only eyewitness. Without the victim, her accounts would link the physical evidence to Phelps, as well as the crime itself. But if Hazzy's suspicions were accurate, why did she have Phelps' diary, and how did she obtain it, he wondered.

Another ten minutes went by, Rosenburg was continuing to study each page of both the crime report and his personal notes and then suddenly, out of nowhere, something caught his attention. At first it was subtle, only a mild hunch or maybe a wild premonition, but certainly it was going to be explored.

Lifting his head up, his hawkish eyes met Carney, who was still a quarter asleep, a quarter exhausted, but half curious as he stared evenly at him.

"Will you check out Phelps' personal property for me?" he asked Carney.

"You got something?"

"I'm not sure."

"Be back in a moment," Carney replied.

Fifteen minutes later, Carney returned with a brown, manila envelope containing Phelps' personal property. Emptying out the contents on Rosenburg's desk, his hands painstakingly sorted out each item. For several moments, his eyes were fixed unwaveringly until finally what he was searching for grabbed his attention. It was the fast-food receipt from Chippy's Diner—the same place where Phelps, according to Morton, purchased routinely his evening meals.

"You found something?" Carney asked inquisitively.

"I think so," Rosenburg half responded, intensely studying the receipt.

"What is it?"

"The time."

"The time?" Carney frowned.

"Yeah, the time of purchase."

"I don't follow you."

"Ms. Morton told me the kidnapping occurred around 4:47 pm, but this fast-food receipt's time is stamped at 4:52, on the same day, only five minutes after the kidnapping."

"I'll be damn," Carney sighed.

"Morton said the SUV left the scene travelling eastbound. In that direction, it's moving away from Chippy's. If he had a screaming, frantic teenager who may have still been struggling inside the vehicle, how in the hell could he make a U-turn and drive to Chippy's to purchase a fuckin cheeseburger and fries? Doing all of that within five minutes? I betcha it takes more than five minutes just to get your order placed."

"Maybe, he could have..."

"... Nah. Nah!" Rosenburg interrupted him, quickly dismissing his potential explanation. "If I'm right, it's impossible for him to be at two places at once."

After consuming a pot of black coffee, and four Krispy Kreme donuts, Rosenburg meticulously developed his next layer of strategy. Although each man was exhausted, they could not stop. They were thinking about Bonnie Chesterfield, perhaps she was seriously injured or maybe dead, and about her parents, the nightmarish ordeal they were continuing to suffer. And as always, their message pads were filled with leads and incoming calls from everywhere about the girl's disappearance.

By now, less than forty-five minutes later, the detectives had reworked their investigation. Rosenburg suddenly had that intuitive feeling to temporarily stop Phelps' interrogation. The unsettling anxiety about the case had fully matured inside his head. Before following-up on the information Ms. Morton had provided him, he had to establish two crucial facts with the employees at Chippy's. Most importantly, it was vital to establish if the electronic cash register's clock had been properly calibrated. Secondly, since Phelps was reportedly a regular customer and the case was less then forty-eight hours old, he required an eyewitness placing him at the scene to support his theory that Phelps, under the circumstances, could not have kidnapped Bonnie Chesterfield.

Arriving at Chippy's, Rosenburg left Carney inside the unmarked police sedan. He had fallen asleep. He chastised himself, too self-absorbed with the case knowing it was utterly asinine ordering donuts with his undisciplined partner's weakness for sweets. Carney's sugar level was elevated again.

Three minutes later, sitting in a small customer's booth with the shift supervisor, he had the corroboration to support his suspicion about the case. Helen Palmer, a tall blonde, with remarkable facial features of Florence (Flo) 'Kiss my Grits'—the boisterously character on the comic sitcom Alice—along with her bleached blonde bouffant hairstyle with a heavy, copious amount of hair spray, was undoubtedly going to be his boiler-plate witness. Palmer checked the cashier's clock on the three to eleven shift. On the date involving the kidnapping, not only did she check the clock, she had personally given Phelps' his order.

"Jimmy the Crickets," she began. "How could I ever forget that creepy little weasel?"

"What do you mean?" Rosenburg asked.

She raised one hand to cover her mouth, looking around, she then slowly lowered her hand, "You know what I mean," she whispered. "He acts kinda like a faggot, or something."

"Or something," Rosenburg winced.

"Yeah, like he was interested in boys. I mean we have young kids working here. He always would stare at them. After a couple of times, we began to notice it. He had them probing eyes. It was a troubling stare, like he was undressing you."

"Do you think his stares were more at the young girls working here?" Palmer thought for a moment, her forehead wrinkled and then with a demurred laugh, she said, "Now that you mentioned it, he did make them nervous."

"Good, very good. So, without a doubt, he was here, the exact time (displaying a photocopy of the cashier's receipt to her) this register receipt displayed?"

"Yep. I remember the order because he's a regular—always ordering a grilled cheeseburger, without onions, with tomatoes, large fries, and a strawberry milkshake. It's always the same, he comes in at least three or four times a week."

"Did he look particularly nervous? Like he was in a hurry?"

"Not really."

"Was he driving a vehicle?"

"I didn't see one. Normally, he takes the bus but I really couldn't say."

"Did you happen to see a brown, Toyota SUV?"

"I don't think so," she hesitated. "It was busy then, almost five o'clock, people getting off work, school out, this place is a real mess, but I don't believe the guy was driving a vehicle, especially a SUV."

Rosenburg scribbled her last comments on his notepad. He then smiled, "You won't mind giving me an official statement later?"

"Sure, no problem."

"Thanks."

"What's going on? Did he do something?"

"Later…" he smiled. "I'll tell you later."

Moments later, Rosenburg returned to the unmarked police sedan. Unlocking the door, the sound startled Carney. He winced, "Why didn't you wake me?" he asked frigidly.

Rosenburg shrugged. "I'm sorry, besides it was quick. We're on the right track now."

"Really?"

"Yeah. I know who kidnapped Bonnie Chesterfield."

"Who?"

"Phelps' cousin, Alfred Singleton."

"Son-of-a-bitch. Let's get the bastard. He and that Morton broad are really fucked up."

"Yeah. I guess for some measly fuckin reward. That's what they were counting on."

"Setting up his poor old creepy-ass cousin," Carney moaned.

"Some people will do anything for some dough."

"I guess so."

"Well, we don't have much time. Let's get this asshole!" Carney snapped.

Collectively, both detectives were feeling a level of relief, especially since the investigation seemed to be a smooth pattern toward their primary suspects.

It was all making sense now. Alfred would be the most obvious person having access to Phelps' diary.

Less than fifteen minutes later, the detectives arrived at the automotive repair shop. Alfred was bent over underneath a car hood, unaware of their arrival. Another fact that seemed to confirm their suspicions about him, he was short and muscular built with massive Oarsman's shoulders, work-swollen, banged-up hands, a body typically similar to a prison weightlifting physique.

It would take significant strength, weightlifting force, to drag a young girl inside a vehicle and control her movements while driving away alone.

Stopping their sedan in front of the shop, instinctively both detectives were now convinced they had found their man. Suddenly, Alfred pulled away from the car. He appeared nervous at the sight of the two stoned-faced detectives.

"Alfred Singleton," Carney barked out. "You're under arrest."

"Under Arrest!" Alfred cried sharply. "For what?" he asked.

"You heard him, asshole," Rosenburg said, twisting the barrel-chested mechanic around. "Put your hands behind your back."

"Hey, wait a minute. I ain't got nothin to do with this crap," he snapped.

"That's what Clara Morton probably gonna say," Carncy huffed.

"What?"

"Your old lady," Carney shouted.

"My... old... lady," Alfred said, flinching with astonishment. "What the hell are you guys talking about. Clara Morton isn't my gal. She's Bart Saunders' ole lady. Whata fuck is going on?"

The detectives' faces were suddenly gazed with both shock and surprise. Rosenburg's eyes were fixed unwaveringly on Alfred's eyes. The situation was tensed. For the next several moments, Alfred vigorously defended his innocence while simultaneously enlightening them about Bart Saunders and Clara Morton's on and off relationship.

Bart periodically worked for him part time. He was his transmission specialist. In fact, it was Bart who actually replaced the transmission in the Toyota. For the first time, the mystery regarding who was actually driving the Toyota had been properly—with Alfred understanding the connection—answered by him when he surprised them by disclosing that it was Bart that delivered the Toyota to Phelps, with Alfred's instructions to drive it over to Gooding and drop off some parts.

It had been a perfect set-up, a closet pedophile with deep seeded, psychological and perverted sexual fantasies about young girls recorded in a black notebook, incapable of rationally distinguishing his demented mind between reality and fantasy, became a perfect scapegoat for them. And with this logic came a sickening feeling inside Rosenburg's stomach that maybe the couple used Phelps' own secret, sexual fantasies about Bonnie Chesterfield to kidnap her. But that was only part of it. How did Clara Morton obtain Phelps' diary, since Alfred wasn't aware that it was missing, if in fact it was Phelps' dairy Morton was reading that morning? This was a question only Morton could answer along with the obvious—where was Bonnie Chesterfield?

Rosenburg seemed to sense the possible dissipation of Alfred and his statements, for it was still quite possible he was lying. As a precaution, he was arrested as being an accomplice and taken to jail. His calls were being monitored in the event he attempted to communicate with Saunders or Morton.

Early afternoon, the detectives parked in front of Cedars Glass Factory to confront Morton. Within ten minutes, Morton entered the employee's breakroom. The moment she saw Rosenburg, the tension worked across her face. She slumped into a seat. Her eyes were readable now. A lost expression made her appear dull, with an empty ache gnawing at her soul. Rosenburg was now in the mood for a chess match. He knew the right pieces to move, gazing at her candidly. The breakroom was unusually empty and perfect conditions to slowly dismantle her earlier witness accounts to him.

"Clara, we know that you may have lied to us. You've been seen with a black notebook, maybe Phelps' notebook. And we've got everything put together, minus a few details, about your relationship with Bart Saunders," Rosenburg said cool and icy, while looking at Carney. It was time for their cat and mouse routine.

Right on cue—"Listen!" Carney began, "I hope that little girl isn't dead or injured. You got a choice. Something like that could be a long prison sentence or even the death penalty."

"Now, now!" Rosenburg interjected. "We don't wanna move that down that road with this nice lady. She has worked in this community all her life and a long employee at Cedars, probably not far from retirement. Is that right Clara?" Rosenburg asked.

For a couple of long minutes, they were all silent. Even as Carney voiced his statement, Morton slumped in her seat. They sensed she was no match for their routine.

Gradually, very gradually, a lump formed up inside her throat. She then wrung her sweaty, soaked hands. Barely opening her mouth, her voice quavering, she spoke defensively. "She's alive," she mumbled. "I'll tell you where Bart took her", she sighed lowering her head. "I knew it was a crazy idea……real damn crazy, ever since he told me about Alfred telling him all those creepy things Lester had written in his black notebook. That's what gave Bart the idea."

"The kidnapping?"

Rosenburg had a brief notion to give her the Miranda Warnings, but Clara continued freely and voluntary speaking with them without hesitation.

"Yeah, taking one of the girls around here."

"Do you have Phelps' black notebook?" Rosenburg asked.

Clara shrugged. "Yeah, I got it."

"How did you get it?" Rosenburg asked.

"Bart was drinking with Alfred and Lester one evening. When he left, he unlocked their back kitchen door. He came back later while Alfred and Lester were in a drunken stupor, searched Lester's bedroom and found it. We had been reading all those crazy, recorded notes Lester had been writing in that black notebook, some real sick stuff," she said. "He told me to keep it for safekeeping."

"Is Bonnie Chesterfield in that black notebook?" Carney asked.

"Uh huh. She and a whole lot more. The guy is a real pyscho. He writes those stories about how he's going to kidnap the girls, and you know..."

"Yeah, we know. Let's get Bonnie Chesterfield," Rosenburg said. "Get a unit over to Saunders' place and lock his fuckin ass up."

With a search team of fifteen police officers, two long, wide-eyed Belgian Malinois, three emergency medical technicians, crime scene technicians, two speleologists, and Morton, the two detectives negotiated their way through a densely wooden terrain giving way to a small, remote cave in the Shoshone Ice Cave area, part of the Black Burte Crater Lava Field. Moving cautiously with flashlights, they sloshed through slush of wet footing, glissaded up and down small, hilly rock formations and finally scaling down over a soft ledge to a narrow, but level cavity inside the cave near a small waterfall, about one eight of a mile from its entrance, where a small campsite was tightly deposited away from the world.

According to Morton, this was a place Saunders periodically used when he was an Explorer Scout and knew this cave and its secrets very well. Morton was also familiar with this campsite having been taken there with Saunders on several occasions. She had visited Bonnie Chesterfield during her ordeal to insure she wasn't injured and to calm the girl's frightening nerves.

The group was initially startled by the soft illuminated surrounding generated by a small portable kerosene heater. The speleologists were amazed at how well the campsite had been preserved. Rosenburg's eyes glinted with relief as he caught sight of a sudden movement inside a dark green sleeping bag.

"She's alive," someone bellowed.

Still bound and blindfolded, amid the small campsite containing several supplies and food items scattered everywhere, Bonnie Chesterfield was nestled inside the canvas bag with her wrists and ankles tightly bound.

Within moments, the Chesterfield girl was quickly untied by an EMT and hustled a few feet away to be examined by them. The campsite was now a crime scene and, now meticulously cordoned off by the Crime Scene Forensic Team as anxious police radios echoed loudly throughout the cave announcing that Bonnie Chesterfield had been found—found alive inside the remote cave.

Meanwhile, a burly Bart Saunders had been arrested at Morton's apartment. A day later armed with a search warrant, Saunders's Chevy Malibu was seized and searched. Duct tape, rope and a green ballcap and sunglasses were recovered. The crime scene technicians also recovered hair fibers, DNA samples that subsequently were confirmed belonging to Bonnie Chesterfield. Morton would later confess that the Chesterfield girl's drugged and unconscious body was stuffed inside the Malibu from the Toyota along with supplies. Saunders drove her to his hiding spot inside the remote cave. He had taken Morton later that evening with the kerosene, portable heater and other camping and food supplies.

And, as for Phelps, in spite of his sexual perversions, fantasies, and recordings of what was obviously his fascination about Bonnie Chesterfield, he was eventually released from custody, cleared of any wrongdoing. Except for his pathetic notebook, all of his personal property had been returned to him. Although he was terminated from Cedars, perhaps due to his irresistible pedophile impulses—a potential liability the company lawyers were unwilling to assume—he was now working full time at Alfred's automotive repair shop. Except for a green ball cap and thick sunglasses, Bonnie Chesterfield couldn't remember much about her abductor after striking her head against the steering wheel.

Even the reality about the strange, young teenage girl rescuing her was only a dream. The head injury, prolonged hours of isolation, blindfolded in utter darkness, dehydration, fear, all essentially caused her to hallucinate, a theory concluded by her attending physicians and psychiatrists. Besides, everyone was undeniably more elated about her being found alive and unharmed and less preoccupied about her mysterious dream who she said it wasn't Morton's voice that she heard. To everyone, except Rosenburg, there was something about her eerie experience—the puzzling information the strange girl shared with her—for some reason, it had got inside his head. He had become confounded by it; wondering was there a connection with her dream.

Days went by, and finally almost with a undefining sense of clairvoyance, the elliptical web of suspense regarding Chesterfield's unthinkable dream inside the cave had come to him. Abruptly, one day sitting at his desk, Rosenburg dropped his pen, whirled up from his chair, filled with a frantic source of energy. He rushed over to his file cabinet searching for the Chesterfield case. Crazy! This thing was driving him crazy, he thought, as his eyes slowly scanned over each page of the crime report.

Shaking his head, like a saturation of a nightmare, it was faintly haunting him about the Chesterfield girl's dream and the crime report. There was a connection—his instincts had thoroughly convinced him about it.

Five hours later somewhat fuzzy-minded, it was the fourth time he began rereading the report. Then as though a heavy jolt of caffeine had struck his mind, his eyes bolted wide. "I'll be damn," he said. "Here it is."

It was those miscellaneous business cards from Spokane, Washington found in Phelps' personal property. He then grabbed his notebook, quickly examining each page until he found what the was looking for—Bonnie Chesterfield's initial statements about the brief conversation she had with the young girl. The information was vague, almost indecipherable, but more like a message or maybe a code, said in such a manner that it could be decipherable.

His eyes then moved slowly over his notes:

> *"I'm in Spokane, off Highway 195, outside of Nine Mile Falls, about a quarter mile from the freeway near an old windmill, by a small lake, next to a large patch of the most beautiful lupines, brown-eyed Susans and golden rods that grow every spring in the field all the way to the road. I've been staying near Highway 195, about twenty-four years now".*

Rosenburg continued on reading further:

> *"My name is Chelsea Marie St. John." This was what Bonnie Chesterfield told him during their initial conversation. An eerie statement that Chesterfield said the young girl had told her. Over time, the statement was lodged in the back of his mind, seemingly whispering to come forward so he could understand there was a*

sobering connection between what was said to Chesterfield and the Spokane business cards found in Phelps' personal property. He just knew there was more to this case!!!

He abruptly stopped. Grabbing the report, there was only one final piece remaining in this unimaginable puzzle. He huffed, hurriedly racing down the stairwell to the property room.

Ten minutes later, he checked out Phelps' notebook. Filtering through page after page of young women's names, lurid sexual fantasies, mindless self-gratifying sexual compulsions, delusions, erotomania about young girls and even a sickening episode of necrophilism with a girl's corpse in a funeral home, his eyes finally settled back, "I-II be a son-of-a-bitch," he groaned.

There it was! It was short—seven choppy lines—but significant words for him.

He took a long breath… another one… and still another breath. His eyes were frigid staring at the twisted notation recorded in his black notebook:

"I left her there, off Hwy 195
naked and smiling at me. Still
smiling when her face disappeared.
I knew she would like the flowers,
lake and the windmill, it was real nice.
I'll be back Chelsea, I promise. I
always keep my word."

His muscles relaxed. His instincts continued to comb through the custodial interrogation recording he and Carney had with Phelps. As he listened intently to the recording, the connection of the puzzle was fully coming in focus. He heard Phelps mumble the name, Chelsea Marie St. John, periodically during his rambling and incoherent statements. It was the precise same name that Bonnie Chesterfield said about the mysterious girl she spoke with during her ordeal inside the cave.

Ironically, Lester Phelps was also residing in Spokane, Washington and, was there some unimaginable connection to him and this Chelsea Marie St. John.

About fifteen minutes later, Roseburg had been contacted the Spokane, Washington's

Missing Persons bureau, and discovered that Chelsea Marie St. John was reported missing for almost twenty-four years.

Less than eighteen hours later, using the information and other details provided from him regarding the lurid description location in Bonnie Chesterfield's dream and notes from Phelps' diary, a Spokane Police Department search team slowly identified the area and rigorously edged through the rich brown soil, meticulously combing with excited, cadaver dogs over every inch of the surface until the skeletal remains of a nude, unidentified woman was uncovered in a shallow grave, near an old windmill, adjacent to small lake and beds of spring flowers—exactly how Bonnie Chesterfield recalled in her dream about the conversation with this mysterious girl near Highway 195.

Forty-eight hours later, through DNA analysis and dental records, the body discovered was, in fact, Chelsea Marie St. John. The coroner ruled it a homicide.

These events wouldn't necessarily make Rosenburg become a believer in spirits or ghosts. He had been a cop for nearly twenty-seven years accustomed with dealing in only factual details. However, maybe her strange dream was a prophecy, a supernatural revelation that made it too difficult for anyone to understand. But in an unthinkable paradox, the existence of ghosts, without the acceptance of any other superstition, might be the only fact a rational person could conclude in this case.

It simply was a fact that Bonnie Chesterfield did experience an extraordinary encounter with something or someone inside that cave that simply goes beyond all human comprehension or explanation.

Rosenburg still remembered the look on Phelps' face—his eyes widened, breathing hard—when he told him he was under arrest for the investigation of Chelsea Marie St. John's murder, in Spokane, Washington and that the Attorney General's Office in Spokane was working on an extradition order for his return to Spokane.

Phelps worked as a maintenance assistant less than three miles from where Chelsea Marie St. John was last reported being seen. She too, like Bonnie Chesterfield, was a product of an interracial marriage which possibly explained his sexual fascination toward her.

Three weeks later, after two meetings with his court appointed attorney, Phelps waived his extradition hearing. For his own part, Rosenburg had felt an enormous sense of self-satisfaction finally having that mental itch sufficiently scratched inside his head. This case was over for him or so he presumed.

A week later, in the corridor outside of his office, it was late on a Wednesday afternoon, Carney was walking quickly toward him with a white man wearing black and gray cowboy boots and carrying a brown leather briefcase.

"There he is," Carney said, pointing to Rosenburg.

The man nodded, smiling.

"Glad to finally meet you face to face. I'm Sergeant Paul Anderson of the Spokane Police Department," he announced.

"Well now," Rosenburg said, with a mild curiosity written across his face.

"I guess you're wondering why I am here?"

Rosenburg shook his head. "You betcha," he said with a half-smile.

"We've got a confession from Lester Phelps."

"Great!"

"But he didn't kill Chelsea, according to him, and we believe him."

Confused and perplexed, Rosenburg said, "But his note mentioned only him at the scene."

"That's because he didn't want anyone else to be a part of his fantasy. It's always just him and the girls, and no one else in his diary."

"Are you shittin me?" Rosenburg asked.

"No. It was Alfred Singleton, his cousin. He killed St. John."

"What!" Rosenburg's mouth flew wide open. "Alfred killed her?" he repeated.

"Yeah, that's right. I wanted to come here personally not only to meet and thank you but to see old Alfred's reaction when you guys serve him with an arrest warrant for murder."

"I'll be damn," Carney moaned.

"Yeah, we got it all put together. Alfred was living in Spokane. In fact, he got Lester the maintenance job where he worked. We've confirmed all of this with their previous employer and also obtained both their employee records and Singleton's lease agreement in Spokane during that same period of the St. John's disappearance. Alfred knew his cousin had a fantasy toward young girls but it was only a game for Lester. He wouldn't harm anybody. The guy has no criminal history, not even a jaywalking ticket. But Alfred—that's a different story."

"Yeah, we knew about the two assault cases," Carney interjected.

"That's right. According to Phelps' written confession, they were drinking one evening, and Alfred has his own perversions, but he acts his out. He grabbed St. John, who was a runaway with an arrest record for prostitution and drove her around several hours—drinking and doing some meth—until they wound up on Highway 195. He drove off to a narrow clearing, near a small lake, and old windmill… much of it isolated. Alfred then raped and later strangled her after Lester refused to act out his fantasy. He made Lester bury her in that shallow grave. Lester told us he returned the next day kinda sorry about what happened. That's why he recorded that entry in his black notebook.

They argued after that, and Alfred quit his job and moved around for a while before coming to Boise. We're still working the case, but we got enough probable cause to arrest him and return him to Spokane, after his extradition proceeding here. We believe the St. John murder has sealed both of their fates. We have linked his DNA from her. We're also examining several similar crimes in the Seattle and Tacoma area as we are developing some possible timelines that Singleton may have been in the area at the time. Phelps told us this was the only incident that involved he and his cousin. Apparently, he was right so far, we can't find anything else in his diary nor do we have any evidence that he was in the Seattle or Tacoma area with Singleton."

Rosenburg sighed. "I'll be damn. I'll be damn", he repeated. Turning his head, meeting Carney evenly in the face, he said, "Well partner, we'll get our coffee and hamburger later after we go lock up this asshole."

Carney sighed, shaking his head in agreement as they gave each other a wordless stare, understanding the incredible events that unfolded in this entire case. Shrugging his narrow shoulders, "This case was real creepy from the beginning." Shaking his head, "We need to hurry up! I am hungry now for my coffee and hamburger. I'll call a marked unit to cover us. We gotta another asshole to lock up," Carney said, with a slight chuckle.

UNWELL
LETTERS

CHAPTER 5

UNWELL LETTERS

HE LIFTED HIS JOWLY CHIN TWISTING HIS HEAD AROUND, DEFIant, full of a strange, unreasoning suspicion. I quickly turned my head avoiding meeting his gaze. I could feel his huge dark eyes beneath those arrow black eyebrows searching every outline of my entire body. His face was a waxy pale, cold, an icy coolness that made me shiver. The rotation of his eyes made me feel weak, ineffective and woozy. The sudden, intermittent shafts of sunlight fell upon my body compounding my apprehension about him.

I tried to resist the sickening intensity that surged up inside me. This moment, a point of time that had become a ritual between us for nearly seven years, while incarcerated at Chillicothe Correctional Institution, adjacent to the Ross Correctional Prison, and Hopewell Culture Historical Park, about 190 miles from my hometown south of Cleveland, Ohio.

Each occasion made me fascinated in a horrified way. He was an icon surrounded by superstition and endless dark tales of strange powers. Possessing strange or peculiar powers in prison wasn't uncommon—but there wasn't anything common about him.

I always remained frozen, deceptively still, at least in my mind, waiting for his gaze to retreat while ignoring my malignant curiosity about him. It would be several moments before the unsettled feeling gradually withdrew from inside my head. My body relaxed and softened the unspeakable dread these moments created for me.

But unlike before, this time I made a sidelong glance at him, and a tense smile creased his face. His eyes never left me. Even at this short distance of twelve feet between us, our lives and thoughts were never connected. However, in this period of irrepressible silence—no movement to ripple the stale air, no voices to rattle our eardrums, no indefinable words to separate our concentration, no thoughts to waver our immutable thinking—the silence, the unusual nature of it, nevertheless seemed to unexpectedly draw me closer to him.

I could feel a stride of courage deep down inside my stomach. Slowly, it was moving up toward my mouth. At first, I wanted to dismiss this feeling—a twisted aberration loomed up inside me. I never felt like this before. "I-I-I don't understand what's happening to me," I muttered softly to myself. My breathing quickened. I struggled to compress this utterly uncomprehending feeling that was rapidly increasing my self-assurance. This uncertain premonition was suppressing my reluctance which now became subordinate to his reputation and hypnotic image.

The feeling now moved up passed my throat, settling inside my dry mouth. It was dominating my psyche forcing my will to speak to him.

Now, our gaze changed to a suspicious glance. He then gestured a subtle wave to me.

I initially hesitated a brief moment before I spoke, "What do you want"? I asked.

"Talk," he mumbled impuissantly. "Just a few words."

He then nodded his head and motioned for me to come over. Our cells doors were unlocked and open. The prison inmate body count had cleared.

I shuffled over and stood by his cell door.

"First time in seven years," I said.

The man clasped his hands behind his head and stared at the ceiling. "Yeah," he mumbled.

"Been meaning to chat with you," I said.

"All right."

"My name is..."

"Conner Davis, some former bank executive from Cleveland."

I shrugged, slightly puzzled by his statement, "Didn't know you knew."

"I know a lotta things," he said dryly. "Haven't you heard about me?" he asked. "The rumors... my reputation... my powers... and the letters," he grinned sharkishly.

I was totally expressionless. Somehow, I knew about the implications of the letters. For several years, I developed a growing suspicion about this man, the letters and the endless inmates visiting him, and oddly some prison staff would also secretly visit.

He shrugged and grinned a baleful grin. "I've seen all those letters you been writing for the inmates and staff. Are you a writer or something?"

He then took a deep breath. "Or something," he repeated.

But I didn't really mean a writer with literary skills, publishing with a compelling hip hop or gangster story, something I envision most prisoners would write with all the elements that might stimulate an editor's interest.

"Calvin. Calvin Kellogg." The man unclasped his hands from behind his head. "But everybody calls me Cal." His words broke my thoughts.

"Okay, Cal. What about 'em?"

"About what?" Cal asked. Cal's face twitched slightly. I immediately recognized that it was a naïve response, even simple-minded. It was the letters that created every aspect of Cal's mysterious reputation in Chillicothe. My curiosity about him never wavered for seven years and I sensed he was keenly aware of this fact about me.

I shook my head. "What I meant to say.." I paused a moment, licking nervously my dry lips several times. "I know you write letters for people, that all I'm saying."

"Hundreds of 'em… maybe thousands of 'em."

"That's cool man," I said.

"You think it's cool?"

I hesitated for a solemn moment. Confused, now, perplexed, even uncertain how to continue the conversation with this shrewd convict. I wanted to avoid Cal getting inside my head.

"I'm sorry. Maybe you misunderstood what I meant. Do you believe it's cool that the letters help people?" Cal asked me.

"Sure," I said for his benefit. He winced. "That cool brother, helping people with pain, with incipient grief walling up inside them for justice, retribution, or just plain old-fashioned revenge. That's exactly how and why I write letters. I personalize their problems, wrapping them up inside words. Words that can expel a problem by eliminating it—completely and utterly alleviating the prolong moments of emotional pain—a tool to satisfy their insatiable rage for justice. Guys in prison know about how fucked up justice is in the Ohio court system. Just ask these black dudes doing time here—injustice for them rather than justice. And the poor Hispanics and even the white guys, they all get a taste of how fucked up the system is. They understand how this so-called justice fucks them over and over again."

"What about the prison staff who come to you?" I asked. He snickered. "Them fuckers only want 'revenge', against a system that fucks them over and this is their 'payback', coming to me."

I glared at him. "How does your letters satisfy justice or revenge for anyone? Hell, that sounds like bullshit to me." I chuckled slightly. "Good god, Cal, do people pay you for that tripe," I said without thinking.

Cal stared at me for a long moment, examining my face, and eyes. I bristled, recognizing that my off-handed, flippant sense of humor wasn't amusing. Grinning, Cal said, "They pay just like you would to have your ex-girlfriend and her boyfriend killed."

Both shock and surprise immediately worked across my stunned face. He shook his head. The statement utterly and completely fucked me up. I mumbled, struggling to move words from my mouth. They seemed to be twisted inside my head. This was some convoluted bullshit—it was so surreal, the unthinkable power that Cal just demonstrated.

"I-I don't understand," my voice trembled. "What do you know about me?" I asked moving slightly inside his cell. "I've never told anybody in here how I felt. Nobody… I mean nobody knows how I feel. So, you…"

"I know," Cal whispered. "I know how you feel. I can feel the anger and thoughts moving across your mind about her and the boyfriend."

"Shut up!" I said mildly shaken by him. "Shut the fuck up," I repeated, moving backward to the edge of his cell door entrance. "Pleaseeee, just shut up," I moaned as my eyes fell to the concrete floor.

"You want her dead," Cal said with an unreasonable smile. "Don't ya, brother Conner?" He giggled quietly.

Now something incredible was occurring between these two Ohio inmates. Conner Davis, former bank operations manager with the Ohio Savings and Loan, and Building Company, the oldest bank in Cleveland which opened in 1889, on the west side of the city. Conner received his first break when Ohio Savings established its vigorous, affirmative action hiring program searching the area for highly qualified women and minority candidates with strong banking resumes and the educational pedigree, making them successful candidates in their banking program. Conner graduated magna cum laude from the prestigious Case Western Reserve University in Cleveland, with an MBA degree in banking after obtaining his BS degree in finance from Akron University. He worked in several community banks, rising up the ranks, and was a prime selection as the company's first African American male banking managerial staff member.

After working for twelve exceptional years in the Ohio Savings and Loan system,

Conners' personal life changed after his divorce, something he was opposed to from his wife who was his high school sweetheart where they met at East High School in Cleveland. This event worked deep inside him, causing a tug-of-war between the quality of his professional banking responsibilities and personal life. In trying to escape the aftermath of his divorce, he began rearranging his personal life with new friends, friends who never climbed the social and career ladder like him. These friends were refined "dope fiends," whom Conner soon found himself on even footing. With a new girlfriend, and what junkies eventually do—search to get high—moving from his addicted cocaine habit to crack cocaine. Conners' addiction was consuming him along with his income and the inability to balance the two—work and his addiction. He was now feeling his drug addiction had become a heterogeneous disorder, his body changing characterized by him going through long cyclic periods of drug use, withdrawal and abstinence and then stronger drug-craving for crack.

His addiction was affecting his work performance and soon his absenteeism caused him to be reprimanded by his supervisor. He knew the end was near and, listening to his girlfriend, he developed a half-baked scheme to embezzle nearly four hundred thousand from a large overseas corporate account from the bank.

About three weeks later, Conner was terminated for embezzlement of the funds and the bank sought criminal charges and restitution from him. Although he was regarded as a first-time offender, the prosecution was aggressive and having a public defender didn't help his case. He was sentenced to three to fifteen years in the Ohio State Criminal Justice and Rehabilitation system and later Chillicothe State Prison.

Conner had a terrible time explaining to the prosecutors how he completely evaporated nearly four hundred thousand dollars; not one cent left from his marathon crack episodes. The prosecutors tried to cut a deal with him—less prison time and more time off for mitigating factors for a reduced sentence if he returned the remaining embezzled funds.

Love! Perhaps because of love for his ex-girlfriend or perhaps without realizing it, she convinced him to conceal the whereabouts of the money and she would keep it for them once he was released from prison.

Although Conners wanted to appear cooperating as any refined first-time offender but his inward nature, at all costs, was willing to do a longer prison sentence foolishly believing he would have both the girlfriend and remaining cash upon his eventual released from prison. She concealed over three hundred thousand.

He was now face-to-face with a fellow convict who was lifting the veil of his most inner thoughts he shielded from police and prosecutors for over seven years.

"Stop it," Conner said firmly. "Just… stop… it," he groaned. Cal didn't flinch. Smiling, he said, "Does the word brother, bother you?" It was an obvious reference as Cal was white and Conner black, Conners frowned. "Nope," his voice was subdued. "What the hell is happening here?"

"The beginning of the end about them. The nightmare that comes inside your dreams about her, him and the money. It keeps coming over and again."

Cal remarked calmly. "Isn't that why you're here this long—for her, the money. You remember, it was her idea to steal it. Remember?" Cal said coldly, "Remember," he repeated.

After a brief hesitation, Conner said, "Yeah, I remember."

Conners groaned dutifully at his previous bad joke now realizing the rumors about Cal were true. He shuttled over to his cell and sat on a square, steel chair, staring at his pinching equilateral confines. The conversation was a radical exchange that somehow became an embarrassment to him. Cal found his dark thoughts, deep dark dreams, nightmarish dreams that would sequester his ex-girlfriend to his personal hell, along with her new boyfriend, and the money she covenant.

Conner gave Cal a dubious look. "How did you know? I've never told anyone. She talked me into it. It was my addiction. For two years, I stole and manipulated funds from my bank. I listened to every stinkin word, all the lies, and never once was I suspicious. Even when she insisted in hiding the money. I got high with her, but I never got one red cent. Nothing!!!!!"

Cal nodded. He stared directly at him. "I'm on your side, brother," he smiled leaning back against the bland, gray wall toying with a pen.

Still confused, Conner cleared his throat. "But this was my private thoughts. Weird. They were too weird to ever discuss 'em." He winced. "How did you know?" Conner shrugged. He stared at him for a long moment, searching his face and eyes. "After all, isn't that why you came over to my cell?" Cal then raised his bushy eyebrows and said, "A letter… do you want me to write a letter for you?'

Conner shook his head. He obviously ignored Cal's question. He stared at him for a long moment, searching his face and eyes. "Isn't this why you came over to my cell?" He repeated the question. Conner stood silent.

Cal edged closer to the entrance of his cell door and now, looking both ways, searching the corridor for any eavesdropping eyes or ears, he said, "I'll not only write you a letter, it will actually take care of your problem. Ya know, for the umpteenth time those dreams you have about her, him and the money."

"Okay…okay!" Conner said. "You don't have to tell me anymore about my damn dreams. I want the fuckin letter. But who will it go to… what will it say? How does this whole thing work?"

Cal paused and twisted his head slightly over his right shoulder. He gazed at a blank sheet of paper. "Kill 'em." He was deliberate, composing a fixed stare at the paper.

"You sure about this?" Conner asked.

"Quite sure." He said, turning around facing Conner with a reassuring smile. "Gonna cost you five hundred bucks. Gimme the money, and you'll get the letter. You sign it and give it back to me. I'll mail it to my sister."

Conners' face went blank for a short moment. "Your sister? Why would we involve her with a murder? I don't want her to use a letter about my interest in killing my ex-girlfriend. That would be potential evidence against me in a criminal prosecution for a conspiracy to commit murder."

There was not a lambent of emotion in Cal's cold, obsidian eyes. His face was strangely rigid. He closed his eyes for a few seconds and shook his head slowly.

"She doesn't open them," he mumbled. "Your letter is sealed tight and placed inside another envelope. When she receives it, she'll know what to do. She done it a thousand times or more. It will be no different for you."

Conner frowned. "What happens next?" he asked anxiously. Cal hesitated abruptly, reeling at the implication of his question. It was his question that involved a highly unlikely scenario.

He looked closely at the tall, light-skinned black man. Even in his prison garb, he was photogenic with his narrow feature, salt and pepper hair around his temples, mustache, and sideburns. Conner was in his middle forties and still looked trim and fit.

Cal then suddenly laughed, scoffing at his question. His behavior created a peculiar intensity about it. He was a member of the Aryan Brotherhood along with his proud Nazi Swastikas on his upper right forearm. He dealt with black inmates before but never had anyone questioned him as much about the letters as Conner. He resisted having a racist edge toward him; this was business.

Conner was too intelligent to believe Cal's sister was the final destination for the letter. In his mind, she was only the panoply in protecting the letter. It was this moment that his meddlesome thoughts wanted to understand Cal's dark and menacing secrets, fact or fiction about the nature of his power, and everything associated with it.

For the first time, Cal perhaps noticed a confused expression in Conners' eyes. Confusion—it wasn't like confusion that he didn't understand but rather confusion about why Conner was asking about something he had endless dreams about.

In Cal's mind, it was now going to happen, the retribution, the punishing justice of a Lacedaemonian Soldier coming in the night, what he was confused about. Both men cast equally penetrating stares at each other.

"What do you want from me?" Cal asked. Conner shook his head.

"A letter—that's what I want. A fuckin letter from you for them," Cal chuckled, stepping back inside his cell. "Every man has his own poison; a well-hidden lace of arsenic stirred up inside him. I systematically transfer it in my letters, but nobody ever wants to know how it's done. I used your hate."

Conner winced. "But I do."

"I don't think you understand, brother Conners." Conner shrugged off Cal's statement. "No deal. I have to know—the police, the letter, witnesses and you. I cannot afford to have a problem with this. I'll be on parole in less than seventy-two hours. If it happens…"

"You're right. I haven't told you everything else. It's my grandmother. The letters are taken to her."

Conner shook his head greenly, seemingly to clear it. The letter, going to his grandmother, it was hardly convincing or believable. It sounded like bullshit again. He rose up from the steel chair inside his cell, "Fuck a Duck," he said, walking to the edge of his cell entrance.

"I don't understand."

Cal then smiled; his neck strained. He looked intently at him. "Because…" he began and then hesitated a few more seconds. It was obvious he didn't want to go into any great length about it. For another brief instant, he thought about changing his mind. But it was a fleeting thought that quickly passed by him. His eyes finally settled deep into Conners' face. His lips parted in a tight smile as he spoke.

"Do you believe in witches, sorcerers, warlocks?" he asked while letting out a long sigh.

A half-dozen thoughts quickly raced through Conners' mind about another convict who visited Cal named Walter Harris. Harris hated Associated Warden James "Hop" Benson; a hatred that created a visit to Cal.

Conner recalled seeing the aggravation in Harris' face, the unmistakable hate that etched across his heavy lined, and pot-marked face.

"What in hell?" Harris said to Cal as Conner recalled him saying nearly two weeks later. "How did you do it? It was just a coincidence, wasn't it?" Harris asked.

Cal looked expectantly at him, smiling as he rotated a pen through his fingers.

"Call it a desire fulfilled, a long story and I don't have time to tell you about it."

Harris gave Cal a "you-don't-really-expect-me-to-believe-that" stare. "This won't come back on me?" he asked Cal.

"About Warden Benson's death." He smiled. "How could it? You didn't have access to his car brakes. Shame, shame on Ol' Hop for not checking his brakes regularly. We'll miss him. I wonder who'll take his place," Cal said sarcastically.

Conner still bristled from the experience when everyone was notified that Warden Hop Benson had died in an automobile accident when his brakes failed.

"Let me know," Cal said, "The letter—do you want the letter?" Cal's statement abruptly disconnected his thoughts. "That's where they go. All of 'em. She'll take care of them. My sister." He paused, smiling a faux bon smile. "She takes them there. Buries them in the dirt above her grave, at the Simons Memorial Cemetery, and leaves."

"Just like that..." Conner responded.

Cal nodded. "Right! Just like that—that simple."

Conner was a pragmatic man. Wishful thinking, witchcraft, spirits were all so foreign to him. Wild skepticism worked across his placid face.

"Surely, there's got to be more to this. Are you telling me she'll read the letter. Read it from her grave?"

Cal shrugged. Stepping backward, he gave Conner a cold stare and thought, "Fuck this uppity ass nigger." His mind quickly set aside his racial bias. "She has answered every letter, all of them. She always do," he said with a stern expression.

Conners couldn't fathom this unimaginable scenario about Cal's grandmother. On the other hand, his reputation was well established in prison. Conners shook his head. He then leaned forward, facing Cal squarely between his eyes.

"Five hundred bucks... that's it?" Cal smiled. "So little for so much, huh?" He grinned. "After you read it, sign it. Give it back with the five hundred bucks. I got ways for you to give it to me. I'll take it in commissary, stamps, or whatever, even green money will be okay, but its gonna cost you five hundred bucks."

Conner stared pensively for a few moments at the pale, gray wall inside his cell. Over the years, he had mastered a leather craft hobby, making hundreds of purses, Bible covers, belts, leather house shoes and practically anything else that was authorized in prison. He also made leather items that were unauthorized—knife leather cases, leather ropes, leather black police night sticks, and even leather dices. He saved nearly eight hundred dollars on his prison account, but several years ago, he opened an account at One United Bank in Cleveland and made regularly monthly deposits through his sister's name.

He had been re-working his exit plan since his scheduled parole release was just in a few days. And before this exchange with Cal, he didn't contemplate any significant expenses until now.

Conner stared at Cal. His suspicion slowly subsided. "It's a deal."

Cal's eyes gleamed. "Ah, I knew we would have one. T'morrow. The letter will be ready t'morrow—I'll have everything in it."

Conner stood up meeting Cal's stretched out hand. He hesitated a brief moment, perhaps wanting to explain his financial circumstances, but instead he just squeezed his hand. "It's a deal," Conners replied. "A deal." Both men then exchanged questioning glances at each other, followed by a slow, appraising glare.

A few moments later, Conner thought about changing his mind, perhaps working out a different payment arrangement, but something wouldn't allow it. Without a word, he watched Cal walk out of his cell. It was a stupid decision, he thought. He swore softly under his breath, angry at himself. He knew it was a half-hearted deal. He had no intentions of paying Cal but, for some reason, his nudging curiosity wanted to read this unwell letter he was writing. He was intrigued about how Cal would describe both the psychological demons that tormented him and the self-induced rage he created inside himself which created his insatiable craving for revenge. His feelings weren't unique. He knew other convicts felt like him, the black convicts refer to it as 'Serving a Motherfucker,' the hood term for getting some payback.

Gang members understood this expression all too well, especially when they learned of a betrayal within their ranks; or when a drug dealer discovers he was snitched out and, even worse, when guys learned how their lawyer sold them out.

But now, at least for the moment, he could be entertained about his hate, a literary fantasy of payback from Cal's crazy-ass delusions. It was so fascinating to him, a clever ex-banker executive with an MBA from *Case Western Reserve University*, was unquestionably more superior than this fucked up prison con. His intellect far surpassed this two-bit, prison charlatan, he reasoned. The notion that this crafty ass Machiavellian-power was real seemed utterly unconvincing to him.

Conner, still mentally toying with Cal, asked "What's her name?"

"Who?"

"Your grandmother—what's her name?" Cal looked at him. "Does it matter?"

Conner sighed. "My man, don't get me wrong. I don't know exactly why I asked. Maybe because I have a hard time believing this."

For an eerie moment, Cal's cold blue eyes shot back at him. The intensity of a frigid scowl made him nervous. He then stood up, his head dropping slowly to the floor. His eyes surveyed the scattered letters about on the concrete floor. "Ya fuckin with me '*Eenie meenie miney moe*'? My time… you fuckin with my time?"

"No sir." Conner demurred, ignoring the racist slur. Walking over to his cell entrance, Cal closed his lumberjack hand tightly around a single bar, his chilly eyes focused on Conner.

"She's a witch. They been in my family for over seven hundred years. I'm a part of 'em."

Conner frowned reflectively. "I-I-I-I…" he stuttered. "I… mean… never… mind… that's… okay… about… her… name," he replied.

"Harriet Rene Rorschire—that's her name. She was born in Southern France, in Aubagne near Marseille," Cal replied.

Conner said nothing. He smiled at Cal, turning around on his steel chair. He had enough of him for today.

By this time, daylight was coming more aggressively on the cell block. Conner's eyes widened as he watched the activity increase among the other convicts. He then moved back inside his cell. Falling on his bunk, he closed his eyes pondering thoughts about his exchange with Cal, the letter, and still later more thoughts about the mysterious Calvin Kellogg.

The following day was very much like the rest of the previous days in prison. Prison life becomes a mental collage. Doing time soon makes all the days vanilla… one day seems like all the rest. Routine! Nothing is ever said, done, performed, purchased, worn or even eaten that isn't routine. There is a blandness about all of it, a rather numbing sensation, especially for the lifers, guys whose lives end inside the joint.

Conner stretched his arms twisting over in his bunk. It took him only a millisecond to notice Cal was standing just outside his cell door waving something at him. It was the letter. For him, something half-good, half-evil; a letter that contained his internecine dream and their unthinkable nightmare.

Conner looked at him, now feeling perfectly substantial about having his grievance satisfied.

"Your letter."

"The way I wanted it?"

"That's right."

"Great!"

Conner stretched his long frame touching his feet to the floor. He shuffled over toward the bars. His cell door was still closed. Cal extended his arm through the bars and handed him an envelope. Conner stared at it briefly, hesitating slightly before he finally took it.

"Read it. Take your time. It's what your dreams are about just the way you wanted it to happen. An intruder coming in the night, shooting both of them to death while they slept inside their bedroom."

"Right?" Cal asked with an evil glee in his eyes. "Shooting them each in the head twice, like an executioner. Isn't that right?" he repeated. "Your thoughts," he grinned.

Conner remained quiet.

Later that day, the unexpected occurred. Conners' parole release arrived a day early. There was a combination of surprise and anxiety that worked inside him about the sudden notification. A few minutes later, Conner was eagerly packing his personal effects. His mind quickly registered about the envelope. At first, he intended to return it; however, Cal was at his prison assignment, and, without an afterthought, he tossed the envelope inside his bags. Looking around his cell block, he chuckled quietly to himself. The con man had just been conned, he thought. He would be long gone before Cal returned on the block. Long gone from this Old Folsom County

Blues, a song written by the great country western singer Johnny Cash who served a stint at Folsom Prison in California.

Conner's exit, of course, didn't create any problems as he meticulously avoided any more contact with Cal.

Several hours later, Conner had returned to society again. Nestling inside a small, efficiency studio apartment, it didn't take long for his compressed regression and schizophrenia to manifest itself inside him. It began as his eyes consumed the cramped and small quarters of his apartment. He bristled as the sight reminded him of his sophomore years, moving out of the dormitory and settling in his first dumpy apartment.

After unpacking, he flopped down on a narrow day bed fanning the air with hands in a show of disgust. He was tired from the abrupt transition and long bus ride back to Cleveland.

Yet, the notion of rest was strangely absent. He was now thinking about her... him... and the money. The cycle never stopped. Always there for seven years of sleepiness nights—endless daydreams—all day, every single damn day of his incarceration. And now, finally he was free to satisfy his inundated psychosis about them.

For the next several days, he slowly worked himself back into the Cleveland area. He was job hunting, staying focused and avoiding the Hough area where he frequented along with ex-girlfriend during his crack addiction. Soon he was gainfully employed with a new job working as a Re-entry Instructor for a non-profit that provided prison re-entry, training, housing and job placement services.

Despite his terrific new start, his continuing hatred loomed up inside him. It became too irresistible. The urge to see her was overwhelming again, and several weeks later he soon found himself driving by the old areas of the Hough neighborhood, hoping to obtain a glance at her and him.

It was an idiotic decision, and relatively a no brainer from his undemonstrative reaction the moment he saw her and very quickly her boyfriend—both of them hanging out and in the same old fucked up dope areas and spending his money.

"That skinny, pencil neck bitch, that stinkin low-down, yellow ass mother fuckin ho," the words scrolled across his mind. The mere sight of them seemingly getting high and in love made him become someone else—the intruder inside his dreams. Someone without either a conscience or morals who would deliver a final coup de gras for him and finish a mental anguish forever.

It was this rage that eventually returned him to the envelope on a cold, rainy Cleveland evening. The raindrops snapped irritably loud and seemed to bark annoyingly at his dark conscience. Despite his reluctance, he nevertheless retrieved the letter. For several undefined moments, his dark eyes swung languidly across each line and then suddenly, he gasped. The contents were amazingly accurate—every single detail had been extracted from his conscience. He abruptly stopped tossing his eyes away from it. The raw skepticism he felt about Cal's weird and narcissistic behavior was flowing away from him. Within seconds, he started trembling and shuddering, confounded by what he always wanted to occur. Just might… was it possible for this to happen?

A letter! Could something like this work, he thought. He shook his head, swinging his doubts back and forth… back and forth… back and forth until the doubts just stopped. His mind froze upon a supernatural composite—maybe, this could be real, so very real, he reasoned.

Once, twice, three times, calmly and coldly, he read the letter over again. His body shook from a strange, twisted stimulation from each detail regarding the murdering scenario. Finally, he signed it, presuming their demise was only days away.

Returning the letter inside the envelope, he gave a wicked sigh now recalling that perhaps he was nearly as crazy as Cal. The only thing left was to locate his grandmother's grave and place it in the soil exactly the way Cal told him how the secret worked.

The next day, Conner located Calvary Cemetery. Thirty minutes later, he stood dripping wet with frustration inside the caretaker's office. He shook his head and stared at the thin white man behind the counter.

"Can you help me? I'm looking for Harriet Rene Rorschire's gravesite. I don't seem to be able to locate it."

"Why certainly," the man responded, scribbling down her name, his right hand waved a helpless gesture.

"Oh! I'm sorry. The last name is spelled 'R.O.R.S.C.H.I.R.E. Rorschire," Conner repeated.

He nodded, quickly searching through his microfiche screen. Several moments later, his face contorted. He softly moaned as his nimble fingers raced across the keyboard rapidly punching the ***Return*** key several times.

Without looking up, he then said, "I'm so sorry, no Harriet Rene Rorschire, in fact, nothing even close to it. You sure this is the right cemetery?"

"I'm sure," Conner moaned.

He shrugged, "Sorry, we don't have her. Everyone out there is inside this microfiche data base. We're very careful about things like this. I have several ways to check." He sighed. "She's not with us. Believe me, we're real sensitive about something like this, sir."

Five minutes later, Conner was clear of the cemetery. His breathing was shallow, now believing the entire episode with Cal was nothing but a cheap con game. Disheartened, he was about to give up when he suddenly remembered the process. He briefly chastised himself, cursed as he distinctly recalled the precise details. The letter was supposed to be mailed to Cal's sister. Desperate. "I'll take it there, but I haven't had time to think of a good excuse," he thought.

Conner shook his head. After driving for nearly forty-five minutes, to his utter surprise, he located the house, the exact same address. Without the slightest hesitation or wasted movements, he quickly leaped from his pick-up truck racing hurriedly to the house. Just briefly, he noticed there was something strange about the house but that observation became an insufficient blockage to any suspicion.

He caught his breath while standing rigid at front of the door. After knocking twice, almost immediately the door opened slowly. He raised an eyebrow, believing he would meet a young woman. Now, standing before him was the diminutive features of an old woman. Conner took a few moments, stared at her along with the darkness in the backdrop behind her. She looked feeble, with long, very long matted silver and gray hair.

He shook his head in an uneasy puzzlement. "I'm looking for Calvin Kellogg's sister."

She gave him a sober grin. "She doesn't live here anymore. Debbie been gone for two years. I'm her grandmother, Harriet." She smiled at him guardedly. "May I help you?"

Conners did not speak for a moment. He glared at her in morbid astonishment. He struggled weakly, helplessly while trying to understand what was occurring to him. "Now this is really a crock of shit," he thought.

"May I help you?" she repeated. Her eyes gradually panned his features. Soon they fell down at the letter still clutched tightly in his soaked hand. Conner stood there, drained. There was a strange silence that welled up inside him. "He told me you were dead. That is exactly what he said."

She smiled, shaking her head. "Do you know my granddaughter?" The question broke through his mental numbness. "No ma-am. I knew your grandson, Cal." Her eyes lit up. "Good. That's so nice. Don't meet many people that know him." Smiling, "Please, please… c'mon inside before you catch your death of cold."

Startled and shocked that he perhaps missed something as he walked passed her. Still smiling, she closed the door immediately behind her. "Now there, how can I help you?" She asked a third time.

He couldn't mask the puzzlement in his voice; perhaps because he was staring at someone he thought was deceased. He hesitated, clearing his throat, and said, "I have…" His voice died before he completed his sentence.

"I know what you have." She extended her hand for the envelope. Her eyes narrowed. She smiled, her cheekbones widening innocently with a gentle head nod. "It's all right. I've seen them before, plenty of them."

Conner' knees felt unsteady. He was highly embarrassed about the contents in the letter. "I don't know."

Strange, it was now easy for him to see that she wasn't uncomfortable about his letter. Reaching for it, he felt a deepening exposure of shame, still embarrassed by his potent thoughts.

Her puny right hand slowly touched the envelope. Her face was expressionless. Conner stood without moving. A slight tug, barely noticeable, and now she was in complete control of it. Her tiny fingers slowly traced around the sealed envelope. "It's a death cry," she whispered. "Death is what your dreams consume, Thanatopsis. I've seen it many times. It's the only thing that satisfies your craving. Your soul is delirious, poisoned with raw hate. It's all here, right here in this letter," she murmured slowly. "Why did she do such a thing? Why? Why?" she continued.

Conner stood flabbergasted. He could feel a rush of heat forming over his face. He clamped and unclamped his teeth, his muscles tensing as he continued to stare at her. She appeared to be in a hypnotic-like state. Her fingers nimbly continued to rotate across and around the sealed envelope. It was though she was reading it. Reading it like a....

"...a Witch," she abruptly interjected.

Conner was now transparent to her as she spoke. Her eyes now wide with a fanatical gaze.

Somehow, Conner developed enough sense not to respond to her remark. He sensed there was something unusual about her. He pushed his attention back to the letter.

"Do you have the five hundred dollars?" She asked. Conner shook his head greenly. Reaching inside his trouser pocket, he removed five twenty dollars bills. Handing them to her, he then said, "I will get the rest t'morrow,

I swear, I gotta get out of my account. You will definitely have it first thing in the morning. Is that cool? I will bring it because I want it to happen so bad."

The silver and gray-haired woman smiled at him placing the five twenty-dollar bills next to the envelope. "I trust you. You need to have this happen and I know you will bring the rest t'morrow."

There was a subtle change in the air. It was though a sudden rush of heat arrived inside the house. Conner felt warm, unusually warm. While loosening his shirt collar, he paused for a brief moment to look around. The front room was meticulously clean, almost sterile, everything positioned so orderly—almost perfect—almost unreal; a ghostly unreal. The scene struck him with wild alarm. His body flinched, while he tried to maintain a cool self-control. "How will it be done?' he asked sheepishly.

His question followed her. She then placed the money and the envelope inside a small, brown wooden box with black metal hinges on this side. She stirred, making a thick sound inside her throat. "Want you go see. T'morrow, want you go see. T'morrow, want you go see," she repeated.

There was a moment of eerie silence. Conner believed he said enough. He then shook his head, turning for the door. "All right. I'll wait unit t'morrow."

Closing the door behind him, he shook his head in wonderment walking back to his truck. 'That lying, white bastard! I ain't giving these con-ass motherfuckers not another damn cent' he laughed to himself.

Moments later, he drove away feeling elated about his dreams soon to become a reality. Later that evening required an all-night celebration between him and Hennessy Cognac, his favorite drinking partner, and an 8 ball of coke.

It was late Saturday afternoon; struggling to move the cobwebs from his head caused by all night alcohol and coke consumption. The potency of the crack was producing an odd feeling of energy and excitement inside him. His thoughts were elevated about the letter and the prospects of learning about their death later today. He was certain they were both going to die.

Reaching over toward a small, wooden framed nightstand, there at the very bottom underneath it, taped securely and well-hidden out of sight, was a nickel-plated Walther PPK, a German-made, semi-automatic pistol known for its accuracy and reliability. Conner owned this gun for several years. He was well acquainted on how to use it. Even before Cal's letter, his agenda was to 'get what was coming to him', created a big revelation in spite of not quite having his head on straight about his plan. He was now void of all consequences and only felt revenge.

Turning on the radio, the R&B popular singer Aretha Franklin's song 'Think' was playing. This was 1968. A collage of social issues was emerging in Cleveland, its political landscape was changing. The Vietnam War was ramping up, black male, teenagers were drafted going straight to the war with many never returning and many returning not the same way they left. Cleveland elected its first African American Mayor, Carl B. Stokes. The anticipation for progress was at Cleveland's front door.

Shaking his head, "Man, fuck that song, I thought about this shit long enough. They better be dead, or I'm going back to see that old woman," he thought.

His hatred now penetrated into his soul, settling deep down where it sauteed and seethed, finally reaching a boiling point of irrational thinking, along with the intensity of it. No longer was he concerned about a life transformation success after prison and learning how to let go. No, not his sentiment. He wanted them both dead, sent to an eternity in Hades, which was the only resolution for him.

He would settle down, re-working his next steps, but a single-minded thought continued to race inside his head. It was the consistent thought of her... him... and the money. The stimuli of his motivation was well transplanted. He would wait until late evening visiting the Hough area, specifically the Fox Hotel, to see both police and ambulance vehicles blaring while feeling elated about their deaths.

Meanwhile, across town on the westside of Cleveland, an ominous scene swirled around a small ash colored brick Victorian style house—the same house Conner visited a day earlier with Harriet Rene Rorschire. During yesterday's visit, in his excitement, revealed his obvious lack of self-awareness or inability to be cognizant of why Cal told him his grandmother was deceased. After all, he was precise, thorough, on how the letters worked being placed on her grave. Conner was highly educated, slightly privileged, conservative. Having experienced much success navigating through the Cleveland Public School system, eventually obtaining two scholarships, suggested a person of his intellect would both ignore and avoid a person of Cal's reputation.

With his life experiences, he moved surprisingly well within the prison's undisciplined subculture by teaching and mentoring inmates. His ability to 'artfully dodge' his personal dilemma by avoiding trouble and avoiding commitments were his strongest assets until, playing his cards close to his chest, was exposed by Calvin Kellogg. This exchange—the letters and the agreement to pay five hundred dollars—was going to be consequences with warnings signs he missed.

His irrational thinking and anger led to a failure to notice the implication that something was wrong. Because Cal wasn't an ordinary person, his reputation (the letters) were like magical powers which made Conner's paranormal experience with him real with life experience consequences. Leaving prison without paying Cal the five hundred dollars was his first mistake. His second mistake was his failure to notice a second envelope lying on a coffee table in front of both him and Rorschire with a printed name on the front—**Conner Davis**. The letter was obviously from Cal and was a problematic situation for him—two combined errors of judgment.

And now, less than six hours until nightfall, Conner was anxiously making plans to visit the Fox Hotel, the transient dope house where his ex-girlfriend and her lover lived along with a host of other dope fiends.

Nighttime finally arrived in Cleveland. It was still chilly. The icy coldness navigated brilliantly among the sleet, cascading the streets with a shining thin blanket of a Navajo white color.

The moment was electrifying and exhilarating to Conner. He was alertly awake watching for the darkness staring out from his bedroom window. He was anxious, ready to go even with his hair and clothing wildly disheveled. Turning simultaneously both the television and radio on, he was relying on Cal's imaginative powers to give him the news story. After a couple of minutes, neither produced the authentic nature of the letter's contents.

"I'll be a cocksucker," he groaned. "Let me check this shit out for myself."

Fifteen minutes later, he was driving around the Hough area. It was nighttime with its makeup off hiding the ugliness of its features and the sleepy-eyed crack houses and cheap hotels that sagged the neighborhood with filth, crime, prostitution and drugs. This was now the pre-nighttime, junkie-zombie hours. They lurched about foraging in and out of hotels where inside they searched for a mistakenly misplaced rock, a stray dollar bill, a John looking for sex, or an unlocked room with an unsuspected victim, still too high to realize their potential victim status.

"Where the hell are the police and ambulance vehicles?" he sighed. Fifteen minutes later, his search ended when he was parked about a half block from the Fox Hotel. He was staring at the entrance. A coldness moved up inside him. He moved from his pick-up truck. Walking slowly toward the Fox Hotel, he began to lick his chapped lips trying to hold off the surging moment of schizophrenia growing inside him. Moments later, he wedged himself in a small dark narrow corner concealing himself from sight of the entrance. His right hand clutched tightly around the handle of the loaded PPK German Revolver inside his coat pocket. The moment gave him an instable urge, spawned by a sudden four-dimensional image inside his head about her… him… the money and betrayal.

Soon, a grimed face, razor thin frame Hispanic woman with a salt and pepper wig wearing a Russian Hat, fake fur collar around a red leather coat, white pants and red plastic leather boots, emerged from the door entrance of the Fox Hotel. She bristled from the driving sleet lighting a Virginia Slim cigarette. Her hand trembled placing it to her mouth. She inhaled three quick puffs from it.

She gave a sidelong glance. Conner's frame was now even with the dark, narrow opening.

"What's up, baby?" she asked.

"Just hanging out," he replied.

"Sheelit… you wanna date? I'll suck the skin off your dick," she said ignorantly, "I'm game for anything, except ass fuckin… don't do no ass shit, baby, if that's your thing. If not straight sex, we can get high… be cool and smoke or snort some crack. Too cold to be out here hustling tonight. I don't wanna be alone. I gotta room… I'm just sayin…" she continued without waiting for a response from Conner.

"Damn… it's cold as a mother fucker out here tonight," she said, stepping backward, pulling out another Virginia Slim. The first one was abruptly extinguished from the now roaring sleet, "These cigarettes cost too damn much money for this bullshit weather," she moaned.

"I'm looking for Lucy Bailey and her ole man. Wanna cop some dope from them. What room are they staying at?"

The question caused an intense reaction from the woman. She then moved cautiously to the edge of the front steps carefully, rubbing her Virginia Slim against the wall. Fire and ashes flickered out immediately against the driving sleet, rapidly disappearing.

She was now positioning herself to examine the stranger in the narrow, dark corner next to the hotel entrance.

"Can't see your face, baby," she said. Squinching her eyes and rubbing her face, edging closer for a look at Conner. "Hmmm baby, you ain't the policeeeee, vice or some narcotic dude, are you?"

"Hell naw! I'm cool, just trying to get high." She shook her head, "I'll don't know about that sheelit."

"Hey baby, don't get worked up. I just wanna get high. We can get high together, do some crazy ass fuckin, but I just like their dope."

"I heard that… is there something for my ass?"

"Hell yeah."

"No bullshit."

"No shit, baby," Conner responded.

"And, you ain't the policeeeee…or them dope boys."

"Hell naw."

"Okay, they staying in 203."

"You sure?"

"I'm sure, but you didn't hear that from me."

"203".

"That's right… 203, their regular spot."

"Cool."

Without moving forward, concealing his face, he handed her a fifty-dollar bill. "What room are you staying in?"

"410. First room next to the elevator on your right. The zero is missing on the door. It looks like 41 but its 410. I got that claustrophobia sheelit, scared to ride on this raggedy ass elevator, so I walk up the stairs. My regular spot is on the first floor but all the rooms were taken tonight."

"Okay, baby, be careful," Conner said.

"Yeah, see ya later baby. I'm going upstairs now." As she moved toward the front door, she stopped, still searching for Conner's face.

"Whatcha your name, baby?"

"Bobby. Bobby Simms but everybody calls me Booths."

"Okay, Booths."

Looking back, shaking her head, she continued to search for his face. "Hmmm...," she said. "See ya later, Booths."

"I'm coming baby. You in 410 with the missing number?"

"Yeah, the missing zero. And they call me Isabella."

"Right. Got it! Isabella. See you later, sweetheart."

His eyes followed the front door closing behind the woman. Conner stepped back, depositing himself back into the dark narrow cavity adjacent to the hotel front door entrance. His mind flashed with uneasiness. He sighed heavily, waiting for some irrational impulses to flood his mind. The smell of Hennessey Cognac and anger thickened the air. He was no longer intrigued by Cal's bullshit letter convinced the crucial end to his seven years of 'bent up' rage was going to be decided by him.

His thoughts began shifting to a psychosis characterized by several impulses of distorted thinking. Waves of delusions were crisscrossing inside his head, washing back and forth hallucinations about his ex-girlfriend leaving him along with seeds of betrayal surfing over these wet disturbances that, in his twisted mind, revenge was the craving he sought for justice. His cold, dark eyes were now staring through the blackness of the raging sleet. His thoughts re-working on the reality that he could get away with murder.

This was no hair-brain plan—he would leave not one scrap of evidence behind. Certain the prostitute caught no sight of his face, he was confident the menacing sleet concealed his pick-up truck, disguised his movements and thoughts. He was giving himself a good talking to, rambling on with a dialogue to himself.

This was all worth seven years, excruciating moments to his soul. He wasn't balancing right or wrong, good or evil or life or death. He was going to be the architect in defining the last moments of their lives.

Without thinking… without hesitating, Conner unbuttoned his dark, navy peacoat, removing his Walther PPK revolver. In an instance, after checking the clip, he flicked the safety off. Time was now… no more apprehensions. He was going to kill them.

Moments later, moving quietly, placing a pair of black leather gloves over his icy-cold hands, Conner's thoughts were manipulated by a strong sense of indifference. Ready!

His steps were deliberate, walking carefully over the slippery ice surface covering the front doorsteps. Looking back, his eyes meticulously surveyed the area for anyone following his movements. The excitement drilled throughout his body. Grabbing the front door hotel doorknob, he understood this moment was craving his satisfaction for revenge.

Within seconds, he was inside the hotel's darkened corridor. The hallway smell of urine, crack, alcohol and lascivious sounds permeated from every hotel room. He momentarily bristled from it, while cautiously stepping up the stairwell toward the second floor. Reaching the top of the stairs, the dimly lit hallway partially blurred his vision. Wiping his eyes, "Whata fuck?" he said to himself. The first room door was missing the second two numbers, only the number two was displayed.

Searching the corridor, his sight settled within the darkened hotel hallway. He now recognized the remaining doors, all with complete numbers starting at room 206.

Slowly he crept purposely toward room 203. A wet stream of wild sweat raced down both cheekbones.

Now, standing directly in front of 203, his mind relaxed. He slowly removed his revolver and with one last check, the safety off, he was ready to go. He then twisted a black muzzle silencer onto to the barrel to suppress the gun discharge from the revolver. This was now a premediated murder, something he planned for seven years.

He knocked once listening intensely for any sounds. Another knock followed quickly, by a soft female voice who weakly responded, "Who is it?"

Conner was certain, the voicc of Lucy Bailey, his ex-girlfriend. "You fuckin bitch," he hissed softly to himself. Without waiting, Conner shot twice striking the doorknob, along with a swift kick and the door flew open wide. He immediately rushed inside to a dimly lit small room.

"I got you now, bitch," Conner shouted, believing this was his moment.

"You crazy bastard," a female voice yelled at him.

Conner fired two shots, striking the woman twice, one in the shoulder and thigh. BAM… BAM…. Two menacing bullets screamed through the darkened room. Finding their target, a woman screamed hysterically. "You mother fucker… you just shot me. I'm shot, Oh Gawd," she cried.

"We did nothin to you, man," another female voice moaned.

"Please don't shoot me no moe, Mister," the woman pleaded. There was a scorching look in Conner's eyes, searching both right and left… right and left… followed by frantic screams by the two women inside room 203.

He hesitated, realizing now the prostitute gave him the wrong room number—a fatal mistake on his behalf.

The woman eyes beamed as Conner was still pointing the gun at her. But suddenly, out of nowhere, a loud thud broke the silence. A butcher knife plunged deep inside his rib cage. His eyes blinked in disbelief. He slowly lowered his gun. The blood seemed to be racing everywhere all at once inside him. Before he could gather himself, the second plunge from the knife wedged deeper into his back striking his left lung. This plunge felt even deeper and deadlier.

He sobbed weakly, dropping the gun and falling to his knees. The second stabbing was causing his heart to race quickly. His legs were numbed and his mind swirling from the two wounds.

"Oh gawd, I'm soooo sorry," he sobbed. "I'm sorry, I should have checked this shit out. I just fucked up. Please forgive me," he pleaded. "Ya'll forgive me. I need a doctor… we all need some medical help right now," he begged.

Conner fell over on his side, his face pale, blood was draining from his lemon face. Looking up at the woman who stabbed him, "It's okay, ma'am… I fucked up… got mad… real stupid shit…," he said, grimacing now in unbearable pain. "Ya'll get me and this lady some help."

His eyes now noticed several people standing at the front door. "I don't wanna die in this nasty ass, flea bitten dump," he moaned to himself. His eyes had now fallen back into a locked position. He wheezed, coughed and wheezed again. His head fell hard against the floor. His breathing was now quickening as he was struggling to breath.

In a few minutes, police officers flooded the second floor of the hotel. Many of the occupants scampered throughout multiple exit doors, running like cockroaches when bright lights reveal their hiding location. This was no aberration—minding your own business, keeping your mouth shut and avoiding the police created no tension, no drama and no snitch jacket for them. Moving among the crowd through the exit doors was Lucy Bailey and her boyfriend. They were staying on the first floor in room 110.

Hysterical screams continued to sprint down the piss-stained hallways as a half-naked, coked-out woman raced blindly toward the front door and into the waiting arms of the police. Pandemonium was everywhere. The rumors of a maniacal rage had descended inside room 203. Cleveland Police cruisers rapidly surrounded the Fox Hotel. Even in the driving snow, many hotel occupants with active arrest warrants, probation and parole violations were tiptoeing over the slippery surface like a panic-stricken herd of excited antelopes running from hungry lions.

In spite of their insane efforts to escape, the police covered the slippery surface like fast-moving cheetahs, twirling and twisting, nabbing slow-footed occupants screaming when cold handcuffs gave an abrupt pause to their momentum. Conner's incident provided sufficient justification for the police to tightly squeeze this community eyesore from the centerpiece which harvested the filth, drugs, crime, and prostitution that plagued the Hough neighborhood for years.

Inside room 203, a trembling and distorted young white girl's hand was shaking as a cigarette dangled loosely between her puny fingers. She had stabbed Conner. She was a runaway teenager from Trenton, New Jersey; a likely drug user, prostitute, or maybe both who was staying with an older, black woman in the room—the same woman who was shot twice by Conner's shooting rampage. Scattered thick dark blood spots and stains were present everywhere on the floor.

Meanwhile, seriously injured, Conner's identity was established. His parole conditions revoked, he was being transported and treated at the Cuyahoga County Hospital's prison ward. Although in much pain, fortunate to be alive, Conner knew his life's journey was over. The event caused him great mental angst, now realizing how foolish he acted. Even more unsettling, it was now clear that Isabella, the prostitute he engaged with about locating his ex-girlfriend, either lied to him or was mistaken. In either case, it was an obvious downright stupid decision.

Lying in a prison ward bed, these were now heart brainstorm moments for Conner. The Fox Hotel incident was a local news delight. The Cleveland Police department Law and Order posture was in full mode: 'Ex-con Nabbed for Attempted Murder' was its headline banner. It was followed up by 'Police raided Fox Hotel; Arresting Multiple Offenders with Arrest Warrants and Other Charges.' The Cleveland City Council and the Mayor's office were in lock step with this news by citing the owner of the Fox Hotel with several city ordinances and fire and safety code violations. A county recommendation included the property be condemned and torn down as a public safety nuisance and fire hazard to the Hough neighborhood.

Likewise, throughout the Ohio Department of Rehabilitation and Correction, and especially at the Chillicothe, the news spread faster than a raging forest fire.

Meanwhile, Cal was smiling, finishing up his third crossword puzzle in the prison recreational area. He understood more than anyone the extraordinary circumstances that occurred to Conner, far beyond any human comprehension about his unimaginable power that he possessed.

"Stupid shithead," he laughed out loud.

Nothing about the lurid details of the incident surprised him. He recognized by now Conner's mind was delirious—he was filled with fear. Fear is the most primal emotion there is and he sensed Conner's thoughts were saturated with fear of the anticipated consequences of his behavior. Cal was the potent architect of these events driving Conner's decisions. He manipulated his rage and irrational judgment which produced this expected outcome for him.

Meanwhile, several miles north in the Cuyahoga County prison ward, Conner finished meeting with a grimed-faced parole officer. The officer provided him with a boat load of charges against him—two counts of Attempted Murder, Aggravated Burglary, Possession of a Gun by an Ex-felon, illegal possession of a silencer, Assault, Destruction of Private Property, Vandalism, Association with Known Offenders, Trespassing and Violation of Parole. Charges that will surely give him life in prison.

His previous support from relatives and few friends had evaporated from this ordeal. He was virtually alone, with no justification or explanation for his irrational behavior.

"I'm a real crash dummy," he groaned himself. "Why didn't I just let this shit go?" Now shaking his head, the letter quickly flashed inside his mind. Cal's impish smile worked across his thoughts.

"I betcha that racist bastard is happy hearing all this shit about me," he sighed.

A cold voice suddenly broke passed the kaleidoscopic thoughts racing inside him. "Are you Davis? Conner Davis?" he asked.

"Yes sir," Conner raised up, sitting upright on his bed. "I'm Conner Davis."

"I have mail for you," a female jail employee said.

"Thank you." Conner replied.

Examining the letter, Conner immediately bristled, noticing the name on the front of it: Harriet Rene Rorschire. It was from Calvin Kellogg's grandmother.

His eyes narrowed with suspicion and dread. He gazed upon it for several seconds, shaking his head. His fingers trembled as he slowly peeled open the taped envelope. His eyes gazed upon its contents immediately dropping it harmlessly onto the floor.

His body slumped over on his back, eyes wide open, fixated up against the inhospitable, gray ceiling. His mind was steadfast about the content of this letter, which read:

> "Hey, You Black Jackass:
>
> Thought you got away from paying me my 500 bucks? Do you realize who you bargained with? Remember... my powers... my letters... my reputation. I hope you liked Isabella! She will send you to the wrong hotel room—203. We will have fun with that and my grandma enjoyed toying with your uppity ass. I sent this letter to Grandma, and it will be there when you see her. Now, when you finally read it, you will soon be back here in Chillicothe with me

forever—remembering her… him… and the money but now also remembering me and this Unwell Letter, asshole.

Cal

P.S. You still owe me 500.00, as bargained!

The Spirit of the San Xavier del Bac

CHAPTER SIX

THE SPIRIT OF THE SAN XAVIER DEL BAC

"EL SOL ESTA CALIENTE... DEMASIADO CALIENTE PARA nosotros. Nos vamos a morir. (The sun is very hot... too hot. We're going to die)," Eugenio De los Punetes Ramos said, rolling over on his back cradling his broken right arm. His vision dark and consumed with a sickening wave of helplessness for them.

The sudden expectation of death chilled his sweat. His arm, broken in three places, was a factor in the equation. Always the unexpected for illegals trying to cross over barren ground in pursuit of a better life in the United States. The price was steep for any missteps. He had parlayed four years of the family's life savings, three thousand American dollars, for a pass over to the promised land. And his haste permitted him to ignore the obvious, that the 1964 Ford Platform truck's motor inexplicably had exhausted its mechanical life. Even his wife's sudden sense of skepticism could not modify his intentions. He was a stubborn individual and demurred at her inquiry about the trip being too risky.

After that, the unforgiving desert's landscape was belligerent toward unsuspected, unprepared migrate farmers whose nomadic journeys never encountered acrid heat and bitterly irritating August temperatures that raced toward one hundred and twenty degrees by noon.

Eugenio inhaled deeply feeling the alien pathogens, diablo dust, moving inside his lungs. After two nights of wandering in the darkness, the terrain was inexorable, and the stress induced his carelessness. Stumbling over a medium-sized boulder and breaking his right arm made him vulnerable. This would be a very uncommon predicament for anyone to be placed in but it was also not uncommon for other farmers. They are people with respectable intentions and spontaneous camaraderie to suddenly detach themselves and move with unmistakable haste from the insensitive dry land, the Mexican police and, of course, local bandidos and the infamous Cartel gangs, lurking the areas for unfortunate stragglers to rob, rape, kidnap and even murder.

"Agarrate… agarrate..." Hang on, hang on, he continued to repeat to himself. He shook his head with bewilderment gazing across the parched dessert, wondering where the twenty-seven others had fled. He remembered the look of mute appeal in their eyes when they were told the motor was dead, like it had no pulse, and just stop breathing. His wife's eyes seemed to squeeze the bravado from him. His stubbornness toward her disquieting voice seemed pathetic in retrospect.

Eugenio took another deep inhale, shaking his head about the $3,000 and what it could have been for his family. They lived in a tiny village, slightly over fifty miles southwest of Cananea, Sonora, Mexico.

"Mi casa de abode," he moaned quietly to himself. "My house," is what he was thinking that $3,000 could have represented. He was a simple man, the simplest when it came to business transactions. He sold his mother's land, an inheritance, for $2,700 dollars, twenty acres, and sweat labor produced another $600 dollars. The Mexican government had made a steal, nothing surreptitious, but a business theft without the benefit of a worrisome lawyer creating some ambivalence for this client. His wife of eighteen years and six children's enthusiasm was stopped by a sharp exclamation.

His grandiose plan offended her, not any of her insecurities, but how transparent he made her feel. She was thinking home; he was thinking escape. Escape!! Most Mexicans understood that word. Escape to America—escape from the nightmare of poverty, oppression, lack of work, poor education, healthcare, crime and many other social and economic problems. He was embattled with kakorrhaphiophobia, it was only too common among men like him, fearing failure.

Everything was failing around him and now the prospect of escaping it all was an impulse to irresistible to retreat from.

Once they twisted passed the border patrol juggernauts, their destiny would be finalized in Denver, Colorado. A 'ready-made' depository awaited him and his family to begin assimilating into America's culture and its economy.

He laid there, turning now to listening to the voices of sneering criticism and mockery. In the meantime, his wife and their youngest son, just two years old, were asleep—exhausted and dehydrated. Feverishly, his mind searched through his very limited options and then, suddenly, a snippet of sound grabbed his attention.

He wasn't alone. The silhouette of her small frame was even more visible from the full moon. Her hair, matted from the heavy humidity and dust, was curled back into two long pigtails. A long minute passed. They stared but remained silent toward each other.

It was pitch-black but, somehow, he could see her lilliputian features. His only daughter's silent gaze seemed to work his adrenaline harder. This was now a moral imperative to save his family from a certain death. At first, the very thought was dismissed as an afterthought practically vanishing from his memory. However, even though it seemed utterly outlandish, it was perhaps the only opportunity any of them had to survive.

"Ana, mi nina Valiente," he said, in a voice dripping with desperation. She was his brave little daughter, he announced with a helpless gesture.

She moved closer toward him allowing his gaze to settled on her pixie-face. Rosalinda always told him that Ana, their daughter, was an iron-jawed little girl. She wasn't quite a tomboy nor a prissy girl but maybe somewhere in between with Rosalinda's wisdom and insight.

Rosalinda was asleep. It would be easier to make this painful decision and later brace himself for her belated remonstrations. This situation, without his wife having to participate in, would create much pain and reticent between them. But on the other hand, it was only his idea. It would be left up to her to brazen the elements to search for help.

He was suffering from high blood pressure and the pain from his broken arm now dramatically increased his hypertension. Without sufficient fluids in his body, the risk of a stroke or heart attack loomed a high probability for him. Rosalinda and Pedro were dehydrated, too weak and too lethargic to travel any further.

To all appearances, Ana looked frail, maybe too fragile to cope with the elements that could bleach flesh lobster red with sinister heat and unwell humidity, all prerequisites of a soon to be memento mori from the events. The desert held its respect, even the wildlife understood the parameters mother nature provided them. There were no unnecessary movements, only what the desert allowed. This was no gross exaggeration. The desert was filled with skeletal and decomposed remains which continuously reminded every one of those who fatally realized their mistakes.

This was now a quiet conversation between father and daughter. Although seven years old, Ana seemed to recognize their dilemma. As her father continued to speak to her, she was silent for a while turning her attention to Rosalinda and Pedro.

Ana seemed subdued, but little by little, she was gaining strength. This was going to be an extraordinary task for a small girl, the likes most adults would hardly consider especially with one bottle of water.

About an hour later, Ana frowned, listening intently to Eugenio's last instructions. Her silence was making him feel uncomfortable but there was no fear in her eyes. Moments later, it was time to leave, leave while the desert slept. She took one sixteen-ounce bottle of water without comment. Her eyes roamed around, reaching her mother and brother's faces. She thought about kissing them, but it was only a fleeting thought. If either had awaken from the gesture, she might cry.

Truthfully, she wanted to cry. This wasn't easy for her. She was afraid to travel at night, terrified of wild animals, especially those fast-moving lizards.

Everything was now set; it was time for her to leave. Eugenio gently hugged his daughter. He tried but couldn't hold back his tears. During their embrace, he reconsidered his plans. Perhaps it was better they all perish together. This was unusually cruel to send his small child away from them, he reasoned.

At this point, Ana slowly pulled away. Eugenio looked awful. His eyes flooded with tears, both hands shaking uncontrollably. And yet, her eyes seemed to tell him there was no other way. Her puny hands slowly moved toward his face. She began rubbing his cheekbones, wiping away his tears. Her hands felt surprisingly firm, steady with confidence sufficiently enough to give him courage to let her go.

He then fell to his knees; his soaked face searched the night sky. Pleading, he then said, "Padre nuestro por favor cuide a mi hija (Our father please look after my little girl)," he continued mumbling to himself.

On the second night, Ana was running aimlessly across a thick bushy area early evening. She had been spooked by a bearded lizard. There was only a sheet of blackness ahead. Gasping, she began hallucinating and shimmering, unable to fix her location where she was going. She was running faster, glancing backwards hoping to distance herself from it. Her tongue was swollen, the saliva was thick inside her mouth. She was only a swallow away from heightening her thirst and drinking the remaining water, but the diablo dust simply would overwhelm her lean frame allowing thirst to evade liberally inside her small body. She had taken small sips, day and night. This nightmare would compound her problem. Anxiety and sweat would eventually force her to drink the final drop.

Moments later, Ana fell to her knees. She began crying but made no noise. It was the lizards; they might hear her voice. Trembling, she would be still, listening beyond the darkness, intending to flee at any sound.

An hour later, sleep had succumbed her fears forcing her to close her eyes and drift away. Occasionally, a slight wind would brush across her soft skin soothing her sore legs and tired feet.

And now two hours later, a lambent of a sound caught her ear. Instinctively, her head snapped up like a timid rabbit in a thick brush catching scent of a stalking bobcat. She moved, back and forth, back and forth. This was no dream. Something was out there; she was certain of it.

And then a brief sound… another…and still another. It was coming from the blackness, coming from all four sides. She stood up, transfixed by the sounds, but still wanting to be brave. Somehow, intuitively she considered running away from the darkness as the sounds grew closer.

Her tiny body shivered. She felt cold and yet sweat dripped heavily from her hands. Her heart began pounding inside her chest so hard that she clutched it, hoping to slow the rhythm down.

The strange, quickly darting movements were creeping closer toward her. She tried to recall what her father's instructions were for something like this but the movements disjointed her memory, replacing it with fright. Ana now realized this was no animal watching her.

Suddenly, without warning, the blackness came alive, the veil of darkness fell upon her, grabbing and swinging her back and forth. Every part of her body was being touched and ruffled. She could smell the stale odor of Tequila and raw sweat from their mephitic mouths. A hyena-like chuckle punched loud through the warm air. She couldn't quite see who was holding her, but it was strong, so very strong.

"La Tenemos, nos van adar Bastante Peso por ella," he continued to cackle.

A sharp light flashed across her pale face. For a rebellish moment or two, her tormentor raked over her entire body, and finally a man's oyster mouth twisted into a guttural laugh. He shook his head. His eyes told her of his delight.

This would be Eugenio's worse nightmare—that Ana had been captured by five Cartel members. For them, this was perfectly natural, hunting down wayward Mexicans and other migrants who made miscalculations or those who encountered unpredictable misfortunes that ultimately relinquished their personal possessions. Sometimes a good bounty, something precious, like a King Ransom of sort, would create much restraint among these human predators.

Ana wasn't just a little, downtrodden Mexican girl. To the contrary, she wasn't stereotyped in part due to her extremely fair complexion and her angelic face, an almost Anglo-Saxon feature but not quite, and strawberry blonde hair. She would command top US dollar for one of the border town brothels. Her age could add a considerable amount of longevity and, quite possibly, a hefty price from some American pervert seeking to smuggle this delicate piece of appetizer for his unsavory menu. They chatted and contemplated among themselves.

Despite this hair-raising predicament, the men seemed taken by Ana's reaction.

Although she was terrified, frightened beyond anyone's comprehension, her psychological defense mechanism would not allow her to cry.

It seemed like an eternity. Two large vans crisscrossed the desert plains. Ana had become depressed, remembering the days she played with her dolls and wrestled with her brothers. She would also remember waving to Eugenio when he left energetically for work and waving to him when he returned feebly from the fields and she missed her favorite meal, Rosalinda's chicken and dumplings.

She closed her tiny eyes still frightened, still choking from the diablo dust. She had become weary but her weariness was pale compared to what she was hearing.

There were frequents stops… gunshots… screams.. and endless quarrels among her kidnappers. She knew they had come in contact with other people, but they never placed anyone inside the van with her.

Perhaps on the eighth or ninth evening, she just finished eating a flour tortilla, a small bowl of bean soup and plain rice when her captors began drinking heavily.

She stared at them confused. She didn't understand the nature of their celebration, but the men were preparing to return to San Luis Potosi. It would be their ending destination and her beginning nightmare. They planned to sell her for several thousand dollars to the highest bidder among several brothel strip owners. And very soon, she would eventually be sold to some horrific monster who specialized in destroying children's souls.

An hour later when the celebration was over, the men fell into a drunken stupor. Both her hands and ankles were tightly wrapped. For some unknown reason, the men had left her alone sitting near the edge of the campfire.

Now there was no sound except an occasional breeze rushing slowly over the dwindling fire. She then tried for a moment to work free of the skin-biting rope that secured her wrist. She shook her head in utter frustration. This was an impossible task. The men never considered the fact she might escape. This was a fact she now quickly recognized.

Before she could consider anything else, something incredible happened. She wasn't imagining things when she first saw it. She blinked, licking her swollen, dry lips. It moved quickly, quietly, circling the campfire with amazing swiftness. Maybe this was a dream, she thought. "No, no," she thought as she shook her head. It was staring directly into her eyes.

"Es un perritto… un negro y blanco (a little dog… a black and white dog)," she mumbled quietly to herself.

It was virtually impossible for her to understand how and why this little creature had wandered into this campsite. Ana suddenly blinked wondering again if she was dreaming. Opening her eyes, she expelled a long breath. The dog was still there. It then moved quickly and unexpectedly toward her. She twitched momentarily stunned by its lizard-like quickness. The dog moved cautiously toward her, a few inches at a time, but never taking its eyes off her face. It was though the animal was telepathically trying to relieve her of any panic or fear.

Sensing the unthinkable, Ana initially sensed she was staring at a frightened animal but instead the dog's bizarre behavior displayed no signs of fear. As it continued to edge closer toward her, its nose finally rubbed against her damp face and, without a moment of hesitation, the dog began licking the tear stain corner of her right eye.

Ana sat very stiff while the dog began quietly circling her. All the tension was building up inside her, fearing one of the men would awaken. But suddenly, a quick tug from behind startled her. She jerked slightly feeling the dog's surprisingly powerful teeth ripping the rope around her wrist to shred.

It took only several seconds until the rope gave way to the dog's determination. Without hesitating, the dog moved to the rope securing her ankles. In less time than before, Ana kicked away the remaining rope threads from her ankles.

Now standing up, her legs felt stiff and rubbery. Without knowing why, she quickly crouched and scampered after the swift moving dog who raced off deep inside the darkness.

Ana was amazed that she could run all night with this strange dog. It was also odd that, even in the daylight with the heat and the heavy, sap-soaking humidity, she continued to follow it. In a peculiar way, Ana felt the dog somehow knew the danger had not disappeared. Stopping periodically, a stretch of thirst moved inside her lungs. For reasons she would never know, the small animal would frequently lick her parched lips, miraculously satisfying her thirst with both moisture and energy.

Finally, in what seemed like hours of non-stop movements, Ana suddenly stopped. She turned and examined the desert's outer horizon listening intently to that familiar noise. She had heard it for several days and there was no mistake in her mind. She was now certain the men were coming for her. The terrifying sound of their roaring truck engine was an unsettling memory that perhaps they had come from hell.

Her heart pounding, she now feared they would recapture and kill her. Her head tilted slightly, believing for a moment she would collapse. Yet, before the horror descended upon them, the dog tugged at her tattered skirt. Again, she rambled along following the small animal around a narrow slope, up a short hill and then suddenly stopping in her tracks.

Both shock and surprise fell over her face. Rubbing her eyes, she initially thought it was a mirage. Even for a small girl of seven years old, this was hard to believe.

Nevertheless, a second eye rub did not make it go away—it was still there, sitting nonchalantly in front of her. For a second or two, Ana just stared with no expression, nothing at all.

The sharp barking yaps broke through her concentration. The dog's tail was arched excitedly high. It raced to the front entrance to an old church mission sitting in the middle of the desert.

At the same time, the Cartel members were rapidly moving closer toward her location.

Recovering instantly, Ana bolted toward the old mission and directly behind the dog, passing by a thick wooden door. Immediately she fell to the floor, naturally exhausted and helpless. She began trembling, biting her lower lip as the noise grew closer.

Lifting up her head, the dog raced down the narrow walkway directly toward the altar. For some reason, Ana could not move. Her eyes searched above the altar stopping at the dome overhead. She had never seen anything like it before, never.

The dome was covered with unusual wood carvings, paintings, scriptures and pictures of Jesus Christ and saints. Her eyes stared at this strange phenomenon. It was so unimaginable to her, especially for someone of her circumscribed background. She then lowered her head and sat perfectly still, silent between rolls of pews on each side of her. She now knew this was no imagination or dream. Everything was so real.

Suddenly, she heard the roaring sound of vehicle engines in front of the mission.

She leaped up racing toward the altar. She caught her breath. Her eyes raced around the sanctuary for the dog, but incredibly it had disappeared. And now a furtive sound was at the front door. Panicking, she quickly moved underneath the front pew, wedging herself tightly in a small ball. She was crying and praying for herself and her small friend.

Locked in a fetal position, she laid perfectly still—continuing to cry and pray, fearing for the worse. Soon the seconds increased to minutes… to hours… and then Ana's fears gave way to exhaustion. She then fell asleep.

The next day, Ana slowly opened her eyes staring at a man's drawn face. She gave herself a mental shake, waiting for him to respond.

"Todo esta bien Anita. Ya encontramos a tu familla todoa pensabamos gue estabas muerta. (Everything is alright little Ana. We have found your family days ago. We thought you were dead)," he said.

Ana stared up at him for a solemn moment. She didn't understand why the stranger was holding her. Her eyes looked passed him and not finding the mission's ceiling, but instead only a bright blue sky.

Puzzled, she frowned. Where was the dog? Where was the mission? Where was the Cartel men? She rambled off a series of questions.

It was the Mexican police who had found her… found her lying alone in the desert. The police officer's soothing voice told her there were no missions anywhere close by, and certainly no dog. He laughed. It was all just an imaginary dream, he insisted. Ana couldn't concentrate; she was confused. Her thoughts continued about the mysterious dog and the mission.

As he picked her up placing her inside his truck, she tried pushing these unsettling thoughts from her mind. By now several police officers had arrived, and literally every single one of them wanted his special glance at her. She couldn't believe all the attention she was receiving. Slowly her pulse rate began to settle down as she listened intently to the police officer's excited voices.

Ana blinked in surprise when the police officers were thankful she had avoided being recaptured by the circling Cartel gang. Her tiny footprints miraculously led them directly to them and they were all arrested by the police.

Ana opened her mouth as if to retort what they were saying but quickly closed it. She would tell her mother and father about her incredible friend, she thought.

Several days later, the story of Ana's survival was an absolute miracle to everyone. How could a small girl survive the desert for ten days with only a mere bottle of water and no food, everyone pondered. But Ana insisted she had been captured by a Cartel gang, but her claim naturally wasn't supported by the abductors. The Cartel gang members had enough problems; surely kidnapping a small child wasn't going to be one of them. And since Ana couldn't identify them, more weight was given to their denial.

Ana's description of what now perhaps was a mixed English Springer and Pointer continued to amaze Rosalinda. She also never wavered about the detailed description of the old mission. Yet, despite the skepticism of many, the fact remained how could a seven-year-old child survive the elements of the brutal desert heat without sufficient water, food and shelter.

Shortly after Ana had settled down with her family, several Mexican news reporters and television stations heard of her incredible story, along with ending a reign of crime by five Cartel gang members who had terrorized the border for three years—torturing, looking, robbing, raping, kidnapping and killing along the way. The articles included Ana's alleged imaginary account of her survival. The dog and mission were printed in precise details about her experience surviving ten days in the desert.

Two days later, it was through one such article about Ana that was discovered over the internet by a 73-year-old retired news reporter from Tucson, Arizona named Adele Ortiz. After reading the article several times, she leaned back in her leather recliner and said, "Hay un-Dios, un-Dios maravilloso, gritto ella suavemente." Mumbling she continued to say, "There is a God, a wonderful God," as she cried softly.

Ms. Ortiz instantly recognized Ana's description of the old mission. She was convinced it was the San Xavier del bac Mission near Tucson. She had visited the historic mission on countless occasions. She just knew, as unthinkable as it was, that Ana somehow saw it in the desert. She read Ana's account of the cat and mouse figurines carved in the concrete on each side of the base archway above the center balcony. She flinched while reading about the description of the two outside wrought iron balconies, the center balcony, and the two towers—one smaller than the other—with a small steeple on top of the large one. Yet, most amazingly was the dog, a Springer or Spaniel bred, black and white in color. That just had to be Rex; she was certain of this fact. Rex lived at the mission, and everybody loved this clever, little dog.

For days, Ms. Ortiz became obsessed with Ana, her story and what she felt was a miracle. On the fifth day, Ms. Ortiz received permission to take Rex, along with several Papago Native Americans who were members of the mission, to Mexico and meet Ana. She had taken several photographs of the Mission still convinced there were some skeptics.

Eventually, she had contacted Eugenio, who by now had received fifteen thousand dollars from an anonymous source stimulated by his family's story. Although he had personally some reservations about her unimaginable claims, he could never explain how he believed she survived. On the other hand, Rosalinda was now the primary decision maker for these funds and this time it would be used to buy a modest dwelling, new clothes for their children, goats, pigs, chickens, and a used plot to start their small farm.

After several days of communication and coordination, the group finally met on Friday afternoon in Cananea, Mexico, at Rosalinda's uncle's small cantina.

Immediately upon getting out of her van, Ms. Ortiz was holding Rex on a polka dot dog leash. Her Bel Air smile put Ana's family to ease. Ana's eyes brimmed with joy as she raced toward Ms. Ortiz and Rex. But suddenly, without warning, she abruptly stopped, frozen in her tracks. Neither the dog nor her seemed to recognize each other.

Perplexed! Ms. Ortiz was absolutely certain they would be eager to see each other again. Stepping backwards, Ana turned and looked at her mother, and said, "No es el Yo Yo. El me dijo que sun ombre era Yo Yo. (That's not Yo Yo. He told me that his name was Yo Yo)," she reported. This was another amazing moment for both Ana's parents and the group who had traveled to meet this remarkable little girl. She was communicating that this dog had actually, in some unimaginable way, told her his name was Yo Yo.

And then something unexplainable occurred among the small group from Tucson.

Stunned! Their faces were gaped in a crippling silence. It was though Ana's bizarre statement had struck them like a bolt of lightning, a rush of heat raced across their shocked faces. They gazed at each other shaking their heads and wringing their hands. From their wordless stares, they then fell slowly to their knees, one by one, as they each looked up toward a gray, overcast sky. This obfuscated moment, paralyzed the small group from Tucson. "God will," a reedy voice spoke among them. Eugenio and Rosalinda looked with suspicious intrigue as they edged closer toward Ana. It had been Ana's most astonishing statement that created this most unpredictable setting. Clearly for Ms. Ortiz and the Papago Native Americans, they understood the real nature of Ana's unthinkable encounter, and the *Spirit of San Xavier del bac.*

The little dog named, Yo Yo, that had mysteriously appeared in the night—this courageous little animal with the valor of a lion and the tenderness of a lamb—had lived at the mission for over a decade, but had been dead for nearly five years. Rex was his last offspring.

Undoubtedly, whether anyone believes in God, a higher power, or a supernatural phenomenon, there was simply no denying Ana's incredible experience which quite possibly suggested that her salvation had come from a miraculous, guardian Angel whose spirit was irrefutably connected with this old mission. It was a connection that perhaps wasn't for anyone to rationally comprehend, but to simply realize that it occurred and that Ana could bear witness of this fact forever.

Author's Note:

"A national historic landmark, San Xavier Mission del bac, was founded as a Catholic mission by Father Eusebio Kino in 1692. The Mission is in Tucson, Arizona, where it continues to serve the residents of the greater Tucson and surrounding areas."

Courage Under Fire

Written by

Raymond Andrew Clark

CHAPTER SEVEN

COURAGE UNDER FIRE (NEW YORK CITY—TERRORISM)

BARAKA FELT A SHARP CHILL SMOOTHING BACK HER LONG, COAL black hair; her face was desolate. She was jittery under the circumstances relying on her superlative instincts about danger. Growing up in Iranian culture where the ruling religious government seldom pulled punches about executions, she become intuitively aware of being cognizant of even the most subtle warnings about danger.

"Just relax," she said soothingly to herself. She had to get deep inside her head. The option, perhaps the only way out of this—certainly to remain alive—would be a radical decision, and the threat of personal harm was theoretically uncomplicated now in her mind.

Earlier (three months ago) when she first learned of this possibility, the fact that someone—a close friend or relatives—were considering, better yet intending, to kill her, she initially tried to be unworried about it. She began threading her thoughts back to Friday afternoon, a warm, but gusty day less than four blocks from the previously majestically twin-arched World

Trade Center Towers, did this ominous conspiracy first give to its nefarious development.

She would never forget that Friday afternoon. It was a perfect day in New York City despite a gusty breeze blowing off the Hudson River. She nestled down at an outdoor deli just off West Street. This was their secret rendezvous. The cool wind made her bristle slightly while waiting for her first cousin, Tamaret, to celebrate her recent graduation from Columbia University with a Master's Degree in Civil Engineering and graduating summa cum laude.

After her first sip of green lemon iced tea, she glanced at her wristwatch. It was a little after noon which meant Tamaret was late, as usual. Naturally she would huff semi-hysterically and blame the subway, a traffic jam, something or anything, but never-ever would she find fault with her own lack of punctuality.

Nearly fifteen minutes later, Baraka's eyes went wide. She stood up holding out her arms to a quick-pacing Tamaret rushing toward her. "It's alright," Baraka said, grabbing first her sweaty hands and then pulling her sinewy body close for a gentle embrace. "Of course, I don't want to hear about the subway, the traffic and the rest," she whispered softly in her ear.

Tamaret moved backwards, wiping the perspiration from her brow. She looked beseechingly at her. "You don't want to hear about all the problems I had coming here? You know I hate taking the subway," she moaned.

"Not really," Baraka replied.

"Not really!" Tamaret snapped.

"Alright, just settle down. I'm not, as you Americans say, pissed at you."

Both women giggled. It was a soothing and satisfying exchange as they sat across from each other, their eyes glinted with pleasure.

Tamaret then gazed oddly at her, then shook her head. "Maybe this is not a good idea."

"Why?"

Tamaret hesitated slightly. Her eyes involuntarily rotated around the narrow street, the immediate surroundings, then the patrons sitting adjacent to them. "I-I don't know…," she floundered. "It's so risky, maybe Basam, or someone is following me."

"Following you?"

"Yeah. Maybe," Tamaret sighed.

"My brother, Basam, following you? But why?" She asked with a demurred giggle. "Why would Basam be following you? We're just having an innocent lunch. Don't be silly," she chuckled.

"I see you don't understand the situation."

Baraka rolled her eyes. She knew perfectly well what Tamaret meant. "I'm getting sick just thinking about it." Tamaret shook her head. "They found out."

"What!" Baraka cried.

"Basam told them. Told them everything about how you were feeling and changing your major at the University to Engineering. You know they wanted you to be a nurse. You can't go back to Shiraz being a stupid Engineer. They will never let you be that in Iran."

"It's not stupid! This is what I want to be," Baraka replied wearily.

"You're right, not stupid—it's crazy. Crazy if you believe they'll let you be an engineer. They need nurses and medical people. How did you think your father would let you leave for England, and then you eventually come here with Basam?"

Sighing, Baraka's expression hardened. "That's enough, I don't want to hear about your personal opinion. You make decisions too—like your boyfriend—he's Christian and black."

Tamaret's jaw dropped. "Excuse me, he is an African American, Baraka. In the name of Allah…"

Baraka merely shrugged. "Black or African American, who cares, your secret is safe with me. But if it makes you feel better, you don't have to tell me anything else about him or what it's like dating a Christian."

"But I want to," Tamaret's fingers twisted nervously, her eyes fell to the ground. "I think I love him."

For a tiniest second, Baraka's mind thought about her twin brother's betrayal. Quickly recovering herself, it was important that she maintained a positive relationship with her younger cousin who gossips insatiably about her family. Especially now, she would be crucial to her if or when her real intentions were known.

"My father is smart!"

"I know," Baraka declared.

"You know he was very suspicious when Basam told him finally that you graduated. They were soooo angry because they couldn't attend the ceremony. I felt so sorry for him."

"But you know why!" Baraka responded.

"Of course."

"They would have known my major had changed."

"I know."

"I c-couldn't do that to them."

"They are critical of you now. Basam is under much pressure but he loves you. But he has greater love for his family—your father, his faith and his honor."

"I know that," Baraka said, frowning. "I'm not… comfortable with the pressure that is on my brother about me."

She saw a stern look on Tamaret's face but she said nothing. Instead, she tapped her fingers on the table thinking about her family in Iran, especially her father, perhaps one of the wealthiest businessmen in Iran. He was a merchant who exported mineral ores and spices to Spain, France, and the United Kingdom. She and Basam benefitted from his financial empire by being educated in England, at Cambridge, and later at Columbia.

Tamaret frowned. "Do you really believe you can go back to Iran like this? It would disgrace Uncle Hahib," she hesitated slightly. "My father told Basam that his brother would flail the desert dust for days praying about your sins, and the men would have torturous and murderous eyes upon him when he goes to the Zurhaneh (House of Strength) for prayer.

Baraka gazed at her, then shook her head. "Maybe I should talk with my father."

"Why would you do that?" Tamaret asked, though she remembered perfectly well that Baraka was Habid's oldest daughter and the most covenant by him. He created some liability for himself by permitting her to escape a pre-arranged marriage under many remonstrations from her mother to a wealthy family friend's son. Tamaret still remembered Baraka telling her how she sobbed daily, pleading with her father for a nursing education, a modest career, not in conflict with Islamic principles, and service to her country.

Baraka knew she could win the debate over her mother's protests. There was no one else in the family that could match her intellect. It was those same irrepressible genes and intellectual qualities that her father saw in her, rather than Basam. But what wasn't so apparent to him was her interest in the Mojahedin-e-Khalq (People's Holy Warriors), their ideology about seeking a democratic and secular (non-religious) government reform. Reform had become a growing sentiment among young people in Iran, especially students.

Baraka broke the silence when she smiled at Tamaret.

"Are you upset with me?"

"How could I be?" she murmured. "Glad I was born in America," she sighed. "I probably would be dead by now if I lived over there."

"It's not so bad."

"Isn't it?"

There was a brief silence between them and then Tamaret shrugged. "You're a woman. You know how the clerics feel about Iranian customs, wearing the chadors, property ownership, and pre-arranged marriages. And, what about the Iranian police, and the liberty they have arresting women, beating them for the simplest infractions and, in some cases, killing them? Heck, I know how important Iranian customs and values are even in America."

Baraka frowned. "You're right. Maybe talking to my father isn't a good idea."

"Probably not. You know, when my father tells Uncle Habib, he will cut off your allowance. How will you survive? I-I have some money, but..."

"That's okay, I have enough. I know, at least this might happen, but Basam...?"

"That's a real problem."

"I-I know."

"Above love... faith and honor scares the heck out of me," Tamaret sighed, fumbling inside her leather purse. She slowly removed a pack of Kool cigarettes. "Have one?" Tamaret asked, motioning the pack toward her.

Baraka shook her head. Surprised!!! "No thanks. Has your boyfriend got you smoking now?"

"Hardly. He's really a nerd, but I like him anyway. He's studying to be a biologist."

Baraka thought quickly. Something was wrong, not about Tamaret's explanation, although she didn't provide any, but she never used tobacco before.

"So, just w-why are you smoking?" Baraka asked.

Tamaret shrugged. She swallowed nervously, licking her collagen-inflated lips. Baraka sensing a problem, took her hand, and pulled her closer.

"What's wrong? I know something isn't right."

Tamaret's eyes flickered, then opened. She looked incurably sad.

"I know you're worried about me, Tamaret, aren't you?"

"Of course, I am," she sighed.

"So, tell me.... tell me what's bothering you?" she pleaded.

Tamaret hesitated a solemn moment, waiting to feel the right way. She could bring herself to talk about what was bothering her. Sensing Baraka's impatience, she then slowly said, "I heard my father talking to someone last night in his den. It was a man's voice. I have never heard that voice before—never. Apparently, he entered the outside of the den's entrance from the rear yard. My father didn't want anyone else to see him." She paused, looking directly at Baraka with eyes of reservation in them. Tamaret's voice was crackling with tenuousness, exposing both her nervous composure and growing apprehension.

Baraka looked at her with suspicion. She continued to resist any feelings of trepidation; however, Tamaret's statement made her uneasy.

Tamaret's lips then moved stubbornly. Four words lifted away from her mouth, barely audible. Her head moved closer to Baraka, "It… was… about… you…"

"About… me?"

"Uh huh."

"What about me?"

"He had spoken to your father and then spoke to this man inside the den. By sheer accident, he hadn't closed the door completely. I was soooo scared but I just had to hear everything they were saying."

"What did you hear?" Baraka asked intently.

"I'd rather not tell you about it, but I don't want anyone hurting you."

"Hurting me!" Baraka gasped. "You must be joking. I'm in no mood for this type of humor. Besides you've told me other things," Baraka sighed.

Tamaret's mouth hung. She suddenly wished she had considered another method, perhaps a meaningful way to articulate what she heard ingeniously to her highly educated cousin.

"It isn't a joke," she winced. "I remembered the entire conversation. I think you have been condemned by your father, maybe your whole family in Iran. They feel you have manipulated your father with a clever scheme to leave Iran for a nursing education, lying to avoid marriage, and changing your major like some liberal-minded American woman."

"There is nothing wrong with being a liberal Iranian," Baraka sighed. "Besides, we voted for reform but still the government ignored our feelings."

Baraka was now staring nervously at Tamaret, a queasiness loomed up inside her stomach. She sniffled slightly, trying to restrain a tear, but a lone

one managed to hang from the corner of her right eye. There was a momentary silence between them.

"I-I didn't manipulate anybody. I love my family, especially my father. I just wanted to be free, the satisfaction of feeling an accomplishment that I pursued. What is wrong with that?"

"Nothing, if you're an American—really nothing. But you're an Iranian, a woman, a reformist—and that's a problem. They want you to feel quilt, remorse, grief, panic, and maybe even fear about this."

"But it's wrong! Doesn't anyone understand that's so terribly wrong."

"That isn't the point in their minds. You have disgraced your father and Basam should do something about it."

"What exactly did your father say?" Baraka asked cautiously.

"That if Basam couldn't do it, he should see that you're taken care before your visa expires."

Baraka's mind reeled. She brushed her hands nervously across her forehead. This was immensely disturbing, even more perplexing that her family would ask her brother to harm her. But immediately a more horrifying thought compressed inside her head, it wasn't harm, like corporal punishment or removing an incentive or even canceling her monthly allowance. It was registering a crazy premonition about a permanent sanction. And as unthinkable as it was, her eyes returned to Tamaret. She then winced, blurting out, "You mean… k-kill me," she groaned.

Tamaret shrugged, her voice lowered an octave, "I think so."

Baraka held her breath for a long moment. She was utterly stunned! "I've got to talk with Emily," she thought quietly to herself.

"What are you thinking about?" Tamaret asked. Baraka sighed. "Help," she exclaimed. "I need some help."

"The police?"

"Of course not."

"Are you sure?"

"Quite sure."

Baraka's thoughts returned to her. Just the memory of that meeting with Tamaret continued to make her nauseated. Then, realizing just how things worked, she had to make a decision before she saw Basam, or anyone else in Tamaret's family. Normally, this would be foolhardy for her to ever consider doing something like this. Things were tumultuous in the Middle East. America's war and liberation in Iraq was rapidly deteriorating restraint everywhere which, by now, was destabilizing Islamic and Arab countries, especially in Iran. The fact that Iran was a bordering neighbor to Iraq and with its unsettling and diplomatic America relationship, anyone was a potential target for any Islamic fundamentalist or youthful group who had morphed itself into a terrorist threat that hated anything and anyone they perceived harboring American values. This was a factor that could ultimately pose much risk to her life.

She realized now that her decision was catastrophic and wouldn't be tolerated in her country. Perhaps, because of her American education, she would be considered arrogant, flouting democratic values among Iranian women whose natural silence might be sufficiently aroused to feel like, behave like and think like herself, she reasoned.

Pushing back her thoughts about these problematic consequences, it was easy for her to rationalize her next decision. Turning, she smiled at Emily's photograph sitting on her nightstand. Her focused disquietness was characteristic of her adroit personality as she attempted to calculate the risks and consequences of her dilemma.

It was less than a week after having lunch with Tamaret when Baraka finally decided to contact Emily about her situation.

As she brushed straight through her long, black hair, her mind revisited that Thursday evening at Emily's upscale apartment on the Upper West Side. Emily Anderson had become Baraka's best friend. She was also attending her final year at Columbia. They met eighteen months earlier in a tutoring laboratory for engineering students where Baraka worked as a tutor's aid. Emily would eventually treat her with differential awe, frequently crediting her for salvaging her engineering degree after being tutored through the degree curriculum's most difficult courses—physics and chemistry.

Emily joined her father in New York, moving from Dayton, Ohio three years ago to complete her undergraduate degree at Columbia.

It was this unending gratitude from her that eventually led Baraka to seek her help. Ironically, it was a relationship also cultivated by Baraka since Emily's father was a senior special agent with the Federal Bureau of Investigation's New York City Counterterrorism Organization, a fact that, somehow, she always remembered.

Opening the door, Emily spread her arms wide to a sudden tearful Baraka. Immediately, she sensed something wasn't quite right, looking at her steadily. "Is something wrong?" Emily asked.

Baraka shrugged. "Yessss… I need to talk."

"Well, you've come to the right place," she said displaying her white beaming teeth. Baraka moved slowly passed her not wanting to make any eye contact. It was obvious to Emily that Baraka's semi-freewheeling attitude toward life suddenly changed. Emily sensed this was far more than a just a problem but perhaps a crisis.

Baraka stared pensively straight ahead, still reluctant to say anything, Emily was cautious. She had never seen Baraka behave like this. It was a very odd moment for both women.

After sitting in silence for several moments, Emily heaved a moderate sigh and said, "Are you sure this is the right time for this?"

Baraka nodded her head and still, for a few more uncomfortable moments, both women sat quietly on Emily's living room sofa gazing at the shafts of intermittent sunlight rays paralleling through pink mini venetian blinds laced across a large bay window.

Gradually, Baraka's eyes then shifted toward Emily's oval Egyptian glass, black coffee table with an embroidered brass trim circling around the edge with four ebony legs anchored on each side with brass lion paws that spread evenly on a black and white speckled Persian area rug. She smiled remembering how excited Emily was when she gave her the rug for a Christmas present. It now seemed as though they been sitting in the silence forever when her fear started to drain from her.

Baraka shook her head. "I think someone in my family is going to kill me," she mumbles slowly.

"Kill you? I don't er..." Emily began to stutter unintelligibly.

"I have disgraced my father, maybe my entire family."

"How?" Emily asked.

"I-I lied to them. I-I told him that I wanted to be a nurse, something that he understood for the country."

Emily's eyes widened in alarm. "Did you tell him that you changed your mind. What's wrong with being a civil engineer in Iran? I would think they would be proud of you, graduating summa cum laude."

Baraka groaned. For the next several moments, she told Emily about her plan to leave Iran to avoid a pre-arranged marriage and to obtain a nursing education as a pre-text to her departure. But changing her major to engineering without her father's permission or knowledge, it has now created a considerable embarrassment to him along with his reputation. This along with the potential damaged relationship with his best friend and his son, his potential son-in-law.

Emily arched her eyebrows. "They would kill you for that?" she protested.

Baraka's head slowly rocked back and forth. "Y-You don't understand Islamic customs," she answered weakly. "A woman does not have much latitude. Anything that she does which offends the family can result in extreme punishment, even death. There are many women killed because they dared to have a secret relationship with a man, someone they have fallen in love with." She paused, with a long sigh. "Or even lying to avoid a pre-arranged marriage can be just as serious. These matters have serious, I mean very serious, consequences for women in Iran."

"Wh-What are you going to do?" Emily asked softly, her face terrified with dread as she stared squarely at her. "How can I help you?"

Baraka hesitated a moment. She then slowly stood up walking toward the bay window, not wanting Emily to see the tears flooding from her eyes.

"I have some information for you. Something that may be useful to your father. In exchange, it may give me political asylum somewhere in America."

Emily's brows rose. A strange feeling moved over her. "What kinda information?" she asked while a benign lump wedged inside her throat, disappearing when she swallowed.

"Maybe about some terrorist activity. Here! Right here in the city."

"Terrorists!" Emily gasped, her mouth abruptly gaped wide open, stunned by Baraka's lethal statement. "Oh, my Gawd, this is crazy. We've must tell my dad. Are you serious?"

"Yesss. I'm serious."

"How did you find out?"

"It came from Tamaret."

"What did she say?"

Baraka surveyed Emily's intense face, immediately registering some doubt for even mentioning the word "terrorist" to anyone, especially to a resident of New York City and specifically to someone connected to a law enforcement agency, particularly the FBI. Emily's Aphrodite face had suddenly appeared glum.

Baraka's mind went blank, while staring at the floor. It was a frigid stare.

She winced. Could she be imagining all of this and was it possible Tamaret misunderstood her father or maybe this was a nightmare, some horrible nightmare, she reasoned.

Emily's voice suddenly interrupted her thoughts. "What did she say?" she repeated.

For a split-second Baraka almost decided this was too sensitive, perhaps even too dangerous to talk about, but opening her mouth to speak, she remembered why she came here—it was her life that was in jeopardy. Baraka then gave a big sigh expelling a long, very long breath. "Well, I don't have many details, just bits and pieces."

"That will do—even bits and pieces can be helpful."

"Tamaret told me about a man she calls 'The Syrian' but he is not from Syria or even Syrian. Maybe he lives somewhere on Staten Island, but he's illegal in this country using Jordanian immigration papers and he's not from Jordan either. Nobody really knows where he is from or his real name but he commands much influence and respect from Tamaret's father and her other relatives in the city. Nothing is ever done over cell phones, computers, and they communicate with cryptic message codes sent by special couriers."

"That's odd," Emily said, shaking her head.

"No. It isn't odd. They want to have a bland cleverness, that is what Tamaret calls it. Anything that gives an electronic footprint is to be avoided. They watch cable news, read all the papers and follow the country's technology and IT capabilities and security measures.

They have their own sophisticated, intelligence network. Tamaret told me that her father and my dad provide him funding. So, it really isn't odd to understand how they are working here. She also told me that one of her cousins said they know a lot about how the CIA's covert activities operate."

Shaking her head, "Well, this all sounds very nerve racking to me," Emily said, her face stiffened as she looked intensely concerned about Baraka's information. "They really do hate us… I mean going through these extreme measures."

"Hate!" Baraka moaned, shaking her head. "You Americans understand that word better than Muslims, Arabs, or Persians like me. It isn't hate that drives them—not the hate you can relate to like intensely disliking someone—but a holy calling, a conviction to destroy this Babylonian empire that protects Israel. They believe America is a Colonial Invader, spreading their western values and culture along with its disease of filth and sin in the Middle East, trying to destroy Islam with their democratic ideology and nation building rhetoric.

"Baraka, good Lord," Emily gasped. "You don't believe that's true?"

"Of course not."

Emily frowned. "Somehow, they try to make us feel guilty," she sighed.

Moving away from the bay window and now looking directly at Emily, Baraka replied, "It's a complicated matter. The government in many Arab countries support America even against the will of their people. And we do see America's foreign policy hypocrisy. I-I mean once they supported King Hussein against my country by investing billions of dollars in credit, providing U.S. military intelligence and advice to the Iraqis and monitoring third country arms sales to Iraq. Later, there was never a growing dissatisfaction from America toward Hussein when he used biological chemicals to kill thousands of Iranian soldiers but when it comes to their soldiers, the circumstances are different. Do you see my point?"

Emily shrugged and sighed. "I'm really not sure. I'm not a Middle Eastern historian on these matters," she moaned. "I guess there is propaganda on both sides and do the average American or Iranian, like us, really know deep down how these diplomatic and political issues are formed in the interest, as they say, for the national security purposes of a given country?"

She paused a moment, recalibrating her thoughts, "What is the name of that Arab cable news station?"

"The Aljazeera." Baraka interjected. "It is a state-owned Arabic language international news network out of Qatar."

"Yeah, that's the one. I have occasionally been interested in listening to their viewpoints on many issues and the wars over there and how the Arabs feel about us. Sometimes their reports leave me sad about my feelings toward the violence in the Middle East, especially how quickly women and children are so vulnerable and that they do suffer the most."

"Yessss, they're very vulnerable."

"And speaking about vulnerability… tell me more about this Syrian character." Emily asked.

Baraka paused for a short moment, perhaps rethinking whether this was a wise decision for her to continue with Emily. Her tongue twitched nervously between her lips. She then shrugged. "I don't know," she hedged.

Emily then stared at her. "Baraka, is someone planning to hurt you?" Baraka nodded.

"Then you need my help."

"What if I can't."

"Can't what?"

"Can't give you any more information?"

"You can't or you won't?" Emily barked.

"I'm not sure."

By now, Emily's smile faded away. Her face hardened looking at Baraka suspiciously. "Do you remember what happened here on September 11? Do you, Baraka?" asked Emily as she stepped closer to her.

"Sure, I do," Baraka replied defensively.

"If you remember that and how it made everyone here feel about terrorists, even across this country and around the world, then you should understand that you must tell me what you know. Tell me, because I know how you feel about America and our values. For God sakes, this is New York City! You know what happened here."

Baraka lowered her eyes, and a slight shudder ran through her body. It was a moment which she regained her courage.

She then sighed. "Okay, I'll tell you as much as I know. I understand that he is ex-military with experience manufacturing and improvising fire-arms, bombs and other explosives. He is heavily financed, Tamaret told me. I-I mean according to her, he receives a lot of money, all cash. Nothing is traced back to any accounts. He also ensures that certain other people are taking care of…"

"… killed," Emily interrupted.

"No, no! He pays individuals across the country on a regular basis with these funds. He has many couriers that travel to many places to pay. They drive their own cars or take the bus or train. Everything is low profile and they never take commercial planes. They carry instructions—nothing in writing. They must memorize everything."

"Hmmmm, tell you what." Emily looked around the room and nodded with satisfaction at the telephone. Whew, lady, this is wayyyyy over my head now. My dad might be in the office. Maybe you should tell him everything you know about this."

"Alright," Baraka shrugged. "I hope I am doing the right thing."

"Of course, you are. We've gotta stop anyone who's involved in any terrorist activities in this country. This city is spending a fortune in security and counterintelligence matters in an effort to make us safe. They're doing so with not much financial support from Washington, according to my dad; so, we have an obligation to share this information with him."

Suddenly, Baraka's cell phone rang. She twitched nervously, uttering an exclamation, and said, "It's Tamaret."

"Where you expecting her call?"

Baraka winced. "Not really. I told her I would call her later this evening."

"Maybe it's a problem. She does keep you informed."

"Maybe," she hesitated. "Maybe I'm a little paranoid, ya know? The call coming while I am here."

"You don't think she's…"

"… that she's following me?" Baraka remarked. "I don't think so. I trust her. Why shouldn't I?"

"Alright, in that case, I think you should answer it."

Answering her cell phone, her voice broke timidly. After a few moments, "Nothing," she stammered, apparently in response to a question.

As she continued to listen, she slowly gazed at Emily, then shook her head. Baraka then bit her lip, her eyes welled up in tears, but somehow, she managed to remain calm.

Emily looked at her questioningly. She then whispered, "Is everything okay?"

Baraka rolled her eyes; Her face quickly became drawn and pinched. She continued to listen; her body gradually stiffened in apprehension. And, of course, at this moment, Emily recognized there was a problem perhaps a serious one being described by Tamaret. Baraka's face seemed intensely blank; her features gradually fallen. It was a one-sided conversation. She was listening without the benefit of any meaningful response.

A few moments later, without saying a word, Baraka's jaw tightened, and her head lowered. She then made a heavy sigh, lifting her head up ever so slightly. Without making any eye contact with Emily, she said, "I've gotta go."

Tapping the 'off' button on her cell phone, Baraka shook her head sadly.

"They've been following me."

"Following you! W-Who's been following you?" Emily gasped.

"She wouldn't say. But they're around here, near your place—real close—maybe inside the building."

"For Christ's sake," Emily blurted out. "I'm gonna call the police and my dad."

Baraka shook her head. "No, no!" she cried. "Please no, don't do that," she pleaded. "They wouldn't come inside. I'll be alright. I think everything will work out."

"How can you be sure?" Emily asked suspiciously. "And was that really Tamaret?"

Baraka gazed at her for a brief moment, then shook her head. "I have to go."

"But, what about my father… your story… the terrorists? What about…?"

Baraka held up both her hands, waving off all further questions with a peremptory gesture. "I really have to go. I'll talk with you later," Baraka said, her eyes now were red and puffy.

"No way," Emily hissed. "No way, I know something is wrong. That wasn't Tamaret on your cell phone. If you don't let me help you, surely they'll kill you. Leaving here is a real mistake. We can call my dad. He'll know exactly what to do. We can…"

"Stop it!" Baraka screeched. "Pleaseee… just stop it. They know who you are and all about your father," Baraka sighed.

"What!" Emily barked.

Baraka frowned. "I'm sorry I came over here."

"What do you mean, they know about me and my father?"

The room was suddenly paralyzed by silence, both women stared at each other. Somehow, Emily knew better than to push her friend. It was now apparent the call had terrified her.

Baraka began to tremble. Her mind was now spinning from the conversation. Her cogent plan for political asylum now might be compromised.

"Did they threaten me?" Emily asked. "Am I in any danger?" Emily asked, breaking through Baraka's thoughts.

"Oh no. No. No!"

"Where are you going to now?"

"I'm going home. I have to sort this out."

"Baraka?" Emily asked. "I gotta t-tell my dad about this Syrian business. It really sounds pretty damn scary to me. His agency's gotta know about this. I hope you'll talk with him, okay?"

Baraka made no response.

Within a few moments, she grabbed her purse and quickly left Emily's apartment.

Baraka stopped brushing her waist long hair. She was now sitting perfectly still thinking about her meeting with Emily nearly a week ago. Unconsciously, her hands dropped to her side. She felt relieved that Emily's calls finally stopped.

Her mind began to drift about Basam. Strangely, she received only two calls from him since Tamaret shared that macabre story about the pressure on him to perhaps kill her. Instinctively, she knew how all this worked. It was a deadly game. She heard the lurid details of the Iranian Secret Police enjoying this type of mental torture in Iran. Always using a waiting game—keeping people under surveillance, always watching, listening, waiting for just the right moment when fear dominated a person's every thought about how and when death might occur. This was a peculiar kind of barbarism that always was an effective tool for non-conformists. In a country where the ruling Islamic government was rapidly growing impatient with Iranians who would foolishly challenge Islamic teachings and customs, even now prostitution and gambling were increasing in Tehran. It was this period that she was now struggling to resist. Holding out a slight thread of hope that somehow, perhaps in some incredible way, Tamaret misunderstood each ominous episode about her.

Slackened by hallucinations, Baraka rubbed her weary face thinking of her recent weeks of purgatory, wondering what would happen next.

Shivering, she was beginning to feel like some scandalous outcast or a complete stranger to her family. She continued to ignore her father's e-mails and telephone calls. Even his letters remained half-read and unanswered.

This self-imposed sequestering was beginning to make her paranoid. She could sense something was happening. The pressure was on both sides gradually forcing her to consider that her safety was paramount to any loyalty she may have toward her family.

Suddenly, without any indication beforehand, the doorbell rang. Baraka quickly bolted from the chair. Her face glazed with surprise. This was clearly unusual for a tightly managed security apartment complex to allow a stranger entry unless they gained access inadvertently by an unsuspecting tenant.

Walking nimbly toward the front door, she paused temporarily listening intently. Her ears strained to grab every movement, sound, something that her mind could define beyond the door.

Standing perfectly rigid, this wasn't a mistake. She heard the doorbell rang and there was someone standing on the opposite side; she was certain of it. Quietly reconciling it was no neighbor as nobody would come to her apartment unannounced. Bracing herself, this was perhaps her Grim Reaper suitor, the lone assassin she waited for the last three months.

Unbuckling her mind, curiosity arrived before fear. She inched closer toward the door's peephole. Her arms blossoming with goosebumps, while her heart fluttered inside her chest. She could feel a rush of heat to her face She just needed a single glimpse of the person they sent to kill her; maybe someone's name she could repeat over a 911 recording, quickly exposing their identity, she thought.

Suddenly, painstakingly, Baraka's left eye was glaring through the peephole. Her eyebrows shot up in surprise. "Basam!" she shrilled. "What are you doing here?" she asked, struggling to control her quavering voice.

"I am checking on you. For three months, you haven't answered my calls. What's wrong with you?"

"Me?" she scowled. "Nothing is wrong with me!" she said in exasperation.

"Well then, open the door."

Baraka froze. She knew her next few words would make her seem psycho. "I-I can't… can't do it," she mumbled.

"What do you mean, you can't?" he asked, obviously agitated.

"I'm not leaving until you open this door."

Moving back quickly, she managed to grab her cell phone. Using her programmed number, she automatically dialed Emily's home. After two short rings, Emily answered but before she could utter a single word, Baraka moaned softly, "Please…. please help me. Basam is here standing outside my front door. Call 911 and your father," she whispered in a desperate tone, clicking off her cell phone without waiting for her reply.

Walking back to her front door, each second that passed was increasing her anxiety. "Basam," she said. "I know why you've come."

"Okay, then you know I am taking you out of here. We must hurry."

"To kill me, Basam. You come here to kill me. I know the whole story."

Basam did not respond.

Then if it had come from out of the blue, Baraka's mind raced to an image from the past of Basam when he was ten years old. His features were red, grimacing as his face twisted, straining forearms, and steady hands gripping her puny wrist, pulling her panic-stricken body out of a partially concealed well that she accidentally fallen into while playing in a large, barren field near their uncle's home. He literally saved her life. And now her eyes focused again, there were other times, many moments, when Basam was always there for her.

Baraka's face was now wet with perspiration. Quickly rubbing her eyes, she edged closer toward the peephole while half-thinking, half-pleading.

"Basam," she sobbed looking through it. Baraka looked blank. There was a quiet shock. Clearing her throat, she meekly asked, "Basam, are you still there?" her neck twisted, straining side to side, wondering what he was doing now.

For the first time, Baraka was feeling a strange premonition about her brother. All the dots weren't connecting about him in this scenario.

Without hesitating, she suddenly swung back the safety door latch, turning two dead bolts locks. She then pulled the door back slowly. Her face creased in a corkscrew expression. She frowned, moving cautiously at first, a single timid step… another… and then another until she was midway in the corridor. She stood staring dubiously down the narrow, placid carpet hallway.

Her utter astonishment soon gave way to an eerie suspicion. A look of uneasy puzzlement loomed over her face. There was no sound of the elevator door's opening or closing. She raised one eyebrow in a questioning slant wondering if she should have waited for Emily's arrival or continue toward the fire stairwell, only a short distance from her. She took no time to consider any other possibility. Basam had rushed off and was inside the stairwell, she was certain of it.

Pacing slowly, she pulled back her long black hair and cradled her arms crisscross around her tiny waist.

Despite her terrible fear, she forced herself, perhaps moving closer toward her death. Somehow, she couldn't bring herself to stop. She agonized expecting her worst fears.

She was shuddering now, finally at the door. She hesitated momentarily, tossing her head down the corridor. A bizarre sensation rushed inside her body. "Run, run, Baraka, run, please run…," a faint voice echoed inside her eardrums.

Her knuckles were white as she grabbed the doorknob with her right hand. Squeezing it tightly, a weird feeling surged inside her mind. Instinctively, without a hint from it, she believed he was waiting for her behind the door.

By now, she mustered a considerable courage about her faith. She wanted to confront him face to face, stare him right between his eyes before… and suddenly, as she continued to reinforce her contemplations, out of nowhere a hand reached from behind the door yanking her abruptly inside. Baraka's eyes blinked with crazed fright. Before she could manage both a scream and struggle, Basam quickly covered her mouth, shaking his head, motioning down the stairwell.

"Shhhh… they have come for you," he whispered. Baraka's face suddenly grew ashen. She could not speak.

"I came here before they got here." Baraka shook her head.

"They have been planning to kill you." Now, slowly moving his hand away from her mouth, Baraka frowned wearily. "Because I changed my major to engineering? B-but, I don't understand. Tamaret said…"

"Tamaret!" Basam said disgustedly. "I should have guessed so. They think you have been recruited by the C.I.A. You're friends with Emily Anderson. They believe you're spying for her father."

"Spying?" Baraka gasped! Her mouth fell open in shock.

At this point, a subtle noise from the bottom stairwell grabbed their attention.

Basam and Baraka exchanged stares, without saying a word, they each knew her assassins had arrived.

Grabbing her right hand, Basam quickly raced up the stairwell. "Hurry," he whispered to her. "They are here—just below us."

As Baraka raced up each flight, she could now hear faint footsteps, voices and the urgency below surging up the stairwell. Hearing sounds of someone gasping for air as they quickly raced up each flight of stairs was quietly shattering her Roman Spirit. By now, she was consumed with fear.

Only four flights away from the roof top, suddenly around each turn, she debated to herself whether to believe Tamaret's honesty or the lack of it. Perhaps it was all a pack of lies about her brother and family, even about the unforgiving problem with her degree. She was clever in persuading her to feel paranoid about her brother's willingness to kill her. Even now, Tamaret's subtle questions about Emily and their relationship was never obvious.

Baraka was now becoming winded. Her lungs starved for more oxygen. She was beginning to feel faint. Her knees started to buckle as she wheezed and coughed. Stumbling, she tried to grab a short breath, but Basam was pulling her harder. "I-I-I can't… go… much… further," her voice strained.

"We're almost to the roof… just a little farther, and we can go down the other side exit," Basam said partially gasping.

Abruptly, Baraka's head snapped backwards. She contemplated a quick second. The remark struck her like a ton of bricks. He had never been on her roof top before—never. Her mind compressed vividly to his three visits and each time they departed together. Baraka stared suspiciously at him as they continued to race up the stairwell. Something inside his waistband caught her attention. She stopped abruptly.

"Basam..." she pleaded. "How did you know there was a fire exit on the other side of the roof?"

Before he could answer, a voice screamed from below. Pushing open the door, Baraka stumbled toward the roof surface, screaming. "H-Help me," she shrieked.

Immediately, as if it were almost simultaneously, a voice from below cried out. "Baraka, it's me—Emily, my dad, and the police."

Baraka was nearly psychologically subdued from the fury. Falling to the ground, a bullet suddenly whistled passed her head ricocheting off the roof's door outside exit sign, landing short two inches from her head.

Without hesitating, Basam suddenly dropped to his knees, remove a gun from his waistband and fired three shots over Baraka's body, directly at the opposite fire exit door.

There were two loud, ear-piercing screams that followed, leaping from the rooftop, colliding against the heavy evening air, scattering down and over a collage of high-rise brick and concrete buildings that seemed to be suffocating the city below.

One scream came from Baraka. Her eyes were clamped shut. Another loud yip-yowling, raspy cry bellowed across the rooftop.

"Police officer—drop your weapon. Drop it or I'll shoot." Still another voice leaped out from just behind the stairwell door's entrance. Everything was now in an insane nightmare. The next moment, footsteps raced passed her and then immediately another voice, a different one, yelled out, "We need an ambulance!"

It was now a general commotion around Baraka. An amazing few seconds erupted as she continued to close her eyes tight, while her arms stretched outward.

"Baraka, are you alright?' Emily asked cautiously kneeling down beside her. "She was planning to kill you."

Baraka slowly opened her eyes. It was though she was dreaming about this unthinkable moment. She then half rolled over, releasing a soft cry. "What do you mean?" she asked incredulously and, without waiting for a reply, "Where is my brother?" she continued.

"He's with my father and the police. He was trying to protect you."

"Protect me?" Baraka frowned. "From who? I thought..."

"I know what you thought," Emily interrupted. "But it wasn't him; it was Tamaret."

Baraka's eyes glazed like saucers, along with a long, searching look. Her face was now turning scarlet and swollen. The reality of what she just heard was gradually coming forward in her mind. "Tamaret," she moaned.

Her body stiffening in apprehension as she forced her head slowly around. There was now a sudden look of mute appeal. She bristled from a wounded look in her eyes. Only less than twenty feet from her, lying on the pavement from the opposite end of the exit, was Tamaret's body spread eagle and, a short distance from her, a small automatic weapon with a silencer. Her eyes then rotated to two Middle Eastern men, handcuffed by the police, lying in a prone position at the entrance of the fire exit door on the opposite end. Two similar weapons were lying near them with police technicians securing them with yellow tape. Up against the wall was a partially opened suitcase. She bristled at seeing large black plastic bags, at least two cordless saws and what appeared to be a large carving knife.

Now refocusing back to Emily, she said, "I think they were going to kill me, cut into pieces and take me away in that suitcase," she moaned softly.

"Gawd, this is so awful," Emily winched.

"The second scream I heard came from Tamaret, but I am still so confused about this."

'I know. My father didn't give me any details. I wouldn't expect him to, but they're investigating Tamaret after our conversation."

"B..but why?"

"Someone has been brainwashing her and had thoroughly convinced her you were a CIA operative and was spying on them because our relationship. You know they must have been so paranoid and hateful toward you."

"Who's they?"

Emily shrugged. "I'm not sure. But she's involved with them… they're here. Even after now, I'll never understand what this terrorist stuff is all about, but Basam was never involved. He really couldn't come to us but telling me about Tamaret probably saved your life, and possibly his as well. When I told my father about her, she was already on their radar. I really don't know to what degree and please don't ask me anymore about her."

"What about this Syrian?"

Emily hesitated, apparently not wanting to say anything else. "They're having some progress, but still haven't actually identified who he is because he moves around a lot, about like a phantom or something."

Baraka then turned, staring evenly at her brother. His eyes looked heavy. He was also in handcuffs. Speaking with him was Emily's father through an Iranian interpreter who had arrived moments after the gunfire on the rooftop.

For a few uncomfortable seconds, Baraka's head surveyed the surroundings. The city that she had fallen in love with, the dreams and aspirations she secretly had wanting to become an American citizen, was displaced by this contemptuous event. Her face stopped extemporaneously in front of Emily. She was expressionless as Emily forced a moderate smile at her.

Satisfied that Baraka's intransigent behavior had somehow acquiesced to some common-sense which prompted the telephone call to her, Emily was relieved that it ultimately saved her life.

As the area rapidly transformed into a frantic crime scene flooded with police, FBI agents, ATF, and several men walking around without any identification taking tons of photographs. Meanwhile, more ambulances could be heard blaring through the streets below. Two large helicopters, one from the New York City Police Department and the other from a local television station, were buzzing over the rooftop. Their long helicopter blades occasionally would push a strong gust of wind over the crime scene.

"Are you alright?" Emily asked again.

"I-I'm not sure," she replied, half-unwillingly.

"I understand."

"No, I really don't think you do."

Emily then shrugged her shoulders. "Maybe you're right. It's all so hard to imagine, she was going…"

"… I know," Baraka interrupted her in mid-sentence. Without waiting for a response, she continued. "What will they do to Basam?"

"Well," Emily sighed. "He shot her," she answered lugubriously.

"He should have come to the police and carrying a gun with a nonimmigrant visa is a violation of the law. I know because one of the students in my class was denied a gun permit due to his nonimmigrant visa status."

Disengaging herself from Emily, Baraka's thoughts were pre-occupied with the FBI and ATF agents who were surrounding Basam. There was something about this twisted scenario that still wasn't making much sense.

She could hear Basam agitatedly eliciting short, abridged answers to Emily's father's questions through the interpreter. Strangely, during the entire affair, Basam was looking directly at her.

"He's part of this," Baraka said dryly. "That figures, doesn't it?"

"Oh no… I don't think so," Emily replied. "He saved your life. Everything is alright. You can go back to your country. That degree business was all just a lie. He told you about Tamaret, what she believed, the CIA connection with me. It all makes sense to me—the lies Tamaret told you and maybe even this Syrian business. I believe now everything is alright."

A frown crossed Baraka's face. "I don't believe everything is alright…. meaning just because this incident was foiled by my brother and the police… things aren't okay. That is not how life works in Iranian politics."

And now there was a quiet silence between them as the EMT's finished their initial evaluation of Baraka and were preparing to transport her to the hospital for follow-up tests. Meanwhile, the lifeless body of Tamaret had been removed several minutes earlier.

A few more moments passed when Emily's father waved a hand airily toward her. She nodded resignedly as she walked over to meet him.

After their conversation, there was a moment of hesitation, then Emily turned pulling back her tarnished sunset, blonde hair. Her face twisted to rugged granite.

Serious faced; Emily paced slowly toward Baraka. "They're going to arrest your brother," she said quietly.

"For shooting Tamaret?"

"For several charges, including that and, if she dies, maybe a homicide or something. I really don't know but my dad said there are a lot of charges and questions he will be facing at the moment."

"Will he be arrested for a long time?"

"I'm not sure," Emily shrugged. "But I know the State Department is willing to allow you to remain here if you decide to do so. I'm certain my dad can assist you in a big way about that issue."

Baraka said nothing.

Emily continued, "Maybe you can apply for some emergency political asylum or something."

Ignoring Emily's last statement, Baraka then said, "I think Tamaret is dead. Basam was coming here to warn me." She paused with a quizzical expression on her face, "Or maybe he shot her to prevent her from exposing the real truth."

"But she had a gun and with a silencer on it," Emily replied.

"Maybe that was to protect me from Basam, I-I-I- just don't know what to believe right now."

"Well, in that case, you definitely can't go back to Iran."

"I have to."

"Honestly, that's insane," Emily spoke in an agitated tone. "Are you gone completely nuts?" Emily asked incredulously, half-whispering, while breathing heavily and annoyed by Baraka's defiance.

"Don't get me wrong. I'm afraid to, but so are many of the Iranian students. It's not easy to go up against that tyrannical, religious hardline regime in power over there." She paused momentarily, still gathering her thoughts. "They want to control your life, thoughts, ways, how you dress, worship... Everything about it is just wrong."

"What about our government? We can help you."

"No. No! I don't want that. We need your support, but only working through the United Nations and other Islamic countries. We don't need American forces. Forces from your military would bring internal destruction inside my country. They would fight and resist like the Iraqi people. You can't force your military or government on our will. The struggle for freedom must come from us—we must do it. That is why, despite some of my fears, I still need to return to speak with my father and family. I have to do it, regardless of how my father feels about things."

Emily thought for a moment, "Alright, then what can I do?" she asked.

Baraka sighed, and replied calmly, "Just pray for me, pray for all of us. Pray for our country and pray for its freedom."

Emily nodded, "I will."

Both women then slowly embraced each other as a swarm of special agents finally circled them, providing them no momentary comfort whatsoever to the tragedy that just occurred. All thoughts were now pre-occupied regarding the insidious nature of terrorism, and what information Baraka could provide them about her brother or anyone else. Emily and two FBI agents walked parallel with an EMT who was escorting her away to an emergency helicopter who was now flying above them, preparing to lift her up inside it and fly her away to the hospital. The authorities were taking extreme precaution not to take her down the stairwell and out the front entrance of the apartment building exposed to a large crowd.

No one knew how deeply depressed Emily was regarding that painful period ten months ago. Even though Baraka finally returned to Iran, Emily was still intent on establishing communication with her. But for the moment, she was silent, examining her last e-mail from her. Strangely, there was no response from Baraka. In fact, she hadn't heard from her in the last three weeks. An irresistible notion flowed through her mind that perhaps something was wrong. Baraka was punctual about answering messages and especially from her.

She was wondering about Baraka's life. The FBI certainly made a nightmare of it, along with their media circus-like announcements about her brother's connection to a small terrorist cell on Staten Island, and the failed capture of the Syrian, a reported Egyptian ringleader who allegedly managed to escape just hours before an early morning dawn raid at his last known residence.

And there was Tamaret, who miraculously survived three near fatal gunshot wounds but was now sequestered by the federal government. Many of her relatives, including her father, had been held in detention with rigorous questioning followed by weeks of intensive investigations.

Certainly, it had been difficult for both women to understand what occurred to them. Emily's life dramatically changed. She had become a heroine, confused perhaps by statements like 'The former, white female, American Army Private's painful saga in Iraq; and the grandiose, embellishment of a role for her that simply didn't exist during her capture from an Iraqi ambush.' Much of what was being reported from the media about her just didn't happen and the constant media and exposure about it was taking its mental and physical toll on her.

Meanwhile, as the days went on, Emily was continuing to send more e-mails and text messages to her best friend eagerly waiting for a lone response from her. It went on for nearly two years until, one day, an eerie call arrived on a late Saturday evening to her.

"Madam Emily Anderson," a voice spoke with a thick French accent.

"Speaking."

"My name is Mr. Janiot. I am a diplomat with the French Embassy here in New York City. This number was given to me by Mr. Lemieux. I didn't have your address, and under the circumstance, I apologize for calling you at this very unusual time."

"That's perfectly alright," Emily said.

"Mr. Lemieux is an attaché in our French Embassy in Tehran. I have a message for you from him."

Emily started trembling, "Oh dear Lord," she cried. "Is it from Baraka?"

"Why yes."

"It is a very short note—no address or telephone number."

Emily suddenly frowned. "No address or telephone number?"

"No Madam, sorry. If Ms. Mahdi hasn't contacted you directly, things can be complicated in Iran. But here's is the message Mr. Lemieux wanted to give you which comes directly from Ms. Baraka Mahdi."

Dearest Emily:

I appreciate everything you have done for me. Our great friendship was so important to me in so many ways. I am happily married now with a nice career as a Civil Engineer. Don't worry about me anymore. Things worked out with my father and family. This will be my final message to you.

With love, your friend forever,

Baraka

"Let me try to understand," Emily snapped. "You're saying Baraka wrote this to me and sent it to someone in your French Embassy, instead of sending it directly to me, and there's no forwarding address or no way I can respond to any of her communication to me?"

"Something like that," Mr. Janiot replied. "I am sorry, but I am only delivering this message. I have no details, and neither can Mr. Lemieux provide me with any other information when I inquired about the brevity of the note." He paused for a moment. "I realize this is very difficult for you and perhaps your friend was even taking a great risk in sending this note to you. But, if you have any more questions, you should contact someone in your State Department that might have a back channel, another way of getting messages in and out of Iran, or someone in the United Nations that has some connection with representatives in Iran. And yet, either one of those methods can be risky for Ms. Madhi. I did ask Mr. Lemieux did he actually see Ms. Madhi and he stated a woman did identify herself, through a third party, that it was she that was the originator of this note, and didn't want anyone to know that she was secretly sending it out to you."

"I see. Thank you so much, Mr. Janiot. I am just grateful to hear something from her and that she is well and safe. I have been worried sick for years about Baraka."

"You are welcome. If there is anything I can do on my end, please do hesitate in contacting my office. You have my number."

That telephone conversation was over four years ago. Emily was now married and working for the state living in Albany, New York. But despite the change in her life, it still had become a daily ritual, an unsettling premonition about the mystery of her best friend's bizarre disappearance. It was a personal failure, she resolved in her mind, about her efforts to locate her in Iran even with some help from her father. If she was plagued with hope, it was dissolved two years ago when a State of Department official told her they were ending their inquiries about Baraka. They considered their investigation had come to a dead end.

Gradually, remembering where she was, Emily shook from her thoughts. She withdrew from them while daydreaming, hunched over her desk, glaring unfocused at several photographs of them. In a crazy kind of way, Emily reasoned, her friend had been very courageous—a rare courage that resulted in the exposure of small and well-organized terrorist cell on Staten Island. Her information was a metal of courage because she didn't have to do it, especially returning to Iran. Even the prosecution of Basam for attempted murder and numerous other criminal charges, didn't weather her resolve.

But there was something very special about Baraka's valor, Emily thought. There was a conviction about her people's freedom, and the vitality she possessed about it. She had been strongly encouraged to remain in the United States; however, she was convinced that reconciling with her father and family was the most important thing in her life and especially with what had occurred with her twin brother. Besides, the officials sealed her identity from the media or so she believed.

Finally, a single tear slowly rolled down Emily's right cheekbone. She sniffed slightly not wanting her co-workers to see it. She then shuffled quietly in her chair, returning the pictures inside her purse. She then mumbled softly, "Thank you Baraka... thank you... thank you for so many things. Wherever you are, my friend, I know God is with you," she moaned quietly to herself. "I just know it."

Pimpin Aint Easy
Story By
Raymond A. Clark.

CHAPTER EIGHT

PIMPIN AIN'T EASY

IT WAS A BLISTERING COLD LATE DAY IN DECEMBER. DUPREE leaned back. He rubbed his hands over his new, elaborate cornrow braids. He laughed to himself. Feeling like a celebrity, similar to the rapper Ludacris, his smug laugh stole Connie's breath. So intimidating, like those feelings you have toward meeting Count Dracula. She bristled slightly, slowly packing her bag filled with beauty products and hair equipment. She was intimidated by him but the money he would pay transcended her fear.

Her anxiety level was understood considering his reputation as a vampire, blood-sucking pimp, a villain who spoke charmingly, but inwardly what he commanded can only be accomplished through his inhuman behavior toward women.

"I look so damn handsome; love this new hair style." Dupree simpered. "This took longer than I expected, but something like this was worth the wait."

"Glad you like it, sir," Connie replied.

"Baby, just call me Dupree… drop that sir shit," he laughed.

Connie shrugged. "Okay then, its Dupree," she said with a teeny-weeny giggle.

"Here is a grand for your work." Dupree handed her ten one-hundred-dollar bills.

"Wow!" Both shock and surprised moved across her face.

"I'm generous regardless of what you heard about me."

Connie said nothing.

Dupree followed the young red bone, black woman as he walked her to the front door of his stylist condo in the Oakland Hills. She was sexy, a trait to her advantage. Her hairy legs caught his attention—that feature was a turn on to him. Her artistic nature also appealed to him. He loved red bones, light-skinned black women and Asians, especially Filipinas, the ones that were born in the Philippines.

She was wearing a brown leather jacket; a heavy wool short green skirt and her hair was casually tied back in a ponytail out of the way.

Connie smiled as Dupree opened the door.

"You have my number, just call me," she said.

"I will. Sooner or later."

"Uh huh. Okay."

"You did a great job, baby."

"Thank you..." she hesitated. "Mr. Dupree."

He laughed. "Yeah, no 'sir' business."

Connie nodded. "Right, no sir."

"Right."

As she walked to her sleek black Hyundai Santa Cruz truck, he smiled that nothing spoils a gorgeous little broad than an unflattering shape beneath her attire. Connie had curves, giving her an enviable hourglass figure.

"Damn," he thought to himself, "I might get after her later."

Closing the door, he walked over and slumped onto his white leather couch. He then turned on an old Nancy Wilson album while watching the gusty winds from his large bay living room window move across the hillside of the Oakland Bay area.

He was exhausted but not too tired to recall his journey up to this point. Sipping a glass of Remy Martin fine cognac, he closed his eyes taking a long, heavy sigh shifting his mind back to his last day on the Oakland Police Department.

What seemed like a hundred years ago, Dupree Evangelista Howard momentarily stared at the cold, light green wall in his lilliputian office inside the Vice Control Unit of the Oakland Police Department (OPD). He groaned softly. The final piece of his personal property was stuffed inside a worn black leather briefcase. This was his last, or rather, final moments with the police department. After seven years on the force, nearly two years working in Vice Control, this was his last day. He fumed, straining to withhold a lone tear, that formed in his right eye. He sniffed, holding it, not wanting his soon-to-be ex-partners in Vice to witness his sadness. A light green envelope was the only remaining item on the bland metal desktop. Inside the envelope contained a letter of employment termination from the Oakland City Human Resources Director. Dupree was fired for being untruthful about his relationship with a well-known drug dealer and pander of prostitution who ironically was his cousin and best friend.

Dupree loved being a black cop and equally proud of being a member of the Oakland Black Officer Association (OBOA). It was 1972. Dupree was among 17 black police officers hired on the force, through a Federal Court Consent Decree, requiring the City of Oakland Police Department to hire blacks and other minorities over a ten-year period to reflect the ever-changing minority population in the city of Oakland.

He remembered how proud his Puerto Rican mother, Catalita, was in his decision in not returning to the southside of Chicago after his discharge from the Navy. On the other hand, his father, a Chicago crane operator at a steel plant, wasn't that jubilant. His dad was promoted to foreman, the first black supervisor in the history of a strong union organization operating in the plant. Sylvester Dwayne Howard dreamed of a future for Dupree somewhere in the company's newly formed "Minority Intern" Management Program, especially after Dupree's honorable discharge from the Navy. He was a decorated Vietnam War veteran, a Hospital Corpsmen, the Navy's specialty technicians who provided medical care; eventually saving three Army servicemen's lives during a 1968 pre-dawn Tet Offensive attack while serving with the 1st Marine Division at Da Nang, Vietnam. He was later awarded a Bronze Star with a citation for heroic act and bravery.

Pouring his second glass of Remy Martin, Dupree sighed continuing to revisit those painful moments on the police department. His thoughts were fixated about his zigzagging past. He understood the depth of his mother's disappointment about his termination while restraining his temper toward his father's condescending and judgmental tone. This was a new life experience for him. It crushed his tactfulness in wanting to navigate in two worlds—one of being a cop (he loved both the power and the authority) and then the admiration of being a pimp (he loved both the lifestyle and the money). Both worlds collided with his termination.

From a little white lie to a full scale, elaborate deceitful coverup, his relationship with a known, seedy, and occasional menace to the community drug-dealer was exposed; hence, his termination was recommended by the Oakland Police Chief without an afterthought.

Even the OBOA's and NAACP's appeals fell on mute ears. Dupree would soon be ancient history on the police force.

His final regret was leaving the brothers and sisters of the OBOA. Although, he was committed to many OBOA's community programs like the Poor People's Picnic, food drives, and mentoring young black Oakland Youths; somehow, in a manner which was difficult for him to actualize in his mind, it was the 'street game' that he craved leaving his commitment toward the organization, and community far behind.

The Nancy Wilson album ended breaking away Dupree's thoughts about his experience on the Oakland Police Department. There was a cold, eerie silence in the room. It was 8:30 pm and soon he would be in full activation checking on his women. Finishing up his third shot of Remy Martin, it was time to finalize his high by smoking a blunt; no cocaine tonight. It was Friday and his women must be in full operation getting paid. He would not tolerate any inappropriate behavior or hear whispers about how he mistreats some of them. Interwoven in his mind, these were his bitches. He took care of them, provided for their needs—food, shelter, clothes, safety and welfare. Regardless of what anyone thought, this was a business—the oldest profession in the world. There was a demand for sex, and he had the product to satisfy that need. As a manager of services, he would insure at all costs that his product was going to be protected and customers who defied the street norms would be dealt with in any manner necessary.

Gone were the days of a mindset of law and order—he evolved into a 'no nonsense' street vampire who created his own idiom of how he conducted business.

Dupree slowly closed his eyes. His thoughts now swung back to the Oakland Police Department and his termination. Without considering whether he would pursue his career at another police department, the termination left him in a mental straight jacket, squeezing his only sense of reasoning. All thoughts now were to vacate Oakland as quick as possible. During his moments of deliberation, an epiphany struck him like a bolt of lightning. Without a plan, without an itinerary, he was returning to the Philippines and to Olongapo City, a large province of Zambales just north of Manila, that nestled just outside the Navy Base where he was previously stationed during his tour in the Navy.

The Navy Base was located adjacent to Subic Bay where both merchant vessels and a plethora of military ships docked, unloading tens of thousands of civilians and military personnel to canvas the local bars, whorehouses, along of string of seedy streets and other establishments in Olongapo.

Fresh in his mind was his arrival at the Olongapo Bus Station, riding from Manila on a non-air-conditioned Victory Liner bus. Stepping off the bus, Dupree was feeling distastefully icky and sweaty from the dry humidity, but his discomfort quickly evaporated when he saw his old Filipino buddy, Jimmy "Glow Boy" Salabao.

Glow Boy was a diminutive, narcissistic sociopath with a Napoleonic complex, self-centered with a volcanic temper and very violent. He was slim; not skinny but extremely fit. He wore white khaki pants, Mango designer shirt with large black and gray leaf design and white patent leather shoes—nothing cheap about his attire. His hair was sleek black, curly and combed back in a Cuban style. He worn light blue designer sunglasses and a Borsalino Federico Panama white Straw hat.

He was born on Samal Island, a large island across from Davao City on Mindanao, the largest southern island in the Philippines, about 360 miles south of Manila.

Glow Boy was a high school dropout. He later became an errand boy for a local drug dealer selling Shabu, crystal methamphetamine, on Samal Island and Davao City. Later, he would be arrested in the Baback Barangay (local neighborhood) district inside a small known, dope house along with the drug dealer and several other occupants.

Without having a private lawyer and no ability to pay his bail, Glow Boy was eventually transferred to the South Cotabato Rehabilitation and Detention Center, located in the south Cotabato province Soccsksargen region of Mindanao. In reality, there was nothing remotely 'rehabilitating' inside the Cotabato prison. The center was severely overcrowded, food was crappy and inmates slept in shifts on hot concrete floors. The place was hot or extremely hotter—nothing in between. It was a gang and drug-infested center.

It was there he gained the nickname of "Glow Boy" because of his small statute and swift movements like fireflies that glow. He grew up hastily in the center, daily surviving by peddling drugs and, as a sex worker, willing and ready to do anything for the right price.

His homosexual activity made him a small fortune by Filipino standards, nearly 350,000 peso, or slightly more than 6,400 US dollars. After ten years of courtroom continuances, a prolonged motion for his freedom was gained by a persistent public defender who finally obtained relief from the Philippines Supreme Court which swiftly ordered his immediate release as a result of violation of his due process and a lack of a speedy trial.

His parents were now deceased; his lone younger sister was estranged working as a nanny somewhere in Dubai and an older brother now worked as a construction laborer for a local company in Davao City. Their small house was destroyed seven years ago from a violent storm that struck the Island. There was virtually nothing left for Glow Boy to return to on Samal Island.

Armed with a small fortune, by Philippines standards, Glow Boy headed north to Olongapo where he heard stories that the hustle of American service men by local bar girls and prostitutes was where he needed to be.

After three years living and hustling in Olongapo bars, hotels, and seedy street locations, he became a pimp with a specialty of hustling young, horny American sailors and marines anxious to fuck young Filipinas. These women were recruited from small, rural and isolated provinces near the city, The women were young, naïve and dirt poor. Many of them were underage girls that were sex trafficked to the city under the shield of older women who helped escort and later groom them into the sex business. This was earning Glow Boy a small fortune and mini sex empire.

It was during this period that Dupree met Glow Boy inside the Supreme Destiny Club that held a reputation of having underaged Filipinas work as bar girls and escorts. Dupree was a frequent customer.

Smiling as both men walked toward each other outside the Victory Liner bus station entrance, Dupree said, "Maayong Buntag! (Good morning) Kamusta!" while hugging Glow Boy.

Stepping backward, Glow Boy let go a loud, hyena cackle; his eyes beaming with unfettered delight. "Maayong Buntag sad. Maayo ang tanan! Dugay nata wala ng kahimamat." (Good morning to you, too. All is well. It has been so long since the last time we spoke.) Glow Boy laughed, "So, you still remember how to speak Cebuano?"

"Hell no," Dupree giggled. "Man, just to say hello." Both men laughed and embraced each other again.

For Dupree, this is a reunion made in heaven with Glow Boy. He previously supplied young, greenhorn white and black Navy sailors to his young prostitutes on a regular basis.

These young men were beyond horny and eager for sex and drugs. Dupree had become a panderer and loan shark working in tandem with Glow Boy. His relationship was tightly shielded from the Navy Base officials since he always worked with sailors who came from ships and wasn't familiar with naval base personnel. He wore civilian clothing to mask his identity and his customers usually assumed he was a black American citizen just residing in Olongapo. He was known as Fuzzy at the time.

That was then... now was a different story. Dupree wasn't in the Navy anymore, and Glow Boy's business had flourished. However, there was a huge difference between the two—Dupree was an ex-cop fired from OPD but, Glow Boy had become a lethal monster with a reputation of sex trafficking, beating women, and even murder. It was the latter part of his behavior that created Dupree's departure from the Philippines after 18 months later and returning to Oakland, California.

Dupree still remembered that unusually cold, rainy night on the mud-soaked street named Star Dust Way on the west side of Olongapo. How could he ever forget that stormy, windy night visiting Glow Boy at his green, bungalow house? Glow Boy was uptight, visually upset by something. Any means of verbal engagement just wasn't coming out of him. They were alone—an aberration of not having a few women over for some kinky and marathon sex should have been a clue to him.

They consumed a six pack of San Miguel beer. Dupree wanted to avoid drinking anymore. For some reason, too many San Miguel beers, gave him a healthy, all day long case of diarrhea. Glow Boy polished off the second six pack and was now elevating his already high level of intoxication by taking out his meth pipe and smoking some Shabu.

Dupree grimaced. "Damn Glow, you trying to kill yourself tonight. You geeking already man. That shit—mixing it with alcohol is going to fuck you up."

Glow Boy sat in silence taking another hit, then another and, finally, a long hit off his Shabu pipe.

"I want you to come with me tonight."

Dupree shrugged. "Tonight? In all this fucking rain?"

"Yep."

"What's up?"

"I gotta see someone."

"Who?"

"I need to pay a bill."

"Can't it wait?"

"Naw."

Dupree sighed.

"You coming with me brother?" Glow Boy asked.

"Yeah, can't let you go by yourself in this condition."

"Okay, give me a minute. I am going to the comfort room. You drive my motorcycle."

"Sure, sure! No problem." Dupree replied.

Dupree's eyes followed Glow Boy as he staggered from the comfort room to his bedroom. Without knowing why, an ominous feeling surged up inside him. Most of the night, Glow Boy's face was flushed; his mood was somber. He spoke intermittently not constantly to him. He rarely behaved like this. Was it a problem with a whore? If so, he always eliminated those issues quickly.

In spite of his (small) frame, Dupree had seen Glow Boy in action—he was a fierce fighter, an ass kicker, with an amazing level of endurance. He was a 'pint size hurricane'—everything would come all at once, full speed, nonstop, with tornado like force and ending only when he stopped. He was a Manny Pacquaio on incredulous steroids. It took only one physical encounter with Glow Boy and no man or woman ever wanted another one. His ass whippings were simply legendary.

Returning from his bedroom, he was now dressed in a black leather jump suit. He motioned to Dupree to grab the motorcycle helmets.

About five minutes later, Dupree was driving Glow Boy's black Harley-Davidson Fat Boy, his pride and joy. He purchased it from the Harley-Davidson dealer in Manila.

Now following Glow Boy's directions, about 25 minutes later on the outskirts of the city, he summoned Dupree to drive slowly and then stop requesting he keep the engine still running.

"Whatcha doin, my man?" Dupree asked.

"I going to that house," Glow pointing to a white, two-story house.

"Ooookay," Dupree responded slowly.

Indeed, this was causing him a great deal of mental anguish, unclear what Glow Boy was about to do. While driving, he attempted to clarify in his mind what was happening. He bristled, realizing he was a foreigner visiting the Philippines on a tourist visa and his association with Glow Boy came with much risk. But now, this was a far different story, a situation and drama he wanted to avoid.

He watched Glow Boy's features grow smaller as he advanced closer to the two-story house. The rain was now pounding hard against his helmet visor, obscuring his vision. He remembered his head was hurting from his heart pounding so hard against his chest. Lifting up the helmet visor, he wiped his face attempting to refocus on Glow Boy's movements. Then suddenly, he saw Glow Boy, as he yelled and kicked in the front door, along with four loud gunshots—boom… boom… boom… boom. The flash from each gunshot lit up the front room as though lightening had struck it. He then heard an ear-piercing scream followed by Glow Boy's maniacal voice, "Putang-Ina Mo" (mother fucker)," he yelled. "Putang-Ina Mo," Glow Boy repeated, sloughing in the mud away from the house. A wave of screams and shrieks were punctuating through the rain. Dupree could feel the horror Glow Boy had just imposed inside that house.

By now, Glow Boy was huffing and puffing as he leaped on the back of the motorcycle. A large clump of mud slapped Dupree across his face from Glow Boy's boots.

"You mother fucker," Dupree screamed. "You stupid little shit." Turning the motorcycle around. "Who did you just shoot, you crazy, sick fuck?" Dupree asked while now driving like a maniac leaving the scene.

"I killed that mother fucker and those two nasty bitches... fuck em." Glow Boy angrily snapped.

Several days later, Dupree was still mentally unsettled by Glow Boy's unthinkable and monstrous behavior. He flinched, trying to process inside his mind straight answers, something to make sense out of something senseless. He knew there were reasons to be nervous. He was an ex-cop. He recognized the investigating resources available from the local police, including the Philippines' National Bureau of Investigation and there was always the FBI and certainly DHS.

In his haste to leave, Glow Boy swore there were no survivors or witnesses to connect them. Them! He remembered that word so thoroughly etched inside his head. He recalled when they returned to Glow Boy's house, he released a verbal tirade, with uncalculated fury toward him.

"You meant to... you meant to," Dupree screamed. "Stupid shit over two funky ass bitches?" he fumed. "You got too many bitches already. Your ego that fucked up? So, they left you for another pimp? You got dozens coming from these dirt poor provinces. Fucks wrong with you, getting me involved with your dumb shit?"

Glow Boy said nothing. He knew getting Dupree, a foreigner involved in his personal grievances was a mistake—perhaps more than a mistake. Murder was no blunder in judgment.

Days later, he still remembered their brief conversation as he retrieved his luggage from the trunk of Glow Boy's car in front of the Manila International Airport.

"You going back to Oakland, brother?" Glow Boy asked.

"Hell naw, I'm heading to Sousa, Dominica Republic. I gotta buddy who lives there. Maybe I might swing over to Haiti from there. I know some brothers living over there, too," Dupree said casually guarding his secrecy from Glow Boy about his whereabouts.

After changing his phone number, it was one afternoon, six weeks separated from the ghastly ordeal in Olongapo, did Dupree discover in the Manila Times newspaper, a small, almost inconsequential article, which read:

SUSPECT FOUND DEAD IN OLONGAPO MURDERS

"Suspect in the Olongapo murders of 3, two women and one man, body was discovered by a bar owner in a ditch behind his bar yesterday afternoon. The man identified as the suspect in the slayings as being James (Jimmy) Gabriel Salabao AKA Glow Boy, had been beaten and shot several times. He was identified by a female victim before she died as the shooter. A second suspect is still at large and the authorities are still continuing their investigation."

Re-reading the article a third time, a flicker of sorrow penetrated into his soul. Glow Boy was his close friend, confidante, a mentor in the game to him. Violence was a part of it, maybe not murder, but he understood the unfiltered, twisted mind of Glow Boy. His wayward 'real life run' for revenge on this matter was a fatal mistake.

Dupree's eyes suddenly opened from the piercing sound of his alarm clock. It was now 11:30 pm breaking him away from his dream.

About forty-five minutes later, he was driving down San Pablo Avenue heading for the Roman Hotel, about three blocks north of the historic California Hotel and his favorite nightclub, the Zanzibar Room—a pimp, whores and hustlers' hotspot.

But unlike the California Hotel, the seedy and funky Roman Hotel was a cheap spot and much desirable location for his business to operate. His parked his red Lexus sedan by the side entrance near the back of the hotel. Now walking down, a narrow alley leading to the back door entrance, he bristled momentarily from the cold winds that whipped through the alley from the East Bay, directly across from San Francisco.

He rotated his broad shoulders, pulling up his leather collar around his neck. He grimaced; his body sloughed up against a dark barren wall inside a narrow corridor.

His nostrils contracted reflectively from the potent smell of dry urine and vomit stains that seemed to be conspiratorially consuming the entire building. He stepped back and turned around raising one eyebrow superciliously. For a brief moment, a tidal wave of disillusionment engulfed him, a soul-searching thought that perhaps there is a better life. Maybe he should have tried to be a cop again, even something far better than fucking around with these crazy-ass bitches. He sighed momentarily feeling some regret for not following his mother's advice. There was a period before joining the Navy that he amused himself about attending Ohio State University on a football scholarship. He was a tremendous running back and made the all-city team in Chicago when he played for the South Shore High School. On more than one occasion, college football scouts told him perhaps he was the best running back in the entire state of Illinois.

Dupree permitted himself a disquieting smile. Although he loved football and police work, neither was his calling. He was better navigating the streets of Oakland and the East Bay areas.

Suddenly, a sharp pain rotated over his toes. His face twisted in anguish. He returned from his abbreviated daydream and now refocused on his business. For the next few minutes, he was concentrating on what Sable was doing in room 107.

His mind was now spinning, wondering why she was taking so long to serve her trick.

This was the part he hated about new broads, especially a young, white cunt fresh out of Connecticut, almost like a welfare case. She was a red-head, youthful and would sell twice as much ass as his other four women combined. There was a premium on white pussy, especially some tight, wet ass that a motherfucker would abuse unless there was some control. Such arrogance wouldn't be tolerated by him. He was fully cognizant of every complexity of the vast and time-consuming business of pimping.

However, he never regarded his lascivious occupation as pandering but rather a social facilitator of pleasure for both men and women. He often delighted himself by comparing his business with the infamous gangster, Alphonse Gabriel Capone, better known as 'Al Capone', the notorious mobster who operated in Chicago in the 1930's and 1940's, running gambling, bootlegging rackets, loan sharking, and prostitution. Dupree remembered during a United States Senate Hearing on organized crime and Capone's activities, he always chuckled at Capone's response to the question of what was his line of business and Capone would reply, "I'm in the entertainment business. I simply give the public what they want." He frequently subscribed to Capone's noted theory by satisfying the public craving for sex.

Moments later, he took a long drag off a filtered, Marlboro cigarette, another and still another one. He then shivered. His mouth now quirked in annoyance as he continued to stare at room 107. At first, he told himself to not be pessimistic. She was a new bitch, and at seventeen years old, perhaps wasn't experienced tricking or following his instruction on point, nor was her alleged experience convincing him at the moment. Initially, he had mixed feelings about a white gal and a minor at that—something that, indisputably, would create some problems for him with his former Vice Control colleagues. Most of the time, they turned their heads and allowed him to operate and make tons of cash. But, a white girl, and minor at that, was now a great risk. But in spite of the risk, he weighed the results and the bottom line was this bitch was receiving cash faster than an ATM machine. That was enough to take the risk from any entanglement with his former colleagues and especially the brothers and sisters who were members of the OBOA.

Finally, after nearly fifteen minutes, the door swung slowly open a few inches and abruptly stopped. Surprised, it was the trick. Dupree's eyes darted maniacally past the large, black man's frame, attempting to locate Sable's silhouette while picking objects out of the gloom inside the dark room.

For a brief moment, the man's eyes narrowed with suspicion. Dupree sensed the heavy-jowled, brawny black man had been caught off guard. He was confused and tensed as he stared at Dupree. It was perhaps understandable. He thought they were alone, isolated while he exceeded the consumption of his lustful contract—something that neither party had agreed with from the beginning.

"You must be her pimp or something," he said rather curt, almost to a point of nastiness.

Dupree hesitated a brief moment. "Whatcha t'ank?" he answered.

Tossing the cigarette to the floor, his mind hardened while he slowly stepped on the cigarette butt, pressing the right heel of his shoe tightly on it while slowly twisting his shoe on its side to side. He was tense now. Sable had yet to emerged from inside the room.

"I-I-I just wanna...," his voice stopped in mid-sentence when Dupree edged closer to him, so close now that he could smell the stale odor of vodka and cigarettes reeking from inside his mouth oozing between his butter scotch teeth.

"Where is she?" Dupree asked, his eyes flashed with anger.

Before the large man realized what was happening to him, Dupree had quickly unbuttoned the top three buttons on his gray overcoat.

"What's up my nigga?" the man asked weakly, his eyes drifting down at Dupree's waistband.

Dupree waved off all further questions with a preemptory gesture. His right hand was settled tightly on his Browning 9mm automatic. He was now past the moment of verbal exchanges and other nebulous inquiries. This mother-fucker had interfered with a business commodity, an investment, the type that would cause him to quickly extinguish this miserable bastard's life with malice afterthought.

On impulse, Dupree said, "Step away from the mother-fuckin door. I'll only tell you once," he said clenching his teeth.

Dupree felt no compunction, no hesitation, and, above all, no remorse. He now seemed repelled by the man's despicable sight.

The stocky, bulldog-like man's eyes darted back and forth… back and forth… and slowly, very slowly, he backpedaled softly away from the door. There was a wounded look in his eyes. His face flushed with worriment, reeling from the prospect of how Dupree would react when he entered the insignificant compartment.

Edging closer toward the door's entrance, Dupree hesitated slightly. He felt a perspicacity of superstition. It was a sudden brainwave, something that raced inside his mind that this would be the way he might die one day. Dying in some nasty-ass, flea bitten, hotel room where God had long since closed HIS eyes and sealed HIS ears from the Sodom and Gomorrah type behavior of those crying out for mercy and forgiveness.

With his arms extending outward, a sudden stab of anxiety formed inside his stomach. It was the gun. His eyes stared catatonically at the veins protruding from Dupree's clenched fist which now circled completely around the butt of the gun.

Trembling, he tried to suppress an all too incriminating smile. "Everythin is alright. I mean we just had a little misunderstanding, but the lady is alright, ain't ya Mssssss?"

Dupree did not answer immediately. His eyes followed the beefy man until the wall abruptly stopped his back pedaling shuffle. He shook his head miserably, pointing toward the bed. "Look at her, she's okay. Just look at her on the bed, man," he mumbled.

Dupree was seething. From the corner of his right eye, he caught the profile of Sable who was sitting on the edge of the bed. A sense of excitement filled the air.

There was a soft moan, a whimper followed by several quick moments of heavy heaves… up and down… up and down… up and down and then she spoke with a deepening hue of shame. "He tried to choke me," she sobbed softly. "Just because I refused to give him a blow job. I told him it was going to cost him one hundred dollars more," she said with a hitch in her voice.

Dupree shook his head, turning evenly at the large man. "Get your clothes on. Wait for me outside," he said to Sable in a voice as cold as death.

Recognizing where these moments perhaps were going, Sable in a quavering voice said, "Let's just go, I'm okay…"

Dupree was infuriated by her statement. He slowly turned squarely facing her. He clamped and unclamped his teeth, a wave of impatience formed inside his mind. He then smiled spastically, "Bitch, did you hear what I just said?" waving his finger at her. "Get your fuckin shit on and wait for me outside."

"Man, I don't want no trouble," the man cried, his eyes widened in alarm.

Dupree then shouted, "Get your ass outta here, now!" His voice now raised several intervals. Sable's cumbersome movements were now a distraction. Her reservation perhaps softened the moment, maybe even softened his undeniable thoughts, thoughts advancing rapidly toward her abusive customer that he required a thorough and convincing pistol whipping.

Grabbing her thin, paperweight jacket, Sable quickly crept between the two men, wincing slightly, her face ashen with a lost expression. She momentarily glanced at the stranger, embarrassed about not handling the situation well. She then looked at Dupree and was slightly mesmerized by the intensity of his gaze. This was a bad omen she thought slipping away into the hallway.

Closing the door carefully behind him, Dupree was angry. He half turned, facing his barrel-chested, roly poly adversary. He looked larger now, much larger, maybe weighing three hundred pounds, more like a diminutive sumo wrestler, a World Wrestling Entertainment wannabe. At any rate, the brawny man outweighed him by nearly seventy-five pounds.

Nonetheless, the stranger's size was disregarded by him. His undisciplined behavior created his own detriment. Nobody fucked with his women especially a premium piece of ass like Sable. He had some extraordinary plans for her and no son-of-a-bitch was going to screw them up.

Suddenly, the man looked him in the eye. Seemingly almost as if he were clairvoyant, the man sensed Dupree unwell intentions and bolted toward him reaching for his waistband. The moment was electrifying. Dupree's heart pounded quickly against his chest; blood surged to his fists. He winced, side-stepping the man's bulldog charge immediately recognizing he was trying to get his gun.

"Mother-fucker," Dupree bellowed ferociously.

The man spoke in ragged bursts, struggling to grab the smaller man. With lighting swiftness, Dupree pulled the Browning from his waistband. Meanwhile, spasm of wild fright raced across the man's face. Desperation! His eyes blinked excessively reaching simultaneously for the gun. His voice strained, half pleading, half defiant, with his teeth grinding. He appeared delirious as he struggled to grab Dupree's right hand.

Dupree's football and Tae Kwon Do skills and instincts never left him. With insane swiftness, he fell backwards giving himself enough time to click off the safety. It was apparent, with the stranger's immense chest and shoulders, he was too powerful for him to outwrestle. In a millisecond, the man lunged toward him… a shot rang out… BAMB!!!

The bullet struck the man in his right chest area hurling his Amazonian body across the bed and slamming him hard to the floor with a loud thump!

He was grunting; his face convulsed in pain. A large spurt of blood seeped through his thick, green sweater quickly flowing down the center of his body. His rheumy eyes were glazed and a thick clot of dark red blood oozed from the side of his mouth. The man was stunned but only for a few seconds.

"Help meeeeeeee," his voice groaned with a nasal whine. "Pleaseeeeeee, somebody call me an ambulance, please!"

Meanwhile, Sable raced inside the room, her eyes brimming with tears.

"What happened?" she sobbed shaking uncontrollably, her face glazed with shock.

Dupree sprang across the bed, undaunted about the shooting or the wounded stranger's pleas. Crouching beside the man, he ignored the feeble gesture the man weakly gave while ruffling through his trousers pockets. There was no connection to this man. His somewhat inhuman appearance completely blurred Dupree's thoughts.

Sable looked quizzical. Her cheeks bloated suddenly as if she were holding back vomit. Dupree quickly stood up, his face puffed up with self-importance, stuffing several bills inside his coat pocket. His eyes narrowed with disdain thoroughly believing this bastard had what was coming to him. It's the game, he thought. Just Vampire shit!

He then grabbed Sable and, with a quick wipe with his handkerchief on the door handle, he hurled her puny ass down the hallway and out the back door, battling forward through the cold wind and now rain down the side entrance and inside his Lexus and off they went.

Moments later, the Oakland Police and ambulances sirens broke through the crisp winter night breaking past the howling winds off the East Bay. It was now early Saturday morning—payday weekend! The whores, hustlers, homosexuals, transgenders, dope sellers, thieves, hooligans, and other social misfits were all collectively deposited down the stripe of San Pablo Avenue waiting for that one successful encounter to play the game with all types of men. Those who frequently used their ghetto visas to escape from their sleepy, suburban areas of the East Bay, all point toward Sacramento and as far as San Jose, craving to satisfy that single-minded fascination of fucking a Black, White, Mexican, Asian whore; or buying some weed or coke; or getting ridiculously humped to a fare-thee well by some young black stud. This was game night, the San Pablo and Shattack Avenues would roll out the red carpet for its guests. The hustling spots were non-discriminatory. Everyone was welcome... welcome to receive its welcoming reception of urban hospitality; however, in the game, anything goes, and the district's legal disclaimer was always to be Held Harmless for the consequences that resulted for anyone playing the game. The night was too busy, too unperturbed, too unassuming, and too uncaring about a wayward gunshot on the first floor in room 107 in the Roman Hotel.

Nearly an hour later, Sable took a deep sigh. Her enthusiasm about the business had wavered. She had never seen anyone shot before. Trembling, "My God," she thought, "what if he dies?"

Dupree was nonchalant about the event. She could hear him verbally chastising Cookie about his money. She was real short—four hours of whoring and with only two hundred dollars? Dupree was pissed. They were now outside of Smitty's bootleg café.

"Where's mah money, bitch?"

"That's it."

Dupree shrugged. "I know you bought some coke."

"I swear."

"Don't swear. I told ya about fuckin off mah money. I gonna find out and if ya bought some coke, that's your ass—you know that."

"Uh huh."

"So, I'm gonna ask you again. Did you buy some coke?"

Cookie's eyes were glazed. She steadied herself, leaning back against his Lexus. She slowly brushed back her blonde wig. Her body stiffening in apprehension. She gave a sidelong glance at Sable who was now looking at her with suspicious bewilderment.

Cookie's nose wrinkled up in disgust. "What's that tramp looking at?" she said with a sneer.

"Never mind her," Dupree replied looking wildly at her. "Where's mah money?" he repeated while they all walked inside Smitty's café.

Cookie shrugged. She was not an ordinary whore. She was a clever whore—bold, treacherous and with a unique element of ruthless in her veins. At thirty-eight years old, she was perhaps his most versatile whore, willing to do anything—things most prostitutes would never consider. She had a hard look on her face; a serious look about getting the money. She was a big, red bone who was Dupree's first woman, the one that got him over in the game. She recruited Roxie and Pam and hustled tens of thousands of dollars for him. However, three years ago things changed, their relationship changed, so it was easy for her to find a new crutch and now she had become a real coke fiend.

This scene with Dupree made her feel sick. Breathing shallowly, she was extremely annoyed. Her brow wrinkled in vexation. She took a long sip from her Long Island Iced Tea.

"Damn, you really sweatin the fuck out of me."

Dupree winced. His lips twitched; this bitch was really making him angry. It had been at least four months since the last time he beat her ass about screwing with his money. Perhaps she needed a reminder.

Cookie forced a smile. She had enough sense not to lie. She then swallowed dryly and said, "I owe Sneaky for two half ounces of coke."

"Two half ounces," Dupree hissed.

"Yeah, two half ounces," she repeated.

There was a crazed look on his face. Dupree's lips pursed with suppressed fury. He then looked at his watch. It was nearly 2:30 am; the early morning hours were just getting started.

He then walked over grabbing her right arm like a ragdoll. Immediately, Cookie tried to resist by pulling back as her breath quickened. "Whatcha doin? L-let my arm go!" she cried out, her voice edged with tension. "Let my arm go," she demanded.

Suddenly, he threw her to the ground, leaping on top of her, and pressing his knees in her abdomen and half his weight on her lower torso. "Who ya talkin to bitch?" he spoke with brutal detachment.

There was now an uncanny silence in Smitty's café, a small, but cozy after hour basement juke-joint where many of the pimps, hustlers and prostitutes hung out after the regular nightclubs closed.

Cookie was stunned. She knew nobody in Smitty's was going to interfere with Dupree's business. Besides, she was his bitch—she knew it, the police knew it, and everybody on the blocks knew it. She was part of the stable; a reality that became apparent as her eyes watched his face turned red then purple with rage.

Dupree moved closer to her, leaning down by her right ear. His eyes narrowed, the muscles in his face were tensed. Clenching his teeth, he spoke deliberately, "Bitch, if you ever—ever front me off again, I'll skin your fuckin ass," he said, his voice dripping with contempt. "I'll have your funky ass chopped to pieces and thrown into the Bay. Your momma will never find you and I'll chase your fuckin soul straight to Hell—to Hell, bitch, cause you'll still owe me. You understand, bitch? You fuckin owe me," he said crudely.

Cookie was having a difficult time trying to absorb the unimaginable rage Dupree was displaying. Although this situation was unnecessary, even unthinkable, since he never displayed this type of temper toward her in public before, somehow she sensed something else was bothering him.

Frowning, Cookie nodded her head wearily, "You know I'll get the money, baby. Don't I always come through? You take care of me, and I take care of you."

Dupree looked around the seedy basement joint recognizing he had lost his composure. His eyes widened innocently. He was too embarrassed, too ignorant, and too simple-minded to apologize to her. Despite his law-enforcement background, his previous compassion for people seemed, at times, to disappear and this moment was handled precisely the same way Glow Boy had frequently beat and taunted his young women in local bars in Olongapo. Dupree enjoyed those moments.

He knew all too well that she needed help with her cocaine addiction. At one point, she loved him and the game. She had always made lots of money and then stood by while she became secondary to his elaborate taste and the other women in his life, specifically, another woman like his new, white cunt.

He stood up, quickly manicuring himself, or maybe his transparent image in front of the on-lookers, many who were high and drunk as a 'brewer's fart'.

He then motioned to Cookie whose face was now unidentifiable; her features fallen as she limped over toward him. Slightly embarrassed, he smiled at her. The palm on his left hand cupped her chin.

"Everything is okay baby. I gotta lot of pressure on me. Ya know, I just wanna do somethin special for everybody." He then let go a crafty smile. "Ya know I love you, and we gonna have it back, just like back in the day—you and me, baby." Leaning over, he kissed her on the cheek while working a sidelong gaze at Sable.

Brushing off his coat, he caught his reflection in a mirror hanging behind the bar. He then flashed a dirty little grin. "Ya'll go together, down at Club Zanzibar. I'll send some hunkies down there. Show Sable whata do, I'll be there later, gonna check on the others, okay?"

Cookie smiled back at him guardedly. "Alright baby, don't worry. I'm gonna make it up, I promise."

Dupree's smugness irritated Sable. Sensing her agitation and believing she was still concerned about the shooting; he reached inside his coat pocket and pull out a large roll of bills. In a mental state of satisfaction, his eyes crinkled mirthfully while he flipped several bills over, peeling them one by one. He hesitated momentarily, wondering if this was enough. He shrugged, "Here....this is part of the business at the Roman."

Sable frowned.

"That's okay."

"Whatcha mean?" Dupree snapped.

"I mean it's okay."

"No, it ain't okay—take it."

Immediately, Cookie was astute, realizing this moment had gone wrong between them. She took a deep breath while stretching her hand out, "Give it to me, I'll hold it for her."

Squinting, Sable looked at Cookie, recognizing her calculated intentions, she immediately dismissed this broken-down cow's benevolent attitude toward her.

"That's alright, I'll take it."

"Four hundred and twenty-five dollars—that's yours on that deal."

Cookie peered out of the corner of her eye. Her curiously had peaked about the business in the Roman Hotel. Ignoring Cookie's reaction and before another exchange occurred among them, Dupree's eyes narrowed speculatively. There was an impeccably dressed, middle-aged, white man with dark straight hair standing at the door's entrance. Both men exchanged questioning glances at each other. An unnatural quietness raced over the junk-joint. Nobody had seen this white dude before—maybe he was a trick, maybe he wanted to buy some dope or just maybe he was an Oakland cop. Everyone's mind rotated these thoughts inside their heads.

"Looka here, ya'll be cool, and gone out there—ya know what to do Cookie. I'll see ya later," Dupree said.

They hesitated, glancing at each other, then at the white dude and back at Dupree. By now, a surge of paranoia raced to every corner of the junk-joint. Someone needed to eventually satisfy the identity of this stranger before the situation became ominous. An impeccably dressed white man unescorted in this dive was like someone about to release the plague.

"Hey man—what's up?"

Dupree's question broke passed the repressive silence and dubious facial expressions. Someone, certainly anyone, had to settle the nerves of fidgety junkies, niggas with arrest warrants, dope dealers, hustlers, misfits, and opportunistic hardcore criminals willing to rob a misdirected, well-dressed white man whose curiosity made him vulnerable for the take.

Smiling, Dupree acknowledged the man by motioning him over to his table. For a few moments, he just stood there perhaps second-guessing himself about the unexpected reaction from the patrons in Smitty's joint especially from those individuals who were owlishly examining his face.

Dupree was puzzled. He scrutinized the man's thin features for clues, sensing something was wrong because Nicole wasn't with him. They dated for nearly four years.

Moments later, he was sitting across from Dupree. He gave him a wry smile. There was a look of voiceless appeal on his face. But before either man would speak to each other, a long legged, light skinned, freckled face black woman with almond-shaped eyes and nut-brown hair styled with several corkscrews curls, spoke to them from a bar stool. She wore a short, tight black dress that strained against her thunder thighs and curvaceous body. You could see her large breasts and sharp nipples pushing hard and erect against her bra. Her charcoal gray nylons accentuated her matching purple purse and shoes. She looked stylish, which complimented her sultry appearance, gazing at them.

You would have been a lunatic to believe she wasn't a terrific piece of ass.

She had been idly sitting at the bar, working a light trick or two—waiting for something to happen. Anything was possible. Hustlers were in and out. Maybe somebody needed a whore to flip a deal.

The conversation between Dupree and Cookie hadn't gone unnoticed by her.

She was curious about the exchange—not that she wanted to work for him but the lack of independence Cookie displayed. When matters cooled between them, she turned, smiled at the bartender, and said, "I need a pimp for that bullshit."

By now, she was also intrigued about the well-dressed white man sitting at the table with Dupree. Equally interested was a low-profile, haggard looking, young black man nursing a beer at the end of the bar. He was an undercover cop working for the Oakland Police Vice Control Unit who was assigned to the unit long after Dupree was terminated.

He was also a member of the OBOA, but Dupree had long since left the organization, and police work was no longer an interest to him. The cop was working Smitty's and assigned to investigate the activities of Dupree and several other known pimps and hustlers in the area. He was working the prostitution detail for nearly six months and his background cover was sealed by a local informant, who worked him into Smitty's juke-joint with several purchases of crack and cocaine from known drug dealers.

It was also during this precise moment, the woman, in her drunkenness, which slightly dulled her reasoning but also heightened her boldness about the stranger, did consider her bold move. She was certain Dupree was hustling him for some good action; maybe they could collaborate on a deal since he was in the for-sale business. Her inquiry was worth the risk, she reasoned.

For a minute of two, she finally combed over her scheme sipping the last of her Singapore Sling. "God this is so damn crazy," she groaned softly. Nevertheless, after the stranger sat across from Dupree, she quickly swiveled around on her bar stool stretching out her long legs and, moments later, she was standing in front of the two men.

"Excuse me," she said, with a tight smile. The white stranger immediately stood up, introducing himself to her, "My name is Dr. Thurston," he said quickly standing up. His commissure smile put her at ease. Walking around the table, he gently pulled out a chair for her.

"Please, take a seat."

"Thank you. My name is Ginger." She paused, glancing at Dupree's frigid stare. "Ginger Robertson, but everyone calls me Gingy, but you can call me whatever you like," she said flirtatiously, crossing her thick legs rocking the crossover leg toward him.

"Hmmmm. I'm thirsty. Would you like to buy me a drink? I hope I'm not interrupting?"

"My pleasure," Dr. Thurston said, with a boyish giggle. "Call the waitress. Order whatever is your pleasure."

"My pleasure," she repeated.

"That's right, your pleasure."

The strange, unusual behavior of the young woman caught Dupree by surprise. For a long time, Dr. Thurston, in reality, wasn't his real name. Although he was a prominent neurologist, his real name was Tennyson Grayline Morris, IV. He used Dr. Thurston to conceal his true identity in his association with Dupree and the women. This concealment was also maintained when he always used a rented, expensive SUV during his visiting time in Oakland.

Dr. Thurston was a weekly customer spending thousands of dollars monthly with Nicole.

He maintained a peculiar sexual need and she was successful in accommodating his unique request. Driving over from Redwood City, he was a highly successful neurologist with an upscale office in Palo Alto and hospital practice in the Kaiser Permanente Hospital in Redwood City. He met Nicole several years ago in San Francisco at the infamous "Hooker's Ball". For some unknown reason and the level of his prominence, Dupree could never fully comprehend how Dr. Thurston was so addictive with their relationship.

Occasionally, for months Nicole would never hear from him. He provided no method of contact with him, except a post office box, located in Redwood City. But as time went by, he would call her, sometimes behaving if a 'crisis' had struck him, desiring for them to meet again. Although he was married, he was somehow successful in taking Nicole on trips to Europe, South America and even on a safari in Kenya. Before then, Nicole suffered from aerophobia, but Dr. Thurston's money, compressed her fears of flying.

And, of course, Dupree experienced a windfall from this relationship which allowed him to live lavishly—cars, clothes, money, trips and the purchase of a sprawling, two level condo in a gated community in the Oakland Hills. He, along with Nicole, exploited his sexual weaknesses for her by manipulating ways to obtain tens of thousands from him.

Over the years and throughout his professional life, he was able to conceal his psychological disorder of having an Oedipus Complex, a strong sexual attraction of a boy to his mother with accompanying feelings of hostility toward his father. Nicole's sexual role-playing roles with him stimulated his sexual desires to new heights when he was with her.

His mother died ten years ago and his father moved to Sweden. He inherited nearly 650 million dollars from her estate. She was a wealthy San Francisco socialite belonging to the Maxwell House Coffee family tree. He was their only child.

After the third date with Nicole, she slowly understood how to enhance his sexual fantasy by playing the role of his mother. It was a stroke of genius by her which allowed her to continue to be Dupree's 'cash cow' with a steady flow of large amounts of cash.

While they talked, Dupree's eyes were blazing murderously at Gingy, "What's this bitch doin," he muttered to himself. The young woman's charm and pleasing personality was stimulating Dr. Thurston.

Dupree stared at her a long moment, searching her face and eyes, hoping they would make eye contact. His annoyance was soon obvious. The worse thing about him was his impatience and the rage that was connected to it. This bitch must be sleep-walking. Coming here and disrespecting him was something he intended to rectify, he reasoned.

Finally, Gingy turned, sensing Dupree was losing control of the situation and she might be in danger if she didn't put a spin on her visit.

"Can I have a smoke?" she asked, her face radiated with good cheer.

Dupree frowned.

"You can't support your own habit?" he asked, his voice tensed and hard.

Dr. Thurston spoke quickly, realizing the tension between them.

"I'll buy you some cigarettes."

"Why thank you, sir!" she smiled.

"You're welcome—what's your brand?"

"Newports... Newport long."

"You know smoking..."

"Yeah, yeah! I know—smoking is bad for your health, etcetera, etcetera," she sighed. "Trying to quit, but it's my nerves. My life is so damn crazy and a good smoke helps calm me down."

"Really?"

"Yeah, really, I'm nervous—really I am." she shrugged.

Meanwhile, Dupree shook his head. "Wonder where is Nicole?"

Dr. Thurston winced. "I don't know, that's why I came here looking for you. She wasn't at the apartment. I drove a few blocks but I didn't see her. I have called her several times and no answer. That's why I am here, thought she might be in Smitty's".

Dupree bristled, "She knows not to fuck up our arrangement with you. I mean, if she had a problem, she's supposed to holler at me."

"Maybe..." Gingy said.

"... maybe my black ass," Dupree interrupted. "Listen here you skank! After your cocktail, get your ass back over to your spot. You're disrespecting me and we don't do any business, unless..."

"Unless, what?" Gingy asked.

"Unless, you wanna be one of my bitches... part of the stable."

"Hell Nawwwww! What makes you think I would be interested in working for you?"

"It's simple bitch... to trick with my clientele—like the good doctor, that the bennies, BITCH!" he said, his voice lifting higher at the end.

Gingy sighed, turning to Dr. Thurston, "Thank you for the drink and cigarettes."

Dr. Thurston sat motionless; his eyes looked at Gingy's features. "You're welcome, Gingy. Maybe some other time, but I need him to find Nicole for me."

"Sure. Sure! That's cool," she said icily. She then stood up, tugging down her tight dress over her thighs. "My gracious," she sighed deeply. "I'm sorry for the interruption, maybe some other time."

"There won't be another time," Dupree snapped, leaning over toward her, lighting tapping his right index finger on the table. "I know this will be the last time, otherwise you might see a real, live vampire on your ass; and, you know what vampires do, don't you?" he asked, with his head shaking up and down, up and down at her.

"I'm gone," she said, walking away with a voluptuous sway.

Dupree then shrugged. "You gone back to the apartment; I'll find Nicole. There must be some mix-up or somethin, but whatever the fuck it is, I'll straighten everything out. She'll be at the apartment, I promise you that,"

Dr. Thurston nodded. "Okay," he said with a soft smile. "I know you would be able to take care of it."

"Don't I always?"

"You do."

Within seconds, both men walked slowly toward the front door. Dupree suddenly stopped and motioned to Dr. Thurston to continue on. "Go ahead, I'm comin."

He was now standing directly behind Gingy. She was suddenly fidgety, trying to clamp off those unwanted thoughts that something was about to occur between them.

Bristling slightly, her facial muscles twitched nervously. Their eyes stared evenly at each other from the mirror behind the bar.

"I'm sorry," she said, her voice cracking. Dupree's eyes took on a hunted look. He then moved closer to her, so close that she could smell the cognac and weed on his breath. She held her head back and winced, hunching up her right shoulder.

"Whatcha doin?" she asked weakly.

She could see the vein protruding in his jaw. "That's the first and last time with me, bitch. The next time, I'll make you disappear—like black magic. You history, bitch—I mean history. You understand me, red gal?" his voice dripping with hot spite.

Gingy shook her head. "Whata the hell is wrong with me?" she briefly thought. She shrugged; her eyes now surveying the room. "My bad, it wasn't cool. Not to worry about that ever happening again."

There was a remarkable silence that temporarily paralyzed the atmosphere in the juke-joint. It seemed to hold time hostage, punctuating the single moment in Gingy's display of disrespect toward Dupree. It was now apparent the residue of her conduct transformed the juke-joint into a peculiar intensity. It was almost seemed like everyone was holding their breath—waiting, just waiting with eyes dazzling, just waiting enthusiastically for the eruption of Dupree's anger to take the full measure of some real pain on a stupid ass, nickel and dime street walker.

"Break that bitch off," a female voice broke passed the silence.

"Fuck off that ho," another belligerent voice shot from the back.

Both remarks appeared to surge the growing hostility inside Dupree. His right hand slowly unbuttoned his last button on his overcoat, a vein on left side of his neck was pulsating and swelling dangerously.

"My man… my man," a thick voice surfaced from the end of the bar. It was George Smith, the owner of Smitty's. "Everything is cool, the little lady had too much to drink, played you too close, it won't happen again. Go ahead, take care of your business. She won't do that shit ever again, you got my word on it, okay?"

There was a monstrous glare in Dupree's eyes. He was contemplating inflicting some major injuries to Gingy; however, Smitty's voice had soothed his maniac anxiety about seriously harming her. Crazy!!! The entire scene was so absurd, but so was the nature of street justice and the consequences of someone interfering with someone else's business, especially Dupree's business.

Dupree's black eyes lifted off Gingy's medium shoulders and fell toward Smitty's face. He caught himself. Buttoning up his overcoat, he meticulously stepped backward. His eyes slowly raked the entire room and then returned to George Smith.

He then said indignantly, "You just saved this skank's life."

George Smith shrugged, "I know... thank you. Something like that to happen in my spot would close me down, I can't have OPD, on my ass and they would be if I had a murder in here. I appreciate you and like I said, it will definitely not happen again."

The appeal from George Smith created a pause from the young, undercover officer. His breathing now shallow, collapsing his shoulders while simultaneously loosening his grip on his snub-nose 38 revolver concealed underneath his black leather jacket on a shoulder holster. The moment was an 'artful dodge' prolonging the undercover operation and prolonging Dupree's freedom, or in this case, perhaps his death. He intended to discharge his weapon, exercising deadly force, in order to save Gingy's life. In the chaotic moments, he pushed himself back into obscurity again. "Holy Fuck!" he moaned softly to himself, relieved from this close encounter, also relieved he wasn't exposed.

Driving around 7th Street and other night spots on International Avenue, a murderous barrage of cold rain and howling wind fell hard against the pavements in Oakland. Without much success, he circled back around San Pablo and Shattuck Avenue toward the Roman Hotel. Dupree stared transfixed by the rapidly changing weather conditions. He couldn't allow himself to succumb to the elements and the realization that his women were scattered about and uncharacteristically absent of his mentoring, or rather, human trafficking and controlling behavior. Odd! Dupree's business was one of adaptability. The elements presented no challenges but opportunities to work the night spots, strip joints, hotels, motels, night clubs, even car dates and, in some rare cases, put on a fucking raincoat and sell some ass. The money needed to be flowing continuously in spite of the elements and not from it was always his instructions to them. In his frame of mind, inclement weather was an obstacle to overcome; no one took a sick day off.

After his third circle around the area, it was now clear Roxie and Pam wasn't working the MacArthur Boulevard areas or motels and hotels. Even more distressful, nobody had seen Nicole. By now, his cell phone was continuously ringing. He knew it was Dr. Thurston, who was becoming paranoid and would soon leave. This was going to be a lot of cash evaporating with his departure. "Mother fuckin bitches……," he moaned, wiping a wild bead of sweat from his rain-soaked face. Frowning, he tapped his fist lightly on the dashboard, pissed that Dr. Thurston's cash was slipping through his fingers on this cold, wet night. "All these bitches, including Nicole, better have some cold ass excuse, because none of them—I mean none of them—are where they are supposed to be," he groaned aloud.

Intuitively, something was telling him this picture wasn't quite right, Nicole was a 'pure-bred hustling whore'. She loved the hustle, especially the money and the real sensation of tricking with those rich, fat, bald-headed white men who enjoyed her dominating and demeaning sex games with them. She was a real narcissist bitch that fucked and sucked her way into their heads. She punctuated their lust to make her financial demands coincide with their lurid fantasies.

She made some of them genuine 'cum freaks'; some even thoroughly convinced that she even cured their erectile dysfunction. They paid tens of thousands for their sexual encounters with her. For Dupree, she was his 'Queen Whore', his best money maker of the group. Although Nicole would never socialize with his other women but because she was bi-racial, mixed Asian and White, petite with big nipples, porcelain skin, long dark hair, cut evenly two inches above her waistline, sexy parted lips, about 110 pounds, small but physically tight looking with a wet kitty that kept them coming back for more, she would accept Sable. Her character, experience and emotion was a perfect match for her to take a naïve, young white girl under her wing. This would require a strong sense of using her direct experience in just how the real sex games worked. The rest is putting it into play and utilizing their fantasies to create an unnatural addiction toward her.

This was Dupree's plan for the newest member of his stable. The two of them would become his 'Mega Whores' raking in tens of thousands for him monthly, while he continued to expand his sex trafficking operation. He was a protégé of Glow Boy, watching him and a small cadre of old Filipina bar whores, sway, manipulate, deceive, and seduce, young poor, underaged girls in indigent provinces outside of Olongapo to become waitress and dancers inside the local bars who catered to service men. In some cases, he bribed the parents with a small amount of pesos and hefty kilograms of rice.

This was enough incentive for the parents to encourage apprehensive girls to join him.

That was the hook but it was too late when many soon realized they were being both trained and forced into prostitution. Those that resisted where either beaten into conformity or, in some cases, would disappear. This was the practice and outlandish behavior Dupree learned from Glow Boy—the indifference of being inconsiderate, impolite, disgusting and profane, with an ugly perception that the young girls were nothing but commodities; valuable only if they sold sex.

Suddenly in the corner of his right eye, something grabbed his attention shaking away his focus on Nicole and Sable. He applied the brakes slowly on his red Lexus. Pulling up in front of the Diamond Hotel, it was Sneaky, the raggedy-ass crack dealer who was supplying coke to Cookie. Normally, Dupree would have ignored him, but this wasn't a normal situation. His women were missing and perhaps Sneaky was aware of their whereabouts. Unknown to him, Sneaky was a pathetic snitch and a working conduit in the undercover investigation of him and other local sex traffickers in the Bay Area.

As he slammed his car door, there were spasms of irritation racing across his face. Leaning into the tempestuous wind, Dupree began fanning the air with his soaked hands in disgust.

"You seen mah women?"

Sneaky was momentarily taken back by the tone in Dupree's voice. He raised an eyebrow in a questioning slant, as if to say, 'Who this mother fucker think he's talking to?' while making a slow, appraising glare at him.

"I just saw Pam and Roxie down at the Roman."

Dupree winced. He pulled out a cigarette, studying Sneaky's eyes as he lit it.

"The Roman."

"Yeah, the Roman."

Dupree sighed. "Were they with someone?"

"I don't know, maybe," Sneaky replied.

"Maybe." Dupree repeated.

"Fuck, its cold out here… I'm busy doin my thing. I wasn't really paying attention to them or who they were with, ya know."

Dupree shook his head. "Cookie owe you for two, half ounces."

"That's right." Sneaky said cooly.

Dupree shrugged his shoulders. "What's the balance?"

"Everything is cool… you don't owe me nothin."

Dupree raised his eyebrows curious about the debt being suddenly squashed.

"Did she pay the balance tonight?" Dupree asked.

"Yeah… about half hour ago."

"That bitch," Dupree said acidly. "That stinkin ass cunt. I just told that ho to get mah money."

With panicked eyes, Sneaky looked at Dupree who, in turn, caught his dubious expression.

"I mean… she gave me my dough, but she got it from this white dude. He paid it off for her."

"A white dude," Dupree hissed.

"Yeah, some white dude was with her."

"That lying stinkin ass bitch just played me again." His voice rose hysterically. "I gonna kill that hussy. I warned her funky ass at Smitty's tonight."

"Where did they go?"

"She was looking for Pam," Sneaky replied.

"Why?"

"She said her asshole was sore from the other night," he paused with a silly chuckle. "She said the white dude, got a humongous dick, and ass fucking was his thing, and ya know; Pam is down with that nasty ass shit."

Dupree nodded. "Was a white gal with her?"

"Yeah, she was riding with them. He got a little brown Mazda with a small dent on the left side of the passenger door. It is a four-door sedan."

By now, Dupree's face had grown scarlet and swollen from the shouting. He shook his head walking toward his Lexus without saying another word to Sneaky. Tossing the cigarette out the window, both men gave each other a voiceless stare. Turning on the ignition, he pulled out a blunt and lit it. "Fuck this shit, somebody is goin to get served this fuckin night!" he yelled.

As he drove around, Dupree was perplexed about his women's behavior. His annoyance was now transfixed in a full-blown rage. The same rage Glow Boy displayed during his many episodes of anger transforming into violence against the young girls.

He continued driving slowly, circling the Oakland area—checking every possible location and hangouts the women might be doing business. Over and over again, the thought about them potentially betraying him for another pimp was a notion he could never ever accept. These were his whores and he would determine how their relationship would end.

Several minutes later, after smoking a second blunt, his apprehension about returning to the Roman Hotel was rapidly diminishing. It was now nearly seven hours since the shooting and robbery of Sable's trick in room 107. Though he hadn't mentioned the incident to anyone inside Smitty's juke-joint, he was certain if someone had identified him, the word would have surfaced inside the night club. The crime was his modus operandi. It was the fourth time he experienced that incredible adrenaline of excitement—watching someone's facial expression upon being shot. This was another revelation of his operation, robbing tricks, especially the ones that appear to have a ton of cash on them.

And, of course, the same was true for robbing those that abused and mistreated his women. The black guy was the consequence of that in room 107 earlier that evening. Interestingly, without understanding why, he regarded his ill-natured behavior as a self-righteous justification for the repercussion of anyone being in the game. Besides, until now, none of his victims died from the assault. His twisted and irrational logic continued to make violence another form of his pattern of a street vampire mentality and his unsavory reputation in the hood.

An hour later, his search finally ended when he decided to park a half block from the Roman Hotel. Dupree stared at the entrance. Perhaps his continued precautions were created by both his former police background and because he wasn't certain of the status of the stranger's injuries. He knew the police were investigating the crime and, hopefully, there were no witnesses. He took a long, deep sigh, relieved that he perceived there were no witnesses, or rather, the only witness was Sable. He then began to lick his wide lips trying to hold a surging moment of schizophrenia. His mind began shifting into a weird form of distorted thoughts; waves of delusions were flooding inside his head.

He was beginning to hallucinate about his women leaving him, along with seeds of betrayal surfing over these wet disturbances that possibly (quite possibly) that Sable, the only witness, told the police about the events in room 107.

In fact, she had been with him for less than a month. He checked out, or so he believed, her background from Hartford, Connecticut. She hung out at the Zanzibar Room at the California Hotel. It was the right spot, the right location and the right environment for a 'newbie' to get their feet wet in the game. After a few encounters, he thought how naïve she appeared eagerly accepting his invitation to join his stable. But now, his paranoia was barking at his mind, snarling at him, about them becoming realistic that maybe, just maybe, they needed another pimp.

Suddenly, he was incapable of thinking rationally any longer. His face became dark with pain. "You mother-fuckin bitches," his mouth erupted. The realization gave him an insatiable urge spawned by a single dimensional thought that obviously both the practice and mannerism of his women's behavior suddenly changed. They would always, in an instant, return his phone calls or text messages. They called him continuously trawling for leads, looking for upscale clientele. It was these repetitions that was screwing, mercifully inside his head.

Everyone knew he suffered from explosive disorders. One minute he would display an amazing charm and gentleness and, within a flash, changing that into violent outbursts. For nearly five years he maintained his psychological control over the four women primarily by fear. It was only recently, when Nicole and Cookie began to complain about the money, did he gradually recognize the slow erosion of his control. Pimping was becoming complex. The women were changing, especially the young prostitutes in Oakland and San Francisco. A new breed was coming—new bitches from Mexico. They were influencing the others as they were brave bitches with some having the Cartel stamp of approval. There were now new situations evolving that was making them feel more like Gingy, or at least independent enough to simply do their own thing. This factor was causing him a problem, because he always told them, "I'm not changing a fuckin thing about me."

As he struggled to work through his rage, his head immediately leaned forward. Two silhouettes emerged from inside the doorway of the dingy hotel. He winced inwardly taking ragged breaths as his right hand raced across the windshield… back and forth… back and forth… back and forth… clearing away the wet moisture of condensation formed by the damp winds.

Now, on the final wipe, he stared through the windshield, and it was clear who those two images were. His focus was fish eyed toward them. It was Cookie and Little Howie, another trifling ass cocaine dealer. Suddenly, Dupree's anger intensified, "I gonna get that bitch," he fumed. "Fuck em," he cried. "I'm gonna fuck em both."

Without thinking, without considering any consequences, Dupree unbuttoned his overcoat removing his 9mm Browning. In an instant after checking the clip, he flicked the safety off and catapulted from the Lexus. His veins throbbing inside his temple.

Despite the blustery wind, the abrupt noise did not go unnoticed by Cookie or Howie. They reacted instinctively. There wasn't time to provide him with an explanation of what he thought he was seeing. Even from this distance and in the tumultuous elements, they could sense the rage inside him. Howie, off the bat, hunched over and with legs pistoling wildly, he twisted and turned down the sidewalk, his chest heaving laboriously while he anticipated gunshots to quickly follow him.

"POP… POP… POP…" Three menacing bullets charged through the howling wind. One bullet ricocheted off the door frame of the Roman Hotel, almost a foot from Cookie's head. Ducking, her eyes became moonbeams lighting up the doorway. Her voice cried out in raw terror, "You crazy bastard, you retarded mother fucker," she shrieked, racing inside the hotel.

The next two bullets chased a stricken Howie, who was now running bowlegged down the slippery sidewalk.

"POP…" A fourth bullet found its mark striking him in his left hip. "Oooooooo gawd…" Howie wailed. "I ain't did nothin Bruh," he yelled, gasping for air. "Don't shoot… please don't shoot me… no mo," his hands waving back and forth, back and forth.

"I swear to gawddddddd," his voice slurring, "I didn't sell her no dope," he cried.

The tension was spreading as Howie limped toward his yellow mustang. Dupree fired a fifth shot. The bullet whistled a hairs breath passed Howie's bony head.

With one squeal, he hurled himself sideways on the cold pavement. A wet stream of blood raced down the side of his left leg. He grimaced, instinctively lying perfectly still. His face nearly paralyzed with fright as he pressed himself tightly against the ground. His eyes widened with enormous panic, knowing any movement, even the slightest body twitch would produce another bullet. This was the moment that required him to do his level best imitation of a dead man.

Meanwhile, the fifth bullet came accompanied by anxious Oakland Police sirens piercing through the snappy wind. The moment shook off Dupree's death wish toward Howie. However, his vampirism for Cookie's blood wouldn't become subordinate to reality and the rapidly approaching OPD patrol vehicles. He then turned, looking wildly, as he galloped full speed toward the hotel's door entrance. His mind blinded now with a combined notion of revenge, coupled with alcohol and weed; the reality of the moment escaped him. It was down to this bizarre, single-minded conquest to kill Cookie no matter what the consequences were at the moment. Racing inside the hotel, he could hear the hysterical screams of Cookie, echoing throughout the hallway pleading for mercy as she staggered, breathing heavily, while begging someone to help her.

The burning smell of gun smoke cascaded throughout the first-floor level. The overwhelming fright inside Cookie barely registered the pain in her right leg. It was a sixth bullet that struck her. Her mind frozen in time numb as she continued to elude his maniacal pursuit. She knew stopping, trying to explain the unexplainable to a madman was futile. For now, the only thing that mattered was to survive and try to outmaneuver his rage.

"SCREAMS... SCREAMS... SCREAMS... "

An onslaught of wrenching sobs forced their way throughout the hotel passageways.

Distressing sobs from Cookie's voice joined them in unison. Everyone now felt the terror of being hunted by a street vampire. His bloodthirsty rage ascended to a murderous falsetto. There was a scorching look in his eyes, searching both right and left… right and left, for any signs of her.

With his gun twirling and twisting in his sweaty right hand, he started kicking open the first two doors on the first floor.

"Somebody call the policeeeee," a voice, dripping in horror, cried out a few doors away.

Dupree hesitated a quick moment, he heard Cookie's urgent pleas coming from a third room. By now, OPD was nearly at the entrance of the hotel escorting frightened occupants away from a potential crime scene.

Cookie, now feeling both blood and the burning sensation of her gunshot wound, was huddled together with Sable but there was another person inside the room with them.

All three could hear Dupree slowly edging closer toward the door, listening and waiting intently for confirmation of another sound from her.

"I know you in there, you stinkin ass bitch," he growled.

They could hear his excited breaths. At the same moment, squeezing Cookie's hand, Sable's fright gave way to a slight whimper. A mistake!

Dupree was poised waiting for that error, a prickling sensation raced up his spine. He turned and quickly rammed his broad shoulder against the door with mammoth force.

Both women screamed but, their shrieks were interrupted by a sharp, crisp, but noticeable sound of a police walkie-talkie inside the room. Dupree blinked; his eyes widened in disbelief. He slowly lowered his gun, pausing for a tinge moment collecting his thoughts but before reality settled in his mind, "Fuck it," he said. With another hard push, the door flew open and, then out of nowhere.

"POP… POP…"

Two sharp flashes came rushing toward him. It was gunfire from the undercover officer's snub nose 38 revolver, the same officer who was at Smitty's earlier that evening. He was present inside the room with Cookie and Sable.

The first bullet struck Dupree in his upper right shoulder, crashing through his shoulder blade. The second bullet struck him directly in his lower left side. He fell backwards from the impact of the first bullet. He was too startled to realize that he dropped his Browning 9mm on the floor.

His eyes beamed as flashlights flooded his traumatized uneven face.

"Police Officer...," a voice raced out from the room. "You... make... another... move... cocksucker... and... it... will... be... your... last...," a voice said in a slow, military tone.

Cookie gawked at him with surprise. By now, Dupree was surrounded by police. It was an astonishing moment of an unimaginable transformation for him..

"Baby, whatcha doin?" Cookie cried. "I didn't mess up ya money," she moaned. "I gotta here... right here with me," she sobbed weakly, falling to her knees.

"Never mind that bullshit," a burly, white, OPD patrol sergeant huffed.

Moving her back across the bed. "Get me those ambulances in here and secure that fuckin automatic on the floor next to that creep," he yelled. "This lady is bleeding pretty bad. So, tell them to hurry," he barked over his walkie-talkie. Looking toward the undercover black officer; his face nodded with pleasure while grinning in approval. "Fuckin aye, dude, way to go," he said. He nodded at Sable who was still working off the fright inside her, "You okay, ma-am?" he asked. "Yeah Sarg, I'm okay." He then walked over to Dupree, who was now in obvious pain, and being administered by the EMT's, "You're just a piece of wild shit," he said softly. "We finally got this douchebag," smiling looking at several OPD officers who were now flooding the hallway.

Several weeks later, Dupree was tightly deposited in the Oakland/Alameda County Hospital (Highland), in the Prison Ward. His body was weak from three operations. A dose of frustration was included in the clarity of his dilemma.

He realized on some level with more 'self-focus' that his criminal liability was enormous. Bristling, while remembering everything leading up to those final delicate moments inside the Roman Hotel.

He was still constructing the events when the heavy, steel door opened to his room. Two well-dressed white men wearing dark blue suits and carrying large, black leather briefcases entered first followed up by a uniform Oakland Police Captain, and finally a petite, well-dressed, uniformed black woman wearing light tan pants, and a black polo shirt with the large emblem of the *United States Homeland Security* on it all entered walking single file. She was carrying a medium-sized, brown leather briefcase.

Right away, Dupree knew these were high ranking people with authority.

He grimaced, raising up on both elbows.

"Ya'll goin to let me call my lawyer?" He asked.

"Why certainly," the larger of the two white men said, stepping over to the side of his bed facing the other three individuals.

"Who is he?"

"Leroy Burris."

He smiled. "I'll be damn, ole Leroy, the former prosecutor from Contra Costa County D.A.'s office." He nodded. "We went to law school together."

"That's him, one of the best," Dupree replied.

"You'll need him," he quipped.

"Who are you people?'

The white man standing beside his bed pointed his finger at the black woman, "I believe ladies first."

The woman nodded.

"Good morning Mr. Howard, my name is Janice Woodard. I am with the Department of Homeland Security, the International Division, for Southeast Asia," she said, her facial expression hardened with displeasure.

The well-dressed white man continued, pointing next to her the Oakland Police Captain.

"I'm Arnold Bridgewater, Commander of the Investigation Division including the Vice Control Unit, of the Oakland Police Department."

"The guy standing at the foot of your bed, is Frank Ortig, field Agent in Charge of the Bay Area, Federal Bureau of Investigation. I'm Philip Harrelson, an FBI agent, working trafficking cases under its Crimes Against Children and Human Trafficking. Program."

Dupree's eyes blinked excessively.

"Here are our four business cards. We will also provide them to Mr. Burris when he arrives."

Confused and perplexed, Dupree said, "I can understand why OPD is here. I don't have a clue why the FBI, wants to talk to me. I haven't done any FED stuff."

Harrelson shook his head. "Well, to be frank, Mr. Howard, there are several pending indictments against you. The doctor will discharge you later today and we are going to take you into federal custody, transferring you to our detention center in San Francisco."

Dupree winced.

"Federal Detention Center," his eyes widened in alarm.

"That's right."

'Nah, I thought I'd just assaulted two people—that's a state matter."

"No, that isn't the case."

"Shooting two people in Oakland and you're telling me I caught a fed charge for that?"

The room was now unusually silent. Then a few moments later, Harrelson walked over and opened the front door and motioned to the OPD officer assigned to stand guard at the entrance to the room. "Excuse me, officer? Can you ask the hospital staff to bring us five chairs, please. I believe this room is large enough to accommodate five chairs." He turned looking at the group. "Is everyone alright if we have our meeting in this room? It's large enough?" The group nodded with approval.

The officer then nodded, "Right away, sir!"

"Thank you."

Moments later, five metal green chairs were placed inside the windowless room. After sitting, Harrelson let go a moderate sigh, "Now, that we're settled, I'll answer your question, as to 'why' federal charges..."

"... yeah, I'm listening," Dupree interrupted him in mid-sentence in a distasteful tone.

Harrelson then opened his large briefcase, removing a huge legal court binder.

"These are federal charges presented by the US Attorney's Office for The Northern District of California, offices in San Francisco, Oakland and San Jose."

Dupree's eyes blinked excessively. His face grew signs of both desperation and confusion.

"You're coming with us, sir!"

"Uh... I guess so. Ain't nothing I can say about that..."

"About a month ago, the FBI received a call on its National Human Trafficking HOTLINE, from a Ms. Bonita Mira Davis. Are you familiar with that name?"

Dupree's elbows suddenly collapsed sending his body flat against the bed. His eyes were blank, staring almost catatonically at the ceiling. Shock waves moved throughout his body. How could she betray me? He felt cheated—she used everybody and now she was using the FBI against me. He remembered her complaining about all the money she had given him—it was her grievance against him. He also recalled telling her, "I ain't changing a fuckin thing about me," the statement was now pummeling inside his head.

He then let go a long and heavy sigh. His chest appeared to collapse in front of them; his face stricken with both surprise and pain.

"Yeah, I know that name. Her street name is Nicole." He then shook his head, adjusting the breathing tube inserted inside his mouth. "Man, ain't this some shit now," he moaned privately to himself.

"We have a signed and sealed affidavit with more than a hundred counts of sex trafficking and exploitation of a person for labor services or commercial sex, under the Trafficking Victims Protection Act of 2000, against you."

"Man, ya'll trying to fuck up my life… I don't have the patience for this. I need my lawyer!"

Harrelson nodded in agreement.

"That is understandable, we aren't here to interrogate you…"

"I ain't saying nothing to self-incriminate myself… I know my rights."

"Understood. Like I said, we are just here sharing the reality of your situation… having your lawyer here is appropriate and necessary."

"Okay, that's cool with me. I just ain't saying nothing anymore."

"Again, that is perfectly alright with us." He paused. "You need to recognize the gravity of the situation you are in."

Dupree shook his head, "I ain't involved in Trafficking of no women, regardless of what Nicole told ya'll. This shit you talking about is just CRAZY!" he said, raising his tone at the end.

The four people wasn't overawed by his outburst. In fact, the police captain, stood up. "Do we need to place shackles on your ankles, completely immobilizing you?" his eyes blazing in annoyance. "I will definitely do that if we see another outburst like that again, you understand. Mr. Howard?'

"That ain't necessary. I just was caught off-guard about what he was telling me about Nicole."

The police captain said nothing to Dupree. He looked at the other three who were shaking their heads in agreement of his statement to him.

"I like to proceed on Mr. Howard, if you don't mind? Are you okay moving forward, so we can get this matter over with?"

"Yeah, I'm okay. It was just a shock about her calling you guys about something she is doing voluntarily but I ain't saying nothing else about it. You go ahead."

"Thank you, sir!"

Harrelson then shuffled capriciously through the large document, searching for something and he went from being excited to anxious in a matter of seconds. And then, his eyes lit up. "Ahh, I have it. We also have sworn affidavits from the two other women who worked for you but I believe her street name is Cookie, she declined to provide us with a statement against you."

Dupree's head slowly bent down to his chest, his chin rubbing against it, sideways, sideways. The statement came as another surprise. "And I was trying to kill the one woman who was loyal to me—even after I shot her, damn," he thought quietly to himself. "But she never gave me a heads up!"

Harrelson continued on, breaking through Dupree's private thoughts.

"We have three things that we want to make you aware of before your lawyer arrives as we have other meetings to attend but I will leave you a copy of the indictments against you." He paused shaking his head slowly, as his eagle eyes searched the outline of his face. "Mr. Howard, what you are hearing from us are very serious matters against you."

Dupree sat silent listening to Agent Harrelson. "After we obtained the sworn affidavits, we proceeded to conduct an undercover sting operation against you. We proceeded to contact several law enforcement agencies throughout California, for a young, white woman to be our informant."

"Informant?" Dupree frowned. "Y'all planted an informant on me?"

"Uh huh…that's right. The woman came from a southern California agency that I will not name at the moment. Her information is contained in another sealed indictment against you. We provided her with a cover story and information… I believe you know her as Sable."

Dupree lifted his head; The news was like hammer blows to him. For once in his life, he was at a loss for words. Harrelson's statement caught him off guard. His head was boiling in anger at himself. He should have vetted her background, checked her story out but he was too damn greedy to do that. He had his new ATM sex machine and the authorities knew he would easily take the bait. She always gave him money, enough not to draw his attention to her. In hindsight, he only saw one customer of hers and that was in room 107 at the Roman Hotel. She was the lone witness of the shooting and robbery of her trick. He also remembered that she was hesitant in taking the proceeds from the robbery.

Harrelson, spoke breaking Dupree's thoughts about Sable. "Now, I am going to turn this next matter over to Agent Ortig."

The smaller white agent stood up holding a slightly smaller document with him in his right hand.

"We are indicting Dr. Tennyson Grayline Morris, IV; however, you know him as Dr. Thurston."

Dupree winced inwardly, "Dr. Thurston, I never knew his real name, but the shit he did was between he and Nicole. They were voluntarily doing their thing. How was that sex trafficking, man?"

Harrelson interrupted, "Mr. Howard, we aren't here to interrogate you and I must admonish you that any statements you make to us, can and will be used against you. Do you fully understand what I am saying to you?"

Dupree nodded, "Uh, huh, I understand the Miranda Warnings."

"Good."

Agent Ortig returned to his seat, "Phil, that's all I have to inform about that matter."

Harrelson then stood up, "Thanks Frank," he turned, looking squarely at Dupree. "Before Captain Bridgewater speaks to you, there is something that has been on my mind after I received this case, and it relates to what Captain Bridgewater and Agent Woodard have to share with you. Is that okay with you?"

Dupree shook his head, "Whatever, man… this is y'all show."

"Good, I know you are a decorated Vietnam War Hero, and received a Bronze Star with citation," he paused, "You saved three American lives at Da Nang. We are proud of your service to our country, Mr. Howard." He then reached inside his right coat pocket, and pulled out a small piece of white paper with a short note written on it. "Here it is, a speech by Sir Winston Churchill, on November 10th, 1942, during a luncheon of some sort. He said and, I quote:

"This is not the end, it's not even the beginning of the end. But, it's the end of the beginning."

Returning the note inside his pocket, Harrelson then said, "This speech might make some sense to you after hearing from Captain Bridgewater and Agent Woodard."

Captain Bridgewater then stood up walking erect, now standing directly at the foot of Dupree's hospital bed. His uniform, a dark blue color with a sparking gold badge and name plate. His leather gun belt was polished; even his holster and gun handle were flawlessly shined with near perfection. He probably took great pride in being an Oakland cop. He was clean shaven, salt and pepper hair, lean frame, not an ounce of fat was protruding from his uniform attire. By all standards, his appearance was the epitome of professional decorum and presentation of what the Oakland Police wanted from their ranking command officers. Perhaps he might even be bucking for chief one day.

"Phil… that's a tough act to follow," he quipped at Agent Harrelson.

Now turning to Dupree. "Mr. Howard, in some small way, perhaps I have some good news to give you before Agent Woodard give you the bad news." He then opened up a manila folder and looked at Dupree. "Mr. Howard, the Alameda County District Attorney's Office is charging you with one count of Attempted Murder on a Police Officer, three counts of Reckless Endangerment, one count of Attempted Murder, Aggravated

Assault, Shooting in an Occupied Dwelling, Aggravated Robbery, multiple counts of Pimping and Pandering. They are looking at additional charges as the police reports come to them and possession of a concealed weapon without a license or permit."

"What!" Dupree snapped in an alarming tone. "Capt., I know I ain't shot no police officer. Y'all trying to really fuck me up."

Captain Bridgewater disregarded Dupree's response shaking his head.

"The man you shot and robbed in room 107 of the Roman Hotel was Sergeant Paul Davis of the Oakland Police Department, Special Operations Unit. He was working undercover with Sable. He was trying a new wire device for her, and it was taking longer than expected which caused you to believe he was mistreating her. Thankfully, he is in fair condition and considering everything you heard, you are fortunate you aren't being charged with Capital Murder of a Police Officer. Incidentally, he is the current President of the OBOA."

There was a screaming tirade going on inside his head. He now recognized the extraordinary law enforcement effort to shut him down with a cogent and calculated investigation of his human trafficking activities. He was berating himself for being so careless.

He stared at Captain Bridgewater for several long moments. "This sounds like entrapment to me, Capt."

"Not in the least."

"I think so."

"Well, I'm not going to debate with you any legal defenses, that's for you and Mr. Burris to decide."

Bridgewater then turned, looking at Harrelson, "Sir, that's all I have to share with Mr. Howard."

"Thank you, Captain Bridgewater," Harrelson said, his eyes now searching for an expression on Dupree's deep drawn, naturally intense gaze.

The room was now uncharacteristically silent. Everybody was looking at Agent Woodard. After all that was shared was enough to put away Dupree for life in prison, but, despite it, she had what was described as 'bad news'.

The silence was broken when Agent Woodard stood up with a medium-sized document in her right hand.

"Mr. Howard, there is an Extradition Treaty between the United States of America and the Republic of the Philippines…"

"… Extradition!" Dupree spoke in utter contempt.

Woodard's cold stare stopped him abruptly.

"Don't interrupt me… just listen. I'm not here to debate a thing with you, do… you… understand… me?" she said with vexation.

"Yeah, I understand," he said with a long, exasperated look of worriment.

"This is a bilateral extradition treaty which allows both governments to request the formal arrest of their respective citizens to appear in their government to answer charges of criminal or civil activities which occurred in their country. Therefore, under Treaty Doc 104-16, signed by the Republic of the Philippines on November 13th, 1994, they have presented formal criminal charges against you, for 67 counts of Human Trafficking and Exploitation of Underage Girls for the Purpose of Prostitution; 9 counts of Racketeering, 1 count of Facilitation of First-Degree Murder, and the potential witness of knowing the whereabouts of 17 missing young, underaged girls."

She paused as she continued to read more of the lengthy extradition order.

"Excuse me, this is a very long order, which you are being served today by me," she said continuing on. "Mr. Howard, they have obtained 27 sworn affidavits identifying you as a person known to them as 'Fuzzy', your alias you used while visiting the country and residing in Olongapo, City. The order later identifies your full alias as being one of Fuzzy Jackson. They didn't identify you until a CCTV camera recorded you at the Manila International Airport retrieving your luggage from Mr. Jimmy Gabriel 'Glow Boy' vehicle days after an execution style murder in Olongapo. The investigators followed you to your flight back to Oakland and were able to obtain your identification from your departure via your passport. All these charges, and maybe more, are in connection with your participation with the former Jimmy Gabriel 'Glow Boy' Salabao who is now deceased.

Agent Woodward paused moving down the extradition order. "You are hereby ordered to appear two weeks from today in the United States District Court of Northern California to show cause why this extradition order shall not be enforced." She stopped, looking at Dupree's wounded look in his face.

"Mr. Howard, unless you have some extraordinary defense, you are going to be extradited to the Republic of the Philippines to answer these criminal charges… and there is no bail on them." She stopped, waiting for a response from Dupree.

Everyone was now staring at him as if they expected him to utter an angry outburst. But he said nothing… absolutely nothing. He was staring at the wall. This was an unbelievable development for him to process. Everything he did with Glow Boy, the ruthless business of their activities, forcing those poor, underage, teenage girls into prostitution and the beatings, and the disappearance of those young girls who resisted Glow Boy. He knew where those bodies were, and now he was going to be held accountable for his reprehensible role in Human Trafficking in the Philippines and murder.

By now, Dupree recognized Harrelson's statement of what Winston Churchill's remarks meant to him—***"But, it's the end of the beginning,"*** and the end of Pimping for him, and the beginning of the realization of the consequences of it. As he would say—Just some Vampire Shit!

"Just like I promised, Mr. Virgil Shelton,
I finished your Memoirs,
And I even got them Published for ya.

May God Bless your soul, son."

Stoney Fox
Correctional Officer on Tennessee's Death Row—
Hearing and finishing condemned men's stories for years